Praise for

WILBUR SMITH

'A thundering good read is virtually the only way of describing Wilbur Smith's books'

THE IRISH TIMES

'Wilbur Smith . . . writes as forcefully as his tough characters act'

EVENING STANDARD

'Wilbur has arguably the best sense of place of any adventure writer since John Buchan'

THE GUARDIAN

'Wilbur Smith is one of those benchmarks against whom others are compared'

THE TIMES

'Best Historical Novelist – I say Wilbur Smith, with his swashbuckling novels of Africa. The bodices rip and the blood flows. You can get lost in Wilbur Smith and misplace all of August'

STEPHEN KING

'Action is the name of Wilbur Smith's game and he is the master'

THE WASHINGTON POST

'A master storyteller'

THE SUNDAY TIMES

Wilbur Smith is a global phenomenon: a distinguished author with a large and established readership built up over fifty-five years of writing, with sales of over 130 million novels worldwide.

Born in Central Africa in 1933, Wilbur became a full-time writer in 1964 following the success of *When the Lion Feeds*, and has since published over forty global bestsellers, including the Courtney Series, the Ballantyne Series, the Egyptian Series, the Hector Cross Series and many successful standalone novels, all meticulously researched on his numerous expeditions worldwide. His books have now been translated into twenty-six languages.

The establishment of the Wilbur & Niso Smith Foundation in 2015 cemented Wilbur's passion for empowering writers, promoting literacy and advancing adventure writing as a genre. The foundation's flagship programme is the Wilbur Smith Adventure Writing Prize.

For all the latest information on Wilbur, visit: www.wilbursmith books.com or facebook.com/WilburSmith

Also by Wilbur Smith

Non-Fiction

On Leopard Rock:
A Life of Adventures

The Courtney Series

When the Lion Feeds
The Sound of Thunder
A Sparrow Falls
The Burning Shore
Power of the Sword
Rage
A Time to Die
Golden Fox
Birds of Prey
Monsoon
Blue Horizon
The Triumph of the Sun
Assegai
Golden Lion
War Cry
The Tiger's Prey

The Ballantyne Series

A Falcon Flies
Men of Men
The Angels Weep
The Leopard Hunts in Darkness
The Triumph of the Sun

The Egyptian Series

River God
The Seventh Scroll
Warlock
The Quest
Desert God
Pharaoh

Hector Cross

Those in Peril
Vicious Circle
Predator

Standalones

The Dark of the Sun
Shout at the Devil
Gold Mine
The Diamond Hunters
The Sunbird
Eagle in the Sky
The Eye of the Tiger
Cry Wolf
Hungry as the Sea
Wild Justice
Elephant Song

WILBUR SMITH

COURTNEY'S WAR

ZAFFRE

First published in Great Britain in 2018 by

ZAFFRE PUBLISHING
80–81 Wimpole St, London W1G 9RE
www.zaffrebooks.co.uk

A CIP catalogue record for this book is
available from the British Library.

ISBN: 978–1–78576–648–0

Also available as an ebook

3 5 7 9 10 8 6 4 2

Typeset by IDSUK (Data Connection) Ltd
Printed and bound in Great Britain by Clays Ltd, Elcograf S.p.A.

Zaffre Publishing is an imprint of Bonnier Zaffre,
a Bonnier Publishing company
www.bonnierzaffre.co.uk
www.bonnierpublishing.co.uk

Every day I thank God for loving you, my lovely wife, Mokhiniso. Your face is the most beautiful picture I have ever seen, your laughter is the most lovely music I have ever heard. Loving you is the most wonderful experience of my life.

It was Paris in the spring: a city built for lovers in the season of romance. And of all the couples strolling arm-in-arm through the Tuileries Garden on that Good Friday afternoon in 1939, none were as transcendently in love as the tall, willowy girl and the man at her side, who looked down at her with a smile of disbelief at his own good fortune. There was still a cold edge to the early April breeze, and the girl snuggled a little closer to his broad shoulders and raised her eyes to his, knowing that he would not be able to resist the temptation to kiss her, and damn the looks of any disapproving passers-by.

Elsewhere the twin pursuits of female perfection and manly elegance might be dismissed as wasteful, trivial fripperies. In Paris, however, beauty has always been regarded as a moral imperative, and this man and woman were two magnificent specimens. She had a figure that would have had any of the couture houses in the Rue Cambon or the Avenue Montaigne vying for her services as a model, were they not already fighting for her custom as a client, and her face was equally striking. Framed by a head of thick, glossy black hair, her features gave some indication of her strength of character. Her jaw and cheekbones were clean-cut, her chin firm, her nose a decisive line rather than an upturned button. But her bones were so fine and her lips so invitingly full that they belied any suggestion of masculinity. And her huge blue eyes, as clear as the African skies under which she had been born, and fringed by thick, black lashes that barely had need for mascara, completed the picture of ravishing femininity.

He was a mate fit for such a paragon. To her delight, he was still a full head taller than her, even when she wore high heels. Any woman walking by would notice the dark blond notes in his casually swept back hair and the film-star glow of that loving smile. This being Paris, she would also have spotted that while his dress was casual – a pair of charcoal-grey flannel trousers and a tweed sports jacket, instead of a suit, and an open shirt with a silk cravat tucked into the collar, instead of a tie – every garment was perfectly cut and his shoes were immaculately polished.

What the girl beside him appreciated, which other women could not, was that this man's grey eyes were windows into a soul that was more sensitive and thoughtful than a passing impression might suggest. She knew that while his forearms were strong and well-muscled, he had an artist's hands. His long, elegant fingers could draw anything on which his eyes might rest, or run along the length of her body, playing with every bit of her and bringing her pleasure that she could never have imagined possible, only for it to be exceeded by the ecstasy that the most thrilling, powerful part of him could bring.

Truly, Saffron Courtney and Gerhard von Meerbach seemed blessed by all the gods, for they were as rich and well connected as they were pleasing to the eye. It would have taken the steeliest heart to begrudge them their good fortune.

'Is it really only three months since we met?' Gerhard said. 'I can't imagine life without you. How could I survive for twenty-seven years and have no idea you even existed? And then . . .'

'Then I landed at your feet,' Saffron said and giggled. 'Upside down, in a big heap, dressed as a man.'

When two people are in love, few things on earth are as fascinating to them as their love itself. Gerhard and Saffron constantly found new ways to recount the tale of their first meeting, like children wanting to hear the same bedtime story every night.

Saffron had pretended to be a man, disguising her femininity with bulky clothes, determined to experience the exhilaration of the Cresta Run in St. Moritz, even though the course was exclusively men only. She had charged down the ice run, refusing to slow down, and eventually was flung off her sled at one of the bends, cartwheeling into the snow. Her dark glasses were thrown off, and it was her eyes that seared into Gerhard's soul.

'I know!' he said. 'I took one look at you and . . . boom! I'd been hit by a million volts, like a Frankenstein film, you know, when the doctor puts all the electricity through the monster. I'd never known anything like it. Truly, love at first sight. And I thought, how can it be? How can I feel like this about a man? And then as you walked away . . .'

'I gave that little wiggle. I know, I had to. I felt the same as you did and I simply had to let you know.'

'And all because you were so brave . . . and so, so stubborn.' Gerhard laughed. 'So Saffron! You had to go down the Cresta Run, even though you knew only men were allowed.'

Saffron grinned. 'Of course! Why should you men have all the fun?'

Suddenly, Gerhard's mood seemed to darken, as if a cloud had crossed the sun. 'Ah, poor Chessi. I still feel bad about her . . . That was supposed to be the night—'

'Ssshhh!' Saffron put a finger to his lips to silence him. Francesca von Schöndorf had been her dearest school friend. They were a pair, Chessi and Saffy: one a sweet, sensible German girl, the other a barely tamed child of Africa, newly arrived in England after being brought up in the Kenyan highlands. More than once, Saffron had gone to Germany to stay with the von Schöndorfs, watching the country change before her eyes as the Nazis recreated an entire nation in their twisted image.

At Christmas, when Saffron was on vacation from Oxford University, staying with relatives in Scotland, Chessi had written to her. The letter explained that she would be in St. Moritz for the New Year, hosting a chalet party at which she expected the man she loved would propose to her. Saffron had dashed across Europe as much because she wanted to be with her friend and share her joy as for the thrill of the Cresta Run. She had no idea that the love of her life would be waiting for her, still less that he would be the man Chessi expected to marry.

But love is ruthless and will not be denied.

'You and Chessi weren't meant to be together,' Saffron said. 'If you were, you would not have met me, and even if you had met me, you'd have picked me up, dusted me down and gone on your way. And I wouldn't have given you a second thought.'

'And then, when we met again, at the party that night . . . ?'

'Then we would have taken a second to recognise one another, and laughed about what had happened, and you would have told Chessi the story and she would have laughed too. None of us would have taken it the slightest bit seriously, because it wouldn't have been serious. You would have been made for Chessi. But you weren't, you were made for me. And . . . Oh!'

Saffron squealed as a gust of wind blew her hat from her head, and the two of them ran down the Grande Allée, laughing like children as they chased after the tumbling confection of black felt and sunny silk flowers.

The happiness stayed with them for the rest of the afternoon. They stopped in front of the Eiffel Tower to have their picture taken by one of the photographers who plied their trade there.

'Where would monsieur wish me to send the finished print?' the snapper asked.

'We're staying at the Ritz.'

The man looked at this gilded couple and smiled. 'But of course.'

They dined at La Tour d'Argent and looked out at the lights of the riverboats on the Seine as they ate the pressed duck for which the restaurant was famous. As was the custom, the proprietor, Monsieur Térail, presented them with numbered postcards as certificates of their meal.

Afterwards, pleasantly drowsy from the champagne cocktail that had preceded her meal and the bottle of 1921 Cheval Blanc that had accompanied the duck, Saffron had rested her head against Gerhard and teased him affectionately.

'I want to go sleep,' she mumbled. 'I'm too tired for hanky-panky.'

Gerhard nodded, frowning with exaggerated thoughtfulness. 'Hmm, I think that's wise. You've had a long day. You should get some rest. You won't mind if I put you to bed and go out on the town, will you? I hear the dancing girls at the Folies Bergère are particularly pretty this year.'

'Beast!' She pouted and slapped him lazily.

They went back to their suite, paying no attention to its elegant cream, beige and gold decorations. They dashed without a second glance past the high glass doors, through which a balcony looked across the Ritz's magnificent garden to the city beyond. There would be time enough in the morning to snuggle on one of the silk-upholstered sofas, or enjoy the view.

Saffron kicked off her shoes, yanked her dress over her head and threw it to the ground without the slightest concern for its delicate chiffon fabric. She unhooked her bra and stepped out of her French knickers, laughing as she gave them one last flick with her toes and sent them flying towards Gerhard, a missile of white satin. She kept her stockings on, knowing how her man loved the contrast of colour and feel.

She threw herself onto the bed and then arranged herself artfully, sitting with her back resting on the pillows propped up against the headboard, brazen and unashamed as she turned her eyes towards Gerhard. He was unbuttoning his shirt with maddening deliberation, one button at a time, gradually revealing his chest, lightly furred with golden hair. Then she could see the ridges of muscle on his stomach. Gerhard looked at her, enjoying her gaze. He paused, his eyes examining every inch of her, and she felt the heat rising within her, the melting beginning.

His smile broadened. He knew what he was doing to her. But she could see as he undid his belt and opened the top button of his trousers that she was having an equally potent effect on him. He took his trousers off.

Good boy, Saffron thought as she saw that his socks had already been removed.

And then he was on her, and in her, and she felt completed by him, as though they were two halves of one single organism. Her moans turned to screams and she gave herself over, body and soul, to the man she loved, as he gave himself to her.

Later, when they were sated and Saffron was lying in his arms, idly running her fingers through the hair on his chest, Gerhard said, 'This will be the last time we can be together, my darling . . . before the storm breaks.'

Saffron felt an icy shock. She wrapped her arms around him, as if she could force him to stay with her. 'Don't say that.'

'The Führer won't stop at Austria and Czechoslovakia. There's all the old Prussian land that was given to Poland. He wants it back. He'll use Danzig as the excuse, you wait and see.'

'Let him have it then. What difference does it make to us?'

Gerhard shrugged. 'None . . . except that Chamberlain and Daladier have promised the Poles that Britain and France will respect their borders.'

'Won't that stop Hitler going in?'

'Why would he stop? He's got away with it so many times before. The British and French have always backed down. He'll assume they'll do it again.'

'What about the Russians? They won't like the German border getting any closer to the Soviet Union.'

'I don't know . . . But I can tell you this: my dear brother Konrad is strutting round telling anyone who'll listen that the whole world is about to tremble. "They're going to get the Reich's iron fist in their faces" is how he likes to put it. Then he tells me to go and get my flying suit, because I'm going to need it.'

'Will he fight too, if it happens?'

'Konrad? No, not him. He'll be back in Berlin, nice and safe, with his head tucked up General Heydrich's arse, same as usual.'

Saffron couldn't help but laugh, but then she stopped herself. 'There's nothing funny about it, is there?' A moment of silence fell and then she said, 'I know it's selfish of me, with the whole world about to go up in flames, but all I can think of is: what's going to become of us?'

'I am putting a system in place with Izzy, a way for us to get letters to each other. It will be complicated and take forever for our messages to get through. But they will, I promise.'

'Will that be safe for him?'

'He says he'll be fine. He spent the last war on the front line; how could he possibly be in any danger spending this one in Switzerland?'

'They could get to him there, though, couldn't they . . . if they found out?'

Saffron felt Gerhard's head nodding as he said, '*Ja*, they could. But Izzy doesn't care. He says it's his repayment for me getting him out of Germany.'

Isidore Solomons had been a hero in the First World War, awarded the Blue Max, Germany's highest award for valour. He'd returned home to Munich and taken over from his father as the von Meerbach family lawyer and their most trusted adviser.

But Solomons was a Jew and Konrad von Meerbach was a fanatical Nazi, whose passion for Adolf Hitler and all his works far outweighed any considerations of loyalty, or decency. He relieved Solomons of his duties, without notice or compensation.

Gerhard, however, was cut from a different cloth to his brother. Ashamed of the way that such a loyal retainer and friend had been treated, he had persuaded Konrad to give him five thousand Reichsmarks from the family trust by claiming that he wanted to buy a Mercedes sports car. Instead, he had given the money to Isidore Solomons, and, in so doing, enabled an entire family to escape to safety in Switzerland.

Within a day of first meeting Gerhard, Saffron had travelled with him to Zurich to meet Solomons. She heard the story from the lawyer's mouth, saw the respect that the local Jewish community had for Gerhard, and she discovered the price that Konrad, disgusted by his 'Jew-lover' brother, had made him pay for the crime of possessing a conscience. Saffron understood then that here was someone who knew the difference between right and wrong, and who was willing to act on that knowledge, whatever the consequences. It made her certain in her heart and mind alike: she had chosen the right man to love.

'I like Izzy,' she said. 'It's so good of him to do this for us.'

'Believe me, he likes you too. He keeps telling me that it's his moral duty to keep us together: "You will never find another woman to match her if I don't."'

'Well, that's true. You won't.'

'And will you ever find another man to match me?'

'No . . . never. I swear. I'll always be yours.'

They made love again . . . and again for the rest of the Easter weekend. On Sunday evening, Saffron saw Gerhard off at the Gare de l'Est, where he boarded the overnight express to Berlin. She managed not to cry until the train had left the station. But then the floodgates opened as the awful truth became impossible to wish away any longer.

Her love for Gerhard von Meerbach had only just begun. But she might never see him again. She might yearn for a time when they could be with one another and build a life together in peace. She might tell herself that their love would survive and their dreams would come true, and try with all her heart to believe it. But then another voice inside her asked: *What chance is there of that?*

• • •

In less than five months, in the early hours of Friday, 1 September 1939, Hitler unleashed the forces of Nazi Germany against Poland.

Two days later, Great Britain declared war on Germany. And slaughter, suffering and horror exploded across the world.

A nother April in another country, on an early spring evening in 1942. Saffron Courtney was wearing baggy black serge overalls that hid her figure. In the heel of one of her hard leather boots was concealed a small fighting knife and the button of the map pocket on her left leg was a disguised suicide pill. She leaned over the railway track and pressed the three-pound block of explosives into the hollow between the base and top rail. The block, comprised of six eight-ounce cartridges of Nobel 808, was as malleable as putty, so that Saffron could squeeze it snugly up against the metal. The night air was filled with the strong smell of almonds, the odour emanating from the nitro-glycerine-based explosives. She pushed in a length of detonating cord, onto which a one-ounce gun-cotton primer had been inserted. Once she was satisfied with its placement, she took a roll of three-quarter-inch adhesive khaki tape from her knapsack, tore a strip off with her teeth and wound it over the plastic explosive and around the track. She then tore a second strip and repeated the procedure so that there were now two strips, roughly three fingers' widths apart, holding the bomb she was making in position.

She sat back on her haunches and looked up and down the track. Then she glanced at each side of the deep cutting. It was almost nine o'clock at night, but in the north fringe of a Nazi empire that extended from the depths of the Sahara Desert to beyond the Arctic Circle, there was still enough light to see without a torch. Saffron satisfied herself that she was not being observed. For a couple of seconds she took in the peaceful, limpid beauty of a northern evening sky, its soft blue streaked with clouds in oyster colours of grey, pearl and palest pink. She breathed in air laced with the soft scent of the gorse, whose brave yellow flowers were blooming through the last patches of winter snow, and the salt and seaweed tang of the sea.

The next item out of her knapsack was a metal button that was a little under two inches in diameter. It was attached to a wire clip, shaped like an inverted 'U'. This fitted over the rail so that the button stood proud on top of it. This device was known in the Special Operations Executive, in which Saffron served, as a 'Fog-Signal Switch' because it resembled the small, explosive-filled detonator caps that were placed on tracks as a means of alerting drivers. The pressure of the train's wheels on the device set off the explosive, which made a noise like a large firecracker. That alerted engine drivers to hazards up ahead, or, when conditions were foggy, let them know that they were nearing a station and should begin to slow down.

No railway worker or train crewman would be surprised to see that button on the track, and it would take a close inspection before they noticed that Saffron had fixed a short length of detonating cord between the button and the block of plastic explosive. When the next train passed over the Fog-Signal Switch, the detonator would initiate the chain of detonating cord, guncotton primer and main 808 charge. And all hell would break loose.

The train was carrying five hundred men of the Waffen SS and it was due in less than ten minutes. If the charge went off, it would derail the train and either kill or injure many of the men on board. More importantly, it would wreck the track and block the cutting. The close confines and precipitous granite walls that hemmed everything in would add to the time and effort required to clear and repair the track, and this would severely hamper German lines of communications.

'Now listen here, Courtney,' her commanding officer, Lieutenant Colonel J. T. 'Jimmy' Young had told her, a week earlier. 'Your language skills aren't quite up to long-term undercover operations. Not yet, at any rate. But this mission should be right up your street. It's a simple in-out affair. Take a look at this.'

He spread a map across the chart table that dominated one side of his spartan office. 'You'll be catching the Shetland Bus,' he began, referring to the fleet of converted fishing trawlers, bristling with hidden machine guns that took agents across the

North Sea. 'They'll drop you at the entrance to this long inlet at 05.00, roughly half an hour before sunrise. Paddle due east, inland. You'll have your compass and the first light of the sun to guide you, so paddle towards the light, aim for the mountains on the horizon and you can't go wrong.'

'Don't worry, sir, I'll find my way to shore.'

'That's the spirit. Now, your landing point is this little bay here . . .' Young pointed at a spot on the map marked 'A'. 'It's unoccupied and the nearest Jerry observation post is way back along the coast, so you should be able to get in unobserved.'

He passed her a black-and-white aerial photograph. 'This was taken last week by RAF reconnaissance. It'll give you an idea of the lay of the land.

'The key thing you have to do at this point is dispose of the dinghy. Can't have Jerry spotting it and getting wind of your presence. Two options: first, get out your knife, puncture the hull and sink it offshore. Then wade in. Of course, that's all very well if it stays on the bottom, but we don't want a semi-deflated dinghy floating ashore, looking sorry for itself, where anyone might see it.'

'Absolutely not, sir.'

There was a hint of amusement in Saffron's voice and Young paused and fixed her with a tough, inquisitive look. He had spent his life commanding, as he put it, 'hairy-arsed fighting men' and was having to adjust to the idea that a significant proportion of his new subordinates were soft-skinned, sweet-smelling young women, who might not look or sound like an average Army squaddie but who were, when properly trained, every bit as deadly. She had cut her hair shorter for easier disguise, and there was a flinty, lean composure about her, but she still retained a compelling femininity when her blue eyes blazed in a smile.

'I'm sorry, sir,' Saffron said. 'But I couldn't help thinking of that sad little boat with all the air gone out. You painted such a wonderful picture.'

Young grunted sceptically, though Saffron knew that he was rather pleased by her compliment. She also knew that his gruff exterior concealed a decent, sensitive man, who cared deeply about his agents, even as he was sending them on missions from which some were unlikely to return.

'My point, Courtney, is that you'll need rocks of some sort to weigh the dinghy down. Impossible for us to know if there'll be any lying around when you get there, d'you see?'

'Yes, sir.'

'Second option: you'll see from the photograph your landing point has a narrow beach with thickets of some kind of brush or gorse growing on the landward side. Those bushes may make a better hiding place, once the boat has been deflated. It's up to you to use your initiative and make a judgement on the spot.'

'I understand, sir.'

'Good show. Now, once you're ashore and the boat has been disposed of, make your way across country to Point B, here.'

He jabbed the map with his index finger. Point B was south-east of Point A and a short way inland. 'Distance is only four miles, but no need to rush it. Hilly terrain, virtually no tree cover, main thing is to avoid being spotted and avoid injury. No bloody use to anyone if you're hopping along on one leg, or broken an arm, that sort of thing. Should still be plenty of time to rest, eat and familiarise yourself with the area before you get to work.'

'Yes, sir.'

'Observe the line of the railway, here. Note how it follows the coast, with a few detours further inland, cutting through any hills that come down to the sea. This is the only line along the coast and there are no roads to speak of, certainly none that would allow the easy movement of lorries and artillery pieces, let alone tanks. If we can break that line, it will seriously hamper Jerry's ability to respond to anything we do. He won't be able to manoeuvre his forces or send in reinforcements.'

Saffron knew better than to ask what 'anything we do' might refer to. Instead she inquired, 'Would you like me to blow the line, sir?'

Now it was Jimmy Young's turn to be amused. 'You sound as if you're asking me whether I would like another slice of cake. And the answer is yes, Miss Courtney, I would like you to blow that line. In fact, I am ordering you to do so.' He looked back at the map. 'Right here, in this cutting, just as a trainload of Herr Himmler's finest goons comes rolling by, at approximately 22.00 hours on the night of the fifteenth, precisely one week from today.'

Young passed Saffron two more reconnaissance photos: one showed the cutting and the surrounding landscape, the other was an extreme close-up. He explained that the line was used by civilian as well as military traffic. 'There's a passenger train that passes by that spot at approximately 20.45. We do not want that to be blown to kingdom come. Can't have the citizens of an occupied country thinking of us as the enemy. Wait for it to go by before you place the explosives on the line. When the troop train passes, stay long enough to be sure that the charge has exploded. If it has, do not wait one second more to examine the effects. The flyboys will do that in the morning and we'll have the pictures long before you could possibly get back here. Wait for the bang, hear the bang, then run. Got that?'

'What if the charge does not explode?'

'It will explode, because these charges always explode if properly assembled and positioned, and you will do your job, won't you, Courtney?'

'Yes, sir.'

'Then you must focus all your energies on making good your escape. Your pick-up point is approximately two miles from the cutting . . . here.' Young pointed at a spot marked 'C' a few miles further down the coast from Saffron's landing site. Together, Points A, B and C formed the three corners of a shallow triangle.

Another black-and-white print was passed across the chart table. It showed a cove with two rocky promontories on either side and a small patch of beach at its head with flatter, grassy ground behind it. On one side there was a path through the rocks that led to steps down to a jetty that stuck out into the cove.

'A member of the local Resistance, with a fast motorboat, will moor beside that jetty at 23.30. He will wait until midnight. You have a half-hour window in which to make good your escape. If you get to him in time, he will take you out to sea to rendezvous with another trawler that will bring you home.

'If for some reason the rendezvous is impossible, and you have no other means of survival, you can contact the local Resistance as follows: go to the bar of the Hotel Armor – it's in the town down the line from the cutting – speak to the chap behind the bar, say, "Is Mrs Andersen in? I have a message from her niece."

'The barman will reply, "Do you mean Julie?" To which you reply, "No, her other niece, Karin." He will take it from there. But Courtney, let me be frank, you must only make contact if you have absolutely no alternative. Don't want to risk you leading Jerry to our people.'

Saffron nodded. She had understood from the moment she signed on for this work that her life was expendable. The security of an entire Resistance network was more important than her individual survival.

But she could at least make the enemy pay a price for her death. And now the time had come. Saffron gave the bomb and its switch one final check. Satisfied that all was well, she stepped away from the track and walked as calmly as possible (for nothing would catch a passing German eye, or provoke suspicion more surely than someone running along the railway line) to the end of the cutting. Then she doubled back on herself, but this time walking along a path that ran up the side of the hill through which the railway had been cut, until she reached a spot a short way down the line from where she had positioned her bomb. It was close enough to get a good view without being within range of the blast, or any flying debris.

The spot offered two other attractions. It was on the seaward side of the line, making her getaway easier. And it was one of the few places where there were trees growing, right up to the edge of the man-made precipice. Tucked away between the trunks of two pines, wearing a black woollen skull-cap and her face covered in black war-paint, she could observe proceedings with minimal risk of being spotted by anyone down on the track.

Then she heard German voices, and footsteps pounding: at least a dozen men, by the sound of it. A sickly chill gripped her stomach as she realised that they were coming along the path that ran past her position, a few yards from where she now was.

They were heading straight towards her. And they were running. Running hard.

• • •

Saffron thanked her lucky stars for the pines that screened her position from the path and for the training she had received in concealment. But no matter how well she hid, there was still a sunless grey light in the sky and anyone who looked hard would surely spot her. Even worse, the more distance she put between her and the path, the closer she was to the edge of the cutting, and the more vulnerable to any prying eyes below.

As she pressed herself against the base of one of the tree trunks, the fear of discovery tore at her while a flurry of questions nagged, like yapping, biting hounds: *Do they know I'm here? Has someone betrayed me? But who?*

The Germans were getting closer. Their voices were more distinct and she could make out what they were saying.

Suddenly it dawned on her. These men were not a patrol, out looking for her. They were on a training run and the voices were those of their leader, shouting, 'Come on, lads! No slacking! Keep up at the back!' to the accompaniment of a low rumble of complaints and one cheeky, or simply desperate, soldier calling out, 'Give us a break, sarge! We're dying back here!'

Saffron knew that feeling. In the past twelve months she had been on countless runs at every hour of the day and night, and each one had taken her to the brink of collapse and then beyond. And always the message was the same: 'You're stronger than you think. You can keep going longer, run faster than you believe possible, reach the point where you know you will die if you take another step . . . and keep running nonetheless.'

She almost felt sorry for the runners. But then she remembered that they were the enemy and would hunt her down mercilessly at the slightest inkling of her presence.

She became aware of the deafening pounding of her heart and the rasping of her breath, and she forced herself to calm her pulse and clear her mind.

They were almost on her, no more than twenty yards away . . . then ten.

A rabbit, frightened by the men's approach, burst out of the undergrowth on the far side of the path. It raced across the bare earth, right in front of the onrushing, boot-clad feet, and hurtled into the shelter of the trees towards Saffron.

The men must have seen it. Their eyes would have followed the rabbit into the pines. They would be looking straight at Saffron's hiding place.

But then the rabbit stopped, catching the smell of another human and dashed away again, back out onto the path, and Saffron heard the men's laughter as they followed the animal's frantic attempts to escape.

They passed right by Saffron and she heard one man say, 'I wouldn't mind some rabbit stew for dinner,' and another answer, 'Mmm . . . The way my mum used to make, with beans soaked overnight and spices and . . .'

The rest of the recipe was lost as they disappeared down the path. The evening calm was restored and Saffron returned her attention to the railway track. The last traces of light had vanished from the sky and she was less nervous than she had expected to be. The fact that the runners had not spotted her felt like a good omen, a sign from above that all would be well. Her only worry was the bomb itself, but she knew that there was no rational basis for that. She had assembled and positioned the device correctly. The Fog-Signal Switch was absolutely reliable. The detonator cord and the Nobel 808 were both in perfect condition.

It will work, you know it will.

Time passed. Saffron looked at her watch: 10.15. She frowned. This was German-occupied territory. And German trains were never late.

Where is the damn thing?

And then, in the distance, she heard the whistle blow and a little while later the puffing of the steam engine and the clackety-clack of steel wheels on the line.

The bomb was in position.

She could see the train approaching the cutting, a dark shadow, blacked out to avoid being spotted by enemy aircraft. Saffron thought of all the times her father had taken her hunting as a girl at Lusima, her family's estate in the Kenyan Highlands. Watching the quarry approach, she felt the same sense of excitement and anticipation as she had done then, yet there was a tinge of melancholy, too. Death was approaching. True, there was a difference between killing a noble, untamed creature or soldiers fighting for a dictator who wanted to crush the world beneath his jackboot heel. But they were young men and not so different, as people, from all the others who wore British, or Canadian, or American uniforms. Saffron knew that Germany's rulers were vile, wicked men, but she also knew that there were German men who were decent, kind, and far from the stereotype of the thick-necked Nazi thug.

One of them was the man she loved.

There would be other men, with other girls who loved them, sitting aboard that train. And now it was her job to kill and maim as many of them as possible.

The moon was almost full that night but it had been hidden behind a patch of cloud. The veil vanished and a silvery wash of moonlight illuminated the train as it entered the cutting. It was making good speed, meaning that the crash, when it came, would be even more devastating.

Saffron looked towards the Fog-Signal Switch. It was less than two inches across but it seemed as wide as a soup plate.

Her heart skipped a beat as the train driver leaned out of his cabin to look up the line. The switch was so obvious, right there on the track.

He would see it. He would slow down.

But then he popped his head back inside the cab.

Two seconds later the train passed over the Fog-Signal Switch.

Everything had gone to plan.

• • •

Saffron leaped into the woods, her hands over her ears, suddenly terrified of the carnage she had inflicted on human lives, the shockwave that would surely fling her into oblivion. The noises in her head were so shrill they were hallucinatory, so intense that she could hear high-pitched screams, and she hoped to God they weren't coming from her own mouth. She could imagine the scene of devastation and bloodshed down below her in the cutting as the train careered off the tracks and the carriages behind it slewed and bucked and smashed into one another. The men aboard would have been taken unaware. They'd have been hurled about the compartments, slammed against walls, doors and seats, or thrown out of the windows against the brutally hard granite that rose on either side, their bones broken, their limbs unnaturally twisted.

All this she could picture in her mind's eye. But any thought about what she had done swiftly gave way to her own immediate danger. Her senses focused on the ground in front of her and she began running for her life.

In the days after Jimmy Young had informed Saffron of her mission, she had pored over maps and photographs until she knew every path, every field, every sheltering copse and every bare expanse of open ground between the cutting and the cove, with the arm of its jetty pointing to freedom. She knew where she was going as she ran through the night, and she was not taken unaware by the springy ground, perforated with dips and holes that could easily twist an ankle or break a leg, or the cruel protrusions of rock that lurked beneath moss or wildflowers. She was used to land like this, every SOE agent was, and her feet instinctively adjusted to the rise and fall of the ground on which her steps landed.

She was about a third of the way towards her destination when she had to slow down to work her way around a village. It cost her almost fifteen minutes, but she had allowed for that when mapping out her route. But there were some things for which no one could plan, such as almost running into a German soldier and a local girl making love behind a hedge.

The first clue Saffron had to their presence was a female voice asking, 'Why did you stop?' and a man answering, 'I thought I heard something.'

Saffron dropped to the ground.

'I should go and look,' the soldier said.

Through the foliage that was all that separated her from the lovers, Saffron saw a hand – so close that she could almost touch it – reach to pick up a rifle. She moved her right hand down her body until she felt the handle of the Fairbairn-Sykes fighting knife that lay in its scabbard against her hip. The knife had a needle-sharp pointed blade that made it a deadly stabbing weapon, but the sides of the blade were as keen as razors and could slice through human flesh like a steak knife through tender filet mignon.

Saffron was not afraid of being shot. She had been trained in combat techniques more deadly than the average infantryman could imagine. She could kill that German soldier before he knew she was there. But then there was the girl. She would have to be eliminated too, before she could scream. Saffron knew that the girl would be too shocked to make any sound for a second or two, which was more than enough time to deal with her. But it was one thing to kill an enemy combatant and another to murder an unarmed female civilian, even a collaborator. And, all moral considerations aside, she would be left with two dead bodies to dispose of.

If the soldier looked over the hedge, Saffron would have to fight. She tensed herself, ready to spring at him. But she heard the girl say, 'Don't be silly. It's probably just an animal – a fox or a badger, or something.' Then her tone changed and became more ingratiating as she purred, 'Come back here. I miss you . . .'

Saffron saw the man stop moving. He was torn, she could tell, between his lust and his sense of duty.

'I really liked what you were doing, it felt soooo good,' the girl sighed.

The rifle fell to the ground. The soldier went back to the girl. Saffron prayed that he was a terrible, inconsiderate lover. *Get a move on. Get what you want. Button up your trousers and go!*

But now of all times she had to bump into a Casanova in uniform. He put his heart into it. He paid attention to his partner. Whatever he was doing, it was working because the girl was being aroused to such ecstasy that he had to clamp his hand over her mouth to stop her from screaming. Saffron felt a brief twinge of jealousy. It had been a long time since she had known pleasure like that.

Five minutes passed, then ten. Saffron considered trying to make her getaway while lover-boy still had his pants down, but if he heard another rustle in the hedgerow he would be bound to investigate.

But finally the mutual passion reached its climax and, to Saffron's surprise, it was the girl who promptly stood, pulled up her underwear and said, 'Better be off, then. My mother will be wondering what's become of me.'

She started walking away, followed by the soldier asking, 'When can I see you again?' and at last Saffron could move.

She told herself there was plenty of time and that she didn't want to arrive too early and have to shelter among the rocks until the Resistance man and his boat arrived. The moon was still out and there was enough light to see where she was going.

Saffron's spirits rose; she was elated. Her mission had been a success and she was half a mile from the cove. Maybe she would get away with it after all. And then she heard a howling sound. For a second she was plunged into a dark fantasy world of witches, wolves and malice, but an instant later she had reined in her fevered imagination and realised that it was dogs.

The hunting hounds had been unleashed, and she was their quarry.

• • •

Saffron ran hard, away from the direct route to the cove. She knew that there was a stream no more than three or four hundred yards ahead, which she could use to put them off her scent. By the time they picked it up again, she might be able to make it to the cove, meet the waiting boat and get away.

The water was snow-melt and icy cold. She ran downstream, slipping on slimy, moss-covered rocks on the stream bed but keeping her balance and maintaining her pace, even if she was being taken further off her course, for the stream met the sea some way north of the cove. The stream ran along a gully, whose bush-and tree-lined banks provided Saffron with some shelter from the hounds and the German soldiers who were following. Soon she would have to get back onto dry land again and turn towards the cove. She glanced upwards. The night sky was smeared with clouds, but none of them seemed to be passing over the moon, which remained gloriously isolated, reflecting its glow onto the earth.

If she wanted concealment, she needed to find a hiding place and stay there, in which case she would miss the boat. But to reach the cove in time, she would have to risk being seen. Her only hope was speed. She had to open a gap that her pursuers could not close and pray that the Resistance man had the nerve to wait for her, even though he would see that the Germans were on her tail, and that his motorboat was fast enough to escape before the enemy's guns could blow them both to pieces.

She kept running, taking the single-lane road, no more than a track that twisted along the coastline, serving the farms and fishing hamlets in the area. It struck her that it had been a few minutes since she had heard the barking of the dogs, but no sooner had the thought occurred than she caught the sound of them drifting over the still night air, faintly audible over the gentle susurration of the sea against the shore.

Run faster! Come on, you lazy cow . . . run faster!

Now Saffron understood why her training had been so brutal and her instructors so merciless. They had been preparing her for a moment such as this, when her life depended on being able to push herself onwards and increase her speed when her lungs were screaming for mercy, her heart felt ready to burst and the muscles in her legs were cramping as lactic acid seeped into them past the pain barrier and beyond.

There was a turning off the road up ahead of her to the right: a track that ran downhill towards a large house that was set back a few hundred yards from the cove, screened from the sea by windblown trees that some long-dead owner must have planted as windbreaks. Saffron had planned to work her way discreetly around the property but it was too late for that now.

She sprinted downhill, then left the track before it arrived in front of the house. Here she scrambled over an ornamental rockery, through which artfully constructed paths, linked by stone steps, wound down the steepest slope of the hill. Once these would have provided agreeably civilised strolls for gentle summer afternoons. Now she was fleeing for her life over the rocks and plants, leaping down the steps three at a time, with enemies and their animals hot on her heels. She emerged from the rockery, almost at sea level, and turned onto a rough path that ran between the beds of a vegetable garden.

The dogs were much louder and Saffron could hear the guttural commands of their handlers. A flash of light behind her caught her eye and she glanced back to see a bedroom window opening on the first floor and the silhouette of someone looking out. But then the window closed and the light went out. Whoever was in there, they didn't want to get involved.

Saffron came to the trees at the end of the vegetable patch, ran across a patch of open ground and discovered a chest-high, barbed-wire fence, marking the perimeter of the property. She stopped, her chest heaving, wondering if she could get over it.

She looked to either side. About ten yards away was a metal gate, facing the sea, held shut by a chain. She ran to it, clambered over and landed on the soft, tussocky sea-grass on the far side.

Saffron could see the cove. The grass spread down to the beach, exactly as the aerial reconnaissance photograph had suggested. She looked to the left, towards the rocks and the steps down to the jetty.

There was no boat.

But then she saw a shadow rising above the line of the jetty. It was a man, and he was beckoning towards her. Of course! He'd moored the boat on the far side, out of sight.

Saffron picked up her speed again. She could hear the dogs on the far side of the fence, barking furiously, but knew that by the time their handlers caught up with them and forced the gate open it would be too late, she'd be on the boat.

I'm going to make it!

As she raced forward, her right foot skidded. Where there should have been firm earth beneath the grass, waterlogged mud was sucking at her leg. She fought to free herself and realised that what appeared to be grassland from the air was actually a marsh. There had to be a path through it to the shore, but she had lost it and the only way to find it again would be to head back to the gate and start again.

But that would take her into the arms of the Germans.

Desperately she tried to struggle on, but her progress was painfully slow. She could never tell whether she would be stepping onto dry land, or watery mud, or a hard, roughly shaped piece of rock.

'Over here!' the man by the jetty shouted. She could see him pointing to her left. That must be the path.

She turned and floundered towards it.

'Come on!' the man shouted.

Saffron heard a burst of gunfire behind her.

The Germans had shot the chain that held the gate.

There was a clamour of shouts and barks, and the rumble of an engine being revved.

The boatman called out to her in desperation. 'Quick, quick!'

The crump of a flare gun being fired echoed across the cove and it burst above Saffron's head, casting a blinding white glare over the entire scene.

She saw the bearded face of her rescuer, a cap on his head, a fisherman's sweater. And then he ducked behind the jetty again and the next thing she knew the boat was racing away across the cove, heading for the open water, and she had to throw herself into the morass of grass and mud and salt water as guns chattered and tracer bullets sparked through the air towards the fleeing vessel.

The gunfire died away, though the sound of the engine disappearing into the distance told Saffron that the Resistance man had got away. She was glad of that. She would not have his death on her conscience.

Saffron dragged herself to her feet.

No more than ten yards away, eight men wearing German army windbreakers were standing, their guns pointed at her, while their dogs paced to and fro, snarling angrily and casting hungry stares in Saffron's direction.

One of the soldiers had a lieutenant's insignia sewn onto his sleeve. He pointed towards Saffron and ordered two of his men to get her while the others kept them covered.

Saffron had her knife and her pistol. If she could move, or take cover, or had the element of surprise on her side, she might have fought it out. But she was stuck up to her shins in mud, without shelter, and she knew that the enemy was armed with MP40 submachine guns – '*Schmeissers*', her instructors had called them – capable of firing 500 rounds a minute. By the time she had reached for her gun they would have torn her body to shreds.

Perhaps she should make the move and get herself killed. That way they couldn't torture her and she couldn't give away what little she knew about the Resistance movement. But something stopped her. It wasn't that she was afraid to die, more that she refused to give up. As long as she was alive there was always the chance she could find a way to escape. All her life she had never let anything or anyone beat her.

Even as the soldiers' hands grabbed her, pulled her from the swamp and dragged her towards the path, Saffron clung to her self-belief. *They haven't beaten me yet.*

• • •

Saffron was taken to the large country house that she knew had been appropriated by the SS. 'It's a branch office for all their various police operations,' Jimmy Young had told her. 'Criminal Police, Secret Police and the SD: the Nazi Party's own intelligence agency. In practice there's a lot of overlap, particularly in the occupied territories. They're all equally unpleasant.'

They took her gun, her knife, her bag and all its contents. They stripped her naked and left her that way for three hours in an unheated underground cell, lit by a bare bulb, with no furniture, no privacy and nothing but a tin pot in which to relieve herself.

There was an opening in the door through which the guards could look into the room, covered by a small slat that slid open or closed. The guards made no secret of opening it and looking at her on a regular basis.

Saffron sat herself against the wall with her arms around her bent knees to provide a degree of modesty. She had been awake since three in the morning. At one point her head dropped down against her kneecaps as she fell asleep. Within seconds, a guard came in, dragged her to her feet, slapped her about the face and threw her back down on the floor. He looked at her, letting his eyes wander over her body, making her feel as vulnerable, exposed and helpless as he could.

Saffron knew that this was part of the softening-up process. Sleep deprivation was a fundamental form of torture, and the crushing of a person's dignity and self-worth was the first stage in destroying their humanity. Well, she could go without sleep. She had been trained for that. And even if she was stuck in this hellhole, her mind was free to go wherever it wanted.

She took herself back to the day she had first reported to Norgeby House, an anonymous modern office block in Baker Street. Mr Brown, the mysterious figure who had recruited Saffron's mother for the Great War in the same way he had Saffron for this Second World War, had greeted her and said, 'I thought you might like to meet someone you know.'

He led her upstairs, knocked on a plain office door, waited for the barked command 'Come!' and led her in.

It took Saffron a second to realise who the man in the officer's uniform, seated at the desk opposite the door, really was. Even then she couldn't quite believe it.

'Mr Amies?' she had gasped. 'Is that really you?'

Hardy Amies had made several of Saffron's favourite dresses before the war. 'Captain Amies, if you don't mind, Miss Courtney,' he said sternly. 'Or "sir" to you.'

'Oh . . .' said Saffron, even more taken aback. 'Yes, sir, of course.'

Amies got up, walked around the desk, smiling, and held out his hand. 'How are you, Saffron?' he asked, then looked at Mr Brown. 'This young lady was one of my favourite clients. Such a perfect figure! She could take a hessian sack and make it look like Paris couture.'

'Diana Cooper once made that same point to me,' Mr Brown agreed. 'I've rarely heard her compliment another woman so fulsomely. Now, if you don't mind, I'm expected in King Charles Street. The Foreign Secretary wants a word. I'll leave you two to get reacquainted. Goodbye, Amies, and goodbye to you, too, Miss Courtney.'

'What a funny old man he is,' remarked Amies once Mr Brown had taken his leave. He sat back against his desk and motioned to Saffron to sit in one of the chairs opposite it.

'No one is ever quite sure what he does, but there are few pies that don't have his fingers in them and almost no one of any importance he doesn't know. I think of him as a sort of earthly God because he moves in mysterious ways.'

'I met him in Oxford,' Saffron said, pulling herself together, 'though I'd heard of him before that.'

'Ah, yes, your family connection. He did vaguely mention it. Now, first things first . . . I imagine Mr Brown has referred to this organisation by a number of different terms – the Inter-Services Research Bureau, Ministry of Ungentlemanly Warfare, and so on . . .'

'He said its real name was the Special Operations—'

Before Saffron could say the word 'Executive', Amies had raised a hand and snapped, 'Hush! That organisation does not officially exist, so far as anyone outside this building and a select few in Whitehall are concerned. We refer to ourselves as "Baker Street". Understood?'

'Yes.'

Amies gave her a look she had not seen before. Instead of a couturier charming a client, he was an officer making it clear to a subordinate that they were not coming up to scratch. It took her a second to realise her mistake.

'Yes, sir,' she said.

'That's better . . . Now, let me be frank, you currently lack the linguistic skills that are normally regarded as essential for a prospective agent. You cannot operate properly in a country unless you are fluent in its language. We have always looked for recruits who are bilingual, and then trained them in the skills required to survive in the field. But you're rather different, aren't you?'

Amies paused, looking at Saffron quizzically, knowing her only as the pretty young thing who used to wear his dresses so elegantly. 'You've already killed a man.'

Saffron had become accustomed, somewhat reluctantly, to the morbid curiosity her wartime exploits provoked in other people. When war broke out in 1939, Saffron wasn't interested in punting leisurely along the River Cherwell at Oxford University when all the men she knew were defending their country. She was determined to get involved, even if it was only driving a car or a lorry.

'More than one,' she replied. 'While I was serving as General Wilson's driver in the Western Desert, we were chased by a car filled with Italian soldiers. I shot the driver. The car crashed and, as far as I know, all the other men in it died too.'

It was 1941, and Saffron was a driver for British Army General Henry Maitland Wilson on the North Africa, Greece and Palestine fronts. When his khaki Humber saloon ended up being pursued by an enemy Italian car, Saffron, armed with her Beretta 418 pistol, had put two rounds into the driver's head.

She paused and added, 'And I shot my uncle Francis. He was a traitor. He deserved it.' She thought back to that ghastly affair. Uncle Francis Courtney had become an embittered, cynical man. He had betrayed Saffron and her father Leon to the Germans and they'd both nearly lost their lives. Saffron confronted Francis and, in the scuffle that followed, she'd put a bullet between his eyes. She would claim it was self-defence.

'I dare say he did. Now, your record shows that Wilson mentioned you in despatches for that desert show. And then you were awarded the George Medal . . .'

'Yes, sir.'

'. . . for defending a merchant ship against an attack by Stukas. I'm looking at your citation: "When enemy fire left one of the ship's batteries of Vickers machine guns unmanned, Miss

Courtney, showing complete disregard for her own safety, ran to the guns and operated them under continuous bombardment. She hit and damaged at least one of the enemy aircraft and remained at her post until the captain gave the order to abandon ship. She then pulled her wounded father to safety and ensured he was rescued by the single lifeboat that survived the sinking. Even then, when unarmed, she stood and waved her fist in defiance at a low-flying enemy aircraft."

'You're smiling . . . May I ask why?'

'I'm just remembering the look on the German pilot's face.'

And also I'm remembering who that pilot was.

'Well, it's quite a tale you have to tell. Mind you, there's nothing more unexpected about your situation than there is about mine. It turns out we both had previously undiscovered talents. Mine appears to be for clandestine operations. I speak French quite fluently, so I was in and out of Belgium a few times in the first year or so of the war.'

Even then, without being told anything about Amies' operations, Saffron had understood that going 'in and out of Belgium' would have required extraordinary courage and skill.

'Nowadays my work consists of selecting prospective agents, supervising their training and preparing them for the field. Tell me, did Mr Brown explain the way we're organised here?'

'No, sir.'

'In that case, I'd better fill you in. As you may have noticed, the world of armed forces and intelligence services runs on a system of initials. Baker Street is no exception. For example, the men who preside over your fate and mine are known by the initials that describe their rank: CD, D/R, A/CD, AD/E . . . the list is endless. But there is only one man whose name you need to have engraved upon your heart, and that name is Gubbins.'

Saffron giggled, assuming Amies was playing some kind of a joke. 'Who is Gubbins?'

'Colonel Colin Gubbins is a small, ferocious artillery man with thrillingly piercing blue eyes, whose precise title is irrelevant because he is, as a matter of fact, the Man Who Makes

Everything Happen. He is not in complete charge of Baker Street yet, but he certainly will be one day. My advice to you, Miss Courtney is, "Beware the Gubbins". Do not displease him. Make him happy to be in your presence. Your future may depend upon it.'

'I'll certainly try.'

'That's the spirit. Now, the operational side of Baker Street is divided into sections, each of which is known by an initial, naturally, which also applies to its boss. This may be because these bosses change regularly, so it is easier to remember one letter than an endless series of new names. The French section is known as F, for France, as is its boss. The Dutch section and boss are known as N, for Netherlands. You and I are now speaking in the section covering Belgium and Luxembourg, which is known as T. Do not ask me why. Now, you may wonder why you have been led into T's embrace. The answer is partly that you and I know one another, but also because your upbringing may help you acquire the particular linguistic skills we require.'

'How so?'

'Because half of Belgium speaks French and the other half speaks Flemish, which is a variation of Dutch. Now, I already knew that you'd been born and raised in Kenya, of course, but I see from your file that you were educated in South Africa . . .'

'Yes, sir, at Roedean in Johannesburg.'

'Pick up any Afrikaans while you were there?'

'A bit.'

'Good. Then you'll know that Afrikaans is also a form of Dutch. So it shouldn't be beyond our powers to improve your Flemish. That would mean we could put you into play in Flanders. I see that your mother was of German descent and you spent some time in Germany before the war . . .'

'That's right, sir. One of my closest girlfriends at school was German. I went to stay with her family a couple of times.'

'I don't suppose you picked up the language at all?'

'Yes . . . I have a little conversational German, too.'

'Well, that's a start. Most of our work in Baker Street consists of liaising with the Resistance networks in various places, helping them grow, giving them equipment and getting them up to scratch. But we have every intention of taking on an active role in due course: sabotage, assassination, that sort of thing.'

'And you have me in mind for that?'

'I'd have thought so. In the meantime, why don't I buy you dinner this evening? The Dorchester feeds one as well as can be expected these days, and Malcolm McAlpine, who built the place, swears that it's bomb-proof.'

'Thank you, sir, that would be lovely,' Saffron said.

'Good. You may call me Hardy while we are at dinner, but I have one condition . . .'

Saffron remembered that she had felt a little uneasy. Everything about SOE was so mysterious that she hesitated to speculate what might be demanded of her. 'What's that, sir?' she asked.

'I insist that you wear one of my dresses.'

'Oh, I think I could manage that, sir,' Saffron had assured him, delighted by his command.

She had gone back to the flat that her father had bought before the war, in Chesham Court, a modern block in one of the smartest parts of London, halfway between Knightsbridge and Sloane Square. Rifling through her wardrobe she felt she was looking at another woman's clothes: the woman she had been before the war, the one who had fallen in love with Gerhard von Meerbach.

That night in London with Amies, Saffron had thought about Gerhard as she picked out a cocktail dress in midnight-blue silk, just as she thought about Gerhard now, as she sat slumped in the cold, stark cell.

No! Don't! she berated herself. *It hurts too much. Think about that outfit, that night with Hardy, nothing else.*

Amies had created the dress in his role as chief designer for the house of Lachasse. Its fabric was so beautiful, its cut so exquisite, that it forced any woman who wanted to wear it well to match the high standards that it set. Before she put it on, Saffon made the kind of effort with her appearance that was once normal, but had now disappeared from her wartime life.

Naked and horribly exposed, struggling to stop herself shivering, with her flesh pressed against a cold damp concrete floor, Saffron relived every lovely, indulgent moment of her preparations that night. In her imagination, she was lying in her bath, watching her skin go pink in the piping-hot, scented water. She patted herself dry and soothed her skin with rich lotions, enjoying the feeling of her fingers spreading the slick, creamy concoctions over her soft, smooth body. She put on her satin dressing gown, walked into her dressing room and chose her prettiest underwear and silk stockings.

It had mattered so much that her hair and make-up be perfect, and that every detail of her jewellery, shoes, coat, gloves and hat should suit one another, herself and the occasion. She felt like a new recruit, preparing his full dress uniform for inspection by a sharp-eyed, unforgiving sergeant major. These delicate touches were her uniform and the Dorchester would be her parade ground.

Before leaving the flat, Saffron had examined herself in the full-length mirror. She knew that people found her beautiful, because she had been told so all her life. But there was no vanity in her appraisal. Her intention was not to congratulate herself, but to spot all the mistakes, the flaws and imperfections. Her hands, for example, had spent most of the past year gripping the steering wheel of Jumbo Wilson's staff car. As his driver she was also, as often as not, his mechanic. A woman who had to be ready at a moment's notice to change a tyre, replace a spark plug, or improvise a fan belt from one of her own stockings could not bother with long painted nails or regular manicures, particularly when she was working in the dust and grit of the Western Desert.

Saffron held her fingers out in front of her, looking at the back of her hands and then turning them over to look at her palms. She had done her best to rub all the calluses away with an emery board and cover her short, cracked nails with paint, but still she sighed to herself. *They're a disgrace.*

She frowned too at the hang of her dress. She had never been overweight, but war appeared to have made her even slimmer, because the skirt was a fraction loose around her waist and hips. No normal man would notice, but Hardy would spot it in an instant.

And of course he did. 'You look utterly ravishing, darling,' he had said when they met in the foyer of the Dorchester. He opened his mouth to speak again, but then shook his head. 'You should give that dress to me in the morning, so that one of my seamstresses could take it in an eighth of an inch at the waist and a quarter round the hips.'

'Do you still have seamstresses? What with the war and everything . . .'

Amies smiled. 'Oh yes. I still design collections. But only for American ladies, I'm afraid.'

'But what about us, here in England? Why can't we get your dresses?'

'Because you don't pay in dollars, my dear. The country desperately needs them to refund America for food and military kit. The Board of Trade has commanded Norman Hartnell and me to come up with chic designs that can be packed off to America. I often sketch while I'm working at Baker Street, actually. Helps me think.'

As they walked towards the hotel restaurant, Amies had continued, 'Now I shall tell you something about Baker Street that is of particular relevance to you. We are the most savage, lawless outfit this country possesses. Our task is to play dirty, harm the enemy by any means possible and ignore all the rules. That's why the stuffier War Office types despise us. And yet despite that, or possibly because of it, Baker Street has more women doing more interesting work than any other branch of the services.'

'I did see an awful lot of girls my sort of age when I came to your office.'

'The place is filled with them: smart, bright, young, fierce creatures. Gubbins swears by them. But still . . .' Amies had paused a few yards from the restaurant door, stepped back and examined Saffron like a connoisseur in front of a work of art. 'There's not a woman in Baker Street, indeed in all of London, lovelier than you tonight.'

Saffron wrapped her arms tighter around her knees, desperately trying to silence her chattering teeth. But she smiled at the recollection of how glorious it had been to feel feminine, pampered and admired again, after all the months of work and war and death. Amies had ordered champagne and entertained her with an hilarious account of his officer training.

'As you can imagine, my dear, they hardly expected a pansy dressmaker, who was far from the ideal of the big, tough, manly secret agent, to last the course. But I'm proud to say that I passed with flying colours. I saw my report once they let me join Baker Street. It said . . .' Amies raised his head in the manner of a Shakespearian actor about to deliver a soliloquy and intoned, '"This officer is far tougher both physically and mentally than his rather precious appearance would suggest."'

Saffron giggled.

'I know!' Amies exclaimed in an exaggeratedly effete voice. 'I may say, I was deeply hurt. Honestly, darling . . . Precious? Me!'

He let Saffron's laughter subside and then went back to his recital. '"He possesses a keen brain and an abundance of shrewd sense." I had no objection to that bit, as you can imagine. Anyway, it concluded that: "His only handicap is his precious appearance and manner . . ."'

He glanced at Saffron, 'I know, dear heart, why did he have to be so beastly all over again? But there was a nice twist at the end: ". . . and these are tending to decrease".

'Well, I should think they were. One thing a couturier does understand is the notion of *comme il faut*. In the Army one has to be butch and there's an end to it.'

• • •

Saffron slipped deeper into the memory of that happy evening. After dinner, Amies had taken her dancing at the Embassy Club on Bond Street. Dreamily, between wakefulness and sleep, she recalled how wonderful it had felt to be arm-in-arm with Hardy Amies, wearing her lovely silk dress and doing the foxtrot, knowing that she did not have to worry about fending off a clumsy pass, for he would never ask for anything more than a dance and a chaste kiss.

The door to her cell slammed open. A squat, hatchet-faced woman walked in, wearing a man's boilersuit, with a belt straining against her spreading waist, and threw a bundle of filthy rags at Saffron's feet.

'Put this on!' she barked.

Saffron reached for the rags, which turned out to be a hessian smock in a drab, pale grey. There were brown marks down the front.

'Bloodstains,' said the woman. 'They don't wash out.'

Saffron pulled the smock over her head and stuck her arms through the short sleeves. The material was rough against her skin. *That's the least of my problems*, she thought.

The woman turned towards the corridor that ran past the cell and called out, 'The prisoner is ready!'

Two soldiers entered. One of them handed the woman a piece of black cloth, which she tucked into her belt. Then he gave her a pair of handcuffs.

'Hands!' she commanded.

Saffron stuck out her arms, with the wrists together, and made no attempt to resist. From now on her aim was to be as passive and mute as possible: to give the enemy nothing.

The woman took the black cloth from her belt. Saffron saw that it was a hood, and the next thing she knew it had been slipped over her head, covering her face and leaving her blind.

She felt the woman grab her shoulders and turn her towards the door.

'Walk!'

Saffron stepped forward a few paces, hesitant for fear that she might hit a wall or the doorframe.

'Stop! Left turn! Walk!'

The commands continued as Saffron was marched out of the cellar of the house and into the cold open air. She felt chilly stone against her bare feet and then painful gravel chips, and then a long stretch of frosty turf. The icy wind cut through her smock, as if she were still naked. She had had no food or drink for many hours and try as she might to remain mentally alert, she was giddy with exhaustion.

They stopped. Saffron heard a metal door being unlocked and opened. She was pushed forward as the door was shut and locked behind her. She was shoved onto a wooden chair. Her wrists were freed from the handcuffs, but then tied tightly to the arms of the chair. Her ankles were also bound against the chair legs. The hood was removed.

Saffron opened her eyes but was instantly dazzled by a blinding light shining directly at her.

Someone slapped her face, hard, and she could not help herself from crying out with the pain and shock.

'Open your eyes!' a voice barked. 'You will keep your eyes open. If you close your eyes, you will be hit.'

Saffron could not help it. Her instincts took over. She closed her eyes again.

She was slapped.

She forced herself to keep her eyes open and look towards the light. Beyond it she could make out a shadowy figure. It spoke in English, with cold, calm menace.

'Ah, so . . . Please allow me to introduce myself. My name is Stark. I am an officer in the *Geheime Staatspolizei*, or Secret Police. You may know it in the abbreviated form: Gestapo. Your life is in my hands. I decide whether you live or die. I keep you awake, or allow you to sleep. I starve you, or feed you. I treat you well, or I torture you in ways that you could never imagine in your darkest nightmares. You have no power, no control over your fate . . . Except in one respect. If you cooperate, you will not go free, for you will never go free again. But you may live a little longer and, above all, you may avoid the agonies that will be inflicted upon you if you do not talk.'

Saffron kept her face expressionless. The light had blinded her now to the point where it hardly made any difference whether her eyes were open or closed.

'Understand this: you have no rights, no protection under the Geneva Convention or any rules of war. You are not a soldier in uniform. You are a spy, a saboteur and a murderer. Many good men have died because of you. Their souls cry out for vengeance. Be assured I will provide it. Let us begin. What is your name?'

Saffron thought of what her instructor, Sergeant Greenwood – a small, wiry, but terrifyingly tough Cockney from the backstreets of East London – had told her group of trainees. 'You can shove that "name, rank and serial number" bollocks right up your arse. You've got no ranks, nor serial numbers, 'cos you're not in the bleeding Army and you haven't got no name, neither, 'cos your cover's a person that doesn't even exist. So you got nothing to tell the bleeding Krauts, do you? So keep your traps shut and don't tell them bugger all.'

She remained silent.

Stark repeated the question. 'What is your name?'

She did not respond.

This time she received a body-shot to the solar plexus, delivered with a man's full force. The punch knocked the air from Saffron's lungs and left her retching, gasping for breath and sick with pain.

Saffron repeated Sergeant Greenwood's favourite saying in her mind: *pain can't hurt you*. Or as he would say, 'Pain can't 'urt ya'.

His reasoning was worthy of a professor of philosophy. 'Now . . . a bullet can 'urt ya. It can bleeding kill you. A bayonet in the guts can mess you right up. But pain, what can that do? Pain is only in the mind. It's a feeling. That's all it is. It don't do nothing to you . . . I mean, what if you get caught by some bloody-minded Nazi bastard who pulls all yer fingernails out, one by one. Is that painful? Course it bleeding is. But will it kill you? Course not. Whoever died of pulled-out fingernails? Bleeding no one, that's who.

'And that's what you gotta remember, right? Them Nazis, they don't want to kill you, do they? Not as long as they think they can still get something from you. So as long as you don't tell 'em nothing – and I mean abso-bleedin'-lutely nothing – what's the worst they can do? Inflict pain, that's what, and, all together now, "Pain . . . can't . . . 'urt ya!"'

So Saffron told them nothing.

Stark asked her the same questions time and time again:

'What is your name?'

'Who is your commanding officer?'

'Where are you based?'

'What were your instructions for contacting the Resistance?'

'Who are your agents in this area?'

But not once did he get an answer.

His men punched Saffron and slapped her till her face was cut and swollen, and her torso, from her belly to her breasts, was a livid mass of purple, black and blue contusions, but still she remained silent.

Two soldiers entered the room, and one of them replaced the hood on her head. Suddenly she was falling backwards as they tipped over the chair she was tied to, but before her head smashed onto the concrete floor, a hand roughly held her neck and halted the impact. She wanted to cry with relief. Seconds later icy-cold water was gushing over her nose and mouth, and instantly panic gripped her as she started to drown. Before she passed out, her chair was returned to its upright position and she vomited copiously, dry heaving and inhaling more water as she sucked at the sodden hood for air. They pushed her to the floor again and water spilled furiously down her nostrils and mouth once more, until all her senses were telling her that she was on the point of death. She thought back to Dr Maguire, another, more gentlemanly instructor than Sergeant Green-wood, who had explained that the survival instinct is the most profound force in any living creature. The body does not want to die. It sends out warning signals the moment there is any prospect of that happening. But those signals are sent out well in advance of the event to give the mind time to organise a response to the threat it faces. The key is to trust one's capacity to stay alive and not be fooled by the panic signals.

More than once Saffron blacked out. But they'd always pull her up and she'd always regain consciousness.

And still she said nothing.

Her life became reduced to a simple, relentless cycle. Stark and another man, Neuer, took it in turns to interrogate her. In between she would be taken back to her cell. Both her cell and the interrogation chamber were windowless, though their lights were always on. On the walks between them she was kept hooded. Soon she had no idea whether it was day or night, or how much time had passed.

They fed her occasionally, she wasn't sure how often. The meal, if one could call it that, was always the same: a bowl of thin gruel with a piece of gristle that must, she imagined, have come from some kind of animal, though none she had ever previously consumed. This came with a small portion of stale, black rye bread.

When she was able to pass water into the tin bowl, it was laced with blood. And they would not let her sleep, not for a moment. She was drunk with fatigue, hallucinating with waking dreams that made her lose all distinction between the nightmares in her head and those in the real world. Her mind and her senses were starting to unravel and it was this gradual mental disintegration that slowly broke her will to resist.

'Try to hold out for at least twenty-four hours,' Dr Maguire had said. 'That will give our people some chance of getting away, or covering their tracks. If you can manage forty-eight hours, that would hugely increase their chances of avoiding discovery, but we know that's asking an awful lot. Just try to do your best. That's all anyone can do.'

• • •

Saffron had tried to do her best. She had tried so hard. But now, as they dragged her down the path to the interrogation chamber, for she could barely stand any more, let alone walk, she knew that she had been taken to her limits. One more beating and she would start to talk. And it would not be because of the beating. It would be because she needed to sleep . . . even if it was the sleep of death.

They shoved her in the chair. They bound her hands and feet.

She opened her eyes to the blinding light, hardly able to keep her head upright any more.

Stark asked his questions.

One last time, Saffron defied him. Then her strength failed her. Her eyes closed . . . Her chin slumped onto her chest.

And the next thing she knew, the ropes around her wrists and ankles were being untied. She half opened her eyes and saw a hand holding a steaming hot cup of tea.

An English voice – it sounded like Sergeant Greenwood – said, 'There you go, love. Get that down yer gob. You earned it.'

She looked up and the light was off, and it was not a Gestapo officer called Stark sitting behind it but Jimmy Young, and he was standing up and there was a crack of raw emotion in his voice as he said, 'By God, Courtney, that was the bravest thing

I've ever seen. Damn near seventy-two hours. No one's ever lasted that long before.'

'I'm sorry, Miss,' Greenwood said. 'Just so you know, I hated doing it . . . We all did. But we had to, see, so's there's nothing them Nazi bastards can ever do that you can't handle.' He gave her a rueful smile. 'Bloody hell, love, you may be as rich as the Queen of Sheba and posh as Lady Muck, but you're a tough little bint. I pity the poor Jerry who tries to get the best of you.'

He looked around. 'Come on, lads, three cheers for Miss Courtney. Hip-hip . . .'

But by the time the first 'hooray!' had echoed around the room, Saffron had collapsed to the floor.

• • •

The sun was nearly over the horizon and a cold, early spring breeze blew across the concrete apron of Berlin's Tempelhof Airport as Dr Walther Hartmann climbed the short flight of steps to the passenger door of the three-engine Junkers Ju 52 transport aircraft. He paused and rubbed the corrugated fuselage that made the Ju 52 so instantly recognisable. He had always been a nervous flyer and now that he spent more time than ever in the air, it had become a superstition of his to touch the body of any plane in which he flew, like a rider patting the horse he was about to mount.

Hartmann was forty-four years old. He was not an imposing individual, being of modest height, with a face that had never been anything other than instantly forgettable, even in his youth. The addition of a toothbrush moustache, shaped in honour of the Führer, had not altered this fact. He wore round, tortoise-shell spectacles, and when he removed his hat to enter the Junkers, he revealed a scalp that was almost bald. But while Hartmann might not have looks on his side, he could boast a degree of power. For he was State Secretary in the

Ministry of the Occupied Territories, and reported directly to the Minister, Alfred Rosenberg, himself. His work took him all over the newly conquered territories that the Reich had acquired thanks to the invasion of the Soviet Union. The distance he had to cover, combined with his seniority, ensured that Hartmann travelled in style.

He was met by a uniformed steward, who directed him through the cabin to his seat. A standard Ju 52 carried its passengers in eight rows of two seats, separated by a centre aisle. This craft, however, had been modified for use by senior government officials, right up to the highest in the land. On entering at the rear of the cabin, Hartmann found two sofas upholstered in red leather, positioned lengthways opposite one another, with the aisle between them. The steward led Hartmann into the next area of the cabin, the conference room, in which four high-backed leather armchairs were arranged in two pairs – one facing forward the other back – with a table between them. The steward offered Hartmann one of the forward-facing chairs. Ahead of him he could see an open door leading to a third part of the cabin, which contained a larger, grander version of the chair in which he was sitting, facing back towards the tail. That was truly a seat fit for the Führer, and it struck Hartmann that the man he worshipped so reverently, to whom his whole life was dedicated, might have travelled on this actual aircraft.

The thought was an inspiring one, but it was overridden by the nervous tension that climbing aboard an aircraft inevitably generated. Hartmann paused for a moment to take the series of slow, deep breaths with which he habitually calmed himself. He considered the day ahead.

He was to travel one thousand kilometres from Berlin to Rivne, the administrative capital of the *Reichskommissariat* Ukraine, as the southern half of Nazi-occupied Russia had been renamed. The journey would take around seven hours, allowing for one refuelling stop. His task upon arrival was to meet with *Reichskommissar* Erich Koch, the master of this vast domain, and a number of his regional subordinates, local officials of the *Reichsbahn*, or state railway, and senior officers of both the SS and *Werhmacht*. Their agenda concerned the practical steps needed to implement a policy document called the Wannsee Protocol. This was an important and sensitive subject, close to the Führer's heart, and required coordination at the highest civil and military levels.

Hartmann gave a curt nod as the steward asked whether he would like a cup of coffee before take-off. He rested his briefcase on the table in front of him, opened it and took out a slim manila file marked *Streng Geheim*, or Top Secret. It contained two documents. The first was a copy of the Protocol and the second consisted of a detailed commentary on the Protocol prepared by his colleague Dr Georg Leibbrandt, who had been present at the conference three months earlier, on 20 January 1942, at which the policy had been discussed and adopted. Hartmann already knew every detail of the Protocol and all of Leibbrandt's observations. But it never hurt to go through it all again. There was nothing more reassuring than sitting down for a meeting with the certainty that one knew more about the subject under discussion than any other man there.

Hartmann removed the case from the table and placed it at his feet. He started skimming through the outline of the administrative problem to which the Protocol proposed a once-and-for-all solution. He could almost recite it by heart, he had read it so many times, and it was hardly a piece of prose that repaid repeated examination. The language was dry, bureaucratic:

> *The work concerned with emigration was, later on, not only a German problem, but also a problem with which the authorities of the countries to which the flow of emigrants was being directed would have to deal.*

It was eight in the morning. Hartmann had been working late the night before. His eyes began to glaze over as he ploughed on:

Financial difficulties, such as the demand by various foreign governments for increasing sums of money to be presented at the time of the landing, the lack of shipping space, increasing restriction of entry permits, or the cancelling of such, increased extraordinarily the difficulties of emigration.

Hartmann reached for the coffee that the steward had placed on the table, served in a cup and saucer of the finest porcelain. He had refused the offer of sugar and cream, and downed the hot, bitter brew. He was about to return to the text of the Protocol when his attention was distracted by the arrival of another passenger. Hartmann frowned. He had been assured that he would be entirely undisturbed on the flight. He glared down the length of the compartment, wondering who had the influence to board a plane that had been set aside for the use of the Ministry.

The newcomer was tall enough that he had to duck as he walked down the aisle to avoid hitting his head on the ceiling. As he bent down, his dark blond hair fell across his brow, causing him to push it back into place. He was wearing a Luftwaffe uniform, and if Hartmann recalled correctly, his rank insignia were those of a *Hauptmann*, or captain, meaning that he would probably command a squadron of a dozen or so aircraft. His jacket also bore an Iron Cross, First Class, multiple campaign ribbons, his Pilot Badge and Ground Assault Badge. These suggested distinguished, but perhaps not exceptional, service to the Fatherland. But the final decoration that caught Hartmann's eye, sewn onto the right-hand side of this unknown airman's uniform, changed everything. It was the German Cross in Gold, awarded for repeated acts of bravery, but only to servicemen who already held at least an Iron Cross, First Class.

Hartmann understood the man's presence aboard the flight. He was a Luftwaffe hero. The Ju 52 was being flown by Luftwaffe personnel. They would be only too happy to take him wherever he wanted to go.

Hartmann returned to his work.

The newcomer took the other forward-facing seat alongside Hartmann, with less than a metre of aisle space between them.

'Good morning,' he said, raising his voice as the engines were fired up. He smiled.

Hartmann looked up at the man. He was enviably handsome, but there were deep lines etched around his grey eyes and dark rings beneath them, and his skin appeared to have been pulled tight across his elegant features. Hartmann saw the look everywhere these days. It was the face of a fighting man who lived with too much stress and too little sleep, month after month in combat.

'Good day,' Hartmann replied. 'Allow me to introduce myself. I am Dr Walther Hartmann and I have the honour of being State Secretary in the Ministry of the Occupied Territories.' Hartmann allowed himself the indulgence of levity. 'It is my flight on which you are . . . what is the modern saying? . . . ah yes, hitching a lift.'

The pilot laughed politely. 'Please forgive me for being so rude,' he said. His accent was Bavarian, but refined, even aristocratic. 'How could I think of climbing aboard your aircraft and not introducing myself?' He held out his right hand. 'Gerhard von Meerbach, at your service. I'm a squadron captain in the Luftwaffe. But I dare say you'd already worked that out for yourself.'

Gerhard had never thought of himself as a warrior. He was an architect by profession. He wanted to build, not destroy. His dream had been to harness the power of the Meerbach industrial empire to create affordable, easily fabricated housing, so that slums became a thing of the past and everyone in German society could live in clean, modern, functional homes.

But everything had changed after he helped the Solomons family to escape to Switzerland. The SS had discovered what he had done and in the feverish mood of Germany in the early thirties, with the new Nazi regime altering not only the country's laws but its entire moral framework, Gerhard's actions were deemed to be criminal. His older brother Konrad was by then making his way up the hierarchy of the SS and had become the Personal Assistant of *SS-Gruppenführer* Reinhard Heydrich, one of the most powerful men in the Reich.

Konrad had never felt brotherly love towards Gerhard. He would have been happy to see him thrown into the newly opened Dachau concentration camp. In the end, however, Heydrich himself had concluded that, on balance, there was more to be lost than gained from imprisoning a scion of one of the Reich's most prominent industrial dynasties. Instead he had imposed a more subtle punishment.

Gerhard, Heydrich declared, was to become a good citizen of the Reich. He was sent to work for Albert Speer, the Führer's personal architect, helping to design the mighty buildings of Germania, the new city, that would be built on the site of Berlin that Adolf Hitler envisaged as the capital of his imperial Reich.

At work, and wherever he socialised, Gerhard was warned never to deviate from Nazi orthodoxy. If he expressed an opinion, it would be one of absolute conformity with the party line. When he threw out his arm and cried 'Heil Hitler', he would do so with sincere enthusiasm, for all the world to see.

'I want your soul,' Heydrich had said, and to ensure that he got it he had made the price of disobedience clear: 'If you defy me in any way, you will be sent to Dachau. And what is more, all your friends, your fellow students, the women you have loved – everyone who has ever had anything to do with you – will find their lives examined in every detail by the Gestapo. They will be arrested and questioned. Their property will be searched. And if my men find anything, no matter how trivial, that suggests that they are undesirable, they will join you in the concentration camp.'

Gerhard would happily have risked his own life to save his principles, but he could not condemn so many other people too. He forced himself to play a role he detested. But all was not lost, for Heydrich had demanded one other visible sign of Gerhard's 'good Nazi' status. He ordered him to spend his summers training as a Luftwaffe reservist, so that when the time for war came, he would be ready to lay down his life for the Third Reich.

It was intended to be another form of servitude. But from the moment Gerhard took the controls of a training glider, he fell in love with the wonder of flight. High in the sky, alone in a cockpit, he felt free of all the shackles that bound him on earth. Down there he lived a lie. Up here he was truly himself. Heydrich had, unknowingly, handed Gerhard von Meerbach a gift that would change his life.

Gerhard was a natural flyer. All the years he spent as a pilot before the war prepared him for combat, when it came. He understood what he could extract from his aircraft. He barely needed instruments to fly with because he could feel how a plane was responding, how much more it had to give and where its limitations lay. And though he despised Nazism with every fibre of his being, and hated it even more each time he had to give the 'Heil Hitler!' salute, he still loved his country, the Germany that had existed before Hitler ever drew breath and would still be there when the self-styled Führer was nothing but a note in the history books.

That was the Germany for which he fought, and as a fighter pilot it was possible to preserve the illusion that one was engaged in an honourable form of combat, one man against another in the last faint echo of the old tradition of military chivalry. The nature of air-to-air combat as a fighter pilot meant that one had to fight to the maximum of one's abilities simply to survive. There was no hiding place, no walls to duck behind or trenches to jump into. Gerhard flew and he fought. And, above all, he survived. He came unscathed through the Polish campaign in 1939, the invasion of France and the Battle of Britain in 1940, the Balkan and Greek campaigns in the spring of 1941, and Operation Barbarossa, the invasion of Russia that had followed.

When Gerhard and his comrades had been escorting the bomber fleets as they blasted the RAF airfields of southern England, and then turned their attentions to London, they had come up against pilots who were their match, flying aircraft that were, in some respects, superior to their own Messerschmitt Bf 109s. But everywhere else, they had enjoyed almost total air superiority. And in those first months in Russia, their missions had been less like combat against equals than shooting fish in a barrel.

The Ivans had terrible aircraft, worse tactics and, most shocking of all to the Luftwaffe men who faced them, many of their pilots were women. They used a heavy fighter called the Sturmovik to support their troops on the ground. It was known as 'the flying tank' because it was so heavily armoured and its 23mm cannons were as powerful as airborne artillery. This made the Sturmovik deadly to German soldiers on the ground, but the only weapon it possessed to defend itself from attack in the air was a single machine gun firing from the rear of the cockpit.

The Soviets massed their Sturmoviks in formations, like bombers, from which individual aircraft could not deviate. If attacked, they kept flying straight ahead, in orderly lines, no matter how close a Luftwaffe fighter came. To break through their armour, Gerhard and his fellow pilots had to fire from point-blank range. But there was almost no chance of being hit while one approached and the only danger was when you destroyed a Sturmovik, the resulting explosion hurled jagged fragments of riveted armour steel through the sky in all directions: that downed more German pilots and destroyed more Messerschmitts than any bullets ever did.

Gerhard lost one plane to shrapnel from a Sturmovik, but he bailed out unhurt and landed behind his own lines. That aside, he remained physically untouched as his total of kills increased, until he could count more than forty enemy aircraft downed in airborne combat, and as many again destroyed on the ground. He had long since ceased to care about any of that. He killed only so that he might live. He accepted one award after another, and promotions because they served to burnish his reputation.

And Gerhard cared about his reputation. He smiled for the war correspondents and allowed himself to be brought back to the fatherland for a series of public appearances, where he was feted like a movie star. The more he was seen as the perfect Nazi warrior, the easier it became to hide his true intention.

One day, he did not know how or when, he would find a way to end Hitler's tyranny and destroy the Nazi Reich.

· · ·

And so, as Gerhard was smiling amiably at his fellow passenger, a more dangerous idea was running through his mind. *State Secretary Hartmann, I want you to talk. I need you to pass on your secrets.*

'Nervous?' Gerhard asked, seeing the white knuckles of Hartmann's hand clasped to the armrest of his chair. 'I understand. I spend my whole life in aeroplanes but even I sometimes wonder how a contraption containing thousands of kilos of metal and wood and aviation fuel can possibly fly. But it does.'

Hartmann gave a nod of acknowledgement. His fear was palpable. Gerhard watched him as the pilot opened the throttles, sent the plane hurtling down the runway and then took off into the Prussian sky. The screaming engines hauled the Junkers up into the air, but this craft was no fighter, it had to work to gain altitude, and there was always that moment when even experienced passengers wondered if the effort would be successful.

Hartmann waited until the pilot had eased the rate of ascent and cut back on the engines enough to make conversation possible.

'We'll be going up to a cruising height of about four thousand metres, maybe a little more,' Gerhard told him, matter-of-factly, slowly turning the screw. 'A long way down, eh? But planes don't drop from the sky for no good reason.

'When I am flying a combat mission, some bastard Ivan might shoot me down. But I assure you, no one is going to shoot us down between Berlin and Rivne. We are flying over our own territory all the way. There is no possibility of encountering enemy aircraft. None.'

He looked quizzically at Hartmann. 'You believe me, don't you, Herr *Doktor*?'

Hartmann nodded.

'Excellent. This Junkers is a good, strong aircraft. It will withstand severe conditions. But it might get caught in a hurricane, or a thunderstorm, or cloud so thick that the pilot can't see where he's going and flies into the side of the mountain.

'But I have checked the weather forecast and we have clear skies, gentle winds and prefect visibility all the way to Rivne. That's reassuring, no?'

'I suppose so,' Hartmann replied. The manila file, with its Top Secret stamp, was clearly visible on the table.

'Maybe an engine might fail. This is extremely unlikely, especially if my family made it, but it might happen.'

Hartmann perked up. 'Your family? You mean you are . . .'

'One of *those* von Meerbachs? Yes, my grandfather founded the company and my older brother Konrad Graf von Meerbach is still the president of the board, when not attending to his duties in the *Schutzstaffel*. You may have come across him in Berlin. He is one of *Obergruppenführer* Heydrich's most trusted subordinates.'

'No . . . no . . .' Hartmann bore the look of a man who suddenly realised that he was in the presence of a power greater than his own. 'But I have heard of him, of course . . . and always in the most complimentary terms.'

'My brother is indeed a most admirable man, and as loyal a National Socialist as you will find in all the Reich. I'm sure that he, more than anyone, would want to assure you that this good, German aircraft can easily fly on two engines, instead of three. But what if two engines fail? Well, now it does not fly quite so easily, but still it could reach the nearest airfield. But what if three engines fail? In almost ten years of flying, I have never heard of three engines failing at once, for purely mechanical reasons, but have no fear, an aircraft at high altitude can glide a long way before it reaches the ground. I'm sure the pilot could find a stretch of road on which to put us down. And if he doesn't feel up to the job, I would feel happy to oblige. I've been known to run out of fuel on a long mission and use a highway for a landing strip. I did it once in Greece. Came down in front of a column of Panzers, advancing on Athens. Their commanding officer was most upset that I was blocking the way. Tremendous fun!'

Hartmann gave a nervous laugh.

'Now, I know just the thing to make you feel much better,' Gerhard said. He beckoned the steward to come over. 'Be a good fellow and make us both strong coffee, nice and sweet, with a healthy shot of schnapps in each cup.'

The steward grinned. 'Certainly, sir!'

'Good man.'

Hartmann made an attempt to protest.

'This will help you, I promise,' Gerhard assured him. 'I've flown almost three hundred combat missions and I should think at least half of them began with me downing a tin cup of coffee and schnapps. We all do it. Helps a man get started, first thing on a cold morning, and keeps him warm in the air. It's damn cold work flying a 109 at high altitude.'

When the coffees arrived, Gerhard raised his cup, 'A toast – to the Führer, and victory.'

Gerhard gestured to the steward to bring two more cups. Then he proposed another toast: 'Death to the Jews, the Bolsheviks and all enemies of the Reich!'

Hartmann felt obliged to join in the toast and drank the coffee. Gerhard was not feeling the slightest effect from the alcohol. Like every other man on the Russian Front, he had drunk an ocean of vodka, smoked a forest of cigarettes and swallowed countless tablets of Pervitin, the methamphetamine drug they all craved for its ability to reduce fatigue, increase stamina and induce a sense of wild, reckless courage. His system was so accustomed to one narcotic or another circulating in his bloodstream that it took a massive dose to have much effect upon him. Hartmann, however, was a mousy civil servant. He was evidently not a drinking man. Two large shots of schnapps, first thing in the morning, would lower his defences and loosen his tongue.

'So, what brings you to *Reichskommissariat* Ukraine?' asked Gerhard. 'Clearly it is sensitive work, as I can see from your file. Let me guess: is your work related to the disposal of the Jews?'

Hartmann looked at Gerhard. His eyes narrowed. 'What makes you say that?'

Gerhard grinned as he shrugged. 'I too am obliged to keep some matters confidential . . . but I have connections, as you know, and move in certain circles, and one is privy to interesting conversations.'

The truth was more prosaic. Gerhard had returned to Germany to take some long-overdue leave at a time when there was little action on the battlefield. While he was there, he received his German Star and carried out some promotional activities for the propaganda boys in Berlin. Then he went south to Bavaria for a board meeting of the Meerbach Motor Works, of which he was still a shareholder and board member, albeit with a smaller stake and less influence than Konrad.

After the meeting, the two brothers had lunched together in the company's private dining room. Konrad, who was more aggressive and spiteful when drunk, had downed a great deal of wine. Gerhard had provoked him further by telling the stories of some of the dogfights and ground-attack missions for which he had received his latest award for gallantry. He knew that Konrad would hate being reminded of the contrast between Gerhard's frontline service and his own war work, which was mostly conducted from behind a desk.

'You think you fool them all, don't you, with this flying-ace act of yours?' Konrad had sneered. 'Well, you don't fool me. I know you for a commie and a Jew-lover. That's what you've always been, and you haven't changed, I know it.'

'If I'm a communist, why have I killed so many of my Russian comrades? I don't just have blood on my hands, I'm up to my damned elbows.'

'Pah! I don't care how many Ivans you shoot down, you're still a traitor and a filthy subversive in my eyes.'

'Tell that to Dr Goebbels. He thinks I'm a hero. It says so in all the newsreels this week.'

'That's not all I know, either . . .'

Gerhard knew what he meant. Almost a year had passed since he had received a letter through the usual channels. But instead of bearing a loving message from Saffron, it had informed him that she had been killed in an air raid. He had been devastated, robbed of the will to live until, by pure chance, he had found out, beyond any shadow of a doubt, that she was still alive.

It had not been difficult to work out what must have happened. Though Konrad was married to another woman, he had taken

Francesca von Schöndorf as his mistress. It saddened Gerhard deeply to discover that he had filled Chessi with such hate that she had chosen to debase herself in that way. At heart, she was a much better woman than that. But if she was willing to give herself to Konrad as some perverted form of revenge, she would certainly have wanted to tell him that his brother had fallen in love with an Englishwoman. It was a piece of information that could do a great deal of damage. Gerhard was certain that Konrad had acted upon it and found a way of intercepting his letters to and from Saffron.

Since then, however, Gerhard had been careful never to give an indication that he was aware Saffron was alive. Konrad could not reveal that he was the author of the false reports of death (Gerhard assumed that Saffron had received one about him, too). They had been Konrad's private act of revenge, hidden even from Heydrich, who had long since ceased to care about the subject of Gerhard von Meerbach, and did not want his subordinate thinking about anything except his official duties.

Gerhard did not rise to Konrad's bait and silence descended upon their table. They were eating Wiener schnitzel made from veal calves raised and slaughtered on their own estate, with richly buttered mashed potatoes, sauerkraut and leeks all from their farms. In wartime Germany this was a feast beyond the wildest dreams of most of their fellow Reich citizens, who would have gazed on in drooling envy had they seen Konrad stuff his face with a forkful of meat and potato, and wash it down with a swig of 1929 La Tâche, one of the greatest red wines in the world.

Konrad picked up his fork and jabbed it in Gerhard's direction. 'You know nothing, nothing at all about what this Reich truly is and what it will become. While you're out there, in the mud and snow and shit of Russia, I'm in Berlin, where the power is, creating destiny. And I have news for you, little brother. You won't have to worry about all your Jewish friends in the future, you won't have to spend any more of our family money on those hook-nosed vermin, and you know why? Because there won't be any!'

'What do you mean?' Gerhard had asked, although he feared he knew the answer.

'Because they will all be dead, every last one of them!' Konrad declared triumphantly. 'Before this war is out, we are going to kill every single Jew in Europe, Russia and North Africa.'

'I thought you were going to transport them out of the Reich. Give them a home of their own.'

'That was the original plan, but it won't work. Costs too much to move them and then where would we put them all? Do you know how many Yids we're talking about?'

'I haven't a clue.'

'Go on, guess.'

Gerhard said nothing.

'Eleven million! That's how many we've got to process. That's the official term, by the way: "processing".'

'Was that what they were doing at Babi Yar last year, "processing"?'

Konrad chewed with the exaggerated thoughtfulness of an inebriated man. 'That's a very interesting question, little brother, very interesting indeed. What makes you mention Babi Yar?'

'I flew over a ravine just outside Kiev last September, coming back from a mission. I thought I saw people being shot. When I landed, I looked on a map and saw the name of the place. Then I asked around and was told that Jews were being rounded up all over the city but no one knew why. I went for another flight and had a proper look. I saw them all being shot, Konrad. Naked men and women, lined up by a huge pit, men with guns behind them. They were being shot, falling in the pit, more lining up . . . That was Babi Yar.'

'Well, that was quite a performance you saw there. If I recall correctly . . . yes, I'm pretty sure the figure was around 35,000 killed in two days. Good work, done by fine, committed men . . .'

Gerhard was so appalled that he could not find the strength to object. His mind was reeling with the number of people killed . . . and in just two days!

He managed to say, 'So were there more Babi Yars, then? More good work done by those fine fellows of yours?'

'Oh yes, many more. Not quite that scale, but a host of smaller actions: a few hundred disposed of here, a few thousand there, it all adds up. But it's too slow, that's the problem. And too many of our men are weak. We assure them they are doing important work, that the world is a better, healthier place for the removal of the Jew-virus. But the shootings are bad for their morale, and they are expensive. As a method it requires too many men, too many bullets. It's not efficient enough.'

'You make it sound like a problem on one of our production lines.'

'Actually, yes, it is very much like that. And, as in industry, so in this enterprise we need to find solutions to our problems. And now we have it: the final solution to the Jewish question. It's Heydrich's doing, you know. The man is a genius, an inspiration to us all. He has masterminded the whole scheme.'

'What is this final solution, then?'

'It is the plan by which we will kill all of those eleven million Jews. It is a marvel of preparation, logistics, transport, processing and disposal. I am not going to tell you how the task will be accomplished. The whole thing is secret. It's a tragedy, if you ask me. One of the greatest undertakings in the history of mankind and yet it cannot be recorded for posterity.'

'Why not? Why not tell the world of this achievement? Why be ashamed of it?'

'It is not a question of shame, but of comprehension. Too many people in the world have been deluded into accepting the Jew, even valuing the Jew. They do not understand the need for eradication.'

'You mean they might object to the killing of eleven million of their fellow men and women. Heavens above! Why on earth would anyone do that?'

Konrad glared at Gerhard. 'Are you mocking me, little brother? Are you questioning our Führer's will? Are you foolish enough to suggest that what we are doing is wrong?'

'I'm not suggesting anything. You are the ones keeping it secret. You've told me that you're worried about what the world will think. It sounds to me as though you are the ones who are in doubt.'

Konrad had made some blustering attempts to deny the logic of Gerhard's point, but he was too full of wine and his arguments petered out into incoherent babble. Gerhard had left the table soon afterwards and headed back to Berlin, his head spinning with the horrors his brother had just revealed. Then he had found himself on a plane with a man from the Ministry for the Occupied Territories, heading to Rivne for high-level discussions about a top-secret matter. There were lots of secrets in a war, but Gerhard had a feeling that he knew what this one was.

He leaned across the aisle, so that he could get his head closer to Hartmann's and said, discreetly, 'So, tell me, man-to-man, what is your opinion on the final solution to the Jewish question?'

• • •

Dr Hartmann's first thought was: *Is this some kind of a test?* But, if so, what was being tested? Should he prove his discretion by refusing to say a word about the outcome of the Wannsee Conference, or should he demonstrate his loyalty by affirming his support for the plans that Heydrich and his subordinate Adolf Eichmann had set before their astonished audience? Perhaps there was no more to von Meerbach's question than met the eye. Maybe he really was a highly decorated war hero, who belonged to one of the richest, best connected and ardently pro-Nazi families in the Reich, and who happened to be flattering a ministry official by asking for his opinion.

Hartmann took a deep breath. 'I believe that the Final Solution is an extraordinary undertaking, of vital importance, and I feel honoured to have a small, but in some ways significant part to play in its execution,' he replied.

Von Meerbach nodded. 'If you are enabling the Occupied Territories to play their full part in the operation then I am sure that you are indeed, if you will excuse me for sounding like an engineer, a vital cog in the machine.'

'Thank you, Squadron Captain, I will certainly endeavour to be so.'

'There is one aspect that intrigues me. I witnessed the, ah, processing operation at Babi Yar last September when my fighter group was based near there. In that instance, the traditional shooting method was used, but I gather that great advances have been made in the means of operation?'

'Oh yes. We have now completed the construction of a number of installations that transform the process from what one might call manual labour, to an industrial form that removes a great deal of the human element.'

'That must be more efficient, I imagine.'

'It is.'

'And more humane, too,' von Meerbach added. 'I mean, in the sense of reducing the strain on those who had previously been required to do the work.'

'As I understand it, *Reichsführer* Himmler was deeply touched by the strain being placed on his SS men and the auxiliary staff assisting them.'

Von Meerbach nodded thoughtfully. 'That says a great deal about the *Reichsführer*. I know my brother greatly admires him.'

'And with good reason.'

Hartmann was pleased at the way the conversation was going. He felt he had covered himself against any possible interpretation of the conversation. He had not, after all, revealed any specific operational details. Yet he was making his enthusiasm for the scheme apparent, and responding to Squadron Captain von Meerbach's questions. Now he decided to be more daring.

'Might I inquire, Squadron Captain, whether you are required back at your unit immediately?'

Von Meerbach gave a shrug. 'I probably should get back. I dread to think what my men are getting up to in my absence!'

Hartmann decided that laughter would be appropriate at this point.

'But I am not officially required at my post for another two days,' von Meerbach went on. 'I had allowed a few days for my travel back from Berlin to the front. But thanks to this flight I have gained a great deal of time. Why do you ask?'

'I happen to know that there is going to be a practical demonstration tomorrow at a village near Rivne. One of our new mobile units is being put through its paces. Perhaps you might care to join me for the display?'

'Thank you, Herr *Doktor*. I would appreciate such an opportunity.'

'In that case, I will arrange to have you added to the inspection party. I will give you more details on our arrival at Rivne. Until then, perhaps you will excuse me. I have a lot of work with which I am obliged to catch up.'

Von Meerbach gave one of his film-star smiles. 'My dear Hartmann, of course, please don't let me disturb you.'

There really had been a Fog-Signal Switch, and a steam engine's wheels had detonated it. But the rest of the charge that Saffron had set against the track was comprised of nothing deadlier than a large lump of modelling clay. And the stopping train from Fort William to Mallaig was not filled with Waffen-SS men travelling through Occupied Europe but was, in fact, empty.

Likewise the soldiers who had come running past Saffron's hiding place above the cutting were her own Baker Street comrades, though they certainly would have seized her if they had spotted her, while the courting couple whom she had to get past without detection were a soldier and a local lass. They never had the slightest idea that their lovemaking had been observed, for Saffron had drawn a discreet veil across those activities in her report, not wanting to get either of them into trouble.

The seaside home that Saffron had fled past on her way to the jetty where the Resistance were supposed to be waiting was actually Arisaig House, on the west coast of Scotland, a short ferry ride from the islands of Eigg, Rum and Skye. This was the headquarters of Baker Street's training operations in the Scottish Highlands. In its vicinity stood a number of country houses, scattered across a breathtaking landscape of lochs, hills and wild, empty beaches. They had been requisitioned as accommodation and training both for Baker Street's British agents and those from Britain, Czechoslovakia, Norway and other European nations now under Nazi control.

The rockery and the vegetable garden across which she had run, the trees, the fence, even the marshy patch between the garden and the beach, where she had stepped off the path and been bogged down in the mud, were all in the grounds of Arisaig House. So too were the two red-brick huts, reached by a path across a field usually occupied by cattle, that had been constructed for use by Baker Street personnel: one as an ammunition store, the other for interrogation training.

Saffron herself was based at Garramore, a Victorian hunting lodge three miles north of Arisaig, set back from the icing-sugar sands of Camusdarach beach. But in the aftermath of three days' brutal interrogation, her condition was deemed serious enough to put her in a room at the main house, where Dr Maguire could keep an eye on her. She did not appear to need any emergency treatment, which was just as well, since the nearest hospital was thirty-five miles away in Fort William. There was, however, half a chance that she might have suffered some internal bleeding, and even if she had not, a few days' rest and recuperation were certainly in order.

After her privations in the cellar and the interrogation hut, Saffron's new accommodation was more to her liking. Arisaig House had been commissioned in 1863 as a shooting lodge, built for a wealthy industrialist from the Midlands of England on a grander scale than Garramore, or any other local property. It had remained unchanged for seventy years until a fire caused such terrible damage that the interior of the house had to be rebuilt. The work was done to the highest standards of the 1930s. The main bedrooms all had their own lavish bathrooms. There was electricity throughout, powered by the house's own generators, since mains power had not reached that remote corner of Scotland. Central heating ensured that Arisaig was immune from the freezing chill that, as Saffron had discovered to her amazement when she first arrived in Britain, still gripped most of the stateliest homes in the country.

She had been assigned a bedroom on one corner of the first floor, which looked out in two directions. The windows opposite her bed provided a view towards the sea, over a small rose garden, which, with the lawns and the trees, would have kept a landscape painter happy for weeks. The window to the right of her bed, and another in her bathroom, overlooked a small yard that was a constant bustle of activity, as scurrying Baker Street staff and trainees went about their labours.

Her bed was large and blissfully comfortable. The bath was deep and she had been told to soak in as much hot water as she liked to ease her battered muscles. The food, too, was excellent, for not only were better rations allocated to the Special Training Schools, as Arisaig and the buildings around it were formally titled, but the large vegetable garden at the house, and the deer, grouse, salmon and seafood that could be harvested from the hills and waters all around provided a splendid variety of delicious fresh ingredients.

Saffron's face and body still ached and the brutality of her treatment was replayed in nightmares that had her waking two or three times a night, with her pulse racing, her body bathed in sweat and her eyes wide open in terror. But in her view, that was to be expected as part of the work for which she had volunteered. A peaceful stay in blissful luxury, however, was an unexpected bonus and she was resolved to make the best of it.

Her mood was improved when the nurse looking after her walked in on the second morning with a tray of tea, some homemade biscuits and a large bundle of letters and cards from the other members of the Baker Street gang, congratulating her on her achievement and wishing her a speedy recovery. One message seemed to have come from even further afield.

The notepaper was headed by an embossed swastika, surrounded by a laurel wreath, beneath which was printed the address of the Reich Chancellery at Wilhelmstrasse 77, Berlin-Mitte. The words beneath it were written by hand in a spidery script that the whole world had learned to recognise.

Dear Fraülein Courtney,

Please for bad English my apology accept. But my glorious destiny requires me to you this letter be writing, so impressed I am by your prolongedinterrogationresistance (that is one word in English, too, no?).

My friends Herr Göring and Herr Himmler both agree. I must say, dear Himmi is such a funny man, you will love him when you get to know him. If you do not, I will have you shot.

Dr Goebbels is crazy about you too. He also asks me to assure you that it is not true what the song is saying, that he has "no balls at all". He says he has two and they are large and very hairy.

I also have two. Not one, that is a total lie. I must that make clear.

Also Eva sends her love, though she ein grosse tempertantrum is having because everyone is saying that you are more red-hot than she is. (I agree. But do not tell Eva).

With regards,

Adolf Hitler

Saffron knew at once that the paper was authentic and that not even the Führer himself would be able to tell that it was not his hand that had scribbled the words. The writer's identity, however, was revealed in tiny letters, on the reverse of the paper: 'As dictated to the Forger'.

Saffron laughed. The Forger, as he was universally known, was a strange little man who acted as the would-be agents' tutor in the dark arts of deception, snooping and fakery. He was always impeccably dressed and somewhat obsequious, like an over-attentive hotel manager or the assistant in a smart menswear emporium. Yet it soon became clear that he possessed a tough mind, a sharp eye and a wicked sense of humour. His meek exterior was, in that sense, one more way of fooling people. Everyone assumed he was a former criminal, specialising in fraud or confidence tricks, though no one had dared ask him to his face.

However he had come by his skills, the Forger was a remarkable craftsman. He always arrived for class carrying a briefcase filled with several bottles of inks of various colours and makes, along with a vast selection of pens, pencils, waxes, scalpels and erasers. With these, he taught his pupils how to forge signatures and create plausible 'official' documents, so that even the most ham-fisted might be able to create, say, a travel-pass good enough to fool a busy conductor on a jolting, poorly lit train, and alter genuine papers to their advantage. They also learned how to extract a letter from an envelope, read it and put it back without leaving any trace at all.

The Forger persuaded each new group of trainees that he was worthy of their attention by learning to reproduce all their individual handwriting styles within a week of their first lesson with him. In fact, once she had read the letter from Hitler, Saffron wondered whether he had written all the other letters as well.

The next few minutes proved to her satisfaction that the signatures at the bottom of all the messages were genuine. The clincher was the message from the Czech trainees, based at Traigh House. The Czechs were greatly liked by the other Baker Street operatives and the local folk both for their determination to rid their country of its Nazi occupiers and for their high spirits. One look at the crazy comments and garish cartoons scribbled over the Czechs' card was enough to convince Saffron that not even the Forger could have come up with such naturally wild exuberance.

Feeling buoyed by all those good wishes, Saffron decided that it might be a good idea if she caught up on some of her studies. She had asked for two books to be brought up from the Arisaig House library. Their titles were: *All-In Fighting* by W. E. Fairbairn and *Shooting to Live*, also by Fairbairn, but co-authored with a certain E. A. Sykes. In many respects, the books possessed the same general tone as any instructional manual produced by English authors for their fellow countrymen and women.

The books shared a format of sensible instructions, accompanied by straightforward illustrations, and delivered in a voice that came from a middle-aged gentleman in a position of authority. Had she asked for a practical homecare manual, or a guide to planting herbaceous borders, Saffron would have come across a similar style and tone. These two books, however, were very different. They were inspired by the experiences the two men had had as policemen fighting gangs in Shanghai, the most dangerous city in the world throughout the twenties and thirties. They were the best guides ever written on the business of defending oneself and killing one's opponent as efficiently as possible. The authors were the principal instructors at Arisaig in hand-to-hand fighting, or, as they preferred to call it, 'silent killing' and shooting. More than anyone else in the Baker Street organisation, it was Fairbairn and Sykes who were responsible for transforming prospective agents from innocent civilians to trained assassins.

It was hardly an amusing field of study, but the books had their lighter aspects, even if the humour was not always intentional.

Saffron had worked her way through the first sections of *All-In Fighting*. These taught the reader how to strike with the edge of the hand, the boot and the knee, and escape a variety of holds, including being strangled and bear-hugged by the enemy. Then something occurred to her.

She went back to the beginning and, as she flicked through the pages, she looked out for the same word, counting to herself, giggling as she did so. She did not notice as the door opened and two men walked in: Fairbairn and Sykes themselves.

They were not, at first glance, obvious candidates for the title of the toughest and deadliest men in the world. They were both short, bespectacled gentlemen in their late fifties. They more closely resembled a pair of Church of England vicars or retired music-hall comedians. Sykes had an amiable, dimpled smile and it was only when Saffron had looked more closely that she noticed the bulldog stubbornness of his jaw and the thickness of his neck. Fairbairn was commonly referred to as 'Shanghai Buster'. He had a longer, thinner face than Sykes, with deep lines defining his sunken cheeks. His most prominent feature was a nose that had been battered so many times that doctors had given up trying to repair it, and a scar that ran from his chin along his jawline to the bottom of his left ear.

Sykes put his fist to his mouth and coughed.

Saffron looked up and the sight of her instructors, both in battle dress, with their captain's pips on their shoulder boards, made her feel as if she were back in a dorm at Rodean, caught reading under the blanket by a patrolling matron.

'Oh, hello, sir . . . and Captain Fairbairn.' She did her best to recover her poise and sat up straight in bed. 'How sweet of you to come and see me. I was just reading Captain Fairbairn's book.'

'You seemed to find it rather amusing, Miss Courtney,' Sykes observed drily. 'I must say, it was not intended to be humorous.'

'I'm sorry,' she said. 'I was amused by the number of times the reader is advised to stick his knee into his opponent's testicles, or grab them. I counted seven or eight in the first few pages, with some vivid illustrations, too.'

Sykes frowned, as if this were a joke he had never heard before. 'Well, I suppose a woman might find that rather more amusing than a man. Most chaps wince just thinking about it.'

Fairbairn never said two words where one would do, or better yet, none at all. Now, though, he was moved to speak. 'Better fighters, women, if you train them properly.'

'Why do you say that, sir?' Saffron asked.

Fairbairn launched into what was, for him, a lengthy soliloquy. 'One: women take instruction better than men. Men always think they know best, think they already know how to fight. Nonsense. Two, women are more ruthless than men, no qualms. Three, women don't play cricket. Don't have their heads filled with twaddle about being a good sport, playing by the rules, giving the other chap a chance. No use for good sports when there's a war on, whatever those idiots at the War Office say.'

There was a feeling among senior military men that the way SOE agents were taught to fight amounted to little more than cheating. This opinion was a constant irritation to everyone involved with Baker Street. Saffron was on Fairbairn's side. The idea that combat was some sort of game, to be played by gentlemen's rules, struck her as absurd.

'It must be realised that, when dealing with a ruthless enemy who has expressed his intention of wiping this nation out of existence, there is no room for any scruple or compunction about the methods to be employed in preventing them,' she said, reciting the words from the introduction to *All-In Fighting*.

'You see, sir, I agree with you so strongly I memorised it.'

Fairbairn nodded. 'Grew up in Africa, eh?'

'Yes, sir.'

'Used to seeing nature red in tooth and claw.'

'Yes, sir.'

'Dare say the natives there don't hold back when they fight.'

'They don't fight as much as they used to, or as much as they'd like,' Saffron said. 'We don't let them. I've grown up around the Masai, sir. They're wonderful people. Manyoro, the chief of our local tribe, was my father's platoon sergeant in the King's African Rifles. He knows how to fight our way.'

Sykes clapped his hands in delight. 'I say, Fairbairn, they'd do jolly well in Shanghai. Your average Triad member would understand that attitude completely.'

Fairbairn nodded. 'No mercy, no quarter. Only dishonour is to be defeated, run away, show weakness.'

Saffron nodded. 'Manyoro would agree with you, sir. The Masai are raised to fight lions with only a shield and spear. My father says they're the bravest men on earth.'

Fairbairn nodded, pondered what he was about to say and then spoke. 'Heard about that Cairo business. Your uncle working as a German spy, had to be dealt with. You killed him, made it look like self-defence.'

Uncle Francis had turned rogue, and, family or not, blood had been spilled.

Saffron sighed, wondering when she would ever be able to escape the violence she had done. *When this ghastly war is over, I suppose.* Keeping her expression non-committal, she said, 'Yes, sir.'

'Good work. Proves my point about women, eh, Sykes?'

'It does! The fact that the whole thing was done without any training whatever was what struck me. I can see why you're taking to Baker Street like a duck to water, Miss Courtney.'

'I'm not sure most girls would take that as a compliment, sir. It rather suggests I have a natural aptitude for murder.'

'Precisely,' said Fairbairn. 'Just what we're looking for. Got a war to win.'

'Without any room for scruple or compunction,' Saffron said.

Fairbairn nodded, there being no need to speak.

'I see you've also got our manual on the use of firearms,' Sykes observed.

'Yes, sir.'

'Well, I'm sure you don't need me to tell you that you're a first-class shot. I dare say you've embarrassed plenty of chaps on the grouse moors.'

'One or two, sir.'

'More than that, I'll be bound. But do remember that there's all the difference between aiming a 12-bore shotgun at a bird who can't shoot back, and getting into a fire fight at point-blank range with an armed opponent.'

'Yes, sir.'

'No use trying to line up your sights; no time for that.'

There were two fundamental rules that Sykes and Fairbairn drilled into all their pupils. First: always hit an opponent with an open hand, rather than a closed fist. Second: always shoot as fast and instinctively as possible.

'I understand, sir,' Saffron assured him. 'I simply look at the target, trust my hand to follow my eye and fire twice.'

'That's right, the Double-Tap.'

'No need for a lecture, Sykes. Girl's already proved she can do it,' Fairbairn said.

'Right you are, old boy. Well, anyway, must be getting on . . .' Sykes was about to leave when he pulled himself up short. 'I say, Fairbairn, I don't believe we revealed the purpose of our visit.'

Saffron smiled. 'Do you need a purpose, sir? It's jolly nice just to have visitors.'

'Good show,' Fairbairn barked. 'That was the point. Bloody good show.'

'Captain Fairbairn is referring to your resistance to interrogation,' said Sykes. 'We were both impressed and we wanted you to know that.'

'Thank you . . . Thank you very much.'

'And do hurry up and get well. We have something amusing laid on for next week.'

'Slaughterhouse,' said Fairbairn

'Is that a new version of the killing house, sir?' Saffron asked.

Fairbairn and Sykes had created a special shooting range near Arisaig. It comprised a converted farm building, filled with figures that popped in and out of view in semi-darkness, challenging trainees to kill enemy soldiers, while keeping innocent civilians alive.

'No, it's an actual slaughterhouse, in Fort William,' Sykes explained. 'We use it for demonstrating the feel of stabbing raw flesh.'

'Soon as the beast is killed. Still warm. Stick your knife in,' said Fairbairn.

'You'll discover that it's nothing like stabbing a straw dummy. The sinews of the flesh seem to grip the blade. It can be surprisingly difficult to withdraw it.'

'Only way to learn . . . Not stabbed anyone, have you?'

'No, sir!' protested Saffron. 'I'm not completely homicidal.'

'You will be,' Captain Fairbairn said.

Gerhard found himself a room in a hotel near Rivne's main railway station. The walls of the building were still pockmarked with bullets from the fighting the previous summer. Half the glass in the window of his room had been replaced by cardboard. The wallpaper was so old and faded that its pattern was barely visible and the sole decoration consisted of a portrait of Hitler. It hung in the middle of less worn-out paper that must once, Gerhard reasoned, have been protected by the presence of a larger picture, presumably a picture of the Tsar, Lenin, Stalin, or all three. There was no hot water in which to wash and no food. But he scrounged some dinner in the officer's mess of the local Luftwaffe headquarters, where he also organised a flight up to his fighter group.

'We've got a bunch of new recruits coming in tomorrow, around lunchtime,' the HQ's adjutant said. 'The plane will refuel. We'll give the new boys a bite to eat and a place to piss, and then we'll send them on to your lot. Jump aboard. You can get to know them on the way.'

Gerhard nodded. 'I'm a couple of men short in my squadron.'

'Then you can pick out the ones who might have a chance of being decent pilots.'

'Or at least spot the ones who are never going to make it.'

'No point wasting time on them.'

Gerhard walked back to his cold, uncomfortable hotel room, musing on the way that, just as small boys always knew which of their class were sure to be bullied, so there were raw pilots who exuded a sense of imminent death. Of course, any pilot could be shot down on any given day, but with some it was not a risk, so much as a certainty. *And yet I seem to survive, no matter what*, he thought as he lay down fully dressed on top of his bed, knowing that only a madman would expose his skin to the bugs that lurked within the bedding. *Perhaps it's because I have to.*

He opened the chest pocket of his uniform jacket and pulled out a battered, dirty, stained envelope, from which he extracted a photograph that was almost as faded as the paper on the walls around him. It showed Gerhard, arm-in-arm with Saffron Courtney in front of the Eiffel Tower. The date on which it had been taken – 07 Avril 1939 – was printed in the bottom right-hand corner. Gerhard didn't need to see the picture. Having it between his fingers was enough to bring back every detail.

Gerhard remembered the light that had sparkled from Saffron's beautiful blue eyes, the joyful radiance of her smile, the breeze that had whipped the hat from her head as they strolled through the Jardins des Tuileries and the sound of their laughter as they had chased after it. He remembered the sweet softness of her lips and the warmth of her mouth as he kissed her. He felt the smoothness of her skin as he ran his hands along the full curves of her breasts, her back, her buttocks, her thighs; the sweet rose of the perfume beneath her ears and the rich, arousing musk of her female scent. He recalled the wild ecstasy of their lovemaking, the blissful exhaustion that followed its conclusion, and the amazing speed with which they seemed to recover their strength and do it all over again.

But for all the sensual delights that a woman as beautiful and as deeply in love as Saffron could offer, what kept her memory most fresh within his mind was her character: spirited, fearless, committed to everything in which she believed. They had both known that war was coming. They were bound to be divided by the chasm between their two nations. But Saffron had never allowed that knowledge, nor even the certainty that she and Gerhard would place their lives at the service of their countries, to lessen her absolute loyalty to their love. Whatever might happen, however far apart they might be blown by the storms of war, she would, she swore, return to him in the end.

Thanks to Konrad's machinations, intercepting their letters and forging reports of their deaths, he had thought, wrongly, that she was dead. And then, one day in the spring of 1941, those capricious, malicious winds had blown them so close that they had each almost killed the other for real. As Greece fell into German hands and the last remaining Allied troops fled across the Aegean on any craft they could find, Gerhard's squadron had escorted the Stuka dive-bombers, who had been ordered to sink an apparently humble merchant ship whose destruction had been ordered, as a matter of necessity, by the highest authorities in Berlin.

Gerhard had done his part to ensure that the order was carried out, unaware that the ship belonged to the Courtney Trading fleet and that Saffron and her father were on it.

As he flew over the ship, strafing the machine-gun batteries, Gerhard had seen a vision of Saffron. He could not believe that it was real: how could it be? She was dead. But the bullets that had hit his plane were real enough. Despite the damage, the Messerschmitt had remained airborne. The ship, however, had been sent to the bottom of the wine-dark sea, as ordered. But Saffron had survived, and he had seen her, standing proudly and defiantly in the only lifeboat, unmistakably real and alive. He had flown down over the tiny boat, low enough and close enough that when he slid back the canopy of his cockpit she had been able to see him, too. He had waved to her and he could have sworn she had smiled back at him.

Each of them had known the truth. That they were both alive. And now, everything he did was considered in the light of that knowledge and in the hope that, when this war was over, he could stand before her and know that he had done the right thing, and that he was worthy to be her man.

• • •

'Squadron Captain von Meerbach, please allow me to introduce you to *SS-Obergruppenführer* Friedrich Jeckeln,' Hartmann said, as the inspection group assembled in the forecourt of the Nazi headquarters building in Rivne.

'Heil Hitler!' Gerhard snapped an immaculate straight-armed salute.

As befitted a superior officer, Jeckeln nodded and returned a more perfunctory salutation.

'As you can see, Squadron Captain von Meerbach is a highly decorated fighter pilot. He was too modest to volunteer his current score, as it were, but I did a little research and am informed that he has shot down forty-six enemy aircraft in airborne combat, and destroyed a further fifty-three on the ground. One more needed to reach a hundred!'

'Congratulations, Squadron Captain, that is indeed impressive,' said Jeckeln. He was a thickset man in his late forties, who looked at the world through piercing eyes sheltered beneath hooded, furrowed brows.

'Thank you, sir.'

'I knew Squadron Captain von Meerbach would be particularly honoured to meet you because he happened to witness some of the Babi Yar operation.'

Jeckeln's frown deepened and his gaze became suspicious. 'Might I ask how you did that, Squadron Captain?'

'My squadron was based outside Kiev. I over-flew the ravine on my way back from a mission, and was struck by what I saw.'

'*Obergruppenführer* Jeckeln has the distinction of being the man who devised the procedure by which Jews in any given area are gathered, transported to a prepared site and then dealt with in the most efficient manner,' Hartmann explained. 'It is known across the Occupied Territories as the Jeckeln System, or "sardine-packing", after the manner in which the Jews are arranged after they have been, ah . . .'

'Processed?' Gerhard volunteered.

'Good.'

'Then it appears it should be I who congratulates you, sir. Your current score is higher than my meagre effort.'

Before Jeckeln could reply, a short man wearing a belted raincoat and an officer's cap appeared and barked, 'Let's see this damn gas van.'

This was *Reichskommissar* Erich Koch. He had total civil power over a personal empire that stretched from the chilly waters of the Baltic, to the Black Sea coast of Ukraine. He led the way across the tarmac, past a number of Mercedes staff cars and a Hanomag half-track armed with a pair of MG-34 and ten infantrymen that would act as their escort vehicle. Koch stopped in front of what looked like a large tradesman's van. Behind the driver's cab was a cargo compartment, tall enough for a man to be able to stand up inside, with the name of the manufacturer painted in large capital letters running down either side.

A man in civilian worker's overalls was standing beside the van, nervously fiddling with the cap he was holding in front of him. As he saw the dignitaries approaching, he snapped to attention.

'Gentlemen, this is Herr Schmidt,' said Dr Hartmann. 'He is a mechanic from the Reich Main Security Office in Berlin and has driven his vehicle all the way here – isn't that right, Schmidt?'

'Yes, sir,' Schmidt said, bobbing his head deferentially.

'Ah, so, please be good enough to explain how this van operates.'

'Yes, sir.' Schmidt frowned as he said, 'The idea of the van came from General Nebe, the Head of the Criminal Police himself. He came home one night and got drunk – I'm not telling tales, gentlemen, that's how the general himself spoke when he explained it to us. He parks the car in the garage and falls asleep without turning off the engine. He wakes, coughing and spluttering and feeling as sick as a pig. He thinks, "I could have died in that car. Why don't we use the exhausts from a truck to get rid of people we don't have no need for?" He gets the scientists at the Main Security Office onto the job, they pass their plans onto the boys in the workshops and this is it. May I show you, gentlemen?'

Koch nodded, so Schmidt led the inspection party to the back of the truck. He pointed. 'There's the exhaust pumping out fumes that'll choke a person in no time. It's the carbon monoxide that does it, see?'

Koch could follow the science of it thus far and Schmidt directed his audience's attention to a metal box attached to the side of the truck. 'In here there's a sixty millimetre hose. I take it out and I fix one end to the exhaust . . . slips over nice and easy. Now, look under the van.'

Gerhard joined the others as they got down on their haunches, tilting their heads to see the underside of the van. Schmidt pointed to a short metal pipe pointing downwards from the floor of the cargo area of the van. 'See that pipe? One end of it is welded to a hole in the floor of the van. You stick the hose on the other end. Now the gas goes from the exhaust along the pipe and into the back of the van. Once you shut the rear doors, it's airtight. They're not breathing anything but exhaust fumes in there, poisonous carbon monoxide, and pretty soon they're not breathing at all.'

'Thank you, Schmidt, that will be all,' said Hartmann. 'So, shall we depart for the test site? I assume everything will be waiting for us when we get there?'

He looked at Jeckeln, who nodded. 'The test subjects were rounded up last night. They have been held under guard in a barn. Seventy Jews, as requested, evenly divided between males and females, covering the ages from ten to sixty-five. They have been stripped of their clothes, and any valuables, including gold teeth, prior to our arrival.'

With every word that was spoken, the horror of what he was about to witness became more apparent to Gerhard. He racked his brain to think of something he could do to sabotage the gas van, or call out a warning to the Jews who would be herded into it. But he knew that while some noble gesture might bring a momentary salve to his conscience in the seconds before he was shot dead, it would do nothing to alter the fate of the men, women and children who were about to be sacrificed.

I have to watch this, he told himself. *I have to bear witness. I have to carry my share of the guilt for the evil my country is doing.*

The staff cars, watched over by the Hanomag, set off across the bare, featureless countryside. In a few months, this would be a golden sea of wheat, but for now it was dark, barren soil, stretching as far as the eye could see. A little more than an hour had passed, when the cars turned off the main track and drove down into a village, small houses built with logs, then roofed with thatch, which were the traditional dwelling places of the Russian peasantry.

The convoy came to a halt in front of another building, windowless and larger than the rest. Two canvas-topped trucks were parked beside it, and a dozen or so men, in Waffen-SS camouflage smocks, were talking and smoking. Gerhard could see a junior officer scurrying to get them into order before the important passengers emerged from the staff cars.

The SS soldiers formed up in two neat rows, standing at ease until Gauleiter Koch emerged from his car, then snapping to attention. Jeckeln went over to the junior officer, a lieutenant by the look of him, exchanged Hitler salutes, and conferred briefly.

Jeckeln returned to the group of observers and addressed Koch. 'Herr Gauleiter, I have the honour to inform you that we are ready to proceed.'

'In that case, carry on,' Koch replied.

The sun was shining and there wasn't a cloud in the sky, but the north wind was freezing and the ground beneath Gerhard's feet was hard with frost. The sub-zero air wasn't the only reason Gerhard pulled his grey overcoat a little tighter around him as he waited for the day's events to unfold. He felt a chill gripping him from within, a dread that only deepened as the doors of the barn opened.

A harsh command of, 'Move! Move! Quickly!' could be heard and the first of the Jews emerged, blinking and shivering into the light.

Schmidt had manoeuvred the gas van into position, with its rear end facing the barn. He got out of the driver's cab, walked around his vehicle, opened the double doors at the back of the cargo bay and pulled down a set of metal steps, so that it was possible to walk straight into the bay. He fetched his hose from the truck, pushed one end over the van's exhaust pipe and disappeared under the van, taking the other end with him.

The SS men herded the Jews, forcing them to move at a run by means of shouts, slaps and blows with whips and clubs, like snarling dogs around a pack of sheep. The stream of naked humanity passed Gerhard, close enough for him to smell their sweat, their excrement and their fear. He caught sudden glimpses of individual people, like single frames in a fast-rolling reel of film: a woman holding her terrified, crying son close against her, trying to calm him, though she must have known that they were both on the way to their deaths; an old man clutching at his bleeding mouth (Gerhard thought at first that he had been hit and then realised, *My God, they have ripped the gold teeth from his jaws*); women placing arms across their breasts or hands over their pudenda as they sought to retain some modesty; middle-aged men, who might once have been doctors or lawyers (an instant realisation: *This could have been Izzy Solomons*). A young man in his early twenties stopped and turned to face one of the SS soldiers, who must have been about the same age as him. He waved a fist, shouted out an insult and spat on the ground. The SS man smashed the butt of his rifle into the Jew's face, knocking him to the ground. A second SS man ran to the scene and helped his comrade pick the young man up under his arms, drag him to the gas van and throw him in.

The cargo bay of the van filled up.

'Will they all fit in?' Hartmann inquired, for there were still a dozen or more Jews making their way from the barn.

Jeckeln nodded. 'Seventy is the standard load for a vehicle of this size.'

Schmidt had emerged from beneath the van. He stated with authority: 'Smaller vans, like the Opels and Renaults, can only hold fifty. But a big Saurer like this, or a Magirus, they'll take seventy comfortably, if they're all packed in tight.'

Gerhard kept his face impassive, though it was all he could do to keep himself screaming out, 'In the name of God, stop!' He longed to punch the stupid grin off Schmidt's face. How could that buffoon talk of the Jews fitting 'comfortably' when he could hear desperate cries for help coming from inside the cargo bay as people were crushed and trampled?

Gerhard forced himself to look unconcerned, to keep playing the part of the hard-bitten Luftwaffe ace, the committed Nazi for whom the Final Solution was the ultimate achievement of the Führer he worshipped.

If I cannot do anything to stop this, can I not at least look away?

How he longed to be a coward and close his eyes and ears to the truth.

No . . . look. Listen. Remember everything, every last detail of this abomination and then, when the time comes, be ready to testify to it all, and to accept whatever punishment you receive for having allowed it to happen.

It took four SS men to force the doors of the van shut and then bar them so that they could not be pushed open from within.

'Are you gentlemen ready to begin?' Schmidt asked.

'Should we stand back?' Koch asked.

'Oh no, sir. The van's completely airtight. No fumes come out, no fresh air goes in. That's the beauty of it: proper German workmanship.'

'Then proceed.'

Schmidt marched around to the driver's cab, got in and fired up the engine.

For a short while, nothing happened. The hose around the exhaust muffled the noise that might normally have emerged from it, as well as the smoke.

'Is it working properly?' Hermann asked.

'Wait,' Jeckeln replied.

Then they heard, faintly through the metal sides of the van, the sounds of people coughing. The coughs turned to curses, cries of panic, pleas to be let out. Next came hands, fists and feet battering against the sides of the van as the people fought to smash their way out. The sound rose to a crescendo of human anguish and desperation, the noise like a beating, howling, cacophonous emanation from the furthest depths of hell.

The sound ebbed away until there was only the faint impact of a human hand on metal, one last moan and then a silence fell that was worse than the ghastly clamour that had preceded it, for it was the soundlessness of lives erased, breath turned to stone.

'I suppose we'd better open up the doors and see what's happened,' said Hartmann, with an attempt at a casual tone that was betrayed by his ashen skin.

Now you know what death sounds like, when you stand right by it, Gerhard thought, with that contempt that fighting men felt for the false bravado of those who had never been near a flying bullet.

'Wait,' Jeckeln repeated. Then he looked towards Koch and added, deferentially, 'I am reliably informed that at this stage the subjects are unconscious, but death does not come for a minute or two more. Our men always allow five minutes before they turn off the engine and another five before opening the doors. To be on the safe side.'

'I see,' said Koch. 'Tell the men that they may have a cigarette while we wait. I believe that coffee and biscuits have been provided for our refreshment, gentlemen. Now is as good a time as any to consume them. It ensures that we do not spend more time here than is necessary.'

One of Koch's staff opened the rear of a car and produced a folding table, a large vacuum flask of coffee, milk, sugar, biscuits and a few polished steel picnic cups. Gerhard took the coffee that was offered to him, drank it in one, the scalding liquid failing to melt the chill in his bones, and lit a cigarette. His hand was shaking as he flicked his lighter and put the flame to the tobacco.

'Please, Squadron Captain, do have one of these delicious biscuits. Our baker is a man of remarkable gifts. Sadly, however, he is a Jew, so we must make the best of his talents while we can.'

Koch and Jeckeln were the only members of the inspection party to touch the biscuits. 'Perhaps the men might be allowed to share the rest,' Jeckeln suggested. 'Good for their morale.'

Koch thought for a second. Gerhard knew he was the type who would never see the need to pay consideration to an underling. But since the suggestion had been mooted, even Koch could perceive that an air of regal generosity would profit him more than meanness. He gave a curt nod. 'Yes . . . but tell them to be quick about eating them.'

The Gauleiter need not have worried. The SS men ate with relish. The plate was cleared in seconds.

Jeckeln checked his watch. Ten minutes had passed. He looked towards the junior SS officer. 'Proceed!'

Orders were given. Two of the men put on gas masks, walked towards the back of the van, removed the bar across the doors and opened them. They looked in and then recoiled, as if hit in the face at the sight that greeted them. One of them staggered unsteadily away from the van, then ripped the mask from his face and vomited onto the frozen earth.

Gerhard waited for the breeze to blow the fumes away, then glanced at Hartmann, Jeckeln and Koch. He knew that none of them wanted to look into the truck. *But they have to. They have to see what they have done.*

He threw his cigarette to the earth and ground it under his heel. He drew himself up tall, and said, 'Well, gentlemen, shall we inspect the damage?'

Gerhard was junior to the three other men. But he was a war hero, with the Iron Cross at his throat; he had deliberately worn it and left the collar buttons of his coat undone to show it off, and none of the others could let themselves be un-manned by him, not in front of the watching SS soldiers.

'If you insist,' said Jeckeln. Gerhard knew that this was just another day's work for him. It was Koch and Hartmann's reactions that he wanted to observe.

Gerhard led them towards the gas van. He felt confident about his own ability to withstand whatever vileness was about to meet his eyes. He had been at war for the best part of three years. He had seen the scorched and mangled remains of what had once been his comrades, even his friends, roasted within their crashed aircraft. He had watched the women who flew the Sturmoviks trying and failing to escape the confines of their cockpits as they plummeted to their doom, their hands clawing at the glass, like the Jews hammering on the side of the van. During the savage Russian winter from which they were only now emerging, he saw men frozen solid in the snow and ice. Gerhard had seen the tortured remnants of German soldiers after the Russian partisans had dealt with them, and smelled the human flesh that had roasted in villages obliterated in reprisal.

But none of that had prepared him for the inside of the gas van. It was the stench that hit him first, the overpowering odour of the blood and urine and vomit and human faeces that swilled around the floor of the van, surrounding the corpses like rancid gravy spilling from meat in a stew. Here and there he could see shanks of hair and sets of false teeth amidst the foetid slurry, ripped from the people to which they had once belonged in the frenzy that had gripped the captive Jews in their last moments of earthly existence.

When he had heard that gas was the means by which the Final Solution would remove the intimacy and expense of shooting millions of human beings individually, there had been a part of him that had clung to the hope – entirely absurd, he now realised – that this would be a less terrible death for the victims. He could not have been more wrong. At least a bullet to the back of the head was quick. But the Grim Reaper took his time in the gas vans. He toyed with his victims. He gave them licence to punch and claw and scream at their confines, at each other, at the bottomless well of futility as they struggled to find a way out, to end their agonies.

Many of the naked bodies bore deep scratches down their flanks and limbs. Some were so flayed they looked as if the wounds had been inflicted by wild animals rather than their fellow men and women. Gerhard saw an old woman whose eyeballs had been torn loose from their sockets; a little girl whose head had flopped at an unnatural angle, for her neck had been broken; two men who had died with their hands still around one another's throats; a man and woman who were holding one another tight; and face after contorted face, whose rictus mouths and staring, sightless eyes would, Gerhard knew, haunt his nightmares forever.

Gerhard saw Koch swallowing hard, struggling not to react like the SS man had done. Hartmann went glassy-eyed, then dropped in a dead faint to the ground. A couple of Koch's junior staff had to revive him and lead him away to one of the cars. Gerhard held himself, forcing himself to look and record, as if there were a camera rolling in his mind's eye, documenting everything he saw.

As he followed Jeckeln back to their staff car, another thought struck him: *I have lost Saffron forever.*

He was tainted, guilty by association with this bestial crime, which was but one tiny part of an infinitely greater offence against all humanity. No matter what he did to atone for his own sin, and that of his people, he could not be redeemed. Nor could he possibly ask, let alone expect her to love him. She would destroy herself in trying to redeem him.

Like most Bavarians, Gerhard had been raised a Catholic. He was unable to believe in God, but the rituals of the church held a powerful grip on his imagination and his conscience. Part of him had a shred of faith in the concept of confession and forgiveness . . . but not for this.

This was a sin that was, in the most literal sense, unforgivable. Nor could he ask anyone to share it or be tainted by it.

As he sat in the staff car, driving across the endless, featureless terrain, he returned to his first thought. He could never again be with Saffron Courtney, no matter how much he loved her, or she loved him. That hope was gone for good.

It no longer mattered to Gerhard whether he lived or died, for what value could there be to a life that had been stripped of love?

The fact of his death was no longer important. Only the manner of it mattered.

I have to do something, however small, to try to put this right. If I am to die, then may I at least die doing something good, something worthwhile.

I must die doing something that matters.

K onrad von Meerbach drew a silk handkerchief across his forehead to wipe away a sheen of sweat. It was a warm spring late afternoon in Lisbon and the hills on which the city was built were proving unexpectedly taxing. From his earliest boyhood, he had been a thickset, powerfully built individual, but he had spent most of his war behind a desk. Now his muscle was turning to fat, his waistband and collar were tighter and physical exercise was more of a strain than a pleasure.

Officially, von Meerbach had come to neutral Portugal to discuss wolframite: the ore from which the metal tungsten was extracted. Tungsten was hard and heat-resistant. This made it useful for several applications, including the one for which both the German and Allied governments most valued: as the tip of penetrating projectiles, such as tank and artillery shells. A compromise had been reached in which Portugal supplied both sides with tungsten, in return for an understanding that they would respect its neutrality and neither would invade.

Adolf Hitler, however, was not given to compromise. He wanted all the tungsten that the Portuguese could produce. As a senior SS officer who was also a major industrialist, Konrad von Meerbach was considered the ideal man to deal with Salazar, Portugal's Prime Minister, and his senior ministers. Von Meerbach had taken a number of meetings with Salazar in which he made the point, with characteristic force, that it was in Portugal's best interests to keep all-conquering Germany happy and abandon its allegiance to the failed, defeated British. Salazar had stubbornly refused. Now von Meerbach was attending to his own, private interests.

Heinrich Himmler had told von Meerbach to take a few days leave while he was abroad. 'Relax, feel the sun on your back, recharge your batteries. You've earned it,' the *SS-Reichsführer* had told him, adding, 'Perhaps you might try some fishing. I hear it's very good in Portugal.'

Von Meerbach was indeed hoping to land a catch, but it would be in a casino or a brothel, where he might go some way to sating his constant, nagging craving for power and debasement.

Von Meerbach relished his rare time alone, in a neutral foreign city, away from the tumult of war and the disappointments of a wife whose indifference to his needs twisted him into a fury. That afternoon, he had lost heavily gambling in the casinos, but found a whore, for the right price, who was willing enough to indulge his darkest urgings.

Von Meerbach stopped close to the summit of the steep cobbled street, gathered his breath and gave his face another wipe. He entered the large, old apartment building where he was staying, whose air of faded grandeur suggested it might once have been an aristocrat's townhouse, and he climbed the creaking wooden staircase to the top floor.

• • •

In the kitchen, von Meerbach made a pot of strong black coffee and took it outside to the balcony. The view was magnificent. He could look out across the Sea of Straw, the sheltered expanse of water into which the River Tagus flowed before it reached the sea. Von Meerbach closed his eyes for a moment, just to feel the sun on his face, as his leader had commanded. He opened them again and took in the sight of the city, marvelling in the absence of the barrage balloons, gun emplacements and burned-out buildings that disfigured every major German city. Out on the water, ferries were plying across the river, taking passengers from one side to the other, as freighters steamed to and from the docks under the watchful eyes of a Portuguese naval frigate.

His sunny reverie started to cloud over as his thoughts probed old wounds that festered in his mind like deep craters pockmarking an idyllic landscape. The Courtneys. He took his hatred of that family very seriously. Without willing it, he zoomed in on the particulars of those he despised.

Centaine Courtney–age: forty-two; date of birth: New Year's Day, 1900. Principal residence: the Weltevreden Estate, Cape Town, South Africa. Owner of the H'ani diamond mine. Only child, Shasa Courtney, age twenty-four, lost an eye last year while serving as a fighter pilot on the South African Air Force in Somaliland.

Von Meerbach took a sip of his coffee, savouring the intoxicating taste of freshly ground beans, as sweet as the revenge he felt percolating through his veins.

Centaine was a cousin of Leon Courtney–age: fifty-four; date of birth: 6 August 1887. Principal residence: the Lusima Estate, Wanjohi Valley, Kenya. Major shareholder in the Courtney Trading Company, whose headquarters are in Cairo, Egypt. Only child, Saffron Courtney, age: twenty-two. Until recently, serving as a driver to the British Army General Henry Maitland Wilson on the North Africa, Greece and Palestine fronts. Her present whereabouts were unknown, though he believed she had returned to Britain.

The Courtneys were of no interest to the Reich, although when the war was won and the world re-ordered to the Führer's satisfaction, there would be no place for British imperial parasites and all their property would be forfeit.

For von Meerbach that would not be enough. He had no need of the Courtney family's money. He was very wealthy. But he had known loss. His father was taken from him when he was a boy of ten. He died in Africa. His killer was Leon Courtney. Von Meerbach grimaced as he recalled the hideous slaughter: his father had been forced to parachute from his airship and had the misfortune to get caught in some trees before he landed. Leon found him there, wriggling like a fish on a line, and he shot him through the chest in cold blood with not a second of remorse. The murdering bastard's accomplice was his father's mistress, a woman who called herself Eva von

Wellberg, though she was a British spy, real name Eva Barry. She ran off with Courtney and bore his daughter.

Von Meerbach stared into the distance, his eyes narrowed, and a surge of pleasure flowed through his body at the thought of the pain and destruction he would cause. A ruthless torturer and killer hid behind the impeccable cut of his suit. He would not be satisfied until he had repaid Leon Courtney in full for what he did to his family. He wanted him to die slowly and pain-fully, the infliction of an agonising death being a process with which he was intimately familiar. As he died and his screams filled the air, and he begged for mercy, Courtney would know that his beloved daughter, the light of his life, had gone before him, and had suffered just as badly.

Meerbach felt an almost erotic thrill as he considered the intricacies of his plan for vengeance.

• • •

Saffron had assumed that one or two decent nights' sleep and a day in bed would be enough to get her back to her normal self. But the physical punishment she had endured during her mock interrogation had taken more out of her than she realised. Three days after the end of her ordeal she still felt as limp as a wrung-out dish cloth, and even if the swelling on her face was beginning to come down, the colour of the bruises there and around her torso were, if anything, more livid. No bones had been broken, so no permanent damage had been done, but for now she was a rather battered-looking beauty.

It was almost midday, but she was dozing, with her copy of *Shooting to Live* lying on the bedspread, when she was woken by a knock on the door and a man's voice asking, 'Excuse me, miss . . . ?'

Saffron managed a wordless groan of acknowledgement. She turned over to face the door and saw a head peering around it.

'Mind if I come in?'

Saffron came to as three thoughts followed each other in quick succession.

That's an American accent.

Oh my God, he's handsome.

And then, *I look awful!*

She ran her hands through her hair to make it look less like a tangled, greasy, lifeless mess and replied, 'May I ask who you are?'

The man walked into the room. He had a relaxed, loose-limbed gait. He wore a pale khaki uniform and his legs were long, his hips slim, and his shoulders broad. The smile that now spread across his face had a confident, almost cheeky charm.

'Hi,' he said, and Saffron could have sworn that her heart had started beating faster, though she hadn't moved a muscle. She was wondering whether she could find an excuse to pop into the bathroom and do something to stop herself looking less like a boxer who lost the big fight when the American said, 'Lieutenant Daniel P. Doherty, US Navy at your service. My buddies call me Danny. Some of the folks round here seem to prefer Danny Boy. The only person who calls me Daniel is my mom.'

You won't get a Danny Boy from me, Saffron thought. *I'm not giving in that easily. And besides, my heart is with Gerhard, even though it has been so long since we loved each other, and this war is stripping raw my soul.*

'Thank you, Lieutenant Doherty,' she said, hoping that she had managed to keep her voice and expression composed. 'That was a thorough briefing. My name is Saffron Courtney. My friends call me Saffy. As a civilian, I have no rank. I'm a simple "Miss".'

Doherty saw the simple wooden chair that most visitors chose, said, 'May I?' and before Saffron could respond, he spun it around so that the seat faced him and the back was towards Saffron. He straddled the chair with his arms across the top and his chin propped on one fist as he looked at her.

He had lovely eyes, Saffron saw, so dark brown they were almost black, but they were warm and welcoming, and it was all she could do to tear hers away. She hardly noticed that he was talking.

'I have a rank, Miss Courtney, but you're one step ahead of me, because you've got a medal for gallantry. George Medal, am I right?'

'Yes . . .' she said, concentrating on anything but his eyes. 'How did you know?'

'Well, you've made quite a name for yourself round here. I arrived when you were still in the hole, getting the Gestapo treatment. Word was, you'd been in a day. Anyhow, a couple of your instructors took me up to the Morar Hotel, said you guys had a private room there.'

'It's more like a private zoo, some nights,' Saffron replied.

Doherty laughed. 'Well, the animals were all talking about you. Someone was starting a sweepstake on how long you'd last. No one had gone above thirty-six hours. I told 'em, "Hell, I say she lasts forty-eight." Turns out I was the closest, so I won.'

'How much was the pot?'

'Seven pounds, nine shillings and sixpence.'

Saffron nodded, impressed by the size of his win. 'Congratulations. You're a rich man.'

'I know. Figured I owed you a thank you.'

'You're welcome. What else did the animals say about me?'

'Oh, you know, that you came from Africa, and your daddy had a big old business empire, and that you were . . .' He stopped, like a man who had seen a landmine where he was about to tread.

'I was what?' Saffron asked.

Doherty tried to shrug it off. 'Oh, nothing . . .'

'Come on, Lieutenant Doherty, you're not getting away with that. You were going to say something?'

Doherty sighed. 'Damn my big Irish mouth . . . And beautiful. That was the missing word: beautiful.'

Saffron had been enjoying the flirtatious battle that had passed between them. Doherty had cheered her up more than any of her other visitors. Now that good mood was punctured, her spirits deflated and she suddenly felt on the verge of tears as she swallowed hard and murmured, 'Oh. I see . . . and then you come here and find me like this.'

Doherty leaned forward, a look of concern on his face and a much gentler, less cocksure tone to his voice, 'Hey . . . hey . . . Please, Miss Courtney, don't say that. For one thing, I didn't come here as a sightseer. And two, well, even if that was the reason I came to see you, take it from me, Miss Courtney, it would not have been a wasted journey. Sure, you've been dinged up some, but hell, you look like a goddamn movie star from where I'm sitting.'

He sounded as though he meant it, but Saffron could not believe that was possible. 'Really?'

'Yes, ma'am.' Doherty leaned back again and let out a long, low whistle as he examined her with frank appraisal. 'Hell, if David O. Selznick had ever seen you, he'd have said, "Screw Vivien Leigh, this is our Scarlett O'Hara!"'

Saffron gave a rueful laugh. 'I know you don't mean it, but that's very sweet.'

Doherty's playfulness vanished and a seriousness replaced it. 'One thing you should know about me, Miss Courtney . . . If I say something, I always mean it.'

'That's unusual.'

'Tell me about it. I've been in England a few months and, you know, people here don't say what they mean, or mean what they say. Sometimes they mean the exact opposite. Took me a while to work out, if an Englishman says, "I say, old boy, we really must have lunch," he doesn't want to get something to eat, chew the fat, maybe drink a couple of beers. He never wants to see you again as long as he lives.'

Saffron laughed. 'That's so true!'

'But me, I'm American. If I say I want to see you it's because I want to see you. And if I don't, you'd best get the hell off my land.'

'Well, you're safe with me, Lieutenant. I'm African, and we take the same view as you. We tell it like it is where I come from.'

'Well, I'm sure glad to hear there's someone round here thinks like that.'

Saffron relaxed a little.

'So, tell me, Lieutenant Doherty, where are you from and what brings you all the way up here to Arisaig House?'

'Guess I'll start with the second question, because it's a shorter answer. I'm here because there are folks in Washington who are mighty curious about this Baker Street set-up and they're asking themselves, "Maybe we should do something like that?" A few of us have come over to, you know, case the joint.'

'Ooh, gangster talk . . .' Saffron smiled. 'You should speak to Captain Fairbairn. He's a great admirer of Al Capone. He believes we can learn a lot about the effective use of a Tommy Gun from Capone and his mob.'

It was Doherty's turn to grin. 'Yeah! I met Fairbairn and his buddy . . . what's his name?'

'Sykes.'

'That's the one. Say, aren't they a pair? They look like a couple of harmless old geezers and I'll be damned if they don't know more ways of killing people than anyone on God's green earth.'

'So you're in the same business we are.'

'Not yet . . .' Doherty shrugged. 'But potentially.'

Saffron nodded. 'Fair enough, I won't ask you any more. I know the form. But what about where you come from? Tell me a bit about that.'

'Whoa . . . how long have you got?'

'Hmm, let me see . . . I don't appear to have any appointments planned for the immediate future.'

'Well, I'm meeting some of the guys from the occupied nations in half an hour – Norwegians and Czechs, I think – so I'll keep it quick.'

Please don't! Saffron thought. *Please take all the time in the world.*

'So . . . I was born and raised on a cattle ranch outside a small town called Thermopolis in the great state of Wyoming.'

'A genuine cowboy!'

'Guess so.'

'How did you end up in the Navy?'

'I joined in thirty-five. Times were hard, real hard . . . you know, the Great Depression and all that. I'm the youngest of four boys and I was in my senior year at high school, had no idea what to do. All I knew was the ranch couldn't give me work or money. One day a recruiting officer from the US Navy came through town. He said the Navy was the best way yet invented for a young man to see the world, and get an education, a fair wage and three square meals a day doing it. I figured, what have I got to lose?'

'Your home, your family?'

'I didn't lose 'em. They're still there. But I did get educated at Annapolis – that's our Naval Academy. I got a great job. I went to California, to Hawaii, now to England and Scotland . . . and the chow was pretty good, too. Till I got to England, anyways.'

'Do you ever miss home?'

'Sure, sometimes . . . You?'

Saffron nodded and said, 'Will you think me very rude if I ask, where is Wyoming?'

'Nope . . . and I'll even tell you, if you tell me where I could find Czechoslovakia.'

Good question . . . Saffron closed her eyes, imagined a map of Europe and said, 'Until Herr Hitler trampled all over it and turned it into the Protectorate of Bohemia and Moravia, you could find Czechoslovakia due east of Germany, directly underneath Poland . . . And before you ask, Poland is, or was, due east of Germany, directly above Czechoslovakia.'

Saffron sat back on her pillows, feeling smug about both her geography and wit.

'OK, then, Miss Smart Alec . . . Wyoming is most of the way over to the west of the States, and most of the way up from the south. If you head any further north you get to Montana, and then the border with Canada . . . You know where Canada is, right?'

Saffron frowned and made a play out of thinking hard before she replied, 'Mmm, I think so . . . more or less.'

For a second, Doherty hesitated.

Ha! He's worried that I might not have been joking!

He carried on. 'So, anyway, the Rockies run right through Wyoming. Where I live, it's hill country, kind of at the foot of the Big Horn range. Golly, I wish I had the words to describe it . . . It's kinda like this part of Scotland, I guess, except it rains about as much every day over here as we get in a year. And it's wilder back home, and a damn sight hotter – in summer, leastways – and about twelve hundred miles from the sea.

'Anyways, I grew up on the Blue Creek Ranch, about twenty miles outside town. It covers damn near two thousand acres and to me it's . . . well, it's just the most beautiful place in the world.'

Saffron understood how that felt. 'Tell me about the ranch.'

'Shoot, where do I start? Yeah, I know . . . with the sky . . . It's bigger there, somehow. My family's land rises from five to around six thousand feet above sea level. The air is so clear and fresh. There are places you can look out at the mountains and see for a hundred miles in all directions, but no buildings or people anywhere.'

He could be talking about Lusima, Saffron thought. The sky, the altitude, the views that go on forever. Lusima, one of the finest estates in East Africa, named in honour of a healer and mystical seer, it was a magical kingdom in which she was Crown Princess, where she felt deep, other-worldly serenity and security.

'If you're standing in the front porch of our ranch house, the nearest house is seven miles away,' Doherty went on. 'I guess you might think that was lonely, but we've got all of nature for company. There are cliffs where golden eagles like to build their nests. You see them, way up in the sky, looking down at the earth, you know, searching for their next meal. At night you can hear the calling of the great horned owls. Say, have you ever gone hunting?'

'You mean, hunting foxes?'

'No, I guess I meant shooting. You know, game birds, deer, that kinda thing.'

'I've done both,' Saffron told him. 'Ridden to hounds and shot pheasant, grouse, wild ducks, all sorts of things, really.'

'Any good at it?'

'Hmm . . . how do I answer that? I hate the British habit of false modesty, and I believe in telling the truth, but I've also been raised not to boast about myself.'

Doherty scratched behind one ear. 'Okay-y-y, so that was like listening to a message in code, but if I've figured it right, what you're saying is, you're damn good on a horse and a crack shot, but being a nice, modest, proper young lady, you don't like to say so . . . though you don't like not to say so, either.'

Saffron grinned. 'That's very good, Lieutenant! You are clearly a natural cryptographer.'

'I got it right?'

'Spot on,' Saffron admitted, loving the fact that he had understood her so well. 'I was given my first pony when I was barely old enough to walk. I imagine you were the same.'

'Uh-huh.' Doherty nodded.

'My darling father didn't have any sons, so he taught me everything that he would have taught them. He had me firing air rifles from when I was six or seven.'

'Me, too.'

Saffron moved onto the offensive. She looked Doherty in the eye and said, 'We should put our training to the test one day . . . You should know, Lieutenant Doherty, that I am highly competitive.'

He looked her back in the eye. 'Even against men?'

'Particularly against men.'

'I'll bear that in mind. Might take you up on that challenge someday.

'Till then, tell me more about your ranch.'

'It's called the Blue Creek because it's blessed by water, but the earth is kind of a deep, rich red. We've got a lot of pasture for the cattle and about thirty acres set aside for hay, but down by the creeks you'll find cottonwoods, and willows growing by the water, then up in the hills there are forests of pine and juniper.'

'What kind of wildlife do you have?'

'Apart from the cattle we've got, let me see . . . elk, mule deer, white-tailed deer, antelope – we don't go short of venison or buckskin, that's for sure. You see moose come by from time to time, too.

'Now, if you've got that much prey, you're gonna get all the predators that hunt them, so that's mountain lions, bobcats, wolves, coyote. Oh, and bear, almost forgot to mention them. When I was a kid, I'd go out looking for wild gooseberries and currants growing wild along the creek. Always had to keep an eye out in case a black bear had the same idea. They love a nice, juicy berry.'

'It sounds like real pioneer country.'

'Oh, it sure was. The stagecoach used to come through our land. But there were Shoshoni Indians and their ancestors living on the creek for thousands of years before the white man ever got there. When I was a kid, some folks came up from Laramie, the University of Wyoming. They started digging around, looking for prehistoric life, and damn it if they didn't find signs of ancient camp sites and rock circles. They told my folks the remains date back ten thousand years or more. We have a couple guys work on our ranch that have Shoshoni blood in them. They say you can still see the spirit people, sprites and ogres, and the Water Ghost Woman walking down by the springs and creeks. Ha, I guess you think that's pretty crazy.'

Saffron shook her head. 'Not at all. I grew up among African tribes . . . Their idea of the world is like those Indians. They see more than we do.'

'Well, I'll be damned,' Doherty said. 'You ride, you shoot, you understand native people. I've got to admit, I didn't expect that. Most English girls look at me like I'm some kind of dumb cowboy straight out of a movie.'

'Well, this Kenyan girl knows how you feel. And it's funny, we grew up on different sides of the world, but so much of what you said about your ranch is just as true of our estate. We're high up, with huge skies and red earth and wild animals . . . though I dare say you don't have quite so many elephants, or zebras, or giraffes.'

'Oh, we did. But I shot 'em all.'

As Saffron was laughing, Doherty looked at his watch. 'Say, is that the time? I got Czechs and Norwegians waiting for me. OK, so Czechoslovakia is east of Germany and, ah, south of Poland. Now, where's Norway?'

'Half-way between here and Russia, long and thin, runs along the North Atlantic from the Baltic to the Arctic.'

'Got it . . . Catch you later!'

Then he was gone. Saffron lay back in bed. All of a sudden she was feeling much better.

• • •

Several weeks had gone by since her ordeal and Saffron was fully recovered. Meanwhile, Danny Doherty's fact-finding mission to Arisaig seemed to be lasting a long time. He swore to Saffron that it was business.

'I got new orders. They don't want me just to observe the training. They want me to do it, too. Get a real feel for how it works.'

Saffron frequently found herself running across the bleak but lovely hillsides with the tall, rangy American beside her, or shooting with him at tin cans dragged on strings by pulley up and down one of the local hillsides, or plunging into the icy blackness of Loch Morar, the deepest and, she was convinced, eeriest body of inland water in all the British Isles.

His toughness, athleticism and marksmanship came as no surprise to her. What else would one expect from a real, live cowboy? But what impressed her more was the understated but razor-sharp intelligence he kept hidden away behind his 'aw-shucks' facade. It wasn't just that he shone in all their classroom work. He approached any task he was asked to perform, and managed to get others to work with him in the way he wanted, without them even realising that he was taking charge, which suggested a shrewd, perceptive mind.

One of their instructors was a young Oxford graduate called Gavin Maxwell. His mother was the daughter of the Duke of Northumberland, and his father was a baronet, whose family home was on the far southwest coast of Scotland. Maxwell was a fount of knowledge about the country and its wildlife.

'It's a thousand feet down to the bottom,' he'd told Saffron as they stood on the loch shore one morning, with the water, the massive lowering hills all around and the sky itself looking like a vast black and white photograph, so absolute was the absence of colour. 'They say there's a monster at the bottom that makes the one in Loch Ness look like a tiddler by comparison.'

From that moment on Saffron discovered that she could not shake the mental image of a great, prehistoric sea creature lurking in the stygian depths. She was beset by the kind of silly, irrational fear that she had always supposed that other, weaker females might fall prey to, but never her.

Danny, however, had other, more mundane concerns on his mind.

'Does the sun ever shine here?' he asked as they were led out for physical training on another miserable morning, with the rain blowing horizontally into their faces by a freezing wind off the sea. As he wiped away the water dripping from his hair and eyes, he was clearly a man who was missing the heat, sun and clear dry air of Wyoming.

'Very occasionally,' Maxwell had replied. 'And when it does, a national holiday is declared.'

· · ·

Danny was billeted in Arisaig House, while Saffron had gone back to her base at Garramore. The hours of training were long and arduous, so there was little time or energy to spare for socialising, and any carousing that did go on happened in a back room at the Morar Hotel. This modest establishment had the only decent bar for miles around, but it closed at nine on weekday evenings, by which time the Baker Street trainees had barely finished their day's work, and was not open on Sundays.

Jimmy Young, realising that his people needed to let off steam, had persuaded the hotel's proprietress, Mary Macdonald, to make special arrangements for Baker Street staff and trainees, and keep that room supplied with as much whisky and beer as was required to restore life to tired minds and aching limbs. The local police agreed to turn a blind eye to the goings-on at the hotel, which were mild compared to the constant shooting, fighting and exploding taking place during daylight hours. The Morar Hotel became the place where the future secret agents went to let down their hair.

One evening in late May, Danny borrowed a car from the Arisaig House garage and drove to Garramore, where he asked for Saffron.

She appeared at the door with a smile that suggested she was surprised to see him, but in a nice way. 'Why, if it isn't Lieutenant Doherty of the United States Navy!' she said. 'Have you come to inspect us?'

He gave a rueful half-smile. 'I just got my marching orders. They want me back in London, writing up my report.'

The joy was wiped from Saffron's face. 'When will you be leaving?'

'First thing in the morning.'

'Oh . . .' Saffron was alarmed by the sudden jolt that had hit her, like a physical blow to her stomach: a feeling of shock, disappointment and, she realised, loss. 'I'll miss you,' she said, seeing no reason to pretend otherwise.

'Yeah, me too . . .' Danny looked downcast, but then he bucked himself up. 'Anyway, seeing as this is my last night, I was wondering if you would consent to join me in a farewell drink, down at the hotel.'

She smiled. 'That would be lovely. But . . .' she looked down at her muddy khaki blouson and trousers, 'I'm still in battle-dress and army boots. Maybe I should get changed.'

'No, you're fine as you are. And I know how long you girls take to get dressed in the evening. Let's go.'

They passed through the gates of the Garramore House grounds and onto the narrow lane that would take them onto the Morar road. A shaft of dazzling sunshine suddenly sliced through the car and it made Danny brake hard.

He shaded his face with his hand . 'Well, will you look at that,' he murmured. 'I'll be damned if it ain't blue sky.'

'There might be a nice sunset this evening, though we won't see it from the road,' Saffron said. 'We need to be down by the shore. Camusdarach's only a couple of minutes away. Let's stop off there on the way to Morar. It won't take a minute to look at the sky. And you know what the hotel's like. People stay there half the night, so we're not going to miss them.'

'Sounds like a plan.'

Danny turned towards the tiny seaside village of Camusdarach, which was half a mile away. They were familiar with the beach because it was one of the places where their instructors liked to take them for the regular long-distance, open-water swims that were one of the most arduous aspects of their training. To Baker Street trainees, the words Camusdarach Beach conjured up a sensation of convulsive shivering, heaving lungs, guts full of salt-water and exhausted limbs, blue with cold.

It wasn't a happy place, but it was the best that Danny and Saffron could manage. He parked the car by the side of the road that ran through the village and they began the walk across the seashore landscape, so typical of the region: lonely, wind-blasted trees dotted about a heath of sandy soil held in place by clumps of grass and heather and broom, with thickets of gorse here and there, and streams running down to the sea. Up ahead a line of tall dunes blocked off the way to the beach and prevented them seeing the setting sun.

They strolled in companionable silence and then Danny said, 'Wait a second, I want to show you something . . .'

He was wearing a brown leather flying jacket. He snapped open the chest pocket, fished out his wallet and extracted a photograph. 'This is Meg. She's my girl, I guess . . .'

Saffron frowned, uncertain why he had chosen this, of all moments, to reveal that he had a sweetheart. 'I guess?' she asked.

'Well, we're not engaged, she's thousands of miles away in Washington DC and there's a war on. Anything could happen, right?'

Is he making a pass at me? she wondered. Or maybe he was using his girlfriend as a way of brushing her off. She forced herself not to jump to conclusions.

'Where did you two meet?' she asked as they started walking again.

'In the Russell Senate Office Building, a stone's throw from the Capitol. I was working at the Pentagon. She was the secretary for a senator who served on the Senate Committee for Naval Affairs. I walked into his office one day, running an errand for my boss, and there she was. I took one look at her and thought, "I have got to find some way to get that girl on a date."'

'I'm not surprised, she's pretty. Do you think you'll marry her?'

'Good question. If the Japs hadn't bombed Pearl, and if we were still at peace, and if I'd stayed in DC . . .'

Saffron gave a dismissive sigh. 'Forget the ifs, why didn't you ask anyway?'

'No time. After Pearl Harbour, the nation had to be put on a war footing pretty much overnight. I was working round the clock, so was Meg, so was everyone. Next thing I knew, I'd been seconded to an outfit called the Office of the Coordinator of Information . . .'

'Ha!'

Danny looked at Saffron quizzically.

'Don't the names they give to units like ours make you laugh? We started life as the Inter-Services Research Bureau.'

'Well, we're getting another name soon, a whole new set-up. That's one of the reasons I'm here. My boss, Bill Donovan, is real impressed by you guys. He came over last year, just to take a look-see. Now we're in this for real, he wants to learn everything he can about the way you do things.'

'So you'll go back to Washington to report. Then you and Meg can get married.'

'Maybe. Or maybe they'll tell me, "Just send a written report and stay there in England." Or maybe I'll get an order telling me to get my ass to Long Beach, California, because I've been posted to a battleship that's sailing for the Pacific. Look, the truth is, none of us know what the heck is going to happen to any of us. I could be blown up by a bomb in London. Meg could fall in love with another guy. I bet there's a line around Capitol Hill right now, guys waiting to try their luck.'

'She'll wait for you,' Saffron said, without thinking, surprising herself with the speed and conviction of her response.

'Really? Do you think?'

'Yes.'

Danny was about to ask her why she thought that, but he stopped himself. There was no need; Saffron had already answered the question in the way she'd spoken.

'Why did you tell me about Meg?' she asked.

'Hell, I don't know.' Danny looked away, avoiding eye contact while he tried to formulate his thoughts. 'I guess I was hoping to learn a little more about you and I thought, maybe if I was honest about myself first, that might . . .'

'Encourage me?'

'I guess.' Now he looked at her again. 'I wasn't being too smart, huh? You're the girl that held out against the Gestapo for three days. Why would you crack for me?'

She looked at him. 'You can always ask.'

'Hmm . . . where do I start? OK, you don't wear a ring on your wedding finger. Is that a Baker Street thing? I mean, if you were a regular civilian . . .'

'If, if, if . . . Not that again!' she said, smiling to let him know she was teasing.

'Yeah, yeah . . . but you know what I mean.'

'No, I'm not married. I'm not engaged.'

'Wow! She talks!'

'Oh, come on, that makes me sound horrible.'

'I didn't mean to do that.'

They had almost reached the line of dunes, close enough to have passed into the shadows they cast. Now it was Saffron's turn to stop walking. She wanted Danny's full attention and waited until he was standing still, facing her before she said, 'Forget about Baker Street. Forget all that secret agent nonsense. Think of me as a girl, going for a walk on the beach with a man she . . . a man who's a dear friend. I've been taught how to do all sorts of things that most girls would never think about in a million years. But I'm no different to them. I like to wear pretty clothes and dance the night away. And love matters more to me than anything else.'

'Have you ever been in love . . . I mean, really in love?' Danny asked.

Her answer was instant. 'Yes.'

'I don't know if I have.'

'Not even with Meg?'

'I don't know. I mean, she's the prettiest girl I've ever seen. And I know for sure she'd be the best wife any man could ever ask for. And I really like her, don't get me wrong. But am I in love? How can you be certain about that?'

'Because you don't have to think about it. Love fills your heart and your soul and every atom of your body. You know you would do anything, anything at all for just one more minute together.'

Danny sighed. 'Wow . . . I envy the guy who makes you feel like that. When you were talking about it, you lit up. You were a different person. Who is he?'

What do I tell him? Simple. Stick to Baker Street rules. Keep your cover story as close to the truth as possible.

'He's a fighter pilot,' Saffron said.

'Impressive. One of The Few, huh?'

'Not exactly. He's—' she searched for the right, non-committal word – 'overseas. We haven't been together since the War began . . .' Saffron gave a rueful smile. 'Well, he flew over me once, about a year ago, and we waved at each other, but . . . I've . . . well, it's easier to tell myself that we won't be together until this whole beastly war is over. No point in getting one's hopes up.'

'What's his name?'

'Gerry . . . with a G.' *That's close enough to Gerhard.*

'Well, that's a relief. Jerry with a J would be a whole other deal. Say, do you have a picture of this guy? Since I showed you my gal and all . . .'

Saffron considered the request for a moment and then decided it would be odd to refuse. She reached inside the canvas satchel that had been her companion all through the War, found her purse and extracted her only memento of Gerhard von Meerbach: the picture of the two of them by the Eiffel Tower.

'There you are. That was Paris, April thirty-nine.'

'Handsome devil, isn't he?'

'Don't worry, that's what Meg's girlfriends all say when she shows them pictures of you,' Saffron said, and though she meant it light-heartedly, she couldn't disguise the fact she meant what she said. She could see Danny heard it too.

'Well, I bet the other guys in Gerry's squadron keep asking him for pictures of his movie-star girlfriend,' he replied, and though his smile said he was kidding, his eyes were looking into hers.

'Not that nonsense again . . .'

'Say, do they paint pictures of beautiful dames on their planes in the R.A.F? Maybe Gerry has you draped across his engine cowling with "Hot Saffy" written underneath.'

He put one hand on his hip and another behind his head and leaned back, like a pin-up.

'I'll get you for that!' She took a step towards him, but Danny darted away up the dune, laughing. She raced after him, but he was faster and she couldn't catch him before he had gone over the top and disappeared down the other side. As fit as she was, the slope was near vertical and the sand was soft and slippery under her feet, so her heart was pounding as she reached the top. She looked around, expecting to see Danny looking back at her, daring her to go after him again. But when she spotted him, he was quite still, with his back to her, staring out to sea. She gathered her breath, pushed her hair away from her face and looked in the same direction. And then she saw why he had lost his interest in their silly game.

The sun was low in the sky, shining between the islands of Rum and Skye, turning them into soft silhouettes of purple and grey. The waters between the shore and the islands were like a black satin, sprinkled with myriad gilt and silver sequins where the sunlight sparkled. The sand on the beach, so gloriously white at midday, was now a pale coral, with every rivulet and undulation marked out in rippling lines of deep grey shadow.

But the most wondrous sight of all was the sky. Saffron could not imagine how any painter or photographer could do justice to the way that the dazzling heart of the sun seemed to burn through the high cloud and turn it into a churning fireball of white gold. To either side, the sunset flamed in vivid pinks, magenta, violet, heliotrope and a deep, imperial purple that faded away into the grey-blue colour of the clouds themselves.

She stood, hardly daring to breathe, trying to imprint this majestic vision on her mind's eye forever. And then she smelled the tang of the sea breeze against her face and listened to the gentle rustle of the calm sea lapping against the beach and the occasional cawing of a gull in the distance.

When she looked down at Danny again, he had turned and was staring up at her. This was not a casual glance, it was a gaze so intense she could feel it and her body responded to it, like a flower opening to the sun. He gave a little nod of the head, inviting her to join him. She walked to the far side of the dune, not racing and tumbling and giggling, as she might have done a short while earlier, but slowly, deliberately, scarcely taking her eyes off his.

She came to him, he opened his arms and she moved between them until her body was touching his. Then he closed his arms tight around her.

It had been so long since she had felt the strong, safe embrace of a man. Her body softened as the tension and resistance went out of it. Her face was leaning against the top of his chest and she caught the faint scent of the sweat from his run up and down the dune. His chest was rising and falling, as if he were still running, though they were both still. She could feel his arousal pressing against her and the melting heat with which her body answered it.

His eyes were so dark in the evening light, and she lifted her hands, which had been pressed against his body, so that she could touch his face and feel the gentle rasp of his stubble against her fingertips.

Then she felt his arms lifting her up and she was standing on tiptoe as she lifted her chin to look at him as he lowered his face towards hers. Their eyes met, and their lips met, and Saffron was carried away by the insistence and passion of his kiss.

•　•　•

They walked back to the car arm in arm, their bodies close, stopping now and then to kiss, hardly saying a word. It was a few minutes' drive to the Morar Hotel and that too passed in silence, though Danny steered one-handed, letting his other hand stray from the gear lever to Saffron's thigh, sending tremors though her whenever he touched her.

She felt a terrible guilt but no shame for what had happened between them. Her heart had been awoken by his kiss, like a fairy-tale princess from a deep sleep. How could that be wrong? She had spent so much time denying herself the possibility of being aroused by another man that it had become a way of life.

Now Danny had come along. She knew he would be gone soon. The chances were they would never meet again. He was just a handsome, attractive, charming man, who was making her feel better than she had done in a long time. He could never be a true rival to Gerhard. But what if Danny came back to her? Was it possible to love two men, as different as they were, with equal passion and unbreakable heart?

They pulled up outside the hotel.

He leaned his face towards her, not for a kiss, but an inspection. 'Do I have lipstick all over me?'

Saffron peered at him through the gloom of the car's interior. 'Not that I can see.'

She checked her own reflection in the rear-view mirror. Her hair needed tidying and lipstick was probably a good idea. As she applied it, she thought, *The other girls will know we've been up to something. They'll see it in me. Oh, what the hell? Let them!*

They walked into the hotel and into the bar, which had officially closed for the night. Mary Macdonald was tidying up the mess on the tables scattered around the room. Saffron smiled to herself as she saw the hotel proprietress look up, see Danny and, without thinking, tuck a stray wisp of hair behind one ear and smooth down the fabric of her dress. *He has the same effect on all of us!*

Then again, Mary Macdonald's adoration of Lieutenant Danny Doherty was known to all the Baker Street crowd and the local folk alike.

Within days of arriving at Arisaig, having been to the Morar Hotel and realising how vital the proprietress was to the training operation, Danny had entered the hotel bar one evening. The locals were still drinking, and he strolled across the room, John Wayne-style, leaned on the counter, pushed his Navy cap to the back of his head, flashed his best cowboy smile and drawled, 'Howdy, Mrs M.'

She had blushed like a schoolgirl.

'What can I get you, Lieutenant?' she had inquired.

'Nothing at all, ma'am, thank you kindly. Today it's what I can get you. I figured you did so much for us folks at Arisaig, you deserved a token of appreciation, courtesy of Uncle Sam. Here you go . . .'

Danny was wearing a brown leather flying jacket. He reached into it and pulled out something, which he laid on the counter-top in front of Mrs Macdonald. She gasped in wonder, for there before her was a packet of actual nylon stockings. She had heard of these modern miracles, of course, as every woman in Britain had done. But never before had she seen them. And now, here they were, and, as if that were not enough, Danny produced two bars of Hershey's chocolate and put them down beside the nylons. In a country half-starved by rationing, they were symbols of unadulterated indulgence.

'Thank you, Lieutenant,' Mrs Macdonald had gasped.

'No, ma'am, thank you. We don't know what we'd do without you.'

Since then, Mary Macdonald had worshipped the ground on which Danny Doherty walked. Nothing was too good for him and her face lit up as he walked into her establishment. But then a puzzled frown crossed Danny's face as he looked through the open door of the room set aside as the Baker Street drinking den and saw darkness and silence.

'Where is everybody?' he asked.

'Och, they've all away and gone,' she replied. 'One of the Czech laddies came in and said that they'd had the most wonderful news and were holding a party at Traigh to celebrate. That's where you'll find everyone.'

Danny thought for a second. 'I'd sure love to stay right here with you, Mrs M, but I kinda need to see everyone and say my goodbyes.'

'Goodbyes?'

'Yeah, I'm shipping out tomorrow morning.'

The disappointment on Mrs Macdonald's face was no less acute than it had been on Saffron's when she had heard the same news.

Danny reached out and took Mary Macdonald's hand, as if he was about to propose, and said, 'I can't thank you enough, Mrs M. I will remember this place and your hospitality as long as I live. And when this damn war is over, I swear I will come back here and we will open a bottle of your finest Scotch and talk about the old times. Is that a deal?'

'Oh, Lieutenant Doherty . . .' Mrs Macdonald wiped away a tear.

'There you go, ma'am,' he said, handing her a fresh hand-kerchief. 'Say, I got a little parting gift for you. Didn't have any more nylons, but I've got one left of these.' He gave her another bar of chocolate. 'Now, you be good and keep that all for yourself. I heard you shared the last one with your regulars.'

'Well, it seemed selfish not to.'

'That's real neighbourly of you, but I insist. This one's for you and you alone. Promise?'

'I promise.'

'That's grand. Now, Miss Courtney and I had better move on down the road, so I'll take my leave . . .'

Danny led Saffron towards the door, with Mrs Macdonald following in their wake. Before they stepped outside, he turned and said, 'I'll be back. I promise.'

They drove along the coast road, past Camusdarach to Traigh House, a modest, whitewashed family home that stood on the shoreline beside a nine-hole golf course that no Baker Street trainee could ever find time to play. An assortment of cars, motorbikes, bicycles and an army truck were scattered along the roadside. Danny pulled up at the end of the line, climbed out and opened the passenger door for Saffron.

When she got out of the car, he kicked the door shut and took her in his arms. 'I want you to know that I think you're an amazing, beautiful, smart . . . ah, you're just a hell of a woman.'

He didn't smile, didn't pretend that he was being light-hearted, and his sincerity made Saffron think that it was the best of all the many compliments he'd paid her.

'Thank you,' she said, and kissed him lightly on the lips.

'If things had been different . . . who knows? Maybe we'd have had a chance, you know . . . for something great.'

'Ifs and maybes,' she said. 'Let's just be thankful for what we had.'

'One last kiss?' he asked. 'To remember you by . . .'

She nodded and he held her tighter and kissed her, and the kiss went on and on because neither of them could bear to part. Finally, Saffron forced herself to pull away because she knew that if she didn't she would not be able to stop herself going all the way, and that, she told herself, without quite convincing herself, would not be a good idea.

'Now you do have lipstick on your face,' she said. 'Here, give me your hankie.'

Saffron wiped Danny clean. 'OK,' she said, 'let's go and see what the Czechs were so happy about.'

The answer, they discovered, was truly worth celebrating.

News had come in from Prague. Two Czechs, working for the British, had ambushed Reinhard Heydrich, the Acting Protector of Bohemia and Moravia, while he was being driven in his open-topped Mercedes-Benz from his country estate to his headquarters in Prague. Heydrich had been wounded by fragments from a grenade, thrown by the agents. His condition was said to be critical.

'We are fighting back!' an exultant Czech trainee declared, waving a bottle of whisky in the air. 'Those Nazi bastards aren't safe any more. We've got them on the run!'

• • •

Konrad von Meerbach heard the news of the attack as soon as word reached Berlin. He was devastated, fearful, overcome with a despair he had not felt since the news that his father had died. He had loved and worshipped Heydrich as a hero-figure, a surrogate father, and the pure, unsullied adoration he felt for him was stronger than he possessed for either his wife or his mistress.

He made certain of a seat on the plane that took Dr Karl Gebhardt, Himmler's personal physician, to oversee Heydrich's care at Bulovka Hospital. Von Meerbach barely left his master's room, or the corridor outside it. In a series of operations, Heydrich's spleen was removed. Damage to his ribs, diaphragm and left lung was repaired. He received massive blood transfusions.

For a while the treatment appeared to have been successful. Heydrich had been feverish but his temperature gradually returned to almost normal. After a few days, Himmler himself arrived and von Meerbach conducted him to Heydrich's room. He was sitting up in bed, chatting.

'As you know, gentlemen, my father composed operas,' Heydrich said. 'I've been thinking about something he wrote.'

He hummed a tune and sang the words, 'The world is just a barrel-organ which the Lord God turns Himself. We all have to dance to the tune which is already on the drum.'

'Well, I'm sure the tune will turn out to be a merry one,' Himmler said, with a smile that did not extend to the beady eyes behind his round, metal-framed glasses.

'Yes, sir,' von Meerbach said, trying to keep the groveling desperation out of his voice. Turning to Heydrich, he said, 'You'll be well in no time, I'm sure of it. You have the constitution of an ox, as well as the courage of a lion.'

Unfortunately, however, there was not a constitution on earth, not even that of the proverbial ox, that was strong enough to resist the deadly poisonous toxin, derived from the bacterium *Clostridium botulinum* and codenamed simply 'X', which had been developed at the Porton Down Laboratory and added to the ingredients of Cecil Clarke's custom-made grenades.

That night, Heydrich fell into a coma from which he never awoke. On 4 June, eight days after the attack at the Holešovice crossroads, Reinhard Heydrich died.

Von Meerbach returned to Berlin for the lavish state funeral, broadcast live on the radio to the entire Reich and all its Occupied Territories. He was utterly bereft, and in his pain he turned to the one characteristic that never deserted him: his desire to hurt other people.

The world had taken his father and his hero. Now Konrad von Meerbach would have his revenge.

• • •

Listening to the funeral as it was broadcast over the tannoy at his aerodrome, Gerhard had a very different response. To him this successful attack on one of the most prominent figures in the entire Nazi hierarchy was a sign of hope, rather than despair.

After all, if those two men could kill Reinhard Heydrich, why couldn't others kill Adolf Hitler?

'Why are you smiling?' Berti Schrumpp asked Gerhard, startling him from his reverie. 'A funeral's hardly a laughing matter.'

'No, you're right . . . my mind was a million kilometres away.'

'Thinking about women, were you, old man?'

'Dear boy, you know me too well. Now, let's go and find a bottle of schnapps. We should drink a toast to Heydrich's memory, don't you think?'

'Of course!'

And, thought Gerhard, *to the splendid news of his death*.

• • •

Saffron went from Arisaig to Ringwood aerodrome, near Manchester, where she was trained as a parachutist so that she could be dropped into enemy territory. She proceeded to the SOE finishing school at Beaulieu Palace House in Hampshire. It was made clear from the moment she arrived that the sort of high jinks to which a blind eye might be turned in the wilds of the Scottish Highlands would not be accepted for one second at Beaulieu.

Agents in training were treated like boarding-school pupils, with strict rules to obey. They were placed into houses under the supervision of a House Commandant and were banned from leaving the grounds unaccompanied, unless ordered to do so. They were never to disclose that they had been at the finishing school, nor to recognise anyone they had met there should they meet again on anything other than official business. Saffron was informed that her paybook, along with any weapons, camera or notebooks in her possession, had to be handed over, likewise any money above the value of £5, and any personal valuables. All outgoing letters had to be given, unsealed, to the House Commandant for censoring. Saffron observed to a fellow trainee that, 'Even the censorship is censored,' because no reference to it was allowed in any letter. Telegrams could only be sent – having first been censored, of course – in cases of dire emergency. No telephone calls were allowed within Beaulieu itself, or in its locality – 'Which we can't visit anyway, because we're not allowed out of the grounds.'

Having been deprived of virtually all their freedoms, the trainees were informed, without irony, that, 'The purpose of this organisation is subversion.' At Arisaig, Saffron had been provided with the raw materials of an agent's trade: the ability to defend herself and kill her enemies; to carry out acts of sabotage; to forge documents; to go without sleep for days on end; and, of course, to resist interrogation.

The purpose of the finishing school was to give her and the other trainees an understanding of the context in which those new talents would be put to work. Their textbook was the SOE manual, *How to Be an Agent in Occupied Europe*. Their instructors used it to teach the art of recruiting and managing groups of Resistance fighters. Saffron learned how to operate undercover in enemy territory and was drilled again and again in the key elements of cover, information, alertness, inconspicuousness, discretion, discipline and planning for emergencies. She was taught to avoid any detail that might give her away, from a single word in English, to an incriminating scrap of paper stuffed in a pocket or the bottom of a handbag and forgotten, only to be discovered by the enemy.

As the course went on she learned that there were political as well as practical considerations when planning and executing missions, communicating with London, or maintaining a sense of unity among individuals and groups in local Resistance movements. At times, the limitations on her freedom drove Saffron half-mad with frustration, and she was bored to tears by the endless hours in the classroom.

It was when the course ended and she made her way back to London that Saffron stopped to count her blessings. No women in history had ever been given the kind of education that she and the SOE's other female trainees received. It wasn't just that Baker Street was creating a new kind of agent, with new skills and technology at their disposal; it was that women were given the same training as the men.

If I can survive this blasted war, there won't be anything I can't do, she told herself as she got off the train at Waterloo.

It was a strange experience to look at the biggest, toughest men strutting around the station platforms in their various uniforms and know that few, if any of them, could hope to defeat her in hand-to-hand combat, or beat her in a gunfight. But that much she had learned in Scotland. What Beaulieu had given her was the confidence to give commands decisively and with assurance so that people instinctively and obediently responded.

When she got back to her flat in Knightsbridge, there was a pile of mail to greet her. Even in wartime, bills had to be paid. But not this minute, Saffron thought, setting the brown envelopes to one side. She saw an envelope covered in Kenyan stamps and tore it open to find a lovely, chatty letter from her stepmother Harriet, mostly describing her father's recovery from the serious leg injuries he received when the Star of Khartoum was sunk.

I need hardly tell you that all that talk of him needing a wheel-chair has turned out to be utter nonsense, Harriet wrote. 'He simply refused to consider the thought. Indeed, it took some persuasion to get him to use a stick, even when he was insisting on trying to walk around the estate. I must say, life was easier when he was bed-ridden. At least I knew where he was!

Saffron laughed at the thought of her father informing his doctors, his wife and anyone else who dared to suggest otherwise that he would let a minor detail like having his leg blown half off stop him from doing what he wanted. In that respect, the Courtneys were a case of 'like father, like daughter'. Then she saw another envelope, addressed in writing she did not recognise. But intuition told Saffron who had sent it, even before she had seen the name at the top of the page. And the fact that the message had to be sent, rather than delivered in person, could only mean one thing. *He's left the country . . . and I missed him.* She steeled herself and read:

Dear Saffron,

I tried to see you, or call you, but no one at your outfit would tell me where you were. Anyone would think they were secret or something!

Anyway, I've got to ship out. We're setting up our own training school and Bill Donovan wants me back on our side of the pond to help out. Truth is, I'd rather be doing, instead of teaching, but if that's what Uncle Sam wants, I guess I can't argue.

I wish I could have seen you again. It feels like unfinished business. But something tells me this war's got a while left to go yet, so maybe we'll meet up again. Like the song says, 'Don't know where, don't know when'.

Meantime, remember me, Saffy. I'll sure remember you.
Your very own,
Danny-Boy

Saffron read the letter and cried, because it felt like unfinished business to her too. But as much as she would have loved to have seen Danny again, and for the two of them to have been in London together, it would have complicated her life in all sorts of ways. She felt herself breaking in two. Her soul was with Gerhard; she wanted to give everything to him, but was he even alive? She saw him that day in the plane; he waved to her. He still loved her, surely? As much as her heart longed to be in love, and her body yearned for a man's touch, her head told her that romance was an indulgence she could not afford.

Men could wait. She had finished her training. Now it was time to go back to war.

• • •

As she walked into Norgeby House the following morning, Saffron felt full of energy and ready for action. In common with Baker Street's other female agents, she was officially listed as an ensign in the First Aid Nursing Yeomanry, a rank equivalent to a military lieutenant. On her way up the stairs and along the corridors that led to T section's offices, she felt she was coming home. The other women she'd met in her time at Baker Street greeted her with friendly smiles. There were cheery hellos from the men and even a couple of jokes about her ability to endure torture. Word of the interrogation had travelled all the way down south from Arisaig.

'Oh, hello, Saffron,' said Hardy Amies' secretary. 'Do come in. You're expected.'

She was shown into her boss's office and saw at once that the captain's three pips on his shoulder tabs had been replaced by a gold and red crown. He was Major Amies now.

'Congratulations, sir,' Saffron said.

Amies gave a gracious nod. 'Thank you, my dear. Now, sit yourself down, have a nice cup of tea, and let's decide what's to be done with you.'

Saffron perched on her seat, leaning forward as eagerly as a dog straining at a leash, waiting for the one thing she hoped for more than anything else, and confidently expected: an assignment in Europe.

Amies, who seemed to have become both grander and more serious since his promotion, paused as he examined a number of typewritten documents, which Saffron realised must be her reports. She smiled to herself as she remembered sitting in her father's study at Lusima, waiting while he read through her school reports and exam results. But there was none of the tension she had felt then, waiting to hear what the verdict had been. She already knew how well she had performed on her various courses. There could surely only be one outcome.

'I've read them all before, of course,' Amies remarked, putting the papers down on his desk. 'I wanted to make sure that they really were as good as I had remembered. Remarkably, they're even better. You did splendidly, Saffron.'

'Thank you, sir.'

'No need to thank me, you have more than earned any compliments I might give. You've caught people's eye, Saffron. Even Brigadier Gubbins has been asking after you. His words were that I must be sure to make the best of such an outstanding prospect.'

'I can't wait, sir. I want to be of use.'

'And so you shall be . . . but not yet.'

Saffron could hardly believe her ears. Was Amies saying she wasn't going to be given a job?

'Why not?' she blurted out, so shocked that she could not keep the indignation out of her voice.

'Because I don't want to send you to your death,' Amies replied. 'And it is my judgement that if I were to put you in the field at the present time, you would be either dead, or captured, or both, within a week of setting foot on Belgian soil.'

'I don't understand . . . What have I done wrong?'

'Nothing, Miss Courtney. You have not failed in the slightest way. But none of your remarkable achievements can disguise the fact that you still could not possibly pass for a Belgian, not even a South African with Flemish Belgian roots.'

Saffron fought to control the tide of furious anger rising within her. It would do her no good whatsoever to lose her temper now. 'I'm sure I could, sir. I have all the necessary field-craft skills.'

'All right, then, imagine we are on a train, travelling from, say, Leuven to Antwerp. I enter the compartment and, seeing a pretty girl, naturally take the seat opposite hers. I am wearing the uniform of an *SS-Hauptsturmführer*, or captain. I begin a conversation with you, speaking in Flemish. You can hardly refuse to talk to me. I say, "I have a couple of days' leave and I'd like to go somewhere really special, off the beaten track. Where do you recommend?"

'Please be so good as to give me your answer to that question, describing somewhere in northern Belgium, in colloquial Flemish, with the familiarity of someone who knows and loves the place.'

Saffron opened her mouth, realised she couldn't think of what to say, or how, and thought a bit more.

'You seem puzzled, Miss . . . ?'

Amies had spoken in Flemish. He paused, as a man would who was expecting a woman to supply her name.

'Cour . . .' Saffron began without thinking, caught off-balance by what Amies had said and what he was doing.

'I'm sorry, I didn't hear you correctly. You said Kor . . . something?' Amies asked.

Saffron wracked her brain for a Dutch or Flemish-sounding name. 'Korpman,' she said, though the closest she had ever heard to that was a Doctor Koopman, who used to tend to sick girls at her school in Johannesburg.

'Ah, so, *Mevrouw* Korpman, would you think it very forward of me if I asked you your first name?'

Amies gave that seemingly polite request the dash of menace that any question posed by an SS officer was bound to contain.

'Eva,' she replied.

'Well then, Eva Korpman, my name is Eberhard Miesel, though my friends call me Hardy. And I realise that I have been most rude. You were about to advise me about my forthcoming leave and where I should be spending it. Please, do proceed . . .'

Saffron shook her head. 'I can't,' she said, in little more than a whisper. All her confidence had disappeared, as if it had never been there at all.

'Don't worry,' Amies replied, in English this time. 'The fact that you couldn't is no reflection at all on you. It's simply the proof of your one great weakness. You still can't think like a young Afrikaner woman, let alone a Belgian one. Your Flemish is competent, but not truly fluent. You need to spend more time with Belgians, talking to them, learning about their country, getting to know what makes them tick.'

'How can I do that, sir, unless I actually go to Belgium?'

'Simple, my dear . . . Belgium will come to you.'

Saffron looked at him quizzically.

'I have thought the whole thing through and I know how to get you into operational shape.'

'Do you, sir?' Saffron asked, feeling the first distant stirring of hope. 'Oh, I would like that so much.'

He flicked open a black lacquer cigarette box on his desk, took one out, lit it and puffed before continuing. 'What I propose is that you should join my staff in T section. I shall then appoint you as my liaison with the exiled Belgian community in London. Wend your way to Eaton Square. The Belgian government-in-exile has taken up residence there. Come to think of it, don't you have a place in that part of the world yourself?'

'Yes, sir, Chesham Court. It's no distance.'

'Excellent. You'll find that, like most governments every-where, they're riven by disputes, rivalries and petty jealousies. They all opposed one another when they had a Belgium to gov-ern, and now they don't even have that to distract them. Never mind, I'm sure that they will unite in their admiration for you, and the more Baker Street can get in with the various regimes that have taken up residence in London, the better it is for us. Of course, the whole point of the exercise is for you to speak Flemish at all times, unless you're dealing with anyone who insists on speaking French.'

'I'm happy to speak Flemish all day, sir, but I've only got a smattering of schoolgirl French.'

'Well, that's a start. I'm sure you'll pick it up in no time, once you have to. I think you'll find the work interesting, and the experience of Belgian life invaluable. Get to know them as people, Saffron. Get a feel for the minutiae of their lives: what they like to eat, their favourite music, the books they read, the stories they tell.'

'And the places they would recommend for a weekend's leave?'

'Particularly them,' Amies said, with a smile. 'And there's one other thing you can do,' he added, extinguishing his cigarette.

'Yes, sir?'

'We're having what one might call an intense political debate with the Belgians, and their Sûreté de l'État chaps, in particular.'

'That's the State Security Service isn't it?' Saffron asked.

'Exactly. The thing is, they're becoming touchy about the work we're doing over there.'

'Really, sir? I thought it was going well.'

'Oh, it is . . . from our point of view. We've derailed trains, sabotaged a number of German aircraft, blown up railway lines, lorries, electricity sub-stations, even bumped off a senior Gestapo officer and some of his Belgian collaborators. That's the problem.'

'I don't quite follow you, sir. Surely the Belgians should be pleased we're striking back at the people who are occupying their country?'

'That's a reasonable assumption, Courtney, but not, I'm afraid, an accurate one. The Belgians take a dim view of our activities and are insisting on having the right to approve and, if they see fit, veto any of our operations. They make one reasonable point, which is that their people suffer if the Germans carry out reprisals for our operations. But I don't think that's the main issue for them. The two things they care about are, first, that they can't bear the loss of face, seeing us in charge of things, and second, that they don't want any damage done to any Belgian industry, or transport, or pretty much anything else.' He arched his eyebrows. 'Honestly, the way they go on, you'd think it was their bloody country.'

Saffron laughed. 'Well, I suppose it is . . . but not while the Germans are in charge. And they can't expect to be the only people in Europe who escape untouched. There's a war on, after all.'

'There is, and if you can persuade our beloved Belgian allies to see that, you will be doing the Allied cause a great service. Now, I have a briefing to give in thirty minutes. We're ferrying three agents into Belgium on a motor torpedo boat. I shall be discussing their operation with them. 'I suggest you take notes, familiarise yourself with the plans and get to know the agents. You never know, you may be working alongside them sooner than you think.'

• • •

Amies had sketched out the pattern for Saffron's new life, as he might sketch the design for a new dress. Now it was her job to make it real. She set about the task with her customary energy. Within weeks, she was a familiar face at the Belgian government headquarters, as well as the pubs, restaurants and cafés where the ministers, officials and their junior staff went to relax.

Saffron's work was helped by being young, female and attractive, and she was often invited to spend time with senior politicians who would show no interest in a man of her age and junior rank. She was in a pub one evening with the Belgian Foreign Minister and the head of the Sûreté, wondering whether the other drinkers realised the eminence of the two foreign gentlemen sitting in one corner of the saloon bar, when the minister said, 'Tell me, Miss Courtney, why are your people so determined to leave my country in ruins?'

'I'm not sure I know what you mean, sir,' replied Saffron, who was delighted to find that the Belgians were introducing the subject Amies had wanted her to discuss.

'What the minister means,' the security chief interrupted, 'is that saboteurs working on British orders are causing a great deal of destruction to our property in our country.'

'Well, sir, I'm sure I don't know the details of any operations.' She smiled sweetly. 'That's man's work, don't you think?'

Before her question could be answered, Saffron spoke up again. 'But I imagine that any operations are aimed at the Germans, with the intention of harming them and helping us win the war, so that Belgium can be free again.'

'Maybe so,' said the minister. 'But we do not want to go back to our country to find it has been reduced to rubble.'

'Hmm . . .' Saffron pondered. 'I wonder what the Londoners in this pub would say about that. They've lived through the Blitz. Think of all the terrible destruction they've seen. They've spent night after night in shelters, wondering if their homes, even their streets would still be there when they emerge. I'm sure everyone in here knows at least one person who has died or been badly wounded, possibly someone they love. Could you look them in the eye and say that Belgium refuses to do its bit?'

The foreign minister had not expected that reply. 'Are you suggesting that the people of Belgium are cowards?'

'Oh no, sir, not at all, I wouldn't dream of saying such a thing. On the contrary, I'm sure Belgians are as brave as the British, and equally determined to beat the Germans. So surely they would be ready to make sacrifices, too.'

'They have,' said the security chief. 'They have sacrificed their freedom.'

'Then we must do what we can to win it back for them, no matter what that takes,' Saffron said. 'I'm sorry if I sound rude. I'm afraid I didn't grow up in England. I'm from Kenya, and where I live we're surrounded by wild animals. Some of them are very dangerous. And if there's one thing my father has taught me, it's that when a lion gets a taste for human flesh, there's no point trying to keep out of its way: you have to kill it. You have to kill it, finish it off for good.'

'And is that what you propose to do to *les Boches*, mademoiselle?'

'I hope to do my duty, sir.'

The security chief nodded thoughtfully. 'And what if that includes – how did you call it – man's work?'

'If that's what I'm ordered to do, sir, then I will obey my orders to the best of my ability.'

'Well, I wish you *bonne chance* in your endeavours. In the meantime, may I invite you to join me for dinner? I spent some time in the Congo as a young man. It would be a pleasure to speak to a fellow African . . .'

• • •

Three days later, Saffron was called into Amies' office. 'You're making quite an impression on our Belgian friends,' he said.

'A good one, I hope, sir.'

'An effective one, certainly. You seemed to have put the argument for conducting sabotage operations on their soil with some force.'

'They raised the subject, sir, and I knew how much it meant for us. I hope I didn't cause offence.'

'You may have pricked the vanity of at least one Belgian minister, but that will only do him good. The main thing is that they know how we feel, and, from what I gather, you've made them consider that it's not wise to tell the British that they don't wish to see any damage done to Belgium.'

'I was sorely tempted to say, "Well, if that's how you feel, maybe we should leave you to the Germans."'

'I'm glad that you didn't say that, Courtney . . . It's a complicated situation.'

'**A**m I going pink, Masha?' Yulia Sokolova asked her best friend Maria Tomascheva as they lay on a patch of grass in one of the neatly tended public gardens on the west bank of the Volga River: two seventeen-year-old girls from Stalingrad, basking in the sun, one glorious, cloudless Sunday morning in August.

Maria groaned, raised herself on one elbow and examined Yulia's bare back. 'No, Yulyushka, you're fine. Now let me sleep, I'm so tired. You know I was on the late shift last night.'

Yulia turned her head, pulled a handful of her straw-blonde hair away from her cornflower eyes so that she could look at Maria and asked, 'Do you know what date it is today?'

'Oh . . .' Maria sighed, shaking her head at this refusal to let her rest. She was as golden-haired and blue-eyed as Yulia. People often said that they were more like sisters than friends. She rubbed her eyes. 'The twenty-third. Why?' And then the answer struck her: 'Oh . . . that again.'

'Don't say "that again". It's three days until my mother's name-day and I still don't know what to get for her present. You know how much it means to her.'

'Oh, I do, my darling, I do . . .'

Before Maria could finish her sentence, the low hum of a city at ease was cut through by the wail of an air-raid siren. The girls jumped to their feet. They fumbled with straps and buttons as they made themselves decent, then packed away their towels and books and flasks of water into their bags.

A second later they heard the first explosions in the distance. They looked in the direction of the sound and saw to their horror that the sky was filled with aircraft, advancing towards them in ordered ranks, as neatly as marching guardsmen.

'Bombers!' shouted Yulia. 'Fascist bombers!'

The girls looked up, awestruck and terrified as more and more of the German planes appeared. The explosions became much louder and the ground began to shake. Maria grabbed Yulia's arm and screamed at the top of her voice, 'Run for the guns!'

• • •

Gerhard was flying at an altitude of six thousand metres. His squadron was arrayed around him in three flights of four planes. They were one element in the vast armada of aircraft, more than twelve-hundred strong, that had flown east over the steppes on this, the first day of the bombing campaign that *Generaloberst* Wolfram Baron von Richthofen, commander of the Fourth Air Fleet was launching against Stalingrad.

Gerhard carried a mental picture of the city they would be attacking. He thought of it as a huge snake, stretching for twenty twisting kilometres along the western bank of the Volga River. To the north, at the serpent's head, was an industrial district centred around four huge factories, each of which was surrounded by its workers' housing. In the belly of the snake lay the city centre, a modern showpiece of offices, shops and apartment buildings, cut through with majestic, wide boulevards. To the south stretched a long, bedraggled tail of wooden houses in which so many Russians lived, most single-storey shacks, whose appearance and construction had barely changed in two hundred years.

A giant grain elevator stood in the heart of the city like a massive rock outcrop rising from a grassy plain. The first wave of Luftwaffe bombers had used it as a beacon, guiding them in towards their targets approaching Stalingrad. There had been virtually no opposition, but three years of almost continuous action had taught Gerhard how, in times like this, the greatest danger was complacency.

Gerhard got on the radio and reminded his men, 'Stay alert. You never know with these Ivans. It could be a trap.'

'Well, if they're hiding, they must have magic blue paint,' replied Berti Schrumpp. 'There's perfect visibility and no Ivans anywhere. Maybe they've given up.'

Gerhard's former wingman had been promoted to the command of one of the squadron's three flights. He was also the squadron's licensed jester. None of the other men could get away with talking to their leader like that.

'Keep your eyes open anyway,' Gerhard insisted. 'Don't ever relax. That's how you get killed.' He looked ahead, narrowing his eyes as they strained towards the east. The sky was dark up ahead, the blue smudged with black and grey. 'Looks like storm clouds on the horizon,' he said. 'Plenty of room for Ivans to hide in there.'

Gerhard's voice was stern, but he could hardly blame Berti. Over the past couple of months, the Wehrmacht's panzers had advanced flat-out across Ukraine and into the Crimea and the Caucasus, only slowing when their fuel supplies could not keep up with them. Countless more casualties had been added to the millions of Russian soldiers captured or killed trying to hold back the invasion of their motherland. Now the Führer and his senior generals felt certain that the Red Army had no more reserves left.

And then Gerhard heard Berti's voice in his ears again, a gasp of wonder: 'God in heaven . . . Look at that!'

The darkness in the midday sky did not come from thunderclouds, but from smoke, a thick black pall of it, hanging over Stalingrad.

The city had only been hit by the first wave of bombers. Gerhard was escorting the second, with a third and fourth to follow. And this was just the first of three days of mass attacks.

Stalingrad was about to be obliterated, its people and buildings wiped from the earth. Gerhard couldn't imagine how anything could survive down there. And once Stalingrad was gone, how long could Russia itself stand?

'This is the end,' Berti said, as if echoing Gerhard's thoughts. 'The Ivans can't take much more of this, surely?'

• • •

Most of the men of fighting age had gone away to the front, so the women and children of Stalingrad had been called up to prepare the city for the coming battle. That spring, Yulia and Maria had been in a meeting of their Komsomol, or Young Communist League group, when a party official came to address them. He stood in battledress, tall and handsome, with his chest covered in medal ribbons, and the empty left sleeve of his jacket folded and pinned against his shoulders.

'Comrades,' he began. 'Young, proud, Leninist women of Stalingrad,' and those words alone had thrilled the girls. To think that such a hero thought of them as his comrades!

'I have one question for you . . . Do you want to defend the Motherland?'

'Yes!' a single girl had shrieked.

And then they all joined in: 'Yes, yes, yes!'

That evening, Yulia, Maria and their group of close friends signed up for duty in the city's anti-aircraft batteries. They had no idea what they were letting themselves in for: no idea of what kind of guns they would be firing, or how they were operated.

They soon learned.

The girls worked at the Stalingrad tractor factory, whose production lines churned out tanks instead of agricultural machinery. Between shifts they were instructed, drilled and trained, day and night in the operation of a 52-K air-defence gun. Yulia, who possessed a sharp eye and a quick, mathematical mind, was chosen to be the gun-aimer. Maria, who was taller and broad-shouldered, formed part of the human chain that kept the heavy shells moving from the ammunition store to the gun.

Now, barely two months after they had first set eyes on an anti-aircraft gun, they were firing it in anger. Their battery was stationed in a gun emplacement on the northwest perimeter of the tractor factory. The huge complex was one of the fascists' key targets and the attacks on it were relentless.

Stukas plummeted almost vertically from the sky like furious black crows diving for scraps of food, travelling at such a speed that the heavy 85mm gun could not track them. Their banshee screams had terrified Yulia as much as the impacts of the bombs. Meanwhile, the heavier bombers, rank upon rank of them, droned across the city.

An instant later, the bombs tipped from the fuselage and dropped faster and faster as gravity took hold. That massed sprint of explosives towards the earth had been as overwhelming as the howl of the Stukas at the start of the day, but now Yulia thought of nothing but the aircraft in her sights, their height and course, and what had to be done to hit them.

She was a speck of defiance, like a scurrying cockroach in the rubble of the most ferocious air assault the Motherland had ever seen.

Maria, meanwhile, was now no more than a human machine, repeating the same routine, hefting the shells passed down the line, over and over. To begin with, the fear had energised her, but as she became inured to terror she was vulnerable to exhaustion. Later still, she felt as though she had separated from her body. Her mind was elsewhere, while the muscles and joints of her back, arms and legs were screaming with pain; fatigue had disappeared, and death itself might just as well be another state of mind.

Hour by hour the air became more foul with smoke and dust. The girls tied bandanas around their mouths and noses to make it easier to breathe. They were coated with sweat and grime until they resembled coal miners deep underground. In the brief gaps between waves of bombers, they were given water to drink and hunks of black bread to eat. Only when they stopped to consume these meagre provisions did they notice how parched their mouths had become, or the way that hunger was clawing at their empty bellies.

Their officer was a junior lieutenant, a young man called Morisov, who was barely older than them. He would shout encouragement at the crews under his command when the guns were firing at a good, fast rate and scream abuse when they slackened. At some point in the early afternoon, he produced a vodka bottle for them all to share, and stimulant pills that he promised would give them fresh energy and courage.

The pills worked. When the next attack began, the girls set out with renewed determination. Everything was faster, from the traversing of the barrel to the transport of the shells. Then they saw a new danger: German fighter planes, a swarm of them, peeling from their formation and hurtling down towards them.

• • •

Fighter pilots hated ground-attack missions. The earth was their enemy: to dive towards it went against all their instincts. Up on high they could dodge, weave and spin their way out of trouble. But a ground-attack required a steady course towards the target, never wavering from the onslaught of the guns below, all pointing in their direction.

Gerhard's squadron had been ordered to protect the bombers they were escorting. There was no danger from the air: for all his warnings, there were still no Russian aircraft in the sky over Stalingrad. Down below, however, many of the anti-aircraft batteries had survived the Stukas' assaults and their aim was getting better all the time. One bomber after another was dropping from the sky. His duty was clear.

His squadron was flying over the industrial district to the north of the city. He saw a cluster of guns massed on the perimeter of one of the giant factory complexes. The air above them was thick with the black pom-poms of exploding shells.

Gerhard spoke into his radio: 'Prepare for ground attack. The targets are the gun emplacements by the factory, two o'clock, low. Attack in flights of four, left echelon formation.'

The twelve aircraft rearranged themselves into the three diagonal lines, each with the flight commander in the top right-hand position.

'Ready?' Gerhard asked. He waited less than five seconds to receive a positive reply, then called out the German hunter's cry, '*Horido!*' and banked hard right, peeling away from the other planes and diving towards the blazing inferno of Stalingrad.

The Messerschmitts dropped almost five thousand metres from the sky, till they were scraping the roofs of Stalingrad's tallest buildings. Then Gerhard flattened out, took his bearings from the bomb-battered silhouette of the factory, adjusted his course a fraction and raced towards the guns.

Beneath his wings he saw the ruination the bombers had inflicted: a cityscape of craters, hollowed-out buildings and obstructed roads. Each crater would provide a soldier with a place to take cover. Another, smaller factory flashed past that must have been constructed from glass and steel. The glass was there no longer, but the steel pillars, girders, struts and window frames lay in a great expanse of twisted, contorted, interwoven metal.

No man could possibly clamber over those ruins, he thought. No tank could smash its way through them. The craters and broken buildings were like an assault course within which any number of defenders could take cover.

My God, what if we haven't destroyed Stalingrad? What if we've made it impregnable?

Gerhard had almost reached the battery. The guns had been depressed so that they were firing directly at the oncoming fighters, like cannons blasting at charging cavalry. He was close enough to see their crews. They were women.

Luftwaffe pilots had long since become accustomed to attacking Russian aircraft operated by female pilots and gunners. But that didn't stop them finding it abhorrent and unnatural. Every instinct told them that war was a man's business, that women's role was to create life, not take it. But the Russian Front had no time for sentiment. It was a brutal, implacable slaughterhouse in which one was either the butcher or the meat.

Gerhard tightened his jaw and banished his scruples. His plane was armed with three MG/FF cannons, firing high explosive 20mm rounds that could tear an enemy aircraft apart. The stationary anti-aircraft guns and their unprotected crews were far easier targets. Gerhard pushed down on the trigger button and saw three lines of explosive impacts hit the ground ahead of him, like sewing needles punching into fabric, heading straight towards the nearest gun.

• • •

The girls were screaming, but Yulia couldn't hear them for the hammering of the German guns and the roar of aero-engines so close overhead that she felt as though she could reach up and touch the bellies of the fighters that were wreaking such havoc on the gun emplacements.

She saw a girl blown in two, her legs ripped from her torso by the force of the bullets. Another was picked up and flung against a wall five metres behind her. The havoc around her was worse than anything the Stukas had inflicted.

Yulia kept her nerve. She knew she would only have time for one shot and she was determined to make it count. The fascists had to pay a price for their murderous invasion. She waited until the barrel of her gun was fully depressed and her gun sights were filled by one of the leading aircraft in the fascists' formation.

She fired.

Her shell obliterated the onrushing aircraft. Yulia threw herself to the ground as the blazing wreckage hurtled overhead and smashed against the side of the factory. She lay there as the rest of the aircraft completed their run.

Then, as quickly as they had arrived, the German aircraft were gone and the deafening noise of their attack was replaced by an eerie silence broken only by the cries and moans of the wounded. Yulia looked around for Maria, the fear rising in her belly as she failed to see her friend amidst the smoke, the dust, the wreckage and the fallen bodies. Then a figure emerged out of the murk. Her blonde hair was matted with blood, which had poured down her forehead and one side of her face.

'Maria!' Yulia screamed and ran to her friend, who was walking unsteadily, with a blank look on her face. The skin beneath the blood and grime on her face was chalk-white. Yulia ran to Maria and took her in her arms. She looked at her head and gently untangled her hair to reveal a deep cut across the crown of her head. At first glance it looked like a serious wound, but Yulia realised that the bone beneath the torn skin was unbroken. Maria was dazed, but she would survive.

Yulia heard Morisov's voice. 'You two, get back to your posts.'

The young lieutenant was rounding up the survivors and reassembling them into teams to man the two remaining guns.

'My friend is injured, Comrade Lieutenant. She needs medical treatment.'

'An orderly is seeing to the wounded,' Morisov replied. 'He is dealing with the most serious cases first. He will attend to your friend when her turn comes. But for now, she can walk. Therefore she can fight.'

He walked up to Yulia and held out another one of his magic pills. 'Give her this.'

The girls walked back to their gun, trying not to look at the bodies strewn in their path. Maria took her place in the shell-line. Yulia waited until the gun-barrel had been elevated again and looked to the sky. Barely two minutes later another wave of enemy bombers appeared above their heads and the battle resumed once again.

• • •

When they got back to Tazi, the pilots debriefed and headed to the mess to drink to the memory of the pilot who had been shot down in the attack on the anti-aircraft guns. Berti Schrumpp did his best to lighten the mood.

'My God those Russian men must be useless,' he scoffed. 'There's nothing their women can't do better than them.'

'Maybe they're cleverer than you think, sir,' a newly arrived junior pilot called Otto Braun had retorted. 'They get their women to do all the dirty work.'

'He's got you there, Berti,' Gerhard said.

'Ah, must be the wisdom of youth,' Schrumpp had conceded.

'Then there's no need to worry, old man. That won't last long around here.'

'True enough,' said Berti. 'Take it from me, Braun, my boy, you'll soon be a stupid, drunken old man, just like the rest of us . . . If you're lucky.'

• • •

The last of the bombers had departed. The sun was low in the sky. Yulia and Maria lay around the anti-aircraft gun with their surviving comrades, unmoving, barely conscious, seemingly no more alive than the corpses that were strewn across the tarmac all around them.

Morisov sat on the low wall that surrounded the emplacement, his head slumped on his chest, hardly able to keep his eyes open. He felt a vibration in the earth. It was not the distinct shock of an exploding bomb, so much as a persistent quivering. Then he heard the noise, that combination of a low, rumbling engine and the metallic clattering of steel tracks that even to a soldier who was still as green as the freshest spring grass could only mean one thing.

Tanks.

And they were coming closer.

Morisov caught the sound of small arms fire and hand grenades.

He reached for his helmet, then ran across to the gun, shouting, 'Tanks! Tanks!'

The girls got to their feet, uncertain what to do next. They had been trained to fire their gun at aircraft. They had no idea what to do about armoured vehicles.

Morisov, however, was a bright enough lad, even if he was just three weeks out of his service academy. He knew that the 85mm guns he commanded were essentially the same weapons that were mounted in the turrets of the T-34 tanks that were the Red Army's most fearsome weapon. The T-34s could knock out any panzer the Germans had ever put on the battlefield. This gun could surely do the same.

'Depress the barrel!' he shouted at the girls. 'Prepare to fire at ground level!'

The battery had been set up beside one corner of a crossroads. From where the girls were positioned, there was one road in front of them and two others to either side.

As the barrel of the 52-K slowly descended, like a clock-hand sweeping from twelve to three, Morisov examined the crossroads. Many of the buildings on all sides had been hit by bombs. Some were on fire, others destroyed, others pock-marked. Debris, some in lumps of brick or concrete the size of large boulders, littered the street.

From behind him, the boy-officer heard shouts and running feet as a group of Red Army soldiers rushed by. One of them peeled off towards the emplacement.

Morisov saw that the running man was a captain. He leaped to attention.

'They're coming from over there!' the captain shouted, pointing down the road in front of them. 'You must knock out the enemy armour. Our lives depend upon it!'

Before Morisov could acknowledge the order, the captain was haring away across the crossroads. He caught up with his men and waved them towards the oncoming Germans.

All around, the sound of battle grew louder. Yulia was adjusting to the sensation of looking through sights that were pointing in a new direction. For the first time in hours she felt afraid. She was struck by a new fear that she might wet herself and be ashamed in front of her friends. She looked around and saw nothing but filthy faces and terrified eyes. Yulia was not alone. They all knew dread.

The clanking and rumbling was growing louder. The street ahead was filled with a mist of dust and cordite as the battle drew nearer. Then came men, Russians, fleeing down the road, taking up new positions, hiding in doorways, ducking behind piles of rubble, anywhere they could find cover.

As the noise of the tanks became ever more deafening, a long, thin barrel emerged from the filthy haze, and the broad, squat, brutally geometric form of a Panzer IV tank appeared, two more on either side, slightly behind it, advancing in an arrow formation.

German infantry, in their coal-scuttle helmets, were coming up behind the panzers. Red Army soldiers were throwing hand grenades at the tanks, but the explosions couldn't stop their advance, which continued forward in a slow, grinding, unstoppable tide. There were machine guns mounted in the body of the tanks, beneath the turrets. They poked to one side and then the other, firing at any sign of Russian life.

Two terrified elderly women were hiding in a doorway. One of them was clutching a young child against her skirt. Yulia saw a machine gun point in their direction. She saw it pause, and then the mighty flickering at its barrel as it cut down the women and child like a sickle through corn.

At the beginning of the day, a lifetime ago, Yulia would have been reduced to a tearful wreck by such a sight. Now her anger steeled her nerve as she looked through her sights, aimed at one of the tanks and gave the order, 'Fire!'

The shell smashed into a building behind the tank, which reacted like a huge steel animal, searching out the source of this new threat. Its turret turned from left to right as it sighted for a target.

'Reload!' Morisov shouted. 'Faster! Faster!'

The tank commander inside the Panzer IV found what he was looking for. His gun settled on the anti-aircraft emplacement.

Yulia felt as though the barrel was pointing directly at her, like an empty eye.

She stared back. She knew that the enemy was bound to fire at any moment, but even though it was only for a fraction of a second, she paused for an apparent eternity, made certain of her aim and screamed once again, 'Fire!'

There was an instant explosion as the tank was hit dead-on. The enemy gun was almost blown out of the turret, which burst into flames. Men scrambled from inside it, trying to escape, but climbing straight into the bullets being fired from the Russian soldiers in front of them.

One of the other guns in the battery had also hit another of the German tanks, but it was only a glancing blow. Morisov saw and shouted, 'Traverse left! Engage that tank!'

The girls got to work, rapidly turning the wheels that rotated the gun. Their focus was on the battle that faced them. As she looked through the sights, something flew into Yulia's eye. It was no more than a speck of dust, but it affected her vision.

She drew her hand away from her sights and wiped her hand across the eye.

And that was when she saw it. The Germans had sent another tank on a flanking manoeuvre. It was coming down one of the sidestreets, unnoticed.

Yulia saw the gun-barrel pointing at her, just like the other one had. But she had no answer to it. They could never turn their own gun to face it.

There wasn't time to get away.

We're all going to die.

The tank fired. It scored a direct hit. Yulia, Maria, Morisov and the rest of the gun crew were killed, vaporised in the blink of an eye.

The Battle of Stalingrad, on the other hand, had only just begun.

A s the weeks went by, not only did Saffron's grasp of both Flemish and French improve, so did her familiarity with the minutiae of Belgian life. She began to feel more certain that if she should find herself opposite an SS officer in a train compartment, she would be able to carry on a conversation that would have him thinking more about her as a woman he might want to impress and seduce, than an agent to be arrested, interrogated and shot.

'That's excellent news,' said Amies when she confided this to him. 'The more you can get a man thinking with his balls, not his brain, the safer you will be.'

'What if I have to give him what his balls demand?'

'Better that than a Gestapo interrogation. Now, please excuse me, I have a pair of agents to brief.'

'Yes, sir,' Saffron replied, finding it hard to hide her disappointment that she would not be going with him.

Amies had, on one memorable occasion, allowed Saffron into the Baker Street room. Its walls were covered with maps, reconnaissance photographs, pictures of Resistance contacts and German targets, and any other documents that might be considered necessary for a mission. As a security measure, because every effort was made to keep each section's operations secret, canvas blinds could be pulled down over material that related to one country, when another country's agents were being briefed.

In the middle of a room there stood a large table on which maps could be unfurled, or large scale models of target areas placed. These models were extraordinarily accurate, with every hill, river, road, railway, important building or any detail of the landscape clearly represented, virtually down to the last tree, so that anyone embarking on a sabotage mission knew what the target area was like. The models were constructed within large, shallow wooden boxes, roughly six-feet square.

'If I'm giving the briefing I stand here,' Amies had told her, resting one foot on the edge of the box. 'Then I use this' – he picked up a long, pointed stick that resembled a billiards cue – 'to indicate the various key features the agents are to bear in mind.'

'Are you sure I can't attend the briefings, sir?' Saffron had pleaded. 'I wouldn't speak out of turn, but I do believe I might be able to make the odd useful contribution.'

'I have no doubt about that,' Amies replied. 'I'd go further. In my view you would be ideally suited to handling agents, both during the preparations for missions and while they are in the field.'

'Then . . .'

Amies finished the sentence for her: 'Why aren't you doing that instead of buttering up the Belgians and touring our training facilities?'

'Yes, sir.'

'Because, Ensign Courtney, there is an unbreakable rule here at Baker Street. Once anyone, myself included, knows about the general strategy of a national section, or its current status, or the names of the agents either in the field or set for missions, then they are forbidden to go on missions themselves. It's too risky. If they were to get caught they could give away our entire network in that country. You do understand that, don't you?'

'Yes, sir.'

'But I am happy to give you the choice. If you would like to come and work in-house, for the duration, I would be delighted to offer you a job. You would be extremely competent, do work that was vital to the war effort and be promoted swiftly up the ranks.'

'I don't want to waste my training. And I'd feel I was running away from the fight.'

'Nonsense. Your training would be of huge assistance in giving you a real insight into the work our agents do and the standards they must reach. As for running away, my dear girl, you have already exposed yourself to more danger than any woman has a duty to do. No one would dream of faulting you for that. We get endless criticism for using women as agents, not for letting them stay at home.'

'Yes, sir.'

'So you have that option, in which case your presence at briefings and many other meetings would, I'm sure, be not only possible, but beneficial. Or, you may continue to work towards a state of readiness for deployment as an agent. But in that case, the meeting room, and all contact with active agents, is *verboten*. The choice is yours.'

'I want to be an agent, sir,' Saffron replied without hesitation.

'Then the next time you see this room will be when it is your mission that we are discussing.'

• • •

Saffron went back to her role as liaison with the Belgian government-in-exile. With every passing day she became more deeply embedded in the strange, unreal world of people who posed as the true rulers of a nation that was under the domination of another, mightier power. She found that Belgian ministers and officials might tell her all about the politics and history of their nation, but it was the women who worked for the government-in-exile who were better sources for the minutiae that Amies had described, the details of daily life in the country they had left behind.

They told her how to carry herself in public to fit in with everyone else, or do her hair, or chat to shopkeepers and market stallholders as they would do. They knew the actors and crooners that she should swoon over, the books and magazines she should read. And they knew the giveaways that would make other women think that there was something suspicious about her. In a world where any man or woman might be a collaborator, only too willing to betray her, those giveaways could cost her life.

Other women were Saffron's best source of information at Baker Street, too. There wasn't a scrap of news about the personal lives of Baker Street's inhabitants that didn't eventually find its way into the female intelligence network. The same went for the endless political intrigues between Baker Street and the rival British and American agencies, which were, in some ways, even greater threats to Baker Street's survival than the Gestapo.

Saffron was given a beginner's guide to the inter-departmental warfare of Britain's intelligence services by Margaret Jackson, Gubbins' beautiful, hazel-eyed, 25-year-old secretary and indispensable right-hand woman. Margaret and Saffron had spent a while conducting an unspoken, but mutually understood, negotiation about their personal relationship. They were both pretty young women, who attracted a large amount of male attention, but made it plain that, while they did not object to being admired, they were not available.

They could either be deadly rivals, or the closest of friends. Each had been concerned that the other might be manipulative, untrustworthy or bitchy. When it became clear that this was not the case and that they shared a plainspoken honesty, they became intimate friends.

One Sunday in October 1942, Saffron invited Margaret to lunch at Chesham Court. She got around the handicap of being hopeless in the kitchen by enlisting the services of a 22-year-old codebreaker called Leo Marks, who was famous for two things. The first was his uncanny ability to decipher impossibly scrambled, wrongly encoded messages from agents in the field – a talent for which all Baker Street agents were grateful, for it was a huge risk to have to send a message twice, knowing that the Germans had signal tracking and direction-finding devices everywhere.

This boy genius's second gift was that he could procure gorgeous foodstuffs that were unavailable through official ration books. He pretended that this was because he was the nephew of Sir Simon Marks, the proprietor of Marks and Spencer. The truth was that he still lived with his parents, a respectable book-seller and his wife, who happened to have the best black-market contacts in London.

Saffron was able to serve Margaret Jackson an illegal, but splendid, selection of cold roast beef, ham and roast chicken, with a fresh green salad, followed by the creamiest custard tarts that either of them had tasted in years. To women who normally survived on a wartime diet, this was a feast fit for royalty.

Afterwards, as they were relaxing over cups of the best coffee Saffron had tasted since she'd left the Middle East, Margaret said, 'Now that we're going to be such great chums, perhaps I should fill you in on how our beloved Ministry of Ungentle-manly Warfare really works.'

'Oh, yes, please,' Saffron replied

'I'll start at the top, with Brigadier Gubbins.'

'You rather like him, don't you?'

Margaret put a hand to her face and felt her cheeks, as if they were blushing. 'Oh dear, is it terribly obvious?'

'Only that you work awfully hard for him. No matter how late I've left work, if I look back at the top floor the light is always on in your office.'

'It's not because I have a pash on him in *that* way, if you know what I mean. He is a married man. But I admire the Brigadier tremendously and I have to be there because he works so hard himself. It's the agents, you see. He feels he has to make sure we do everything we can to help them. I can't let him down.'

'He's very fierce, though, isn't he? I've only bumped into him a couple of times, but the way he looks at one with those cold blue eyes . . . like he can see into your soul. I'd hate to get on the wrong side of him!'

'He can be quite hard, I know,' Margaret agreed, 'but he's hardest on himself. And you have no idea how much of his time is spent keeping Baker Street in business.'

'Really? I thought Churchill loved us. Didn't he say we should "set Europe ablaze"?'

'The PM's a supporter, but there are plenty of people in his ear all day long, telling him to get rid of us.'

Saffron nodded. 'Well, I do know the War Office chaps don't like us. They think we don't play fair.'

'Yes, but they're not the worst. The real problem is C . . .'

'Ah . . . the Bastards of Broadway,' Saffron said. As Amies had predicted, she had spent enough time in Baker Street to become accustomed to the endless blizzard of initials. But C was perhaps the most arcane of all. It referred to the Secret Intelligence Service, or SIS, which was better known to the wider world as MI6. For those in the business of spying and sabotage, however, it was known as C because that was the initial with which its boss signed all his letters and memos. And its offices were located on a street called Broadway, not far from the Houses of Parliament.

'So,' she went on, 'why do the bastards want to get rid of us? Aren't we all on the same side?'

Margaret laughed. 'I've long ago given up any hope of that! They're behaving like schoolboys. As far as they're concerned, they were in the spying game before us, and they don't see why we should be allowed to spoil their fun.'

'Aren't we doing something different?' Saffron asked. 'We send our agents in to help Resistance groups and commit acts of sabotage. It's another way of fighting, halfway between spies and normal soldiers.'

'I couldn't agree more. But C have the full might of the Foreign Office behind them and they're working hard to persuade the PM that he's wasting resources on us and we'll never come to anything. That's one of the reasons the Brigadier is keen to make sure that all our operations go well. He can't afford a slip-up.'

Margaret paused. Something was bothering her.

'Would you like some more coffee?' Saffron asked.

Margaret nodded. 'Thank you.'

Saffron let her friend sip some of the drink and then asked, 'What's the matter? I can see there's something on your mind. Is there anything I can do to help?'

'That's terribly sweet of you, but no . . . it's nothing either of us can do.'

Sometimes, the most effective form of interrogation is to say nothing. It was a lovely afternoon, warm enough to have the windows half open, and Saffron drank her coffee and took pleasure in the light of the autumn sun pouring into her drawing room. She listened to the cars passing outside, the voices of children chattering as they walked by. She thought she could smell something in the air, a delicious, smoky aroma. When she went to the window and looked down to the street, there on the corner of Chesham Square was the first roast chestnut seller of the year.

Margaret said, 'If I tell you something I shouldn't, will you promise me, on your honour, not to tell another living soul?'

'Of course . . . but don't feel you have to say anything. Not if you'll feel bad for saying it.'

Margaret sighed. 'I've been carrying it around like a weight round my neck for weeks.'

'What is it?' Saffron asked.

'I think that something's not quite right . . . out in the field, I mean. I can't say where . . .'

'Of course not, I understand.'

'But . . . well . . . there may be a serious problem in one particular country. It's the sort of thing that C has been hoping for.'

'To help them get what they want, you mean?'

'Yes. If this is as bad as it looks, this could be the end for all of us. They'll be closing down Baker Street for good.'

It was early November, well into the third month of the Stalingrad campaign, and the city had become a hell of bombs, shells and howling Katyusha rockets; an inferno of flame and choking smoke; a grinder of human meat. Hundreds of thousands of men had been thrown into the battle, new corpses lying on the rotting remains of the old, but still the Russians were hanging onto one last pocket of the city on the west bank of the Volga. As long as they held that, they could be supplied and reinforced from the far bank, to the east, which was still in Soviet hands. The red army could keep feeding the furnace with bullets, shells and men, and the carnage was bound to continue.

Attrition was taking its toll on the fighter squadrons. Every day Gerhard's fighters seemed to face more Soviet aircraft, and the weight of numbers was becoming overwhelming. Gerhard's squadron had halved from twelve pilots to six – young Otto Braun, among many others, had long since been blasted out of the sky – and there were often not enough working aircraft or fuel to put them in the air.

Gerhard had spent the morning in the hangers at Pitomnik, the airfield twenty kilometres west of Stalingrad that had been his base since mid-September, going over every millimetre of the squadron's surviving Messerchmitts with a couple of senior ground crewmen. Virtual zero visibility, caused by thick, freezing fog, had kept German and Russian aircraft on the ground since dawn. But there was a chance of operations later in the day, so he wanted to make sure that some of his aircraft were ready to go.

With the job done, he headed towards the officers' mess. The Führer was giving a speech, to be broadcast on the radio, and woe betide the serviceman who failed to listen to it. Gerhard had no option but to take in the ravings of a man he now considered to be a homicidal maniac, but he was damned if he was going to get through the ordeal without the aid of a large drink.

As he made his way across the airfield, the fog had lifted, but it was still impossible to see even ten metres in front of his face. Suddenly another figure emerged from the gloom, an Army officer, with his greatcoat wrapped around him, head down, apparently oblivious to his surroundings.

'Watch out!' Gerhard shouted.

The soldier came to a halt within touching distance of Gerhard. His greatcoat was as filthy and torn as a beggar's rags, but his shoulder tabs were those of a major, the same rank as Gerhard. He raised his head, revealing the chalky skin and hollow, red-rimmed, half-dead eyes that every German foot-soldier Gerhard met now possessed.

'My apologies,' he said. 'Name's Werth . . . Major Andreas Werth.'

'Major Gerhard von Meerbach.' He took pity on a brother officer. 'If you don't mind me saying, Werth, you look as though you could use a square meal. And a drink. I plan to have both myself while I listen to the Führer bless us with his wisdom. May I invite you to join me?'

'A square meal . . . what's that?'

Gerhard grinned. 'A quaint old tradition. You might enjoy it.'

'Then how can I refuse? Thank you, von Meerbach. Damn kind of you.'

Pitomnik was the point from which seriously wounded men were flown out of Stalingrad. It was no surprise when they came upon an army doctor on the way to the officers' mess, who introduced himself as Staff Physician Klaus Preuss. His rank was equivalent to that of an army or Luftwaffe captain, which made him their junior in military terms. But a doctor always has a certain status, and Preuss seemed in greater need of sustenance than Werth. Gerhard added him to the party.

The meal for the day consisted of a stew of some indefinable meat, most of which appeared to be fat, bone or gristle, accompanied by mashed turnips and black bread. The two army men wolfed this unappetising dish down as if it were the finest gourmet cuisine. When Gerhard offered them each a bottle of proper German beer with which to wash their meal down, they almost wept in gratitude.

'My God, you Luftwaffe boys do well for yourselves,' Werth declared, having cleared his plate and emptied his bottle.

'It helps to oversee the supply planes,' Gerhard observed.

'That's for sure. I must visit this establishment again.'

'*Monsieur* is always welcome.'

'Ahh . . .' Werth sighed. 'Don't remind me of France. Easy fighting, sunny weather, glorious food and welcoming women . . . Those were the days.'

Before either of them could say another word a fanfare came over the loudspeaker system and a voice announced: '*Achtung! Achtung!* The Führer is about to speak'

A hush fell. The only sound in the room was the voice of Adolf Hitler.

Gerhard paid only the barest attention until, around halfway through the oration, he heard the words: 'I wanted to come to the Volga, to a definite place, to a definite city.' Now he, along with every other man in Pitomnik, in the Stalingrad salient, and across the vast expanse of the Eastern Front, leaned a little closer to the loudspeakers as, their Führer continued in a casual, offhand tone, 'It accidentally bears the name of Stalin himself, but do not think that I went after it on that account. Indeed, it could have an altogether different name.

'A gigantic terminal was there; I wanted to take it. And do you know, we have it; there are only a couple of very small places left.' Hitler gave a casual chuckle as he added, 'I will take them with a few small shock units. I don't want to make a second Verdun!'

The contrast between the bantering tone of the speech and the bitter reality of the battle for Stalingrad was grotesque. Gerhard glanced across to Werth, who had raised his eyes to the ceiling and was biting his lip as he fought the urge to shout back at the radio.

Werth caught Gerhard's eye and shook his head in silent disbelief. Then he moved closer to Gerhard and whispered, 'Do you think he knows? Does he have the first idea?'

Gerhard looked back and said, 'Tell me, out of "yes" or "no", which do you think would be the worst answer?'

• • •

At the end of the speech, Gerhard turned to his two guests. 'Can I get you gentlemen a drink?' he asked.

Both accepted. Gerhard was about to ask them what they wanted when he saw the figure of Berti Schrumpp walking towards them with a bottle of vodka in one hand and four glasses clasped in the fingers of the other.

Gerhard grinned. 'Ah, it appears that one of the waiters has anticipated our needs.'

'You looked thirsty,' Schrumpp explained, handing out glasses, then filling each to the brim with vodka. 'An excellent speech, I thought,' he said. 'I particularly enjoyed the reference to using, what was it, "small shock units"? I dare say you'll know all about that, eh, Herr Major?'

A silence fell as Werth considered his response. The politically appropriate reply would have been to agree that, as always, the Führer had judged the strategic situation perfectly and that victory was sure to follow. Instead, however, Werth replied, 'Funnily enough, I was leading that sort of shock unit a couple of days ago, making another assault on that damned Red October factory. It was a compact group, about thirty-five men, all told. It used to be a full Engineer Battalion of eight hundred men, but if the Führer calls for smaller units, we're happy to oblige.'

Nicely done, Gerhard thought. It would be difficult for anyone to prove that there was anything treacherous in those words. But they all knew what Werth meant.

He felt honour-bound to reply in kind. 'I'll have you know that we "fly-boys", as you call us, are doing our part, too. Our squadrons each used to have a dozen planes. Now they have six at most, sometimes as few as two or three, and we find they are considerably more nimble. Wouldn't you agree, Schrumpp?'

'I do. Though I won't feel we have achieved our peak potential until we are each flying individual missions, one plane at a time.'

Preuss shook his head with such a sorrowful expression that for a moment Gerhard feared he might be about to object to the tone in which they had been talking. But then the doctor said, 'I am sorry, and somewhat ashamed to confess that the Führer's message hasn't got through to the field hospitals.

'Our units keep getting bigger and bigger. More men are arriving all the time. We're having to dig caves into the sides of ravines to make space for new arrivals. I fear our leaders would have a very poor impression of us.'

'Don't worry,' Schrumpp assured him. 'We won't tell anyone. Here, have another drink.'

'What's it like down there on the front line?' Gerhard asked Werth. 'I can see it from the air, of course, but . . .'

Werth took a swig, then said, 'Yesterday morning, we had some food to eat, and a swallow of water while it was still dark. Then we attacked at dawn. We were in the remains of one factory building. The Ivans were in another hollowed-out shell about thirty metres away.

'It took all morning to cross the ground to the Russian position. They had us pinned down with a pair of heavy machine-guns. When we got there, there were only about ten of them, so we managed to drive them away, and we took their guns and ammunition. But before we could secure the position they counter-attacked in greater strength. By the time night fell we were back where we had started. Only now we were down to less than twenty men, an even smaller shock unit. I lost nine killed. Three were so badly wounded that we couldn't get them back to our starting point.'

'Did the Russians get them?' Gerhard asked, and then felt like an idiot as Werth looked at him with cold, emotionless eyes and said, 'We never let the Russians take one of our wounded.'

No one had to ask what that meant. Werth was the kind of officer who would insist on doing the worst jobs himself, so the odds were he'd been the one to shoot them.

'Anyway,' he said, pulling his eyes away from Gerhard's, 'five more men were wounded badly enough to be unfit for battle, but we managed to carry them out. We're not in action today, thank Christ, so I came down here to make sure that they got on a plane. No luck yet.'

'The fog has almost lifted,' Gerhard said. 'We should be flying soon. If you point your men out to me, I'll do what I can to make sure they're looked after.'

Werth nodded and did his best to muster a smile. 'Thank you, Major, I would greatly appreciate your help.'

'Meanwhile,' Schrumpp interjected, 'we had a weather report this morning from the Luftwaffe meteorologists. There's a cold front moving in from the Arctic. It should arrive within the next two or three days. It won't be a week before the Volga's completely iced over.'

'And we begin another Russian winter,' said Werth.

'Indeed,' agreed Schrumpp. 'And how many of us will still be here to see the spring?' He looked around at the other three men. 'More vodka, anyone?'

S affron was at Norgeby House, typing up her latest report on the activities and opinions of the Belgian government in exile, when Margaret Jackson appeared beside her desk. 'The Brigadier wants to see you.'

'Me?' Saffron wracked her brain in search of any offence she might have committed that was serious enough to require the intervention of the Head of Operations. 'Oh dear, have I offended the Belgians in some way?'

'No, nothing like that, it's . . .' Margaret paused as she tried to find a compromise between her natural desire to tell a friend what was going on, and the overriding need for security that was drilled into every inhabitant of Baker Street. As they stepped onto the staircase up to the top floor, where Gubbins and the other senior officers were situated, she added, 'It's an operational matter. Something to do with, you know, that thing we talked about . . . at your flat.'

It took a second for the penny to drop. Then Saffron recalled their conversation over Sunday lunch about something that might have gone wrong with Baker Street's operations: something so serious that it could mean the end of the SOE itself.

'Ah, yes,' she said.

Margaret still hadn't told Saffron the precise nature of the problems. But she had a strong suspicion that she was about to find out. A minute later they were at the door of Brigadier Gubbins' office. Margaret knocked.

'Come!' barked from within.

She led Saffron in and said, 'Ensign Courtney's here, sir, as you requested.'

Standing behind Margaret, Saffron's view was partially obscured, so it wasn't until her friend had departed that she had a chance to get a good look at Brigadier Gubbins, who was peering from a document on his desk and fixing her with eyes that glared at her from beneath two thick, bushy eyebrows. She knew at once that this was a man who would see through any lie, any excuse, any poorly considered idea in an instant.

Saffron snapped to attention, for standing at ease was not an option in this man's company, unless he permitted it. She had a habit, ingrained in her by her African childhood, of judging men in animal terms, dividing the few dominant males from the many subservient members of the herd; the powerful from the vulnerable; the fit and strong from the weak and unhealthy. Even though he was seated, she could tell Gubbins was not a large man. She felt sure she would be three or four inches taller than him in stockinged feet, and tower over him in heels. But that lack of size was irrelevant, because he exuded an air of energy, mental toughness, overpowering will and natural leadership.

No wonder Margaret's so dazzled by him, she thought. Out of the corner of her eye, she saw Hardy Amies sitting on a plain wooden office chair, with a younger man – Saffron realised it was Leo Marks – next to him. Like her, they were waiting for Gubbins to begin the conversation.

He kept looking at Saffron, drumming the table with his fingertips as he did so. She was accustomed to men giving her the once-over, but there was nothing sexual about Gubbins' examination; he was assessing her on different grounds.

He pointed to a third wooden chair and said, 'Sit.'

Saffron did as she was told.

Gubbins spoke. 'Good afternoon, Courtney.'

'Good afternoon, sir,' she replied.

'Before we go any further, let me make one thing clear. We shall be discussing an extremely secret and highly dangerous mission. I am therefore ordering you not to discuss anything said at this meeting with anyone who was not here, unless specifically ordered to do so. Understood?'

'Yes, sir.'

'Good . . . Now, while it is in my power to demand your discretion, I do not have the right, as an army officer, to order you, as a civilian, to undertake hazardous operations on enemy soil, or anywhere else, come to that. What's more, many decent people would think it wrong for a man such as myself to knowingly and deliberately place a young woman in danger of losing her life. I cannot therefore oblige you to agree to undertake this operation, nor will it be held against you if you refuse it.'

'I won't, sir,' Saffron said. 'I knew what I was letting myself in for when I came to Baker Street. I've been trained to do a job and I'm keen for an opportunity to put that training to good use.'

Gubbins nodded. 'Very well, then, let me explain our purpose here today. We are trying to answer a question that may have serious implications for our work in the Low Countries, and, by extension, throughout Occupied Europe. We fear – we cannot be certain, but we fear – that we may be facing a serious breach of security in the Netherlands. It is possible, though this is speculation, that a similar situation may apply in Belgium. You will notice that neither the head of the Belgian nor of the Dutch section is with us today. I am, reluctantly, operating behind the backs of the officers most affected by this crisis. This is for their protection. I can envisage circumstances in which it would be good for them to be able to deny knowledge of the operation I am about to describe, and to be telling the truth when they do so.'

Gubbins paused, as if giving Saffron time to take in what he had said before he continued. 'To cut a long story short, our fear is that the Germans have broken our radio codes. If so, they may have been aware of all our operations this year. They may have captured many of our agents. And it is possible that they may have turned at least one of them and used him as a double against us.'

Saffron now understood why Margaret had been so upset. If the Germans had been acting as puppeteers, using British agents as weapons against London, then that was a disaster. And if MI6 wanted to get SOE closed down, this would provide them with justification.

'I'm sure you know Marks,' Gubbins said.

'Yes, sir.'

Saffron glanced across at Leo Marks, who flashed a mischievous grin. He, like Gubbins, was a small, sharp-eyed man bursting with a big man's energy. Marks, however, was younger than Saffron, just past his twenty-second birthday, and his was a boyish, almost madcap genius. He was an intuitive expert at decoding barely audible signal and turning it into meaningful English text.

His uncanny ability with codes was regarded with awe by the Baker Street operatives, who knew what Marks did, without having the first idea how. Even more remarkably, he worked his miracles with the assistance of a team of women who were mostly younger than him. Virtually none had any of the formal mathematical training that was regarded as essential for high-level cryptography. Yet he had successfully trained them to go over messages again and again, trying one possible cipher after another, until the scrambled letters revealed their hidden meaning.

'You'd better explain your theory to Ensign Courtney,' Gubbins said.

Perhaps because his mind was on higher things, or because it worked so fast that he found it hard to respect lesser intellects, Marks found it difficult to adopt a deferential manner when in the company of senior officers.

'I could explain the facts, sir, certainly. And, of course, what I deduce from them. So, Saffron – may I call you that?'

'If Brigadier Gubbins does not mind . . .' she replied, looking at the grim-faced man behind the desk.

'Call her whatever you like, man. Just give her the gen.'

'Very well. I take it you've had the full agent training . . .'

'Yes.'

'Then you know how we have always used a code that combines text from a particular poem, with a numerical formula, to convert text into code. Both the agent, and the person decrypting their message, know the poem and the numbers. No one else does. And every agent works from a different poem to generate his or her specific code, so that even if one agent is broken, the others are not.'

'I understand the principle,' Saffron said, 'and I've been taught how to do it.'

'Then you may or may not be aware that this code has one glaring weakness. It works well up to the moment when someone like, say, an officer in the Gestapo or *Abwehr* discovers what poem an agent is using. If that person possesses a grasp of cryptography themselves, or has access to trained codebreakers, then the code can be broken with relative ease. Worse, once it's broken, the enemy can use it to transmit messages back to us.'

Saffron frowned. 'But that shouldn't be possible. We were taught how to use security checks – at the start of messages and in the text itself – specifically to prevent anyone passing themselves off as one of us.'

'Yes, you were. But far too many agents don't use them. And even when they do use them, or try to send us warnings by entering their checks wrongly, those warnings are ignored by fools who aren't paying attention, or don't want to believe what's in front of their eyes.'

Gubbins glowered. 'That's enough, Marks. You can't be certain that's what's happening.'

'On the contrary, sir, I'm as certain as I could possibly be. In any case, we now have what I consider to be proof. As you know, all agents operate on "skeds": their scheduled times for making and receiving messages. Well, there's one agent whose skeds have all, in my view, been under German control. We are here now because those suspicions are becoming shared more widely.'

'And suspicions are all they are,' Gubbins said. 'Stick to the facts.'

'Very well, sir. The fact is that the chief signal master, Howells, was on duty for this agent's last sked. He had a sense, indeed a suspicion, that something was not quite right.'

'What made him think that?' Saffron asked.

'Because the coding was perfect, not a mistake anywhere. You see, Saffron, the thing about agents is that they operate in conditions of extreme anxiety, fearing discovery at any time. They're bound to make mistakes. Unless, that is, they're not anxious, because they're not in danger . . . because they're German. As the sked was ending, Howells had an idea. The Germans habitually close all signals with the two letters "HH", which stands for "Heil Hitler". And as soon as one Jerry says "Heil", the chap he's just Heiled – the Heilee, as it were – is obliged to respond in kind. Howells signed off with "HH" and the next thing he knew, the reply came back an instant later "HH". It wasn't the agent operating the wireless. It was a German.'

'Oh . . .' Saffron said.

'I briefed the agent in question not four weeks ago. He was dropped over Holland shortly afterwards and he began transmitting a week after that. If all his communications have, in fact, been coming from the office of Herr Giskes, the Abwehr's man in The Hague, then that suggests the agent must have been picked up on arrival, or soon after.'

'You mean, they knew he was coming?' Saffron asked.

'Yes, that's what I was implying. Which in turn can only mean one of two things. Either there is a double agent here in the Dutch section telling the Germans everything that we're up to, which I do not believe, despite my almost total lack of faith in the wit or imagination of some of the officers concerned.'

Marks glanced at Gubbins and, before the brigadier could reprimand him, added, 'Sorry, sir, can't help myself sometimes.'

He then continued, 'Or, which I believe, the Germans knew because they were receiving all the messages to Holland setting up the drop, the landing zone, the date, the time . . . every detail of the operation, in fact.'

'So they've captured and turned previous agents, too.'

'I'm sure of it. Even if others are not.'

Gubbins sighed. 'I've told you before, Marks, there's room in this organisation for eccentricity, but not for insubordination. I am aware of your ability and of your value. But there are limits to my indulgence. Watch your tongue.'

'Yes, sir. But you know I'm right, sir. You may not say so, but I know you agree with me.'

'I agree that there are questions to be answered,' Gubbins conceded. 'That is why I want you, Courtney, under Major Amies' supervision, to try and get us those answers. Now, if Marks here is correct, then there may be an unreasonable level of risk attached to sending you into Holland. It may also be unwise to use the normal channels of communication to set up a reception for you.'

'Not unless you want to be met at the landing point by a bunch of nasty-looking chaps in coal-scuttle helmets, smelling of sauerkraut,' Marks interjected.

Gubbins ignored the remark and continued, 'You will therefore be dropped into Belgium blind, without anyone in the Resistance being told in advance. Major Amies will give you contact details for those members of the Belgian Resistance in whom he has absolute faith. You are not, under any circumstances, to follow the example of far too many agents and write these details down. An agent should not require a damn crib sheet with you on their assignment.'

'No, sir.'

'On making contact, you are to ascertain, as best you can, the situation currently pertaining in Belgium. Communicate that situation to Major Amies. You are then to cross over into Holland. Once there, you will undertake a similar reconnaissance, acting on the basis that no one you meet, or attempt to meet, is to be trusted. You will be given contact details for Holland, just as for Belgium, but you must treat them with suspicion. Observe individuals and their premises, both professional and domestic. Do not make any contact unless you are satisfied that they can be trusted.'

'I won't, sir.'

Now Amies spoke up for the first time. 'Remember, Courtney, it's just as important for us to be aware of any doubts you have about our agents or local contacts as it is to know about those who can be trusted. So keep me posted, either way.'

Gubbins nodded in agreement, then said, 'If you decide that our network has been broken, then you must try to find out what has happened to our agents, in as much detail as possible. We need to know how many the Germans have got, and what they are doing with them.'

Gubbins paused, knowing that he was coming to the greatest of his demands, before he said, 'The only people in Holland who know all the information we require are the senior officers of the Abwehr, and above all Herr Giskes. I have a great deal of respect for Giskes as an adversary. He's not some caricature Nazi bully-boy. He's a clever, ruthless intelligence officer, who may be laughing at us now. I must tell you, Courtney, it would give me great pleasure to wipe that smile off his face.'

'I'd better get close to him, then,' Saffron said.

'If you can, yes. Work your way into the pro-Nazi movement in Belgium. Find an excuse to get to Holland. Then find out what in God's name Giskes knows about us and our agents.'

'Yes, sir.'

Gubbins looked at Leo Marks, who was fidgeting in his seat like a bright schoolboy in class, desperate for the chance to show how much he knows. 'Anything you'd care to add, Marks?'

'Only that you won't have to worry about learning a poem, Saffron. I have a much better coding method. One the Germans cannot break . . . If Brigadier Gubbins will allow me to employ it, of course.'

The glance that Gubbins flashed in Marks' direction told Saffron that this was one of the issues that had caused trouble between the two men.

'That's a matter for another time,' the brigadier said. 'The priority is for you, Amies, to brief Courtney on the various pro-Nazi groups and work out a plan of attack. Let me have your thoughts by the end of the week.'

'Yes, sir.'

'Good show. Now, if you'll excuse me, Ensign Courtney, Mr Marks, there are a couple of matters I must discuss with Major Amies in private. Margaret will show you out.'

• • •

Gubbins waited until the door had closed behind Saffron and Leo, allowed a few more seconds for them to make their way through the outer office, where Margaret and the other secretaries worked, and then asked Amies, 'Do you think she's up to it?'

'Honestly, sir, I'm not sure that anyone in Baker Street is up to what we are asking.'

'Are you saying we should abandon the mission?'

'No, it's too important. And, to be blunt, it's worth the risk of a single agent's life.'

'Which brings us to my question: is this the right agent?'

Amies gave a half shrug, pursed his lips in concentration and replied, 'Ensign Courtney's linguistic fluency is greatly improved, and we've never had a woman with her fighting skills.'

'This mission doesn't really call for that.'

'It may do, sir, if things get tricky. But it's more than that. This girl has got a cool head. Some might call it cold. I'd pay good money to see her go fifteen rounds with Herr Giskes. He might discover that he'd met his match.'

'It would be nice to see him get his comeuppance,' Gubbins conceded.

'And then there's her advantage: the power of seduction. Whoever undertakes this mission has to make some nasty, mean-spirited individuals want to help them. They must identify someone on the other side who possesses crucial information about our agents and then beguile them into revealing it. I can think of few agents, of either sex, better equipped to do that than Saffron Courtney.'

Gubbins grimaced. 'Bloody awful, isn't it, the way one has to think in this job? Here we are, agreeing that a young woman's life is worth risking to obtain information we want, and now you're saying that we're going to prostitute her in the process.'

'I suppose I am. I apologise, sir, it was bad form.'

'Maybe . . . but I agree with you. Courtney may have to seduce a man, and she has the attributes to do it. I am convinced that she is the best agent we have for this mission. But I want to give her a fighting chance. I'm not going to give the green light unless I'm certain that we have come up with the best plan and the greatest chance of success. Do I make myself clear?'

'Yes, sir,' said Amies.

But as he left the room he found that he was torn. He wanted to come up with something that would satisfy Brigadier Gubbins. He knew that Saffron would want that too. But part of him hoped that they would fail, if only to prevent the awful moment when he had to send her to what, by any rational calculation, would be almost certain death.

• • •

That evening as she left work, Saffron picked up a copy of the *Evening Standard* from one of the newspaper sellers on Baker Street. The front page was filled with news from North Africa. General Montgomery had won the British Army's first major victory of the war, defeating General Rommel and his elite Afrika Korps at El Alamein. Now American troops had landed on the Atlantic coast of North Africa. They were attacking

Rommel's forces from the rear, as Montgomery's Eighth Army was pummelling them on the front line.

Winston Churchill had told the country a day earlier, after all the years of hardship and defeat, 'the bright gleam of victory' was finally visible ahead. 'Now this is not the end,' the Prime Minster had declared. 'It is not even the beginning of the end. But it is, perhaps, the end of the beginning.'

A tear came unbidden to Saffron's eye as she suddenly thought of Gerhard. If there was victory ahead there would be a vanquished people, and more death and cruelty and hatred. How could he survive? Gerhard would be destroyed in the tide of vengeance. But their love transcended the everyday, the dirt and the rubble; it was a spiritual coupling, it could surely never die. Her throat constricted, and she sobbed, turning away to hide her tears from passers-by, from her own doubt.

Saffron stood at a bus stop, her overcoat buttoned-up, the collar raised against the cold and drizzle, listening to the cheerful chatter all around her. What a contrast the Londoners' good-humoured confidence made to the grim faces and anxious minds of the senior staff at Norgeby House.

The half-dozen people waiting at the stop pressed close to the edge of the pavement as a bus, its interior lights switched off because of the blackout and only the faintest sliver of head-light showing emerged from the murky darkness. It was a 74, her bus, and Saffron stepped onto the platform at the back, handed a three-penny bit to the conductor and said, 'Single to Knightsbridge, please.'

The conductor turned the handle on his ticket machine, tore off the sliver of paper and handed it to Saffron. 'Cheer up, love, it might never happen. Mind your step,' he said, reaching up to ring the bell that told the driver to depart. He stood on the open platform like an operatic tenor preparing for his big aria, and in a voice which reached to every corner of the double-decker bus, called out, 'All aboard the number seventy-four bus, going all the way to Benghazi, via Mersa Matruh, Sidi Barhani and Tobruk . . .'

The passengers laughed, for the names of those obscure spots on the North African map had become as familiar to them as any English city over the past two years. The battle lines had ebbed and flowed across the desert as the same places changed hands time and time and again. Now, though, the tide had turned for good.

Someone a few seats ahead of Saffron shouted, 'Three cheers for Monty!' and she found herself joining in as lustily as everyone else as each 'hip-hip!' was answered by an even louder 'hooray!'.

As the mood calmed, however, Saffron's mind turned to something that had been bothering her about her meetings with Gubbins and Amies, one aspect of the plan they had in mind that didn't make sense to her.

She contemplated the problem as she cooked herself an omelette of powdered eggs and cheese, followed by a slice of bread topped by her greatest luxury: raspberry jam made by her cousin Marjorie Ballantyne from fruit grown in the walled vegetable garden of her home in the Scottish Borders.

It was only when she was lying in bed that night, reading the latest Agatha Christie, that, with the same pleasure that she would have received from working out the killer's identity, the solution popped, fully-formed, into her mind.

• • •

The following morning she presented herself in Hardy Amies' office and asked for a few minutes of his time.

'By all means,' he said. 'What can I do for you?'

'It's about the Low Countries plan, sir. Something about it was bothering me last night.'

'I'm not surprised. It's a risky scheme. Anything in particular?'

'Yes, sir, I was concerned about how I'd introduce myself to the local fascists. Suppose I pitched up at their party offices and introduced myself as a young woman who wanted to do her bit for National Socialism . . .'

Amies leaned back and looked at her through a puff of cigarette smoke. 'Ye-e-s . . .'

'Well, wouldn't they wonder what took me so long? I mean, the war's been going on for more than three years, and the Germans have been in Belgium for most of that time. What have I been up to?'

'Well, I'm sure we could come up with a cover story. You've been nursing an aged relative, or running the family business in the absence of all your menfolk, who've gone off to fight in the Belgian divisions of the Waffen SS, being just as ardent as you are. Something like that.'

'That's what I thought too. But then it occurred to me that even the most blockheaded pro-Nazi party official might be a little suspicious and think he ought to check to see who my family were. At the least I'd have to produce papers backing up my story.'

'I can see the problem. I'm sure we can come up with an answer, though I don't have time for that now.'

'Don't worry, sir. There's no need. The way for me to be convincing –' she hesitated a fraction for dramatic effect – 'is to arrive in Belgium with the Germans' help. Under their protection, in fact.'

That startled Amies. He stubbed his cigarette, leaned forward, frowned at Saffron and said, 'Are you seriously suggesting that you are going to use the Germans to get you into Occupied Europe?'

'Yes, sir . . . but first I'll have to go to Africa.'

'And how do you propose to do any of this?'

'I can't tell you yet, sir, not exactly. But I'm working on it.'

• • •

Two minutes later, Saffron was walking down the corridor when she saw Leo Marks up ahead.

'Leo! Leo!' she cried. 'Wait!'

Marks beamed cheerfully as she dashed towards him. 'It had to happen,' he said. 'You've finally fallen for me. I knew you would in the end.'

'It's all that lovely food you get me,' Saffron cooed, playing along. 'These days the way to a girl's heart really is through her stomach.'

'What can I say? Whatever it takes to get the job done . . . Now, before we start planning our honeymoon, what can I do for you?'

'I was wondering . . . suppose I wanted to get a message to the South African Interior Ministry in Pretoria, how would I do that?'

'It depends what the message says. If it's sensitive, I'll have to send something in the standard Foreign Office code to our High Commission in Pretoria, and someone could then decode it and deliver the text, preferably by hand to the intended recipient. Alternatively, if it's not a matter of strategic interest to Berlin, you could send a telegram.'

Saffron told Leo what she had in mind. He considered it for a moment and said, 'Telegram would be fine. The Germans have better things to worry about than the local politics of South Africa.'

'Thank you.'

'You're welcome. By the way, my mother will want to know, do you have a date for the wedding?'

•   •   •

Two days later, Saffron walked into a pub off Trafalgar Square, a stone's throw from South Africa House. She looked around and saw a ginger-haired, moustachioed man with a ruddy complexion waving at her from a table in the corner. By the time she had walked across to him, he was on his feet, holding out a hand.

'Howzit,' he said. 'Eddie McGilvray. You must be Saffron Courtney, eh?'

'That's right.'

'You have some powerful friends, Miss Courtney. The Interior Minister himself, Mr Malcomess, told me to answer any questions you cared to put to me. I'll do my best.'

'Thank you.'

'And the minister's right-hand man, Mr Courtney, sent me a separate message. It read, and I quote: "Beware Saffron Courtney. Tough as rhino, mean as angry mamba."'

McGilvray waited for Saffron's laughter to subside and then remarked, 'I take it you're related.'

'I'm afraid so.'

'Right then, can I get you a drink before we get down to work?'

'Gin and tonic, please.'

'Coming right up.'

McGilvray went to the bar while Saffron spent an enjoyable few minutes contemplating the ways in which she could get her revenge on her cousin. He returned with the drinks, sat down and said, 'So you'd like to know about our South African fascists?'

'Yes please.'

'Can I ask, how familiar are you with South Africa and its history?'

'Reasonably. I grew up in Kenya, but I went to school for a few years in Jo'burg and I visited my cousins in Cape Town.'

'So you know that what is now South Africa was settled by the Dutch and then the British.'

'Of course. The Dutch became the Afrikaners. They fought against the British in the Boer Wars and a lot of them still hate us to this day. That's what I wanted to talk to you about.'

'Well, not all Afrikaners hate the *rooineks* . . .'

McGilvray was testing her. 'That means rednecks,' Saffron replied. 'It's their name for us. And I know that some Afrikaners argued for reconciliation with the British Empire – Prime Minister Smuts, for one. Ou Bas is a friend, and hero to my family.' She smiled. 'And that means the old boss.'

McGilvray smiled. 'Point taken, Miss Courtney. You know your stuff. So how can I help you?'

'Tell me about the fascist elements in the Afrikaner community. I know they exist. I know they have a lot of the same opinions about the superiority of the white race as the Nazis. But I need to know who they are.'

'May I ask why?'

'You may . . . but I can't give you an answer.'

'Hush-hush, eh?'

Saffron gave a noncommittal shrug.

McGilvray drank some beer, wiped the foam from his moustache and began. 'There are two main strands to the right wing of Afrikaner politics: the conventional and the extreme. The conventional wing can be found in the National Party. These fellows don't like the British, refuse to accept the idea of equal rights for black people and did not want South Africa to side with the British Empire in the war against Hitler. But, for the most part, their opposition is a matter of legitimate political disagreement. It does not constitute any kind of subversion or treachery, and they are free to do and say what they please. I don't vote for the National Party, but I have colleagues who do. It's a free country.'

If you're white, Saffron thought.

'What about the extremists?' she asked.

'Now you're talking. There is a Nazi party in South Africa. Their full name is the South African Gentile National Socialist Movement.'

'So they make their position on Jews fairly obvious from the start.'

'They do. And they have plenty of friends in the National Party, right to the top. But they aren't the most significant fascist group, in terms of threat. That honour is reserved for a mob called the Ossewabrandwag. Let's refer to them as the "OB", for simplicity's sake, eh? They actively support Hitler and want him to win the war. Hitler's returned the compliment. The Germans have sent at least one agent into South

Africa, to our knowledge, and we're sure he was helped by the OB.'

'Tell me about them,' she said.

'Their leader is a man called Johannes van Rensburg – Hans to his friends. He trained as a lawyer and served in government as the Justice Secretary before the war. He travelled to Germany on government business and was introduced to all the high-ups: Göring, Himmler, even Adolf himself. Fell for the whole thing, hook, line and sinker. He left the Nationalists, hopped across to the OB and rose all the way to the top.

'But our Hans is a sly old fox, hey? He doesn't do any of the dirty work. He leaves that to the party's hotheads. They call themselves the *Stormjaers*, or assault troops, and they've done all sorts of nasty stuff. They started riots in Jo'burg, attacking men in uniform and calling them traitors. They've carried out numerous acts of sabotage, blowing up railways, bringing down power cables, cutting telephone lines . . .'

Saffron refrained from telling McGilvray that she had been trained to do all those things, as he added, 'We rounded up the worst of them, and the men who were masterminding their operations, and stuck them in a camp. It's a place in the Free State called Koffiefontein. If you're looking for somewhere nice to go on holiday, I wouldn't recommend it.'

'It sounds fascinating,' Saffron said. 'Now, one last thing . . . what do they think about women?'

• • •

Leo Marks had not come up with any fresh blackmarket goodies, so when Saffron and Amies met the next day, they had to make do with limp fish-paste sandwiches and a cup of tea each to sustain them.

Amies took one bite from his sandwich, wrinkled his face and reached for a cigarette, muttering, 'Ugh! That tasted disgusting. And the smell . . . there's no polite way to describe it.'

Saffron laughed. 'You don't have to worry about my delicate, ladylike sensibilities, sir.'

'Yes, but what about mine?' Amies took a lungful of smoke, expelled it slowly and then sighed. 'Right, that's better.' He took one more drag, stubbed the cigarette out, then turned his attention to Saffron and asked, 'Can you please tell me how you intend to enter Occupied Europe, courtesy of the Third Reich?'

'The key is my cover story. To be honest, I'm not sure I could be a convincing Belgian, even after all the time I've spent among them here. But what if I posed as a South African, who had family ties with the Flemish part of Belgium?'

'Yes, that would explain any lack of local knowledge . . . and you might find an Afrikaans accent easier than a Flemish one.'

'Plus, it would account for where I've been for the past few years. Imagine if a young woman turns up at one of the fascist parties in the Low Countries. Suppose she can prove that she is a passionate follower of the pro-Nazi movement in South Africa, she's got letters of introduction from the top men, and photographs with them, that sort of thing. Not to mention a South African birth certificate and a passport, and a Belgian passport too.'

'And you seriously believe you can lay your hands on all that?'

'You may have to help me with the South African passport, but the rest of it I think I can manage. But it would help if I went to South Africa to get it all. And if I did, then I could make my way to Europe from there. We get agents in and out via Lisbon, don't we?'

Amies said nothing, but the fractional shrug of his shoulder was all Saffron needed to know.

'I need to know how you're going to get this material. I want to be certain that it won't risk a breach of security.'

'I'm going to work with the Interior Minister. He's a . . .' *He's my cousin's lover and everyone in Cape Town knows it* . . . 'A friend of the family. His closest aide is my cousin, Shasa Courtney.

They've already set me up with someone at the South African High Commission to get the gen on the OB. And no, I didn't say a word about why I needed to know.'

Amies lit another cigarette and thought through the proposition. 'I think your plan has a lot to be said for it. I can also think of a thousand different reasons why it should all go horribly wrong, but that's the case with every operation we undertake. Whatever we do, though, it can't be a matter of you batting your eyelashes and asking chums for a favour. It must go through proper channels. That way everyone's backside is covered. And for any of it to happen, Gubbins has to give us his approval. He won't do that unless we get all our ducks in a row.

'So, let's imagine that you pitch up in Lisbon. Let's also suppose that it all goes swimmingly. You present yourself to the German Consulate and they believe your story. The next thing you know, you're arriving in Belgium in fine style. If you play your cards right, you won't have to meet the local Nazis. They'll come and meet you at the airport with a brass band and a red carpet. The question is: which Belgian Nazis do we want you to meet? Do you have any thoughts on the subject? You seem to have everything else sorted out.'

Saffron gave an embarrassed shake of the head. 'I'm afraid not, sir. The Belgians at Eaton Square don't say much about the fascists back home. I catch the occasional muttered curse about some traitor or another who's behaving appallingly, but it's not a subject they openly discuss with me.'

'I'm not surprised. Doesn't do them much good to admit that a few of their fellow countrymen greeted the Germans like long-lost brothers.'

'I dare say it would have been just the same here.'

'I'm certain it would.'

'What should I know that the people in Eaton Square haven't been telling me?'

'As usual in Belgium, there's two of everything: a French fascist party and a Flemish one. Your South African girl is going to have a natural affinity with the Flemish, so let's concentrate on them.'

As Amies outlined the situation in Belgium, the parallels with South Africa became clear. Once again there was a conventional party, the *Vlaams Nationaal Verbond*, or VNV, and various more extreme offshoots.

As Amies explained, 'Two of the most senior VNV members left the party to found a Flemish version of the SS. They have the same uniforms, ranks and nasty habits as the Jerry version, and happily take all the dirty work that Himmler cares to give them. Rounding up Jews for exile in the East is one of their favourite tasks.

'Finally there's a bunch called *DeVlag*, who are funded by the SS. They're not a political party as such, but they have a fierce rivalry with the other Belgian fascists, if only to see who can suck up to the Germans most assiduously. You do realise that you are going to have to do that too?'

'Yes, sir.'

'But do you realise what that means? If you go into this, it has to be heart and soul. From now on, you will convince yourself that you love National Socialism and everything it stands for. You will stand in front of Nazis and agree heartily with every vile, hateful word they say. And then you will reply with more hateful thoughts of your own. That will win their trust . . . and without that you've got no chance.'

'I know how much this matters, sir. Whatever I have to do, or say, it's worth it.'

Amis softened. 'You're doing a brave thing, Saffron. Now, let's think about this false identity of yours. You'll never get past the German authorities if you're carrying Belgian documents issued by the government-in-exile, so we'll need Eaton Square to supply a blank passport, of the sort issued before the war. To establish your false identity as realistically as possible, this passport should bear the name and date of birth of an actual South African woman of about your age, with a genuine birth certificate.'

'I can hardly steal another girl's identity. What if she objects?'

'She won't. We need to find someone who has the misfortune to be dead. If her parents are also deceased, so much the better.' He rubbed his hands together energetically. 'Right then, no time to waste. We'd better get down to work.'

'Hang on, Berti, hang on!' Gerhard shouted. 'It's less than five kilometres . . . you can make it.'

Gerhard looked down at the stricken Messerschmitt, trailing a plume of black, oily smoke as it staggered across the snow-covered wasteland towards Pitomnik.

Schrumpp did not reply. He was employing his fading strength to keep his plane from crashing to the rock-hard, frozen ground that was now a hundred metres or so below him. He was badly wounded. The burst of heavy machine-gun fire that had torn through the underside of his 109's wings and fuselage had ripped into his right leg.

'Got a slight scratch,' Schrumpp had muttered, but Gerhard dreaded to think what the wound was really like.

They had been out on a ground-attack mission, a futile gesture in support of the last remnants of a Panzer division that was trying to hold an entire Russian army at bay without artillery, armoured support or even ammunition. Two months had passed since the Soviets had carried out a pincer movement that had smashed through the Romanian, Hungarian and Italian forces arrayed to the north and south of Stalingrad. The Russians had only taken a couple of days to surround the city, trapping the Sixth Army in what its soldiers called *der Kessel*: the cauldron.

The Führer had refused to allow the German army's commander General Paulus to retreat. They and the Luftwaffe pilots supporting them had been left to fight, starve and die where they stood. All through December, the Russians had toyed with their helpless prey. Stalin had massed seven armies around the city and bided his time, knowing that every day that passed left the Germans hungrier, colder and more desperately short of weaponry, fuel and bullets than before. The city itself had never been entirely conquered. Yet the unrelenting slaughter continued as the ruins of shelled and bombed-out buildings became miniature battlegrounds, piling up its own casualties as the battle lines ebbed and flowed, while all the time the con- clusion of this carnage came closer, as grimly inexorable as the march of death itself.

And then, on 9 January 1943, a huge barrage of exploding artillery shells and screaming 'Katyusha' rockets heralded the start of the final Russian assault. Those few Wehrmacht soldiers who were able to fire a gun did their best to resist, but the strug- gle was becoming as pitiful as it was desperate.

By sheer survival, Gerhard had found himself promoted to the rank of *Oberstleutnant*, or lieutenant colonel. He was notionally in command of an entire fighter group, even if it consisted of no more than a dozen patched-up fighters from squadrons that no longer existed. In that group, he and Schrumpp, now offi- cially the captain of one of those non-existent squadrons, were the last survivors of the men who had flown over Poland in September 1939. Neither of them could remember when they last had a proper meal or night's sleep. They were unshaven, red-eyed, emaciated shadows of their former selves. Yet they had survived.

Until now.

They were in sight of the airfield. The runways were pock- marked with shell holes and bomb craters. Along one side of the field ran a huge scrapyard, filled with the wreckage of German tanks, trucks, half-tracks and guns that had been destroyed in the fighting. Amidst them were strewn the planes, hundreds of them, that had been smashed by the incessant Russian attacks. There lay two metal corpses that dwarfed all the others, a pair of giant, four-engined Focke-Wulf Condors, the cream of the Luftwaffe fleet. One was broken-backed. The other was missing a wing. And every time Gerhard flew over them they seemed more and more like the symbols of Germany's impending ruin.

But this was nothing compared to the anarchy around the other three sides of the airfield. On any given day, when the weather was not so bad that all planes were grounded, a few lucky men, two hundred at most, managed to get aboard one of the Heinkel bombers that were being used to transport them back to a field hospital in German-held territory. The aircraft had to run a gauntlet of Russian anti-aircraft guns and then pray they weren't jumped by enemy fighters before they could reach their destination. There was a chance of escape that way, and the airfield had become a magnet for the wounded men of Stalingrad. They hobbled, crawled or were carried to its perimeter. Their faces were a waxy grey-white with cold and malnutrition. If frostbite had taken hold of their cheeks and lips and noses, their complexion turned blue-black, as if their barely living bodies were already starting to putrefy. In many cases they were, for there were no medicines to treat gangrenous wounds, nor bandages, other than strips of cloth ripped from dead men's uniforms.

These zombie soldiers had formed an encampment around Pitomnik. Every time a bomber or transport aircraft landed, those of the injured who were capable of movement – or those who were feigning injury – surged over the broken-down fences, through the hangers and dispersal areas and towards the tarmac where the plane was coming to a halt. Platoons of military police, the *Feldgendarmerie*, known as 'chained dogs' because of the small metal shields they wore on chains around their necks, had been deployed to control the men. They carried out their task with threats, punches and rifle butts, and, when the press of desperate men threatened to overrun the aircraft, with volleys of gunfire.

Gerhard saw that there was a fight going on at this very moment. A Junkers 52 transport plane was sitting on the taxiway, preparing to take off. But its doors were open and men were getting aboard while the chained dogs kept the horde of injured men at bay.

'Berti, do you see that Ju 52?' Gerhard called over the radio. 'We're going to get you on that plane. I swear it. I'm going to get you out of this shithole. But you have to make a landing. That's an order!'

In his headphones Gerhard heard Schrumpp reply, '*Jawohl, mein Führer,*' and now he smiled, because if his friend still had his sense of humour, he might have enough life in him to land his plane.

He'd have to do it alone because there were no emergency crews and fire tender waiting to greet them. Those days were long gone. It was every man for himself.

'This is what we're going to do,' Gerhard said. It was vital that Schrumpp believed there was still hope. 'First, you are going to land. I'll be coming in behind you. If you mess up when you're landing, I'll crash straight into you and we'll both be dead. But you won't mess it up. You'll land. I'll land. I'll come and get you out of your plane and I'll take you to that Heinkel and order the pilot to let you come aboard. He will say, "Yes, *Herr Oberstleutnant*, at once!" And he and I will shout at everyone who can hear us, and you'll be put on that plane and the next thing you know you'll be in hospital with some pretty nurse tending to your every need, thinking how much better off you are than your poor bastard friend who's still stuck in Stalingrad. Got that?'

There was no answer. The runway was getting closer. Schrump's plane was almost scraping the wings and tailfins that stood up from the scrapheap.

'Perhaps you could start by lowering your landing gear, old man. That always helps,' Gerhard suggested.

To his amazement, the undercarriage of Schrumpp's 109 began to descend from the wings. But the ground was getting closer and the wheels were still almost horizontal.

For God's sake get them down!

Gerhard tried to stay calm. He had to have his wits about him if he was to land close enough to Schrumpp to be able to rescue him, without getting caught up in the debris of a crash-landing.

It took a few seconds for a 109 to lower its wheels, but time seemed to be running in two speeds at once: the undercarriage deployment had slowed to a crawl while the ground was rushing towards both incoming Messerchmitts at ten times the normal speed.

And then those two streams became one as Schrumpp's wheel came down and an instant later touched the ground. Gerhard saw the aircraft in front of him slew, but stay upright as he landed in its slipstream, realising that this made his speed much higher than it would have been, if he'd landed in clean air. He raced up behind Schrumpp's plane so that his propeller was almost churning up its tail, then, like a racing driver making an overtaking manoeuvre, he managed to slingshot past without the two sets of wings colliding.

It was all about stopping the plane and throwing open the canopy above his head. Gerhard unclipped his harness, clambered out onto the wing, jumped down and he was running across the fifty metres of tarmac between his plane and Schrumpp's.

He could see tongues of flame escaping from the engine cowling and licking at the fuselage. There was barely any fuel left in the tanks, but there was enough to ignite a fire that would set the whole aircraft ablaze.

Gerhard reached the 109, his fatigue and malnutrition leaving him exhausted, even after that short sprint. It took all his strength to pull himself onto the wing and wrench open the canopy. Schrumpp was collapsed over his controls in the cockpit. The landing had taken every scrap of energy out of him.

Gerhard looked down into the footwell beneath the control panel and swallowed hard at what he saw. From below the shin it was only skin and bone. It would have to be amputated.

He'll probably never fly again, Gerhard thought. And then, *Lucky bastard.*

But if he didn't get that amputation, Shrumpp would die. Blood was pulsing out of his leg and pooling on the cockpit floor.

'Let's get you out of here,' Gerhard said, freeing Schrumpp from his harness. He reached into the cockpit, between his friend's back and his seat, and managed to get his hands under Schrumpp's armpits.

Gerhard braced his legs and pulled as hard as he could.

Schrumpp didn't budge.

He could feel heat against the side of his right leg. The flames were drawing closer. Out of the corner of his eye he was aware of a crowd of men moving towards him. He glanced around and saw the horde of wounded men. Beaten away from the Junkers, they were making for another destination. No matter that the Messerchmitts were single-seater aircraft, with no fuel in their tanks. In the eyes of the damned, they were a ticket out of Hell.

'Come on, Berti. I can't do this alone. Can you hear me?'

He caught a faint groan and a nod of the head.

'Right then, on the count of three, push with your good leg. One . . . two . . . three!'

A terrible groan emerged from Schrumpp. It rose to a high-pitched howl of pain as Gerhard managed to drag him from the cockpit, his shattered leg scraping against the side of the cockpit, before dropping him onto the wing.

Gerhard scrambled off the wing to the ground and dragged his friend after him. Schrumpp's weight knocked Gerhard off his feet and by the time he'd pulled himself up, the crowd of shuffling, dead-eyed wounded men had surrounded his own plane, fighting to get into the cockpit, while others of the living dead trudged towards the second plane.

Gerhard stood, faced the mob, took out the service revolver strapped to his hip and fired two shots over their heads. It stopped the oncoming men for a few seconds – long enough for Gerhard to lift Schrumpp onto his back and stagger in the direction of the control tower.

He saw three more men dashing towards him. For a second, Gerhard thought he would have to drop Schrumpp and fight them off. Then he realised that they were ground crew, good men who had worked day and night to keep him and the other pilots flying.

'Are you all right, sir?' one of them asked.

'What happened to Herr Hauptmann Schrumpp, sir?'

'He was shot up. He needs a tourniquet round his leg, fast. Use some harness strapping, anything that can be tied tight. Then carry him over to the Ju 52 and tell the pilot he doesn't move until I tell him to. Got that?'

'Yes, sir!'

'Good. I'll be there in a minute. Got to get Hauptmann Schrumpp something for his journey.'

Gerhard ran across the airfield to the buildings clustered around the control tower. One of them contained the sick bay where their medical officer had worked until a Heinkel left one day and a short while later the pilots discovered that their doc had been on it. His medicine cabinet was in place, however, and because they ran the transport planes, the Luftwaffe had a few supplies. Gerhard opened the cabinet and extracted several ampules of opium and as much bandaging as he could stuff into the pockets of his trousers and flight jacket. He noticed a pair of crutches lying on the floor and picked them up. Then he ran to the officers' mess. It was as filthy and chaotic as everything else in the Kessel, but there was half a case of vodka left and Gerhard grabbed a bottle.

He raced over to the Junkers. He opened his leather flight jacket to reveal the uniform underneath, with its badges of rank and medal ribbons. Schrumpp was lying on the ground beneath the fuselage of the Ju 52 with his leg bound tight below the knee.

'Why isn't he aboard?' Gerhard asked.

'It's the pilot, sir,' one of the ground crew replied. 'Says he can only take walking wounded. It's an order from High Command, sir. He can't disobey it.'

'Well, we'd better get Hauptmann Schrumpp on his feet then, hadn't we?'

Gerhard fished the opium ampules out of one pocket. 'Give him a couple of these in the leg, and put the others in his pockets.

Pour as much of this vodka down his throat as you can. Wrap these bandages around his leg. See if you can pull him upright onto the crutches. I want him standing upright by the door of the plane in less than two minutes. Go!'

As the men set to work, Gerhard came out from under the Junkers and made his way to the door. He'd hoped that the pilot would turn a blind eye if presented with a fellow Luftwaffe man, but he understood why he had refused to do so. A man on a stretcher took up as much room on a plane as four men standing upright. He was also less likely to return to fighting fitness. Evacuation had been restricted to the walking wounded.

Gerhard arrived by the aircraft door. A large, stone-faced chained dog was standing there, sub machine gun in hand, barring the way.

There was a loud mechanical sound. The engines were starting up.

'Got a pass, sir?' the military policeman asked, having to shout to make himself heard as the engines burst into life.

'No,' Gerhard yelled. 'But I'm not taking this flight. Just need to speak to the pilot. Let me aboard. If I don't get off, you can shoot me.'

The chained dog frowned, not certain how to respond.

'I would remind you, I am a lieutenant colonel.'

The dog considered the grief an angry colonel could cause him and got out of the way.

Gerhard clambered up into the cabin of the aircraft, made his way through the ranks of wounded to the cabin door, and opened it.

The pilot turned and had already started shouting, 'What the hell are—' before he saw he was addressing a senior officer of his own service and stopped himself. 'I'm sorry, Herr *Oberstleutnant*, I had no idea . . .'

Gerhard nodded brusquely. It didn't hurt if this babe-in-arms – there were still spots on the boy's barely shaven face – felt intimidated by his presence. 'I understand you refused passage for a fellow Luftwaffe officer.'

'Yes, sir, but—'

Gerhard held up a hand to stop him. 'But nothing. I understand the rule. Walking wounded only. That is why Hauptmann Schrumpp, a fighter ace who has fought for the Reich since the first day of this war, will enter this aircraft on his feet. And you will carry him out of here. You may be sure that I will call *Generaloberst* von Richtofen's headquarters to make sure that he has arrived safely. Do you understand?'

'But sir—'

'But nothing. Hauptmann Schrumpp flies aboard this plane, or I will make sure, before this damned city falls, that every man in the Luftwaffe, from Göring himself on down, knows that you turned your back on a fellow officer in his time of need. So, I will ask you for the last time: may I have Hauptmann Schrumpp brought aboard?'

'Yes, Herr *Oberstleutnant*.'

'Good man. I knew you'd see sense.'

As the chained dogs opened fire on the men, their fellow Germans who were fighting to get on the plane, Gerhard had Schrumpp, held upright by the ground crewmen on either side of him, carried aboard the plane. Once aboard, he would remain standing by the sheer press of bodies.

Gerhard made sure the aircrew supervising the cabin knew that they were looking after one of their own. Schrumpp was barely conscious, rescued from his pain by a fog of opium and alcohol. Gerhard patted him on the shoulder.

'Goodbye, old friend. Fly safely . . . And good luck with the nurses.'

The moment Gerhard jumped back onto the tarmac, the door of the Junkers closed behind him, the chocks were pulled away from its wheels and it taxied towards the runway.

Gerhard watched as it ascended into the sunless grey sky and saw the bursts of the anti-aircraft shells peppering the air around it as it clawed its way upwards.

The Junkers ran the gauntlet without a scratch. It flew across enemy territory without interruption and landed safely at Salsk, an airfield some way to the west of Tatsinskaya, which had fallen to the advancing Red Army on Christmas Eve.

Late on the night of 12 January a message was received by the Luftwaffe radio operator at Pitomnik. Squadron Captain Schrumpp had survived his flight out of Stalingrad and been taken into surgery. His right leg was amputated below the knee, but he survived the operation.

Gerhard, however, was trapped in Stalingrad. And there the ordeal was about to get worse.

• • •

By dawn on 16 January the Russians had advanced so far into the Kessel that they were on the verge of capturing Pitomnik. Gerhard and his fellow pilots were ordered to fly their planes to another airfield, Gumrak, which was a dozen kilometres closer to the city itself. Their journey was completed in a matter of minutes, though the landing was complicated by the discovery that no one had been alerted to their arrival, so the airfield was still covered in thick snow.

A young pilot's voice echoed in Gerhard's headphones. 'What shall we do, sir? We can't see the runway.'

'Land, of course. We've got nowhere else to go.'

It made no difference where they touched down. The cold made every piece of ground as hard as concrete, and it was a matter of chance whether one ended up in any of the craters left by Russian bombs and artillery shells.

Gerhard had never flown in or out of Gumrak before, so was not familiar with its layout. He circled the field to size it up, then used the position of the tower and hangars – all of which had been virtually destroyed – to make a guess as to the likely orientation of the main runway. Then he led his men into land. A couple of the less-experienced pilots had trouble control- ling their aircraft on the slippery ground, but they and their machines all survived unscathed.

For the ground crews, however, going by road in trucks filled with equipment and spares, which was normally a short drive, became a three-hour descent into a frozen hell.

The road was swamped by retreating troops, exhausted, frozen, their eyes blank and their hands and feet swaddled in strips torn from bandages, old blankets and dead men's uniforms. The units these men had once belonged to had all disintegrated: infantrymen, engineers, grenadiers, gunners and tank crews, regular soldiers and SS men alike were intermingled in a single, formless, shuffling mass of beaten and battered humanity. Many had thrown their weapons away: there was no point in carrying them any further for their ammunition had long since run out.

As the trucks tried to force their way through, they came under siege from retreating soldiers trying to climb aboard. Desperate, exhausted and past caring about any consequences, the soldiers pleaded for the chance of a ride, or begged for fuel to feed their own abandoned vehicles. When their pleas were ignored they resorted to threats and then assaults, which had to be beaten off with fists, rifle butts and any hammers and wrenches that the mechanics could grab to use as weapons.

The attacks never lasted long. The men who mounted them had little strength and soon collapsed in the filthy, bloodstained snow.

And these were the men who were fit and healthy.

For the injured and diseased, the situation was incomparably worse. Those whose condition meant that they could not be moved were left to their fate at Pitomnik. A handful of doctors and orderlies stayed behind to look after their patients, though they knew that as soon as the Russians arrived they would shoot them all.

Anyone who could move set off for Gumrak, propped on comrades' shoulders, hauling themselves on crutches, or lying on improvised sleds hauled by fellow Germans who were barely any stronger than the men they were pulling behind them.

Stalingrad had become a vast experiment in finding new ways to die. A week earlier, a consignment of meat paste had been aboard one of the few successful flights to drop supplies to the Sixth Army by parachute. On the advice of the Wehrmacht's top nutritionists, the paste had been enriched with extra fat to provide more energy to the men who ate it.

Instead, when the tins were forced open and their contents consumed by the ravenous soldiers, men started dropping like flies. Their starved bodies could not process the fatty paste. The attempt to feed them had ended up killing them.

Men who had survived every attack from the Russians, the weather and their own High Command found themselves on a death march along which every metre of road claimed more victims. Men lay where they fell and died where they lay. Their passing was marked by the lice, with which every man in the army was infested. The moment the supply of warm blood ceased, the insects scuttled out of their former host's hair and clothing, in search of new, living bodies to colonise.

Crows flocked from their perches on silent gun barrels, burned-out tanks or the semi-demolished cottages of the peasants who had once farmed the land, clustered on the chilling corpses and picked out eyeballs before they could freeze into pebbles of ice.

• • •

'That wasn't the worst part, sir,' the crew chief told Gerhard when they arrived at the airfield. 'There's a camp half a kilometre from the gates to the airfield. They've got Russians there, captured when the army came through in August: two thousand of them. When we went by there were hundreds pushed up against the fence, holding their hands through the wire, like beggars. I swear to God, sir, our lot look half-starved, but the Ivans . . . they were human skeletons. Someone on the road said the camp quartermaster forgot to order their rations. Word is, they've not had any food since before Christmas, so they've taken to eating each other.'

Gerhard had no response. There came a point when one's senses could not register any more suffering, when compassion ran out like the diesel in all the abandoned trucks and cars and motorbikes that littered the Stalingrad landscape.

'Huh,' he said dully, when the crew chief had finished.

The two men stood opposite one another, too exhausted to know what to do, and then Gerhard said, 'You think that's bad? The hospital here makes the slaughterhouse at Pitomnik look like a fancy Swiss sanatorium.'

'Will any of them get out, sir?'

'God knows, I—'

Before Gerhard could finish the sentence, he was interrupted by one of his pilots running towards him, saying, 'Sir, sir, you're wanted in the control room.' The pilot reached Gerhard, gave a breathless smile and said, 'I can't be certain, sir, but I think we're getting out of here.'

'Is it true? Have we been told to leave the Stalingrad front?' Gerhard asked when he arrived at the tent that had been used as the airfield's control centre since the tower had been put out of action.

The station commander nodded. 'It seems von Richtofen decided that the order to stand and fight to the last man did not apply to Luftwaffe personnel.'

'We don't *stand* and fight,' Gerhard said. 'We fly.'

'That was Richtofen's point. Von Manstein tried to overrule him, but he called Göring and received his authority to pull out. You are to be on your way as soon as possible.'

'Where to?'

'Good question. Salsk was overrun yesterday.'

'What?' Gerhard asked, thinking of Berti Schrumpp. 'Are the Russians attacking there too?'

'They're attacking everywhere.'

'But did everyone get out in time?'

'I believe so,' the station commander said.

'Thank Christ,' Gerhard muttered.

'Last I heard, everyone was relocating to some place called Zverevo, near Shakhty. If you ask my advice, you should aim for Taganrog. That's where von Manstein's got his Army Group Don headquarters, and there's an airstrip, so you should be safe there.'

'And if we aren't?'

'Then what does it matter? The war will be as good as over.'

Gerhard nodded and asked, 'What about the ground crew? I'm not leaving them behind.'

'We're falling back to the last runway. The Stalingradsky Flying School. There's a couple of Ju 52's coming in for them today. I'll be leaving with them.'

'Then I wish you good luck.'

'You too, Herr *Oberstleutnant*.'

The Messerschmitts filled their tanks to the brim with virtually the last aviation fuel that Stalingrad had to offer, for they would need every drop to take them more than five hundred kilometres southwest to Taganrog. They took off again at midday and as their wheels left the runway and the pilots pulled into the steepest climb they could manage to escape the guns of the Russian tanks, they could see beneath them the first long rows of Red Army soldiers, rank upon rank marching towards the airfield's western perimeter.

● ● ●

When they reached Taganrog, Gerhard went in search of news about Berti. But with the loss of Stalingrad only days away and the Russians applying pressure that threatened to open the southern half of the Eastern Front, no one cared about the fate of a single airman. With no fighter wing left to command, he found himself idle for the first time in more than three years while the pen-pushers of the Fourth Air Fleet worked their way around to finding him a new job.

Almost a month had gone by, Stalingrad had been taken by the Russians and every remaining man in the Sixth Army had either been killed or captured before Gerhard received a message saying that a clerk from Luftwaffe regional headquarters at Poltava had called with the information Gerhard had requested. The man was a clerk, with the rank of corporal. He'd left his name as *Underfeldwebel* Götz

'Good day, Herr *Oberstleutnant*,' Götz's voice intoned, oozing the bureaucratic attitude of boredom, obstruction and mild resentment from every syllable, when Gerhard got through to the correct department at Poltava. 'I gather you were inquiring about one of your officers, Squadron Captain Albrecht Schrumpp.'

'That's right, Corporal. He was wounded on the ninth of January, flown out of Pitomnik to Salsk, where he was treated for his wounds. I want to know about his present condition. The last I heard, the operation had been a success.'

There was a silence on the other end of the line, then a grunt and Götz replied, 'That's not what it says here, Herr *Oberstleutnant*.'

'What do you mean?'

'According to our records, and I have no reason to doubt them, squadron captain Schrumpp died on the morning of the tenth of January. There were complications.'

'What do you mean, complications?' Gerhard's voice rose, as if he could will his words to be true. 'I told you, the operation was a success.'

'Well, sir, I don't know about that. But I do know that the death has been confirmed, the squadron captain's family are being notified, though the process is taking longer than usual at the present time. There are a lot of deaths to be dealt with.'

'I don't care about that!' Gerhard shouted 'I . . .' He fell silent, unable to say the words. *I want Berti to be alive.*

'Try to look on the positive side, sir,' Götz said, sounding a little more like a human being. 'There was time to bury your comrade before the Russians arrived. He is lying in peace, which is more than can be said for a lot of good German men. And the Russians didn't take him alive. That's a true mercy, sir, from what I've heard.'

Gerhard sighed. 'I apologise if I was short with you, Corporal. You're right, that is a mercy. Thank you for your assistance.'

Gerhard drove to a bar in Taganrog, where men from the Wehrmacht forces attached to Army Group South had once gathered to celebrate their triumphs, but nowadays sought nothing more than a brief release from the hell of the Eastern Front. He procured a bottle of schnapps and settled down to drink it in Berti's honour.

'To you, old friend,' he said, raising his glass and downing it in one.

He was pouring another drink when a young army officer approached him, a captain. The man came up close to Gerhard's bar stool and stood belligerently, unsteady on his feet, red-faced, sweaty, obviously drunk.

'Herr *Oberst*,' he said. 'Is it true you were at Stalingrad?'

Gerhard looked at him through narrowed eyes. 'Not now, captain. I'm mourning the death of a close friend.'

The man shuffled closer, so that Gerhard could smell the alcohol on his stinking breath. 'I said, were . . . you . . . at . . . Stalingrad?'

'Yes, I was. Now go.'

'And you ran away . . . you and the other Luftwaffe cowards.'

'I'm giving you one last chance. Walk away . . . now.'

'What, like you did? You flew away, you shithead pansy fly boys . . . and left an army of good German men to die. You deserted . . . You disobeyed a Führer-order . . .'

Another army officer hurried across and grabbed the captain's sleeve. 'Come on, Hansi, leave the colonel alone . . .'

The captain brushed him away. He was lost in his anger, his eyes bulging as he raged at Gerhard, 'And now they're all gone! All those brave men! And you deserted them . . . you filthy, goddamned coward!'

'Please, Herr *Oberstleutnant*,' the second soldier pleaded. 'He's not in his right mind. His brother was at Stalingrad, taken prisoner by the Reds.'

Gerhard poured another glass of schnapps, downed it, then he got up from his stool, looked the captain in the eye and said, 'Screw you . . . and screw your goddamned Führer too. I was at Stalingrad from the first bombing raid on the twenty-third of August through to the last flight out of Gumrak when the Ivans were so close we could see them coming onto the airfield as we took off. I saw it all, you drunken shit. I saw an entire army, and most of my own men thrown away . . . and for what?' He looked around the bar, daring anyone to answer him. 'For what? We never even captured the city. We never had control of the river, which was the whole point of the exercise, wasn't it? I mean, that's what the man said, standing safe and sound in a bierkeller in Munich.'

Men looked at one another. Gerhard's words echoed the thoughts that many of them shared. But what in God's name had possessed him to speak them aloud?

Gerhard was past caring. 'It was all a waste. It achieved nothing, except for turning men into savages, dressed in rags, half-mad with starvation . . . the wounded with no dressings, no morphine . . . the men who could still fight throwing away their guns because they didn't have any bullets. So . . . Hansi, is it?'

The captain nodded.

'Well, Hansi, I don't know what your brother looked like the last time you saw him. But I can promise you wouldn't recognise him now. I'll bet he doesn't recognise himself. And I'll tell you something else: they could have sent every plane in the Luftwaffe to Stalingrad and it wouldn't have made a damn bit of difference. So don't blame me. Blame the lunatic who refused to retreat and the generals who wouldn't defy him. I was there one hundred and forty-six days. I counted them. And I flew one hundred and seventy-three sorties. I did my duty and so did my men. Don't you damn well blame me.'

Silence had fallen on the bar. It was as if everyone was waiting for the Gestapo, or SD, or even the chained dogs to appear in their midst and drag the colonel away for words that amounted to treason. But no one came. No arrest was made.

Instead, Gerhard picked up his bottle, shoved it at Hansi and said, 'Here, drink to your poor bastard brother.'

He headed towards the door, men getting out of his path as if fearing to be seen anywhere near him. Now that his temper had settled, Gerhard was thinking more clearly about what he had said. There were plenty of men whose faith in the Führer was undimmed. If anything they felt more bound to stand by him when things were going badly. That was the proof of their devotion. But even so, would anyone speak out about what they had seen and heard? As he looked at the men around him, he knew what they were thinking.

He was a senior officer, covered in medals. Maybe he had said things he shouldn't. But a man could easily find himself in trouble for making an issue of it. Why get involved, if you didn't have to?

Gerhard was almost in touching distance of the door. He was about to walk out onto the street. He thought he'd made it. Then a tall, thin man in an immaculately cleaned and pressed uniform, with full colonel's tabs on his shoulders, rose from his seat at a nearby table.

'A word, if you please, *Oberstleutnant*,' he said, barely raising his voice.

Gerhard stopped and waited as the colonel made his way towards him. 'Your name, please,' the colonel said.

'*Oberstleutnant* Gerhard von Meerbach.'

'Your unit?'

'That's hard to say, sir. The fighter group I commanded no longer exists. I am on a temporary attachment, awaiting a new posting.'

'I see.'

'If you need to get hold of me, I'm sure that General von Richtofen's headquarters will be able to help you. Might I ask who you are, sir?'

The colonel ignored the question. He replied, 'You have not heard the last of this incident, *Oberstleutnant*. You may rest assured of that.'

Men who had been looking at the confrontation by the bar door turned their eyes back to their own drinks. No one looked at Gerhard as he left. No one caught the colonel's eye as he returned to his table. They thanked God that they had not been the ones to open their mouths in the way the Luftwaffe officer had done. And they pitied him for being so foolish.

Saffron sailed for South Africa in one of the 'Winston Specials', as the convoys taking troops south along the west coast of Africa on their way to the campaigns in the desert and the Far East were known. One blazing hot morning in mid-January 1943, she disembarked at Cape Town and was met at the foot of the gangway by her cousin Centaine Courtney.

Many of the troops who had been travelling on the same ship, and whose voyage had been enlivened by the presence of a beautiful young woman on board, had gathered at the rails to watch as they docked below the looming mass of Table Mountain.

'Bloody hell, there's two of them,' one of them remarked with a low whistle of appreciation as the cousins embraced at the foot of the gangway.

Centaine was forty-three years old, having been born on the first day of the twentieth century, but she was wearing the years spectacularly well. She was as slim as she had been when she first set foot on African soil, more than a quarter of a century earlier. Her wavy, dark hair was thick and glossy, and there was hardly a line beneath her huge, lustrous black eyes.

'You look lovely, as always, Cousin Centaine,' Saffron said.

'As do you, my darling, but I think you should stop calling me Cousin Centaine. You're not a child any more, and it makes me feel less like a cousin than an ancient maiden aunt!'

Saffron laughed. 'No one would ever mistake you for that.'

They walked towards Centaine's car, a splendid convertible, painted midnight blue, with sweeping, aerodynamic lines and creamy beige leather upholstery. Centaine was able to afford a chauffeur, but always liked to drive herself, unless there was a good reason not to. The two women put Saffron's cases in the boot, then Centaine slipped behind the wheel and Saffron took the seat next to her. The engine started up with a deep, rumbling growl.

'Mmm . . .' sighed Saffron appreciatively. 'This is a splendid car, Centaine. What is it?'

'A Cadillac Series 62. I had it shipped from America.'

'Well, it's gorgeous. I love the sound of that engine. I bet it's incredibly powerful . . .' Saffron noticed the quizzical look her cousin was giving her. 'Sorry! That's what comes from working as a driver for a year. One starts to take an interest in that sort of thing.'

'Well, if I remember all the salesman's bumph correctly, it's a V-8 and it produces a hundred and thirty-five horsepower. Does that help?'

'Yes, thank you,' Saffron said. She could tell that a more interesting topic of conversation was required. 'Do tell me all about Tara. Is she completely divine? Shasa's clearly quite potty about her.'

As Centaine drove the car onto the road that led towards the lush pastures and vineyards of her estate at Weltevreden, she smiled, almost wistfully, and said, 'You know, I can remember Tara when she was a little girl with a straw hat on her head, decorated with pretty ribbons, running towards her father, holding up her skirt to stop herself from tripping over, and shrieking with excitement at the top of her voice.'

Saffron said nothing. It sounded as if it should be a happy memory, but there was pain in her cousin's voice, not too far beneath the surface. Then Centaine cheered up as she said, 'But now Tara's grown up. She's beautiful to look at, of course. Gorgeous grey eyes, a perfect, oval face like a Raphael Madonna and a tall, slender figure, just like yours. But she's lovely as a person, too. It would be very easy to take advantage, marrying into this family. You know, insist on the best of everything, always driving your husband round the bend asking for more, more, more.'

'But Tara's not like that?'

'No, quite the opposite. She spends half her life in the Cape Flats, where the worst slums are, setting up soup kitchens and clinics for the poor and needy. Any other girl would spend Shasa's money on dresses and new curtains. She puts it all into her charity ventures.'

'How wonderful,' Saffron said, meaning it. 'Makes me feel ashamed I don't do more.'

'You're doing plenty . . . but in a different way. And each is as important as the other.'

'I hope so. The war effort has to be about more than beating Hitler. We must make something better than before, for everyone. But anyway . . . do tell me about Tara.'

'She's kept her maiden name. The children will all be Courtneys, but she's still Tara Malcomess.'

'How modern! I'm amazed she can manage all her charity work when she's got a young son. Does she leave him with a nanny?'

'A little bit more, now that Sean's less portable. When he was a newborn, though, she charged around the slums with him on her hip. All the women loved it. You never saw a baby boy more doted on than him.'

They were leaving the city now. 'I thought I'd take you by the scenic route,' Centaine said, turning onto a road that twisted and turned along the flanks of Table Mountain.

A deep, warm feeling of contentment suffused Saffron, the cares of the world falling away as they passed into a forest of blue gum trees, their slender trunks, wrapped in peeling pale grey bark, rising one hundred and fifty feet around them, and dappling the road with the cool, dark shadows from their narrow canopies of evergreen foliage.

As she was closing her eyes, Centaine asked her, 'So, dearest Saffron, what really brings you to South Africa?'

Suddenly she was wide awake again. 'I'm sorry, but I'm not allowed to tell you.'

'Come now, we're family. You know your secret is safe with me.'

'Being family makes no difference, I'm afraid. The point of a secret is that it's secret from everyone.'

'Even from your sweet old maiden aunt, Centaine?' she wheedled.

'Even from you,' Saffron said, intrigued by the change of tone.

'Are you sure?'

'I think you should know that I'm rather good at holding out against interrogation. I'm really not going to blab.'

'Damn!' Centaine slapped a hand against the steering wheel. 'That bloody boy!'

Centaine was one of life's winners and Saffron was amused to see her on the losing side for once. 'I presume you mean Shasa,' she said.

'Yes. The sneaky weasel bet me that you wouldn't talk and, like an idiot, I accepted.'

'What were the stakes?'

Centaine huffed crossly. 'The loser has to say, "I apologise. You were right and I was wrong."'

'Ouch! That's going to hurt.'

'In front of the whole table at dinner, what's more,' Centaine added.

'Gosh, I'm almost tempted to tell you, to spare you the punishment.'

'Oh, would you do that? You dear, sweet girl, I—'

'No, I can't. But I was just a teeny bit tempted.'

'Bah, you're just as bad as he is.'

'Oh no, I couldn't possibly be *that* bad!' Saffron grinned, knowing full well that she occupied a high position on the list of the people Centaine Courtney loved most, a list on which Shasa occupied top spot.

They approached the gateway to the estate and passed underneath the ornate pediment, decorated with a frieze of dancing nymphs bearing bunches of grapes and topped by the carved inscription: WELTEVREDEN 1790.

'Well satisfied,' purred Saffron, translating the name. 'How perfect.'

In the last, deep golden rays of the setting sun, they drove through the vineyards and past the polo field, where she and

Shasa had first tested one another's mettle, charging head-on at one another – 'down the throat', as the saying went – their ponies at full gallop until, at the last second, Shasa had pulled to one side. Even then, as a girl of thirteen, she knew he had only done it to save her from being hurt. He would never have given way to another boy.

With a start she realised it was almost ten years since that first meeting. It seemed like a lifetime ago, and yet Weltevreden was the still the same paradise as before. The main house, built in the style of a French chateau, was as beautiful and imposing as ever. And there, at the door, was Shasa himself, a fully grown man now, with a patch over one eye, but still immediately recognisable.

The patch makes him look rather dashing, thought Saffron, and then, almost before Centaine had brought the car to a halt, she was leaping from the passenger seat, as excitable as her thirteen-year-old self, screaming, 'Shasa!' and almost throwing herself into his arms.

He caught her, hugged her, kissed her and then set her down in front of him. 'So, I see that you haven't grown up at all,' he said. 'Still the same little brat.'

'Whereas you are now a broken-down old man,' she replied. 'I like the patch. All you need is a parrot and a peg leg.'

'For goodness' sakes, you two,' Centaine said with maternal severity, though her heart was bursting with joy at seeing these two cousins slipping into their old relationship. They were both only children of single parents and they had adopted one another as honorary siblings, which included the right to tease one another mercilessly.

'Shasa, darling, mind your manners,' Centaine added. 'Don't you think you should be making introductions?'

'Oh yes . . . Saffron, this is my wife, Tara Malcomess. And Tara, here's my cousin, Saffron Courtney.'

• • •

Tara was hardly the nervous type, but the pending arrival of Saffron Courtney had caused flutters of apprehension in her stomach. She had heard so much about this paragon of beauty, brains and courage. How could she compete? And how could she not feel that she was letting Shasa down by being so inferior to his cousin?

But then she saw the whirlwind of arms and legs and flying hair leaping from the car and yelling at the top of her voice, and Tara thought, *Oh, she's a perfectly normal girl, just like me*. And when she heard the two of them pulling one another's legs in the way they did, she knew that Shasa did not think of Saffron as anything other than a beloved, bratty kid sister, and that it would not occur to him to judge Tara alongside her.

When she was introduced to Saffron, Tara kissed her on both cheeks and gave her a little hug, and, to her delight, found that she was hugged back.

Saffron said, 'Centaine told me how gorgeous you are and she was quite right. You are much, much too beautiful for Shasa!' They were both laughing and Saffron was linking their arms and walking with her into the house, saying, 'I'm dying to see your baby. Clever you, popping out a Courtney heir at the first time of asking. That'll make you popular! And Centaine said you do amazing work down in the Cape Flats. You must tell me all about it.'

Behind them, Shasa called out, 'Wait for me!' and was about to hurry after the two young women when Centaine caught his arm and said, 'Wait. Let them be. Your wife and your cousin are two alpha females. If they bond as friends, they will be the strength of this family for decades to come. But if they should be enemies, woe betide us all.'

Shasa frowned. 'They don't seem like enemies. They look as though they're getting on splendidly.'

'Yes, they are. It could not have started better. So leave them alone to work out their relationship for themselves.'

'Well, you know best, Mama . . . Or do you?' A grin spread across Shasa's face as a thought occurred to him. 'You haven't said a word about our bet. Which means that I won. Admit it – I won!'

Centaine struggled but managed to get the words out: 'Yes . . . you won. She wouldn't say a word.'

'Well, if it's any consolation, she and her people have barely told Blaine and me anything, either. I'll do my best to find out more after dinner. But don't hold out too much hope.'

• • •

Saffron could not have wanted a better cousin-in-law. They could both understand the pleasures and irritations of being taller than most other women, and quite a few men, but their looks were so sufficiently different that there was no sense of competition. Tara was intelligent, competent and awesomely efficient. She had her house, her husband, her child and the poor of Cape Town scheduled and organised with a skill that would have made her an instant success in Baker Street.

'My commanding officer would love you,' Saffron told Tara. 'He's the fiercest, most determined, hard-working man you'll ever meet, but he's a great believer in women. The brighter and busier they are, the better he likes them. You'd be right up his street. You'd be running the whole show in no time.'

'Thank you,' said Tara, beaming with pleasure.

'I mean it. By the way, I'm not quite sure how to put this, but what exactly is happening between Centaine and your father? I mean, what is one supposed to say?'

Tara giggled. 'It is complicated, isn't it? The simplest way of putting it is that they're both madly in love and have been for years and years. Everyone knows that they're a couple, and since they're both unattached and grown up, I can't see that there's the slightest thing wrong about it. They have to be discreet in public, though, because Daddy's a government minister and it wouldn't do to offend the voters.'

'Well, I'm not going to be offended, so that's all right.'

• • •

Blaine Malcomess arrived and Saffron saw at once why Centaine had fallen in love with him. Blaine was tall, with rough-hewn features and that indefinable yet unmistakable air of a man whose strength is as much moral as physical. In his younger days he had been a fine polo player and a distinguished soldier, who'd won the Military Cross in the First World War. Now, at fifty, he was still in his prime, but moving from the life of a man of action to the gravitas of a statesman.

'Look at you, Saffron,' he said, standing back and examining her admiringly. 'One minute you're a Roedean schoolgirl and now here's this ravishing woman of the world. How times fly, eh?'

A little later, before the gong sounded for dinner, he took Saffron to one side and said, 'Look, I don't want to make a fuss about this in front of everyone. Suspect you wouldn't like it. But I want you to know that we're damn proud of you. I spoke to *Ou Baas* today. He asked me to send you his special regards. Said you were a credit to the Courtney name.'

'Oh,' said Saffron, who was taken aback at the thought that Smuts should even think about her, let alone give her so fine a compliment. 'I . . . I don't know what to say.'

'You don't have to say a thing,' Blaine assured her. He raised his voice and announced, 'I shall have the honour of escorting our guest into dinner . . . Ready?' he asked.

Saffron nodded.

'Then let's go in. And I mean it . . . damn proud.'

• • •

There was no rationing in South Africa and the dinner Centaine laid on for Saffron's arrival at Weltevreden was a feast. They started with a mousse made from fish bought in the market that morning, within hours of being caught, accompanied by a salad of fresh green leaves and herbs picked from the house's own vegetable garden. The main course was roast beef with all the trimmings. Thick slices of meat, still pink and bloody in the middle, were accompanied by Yorkshire puddings that were crisp to the bite, but soft in the middle, with perfectly roasted potatoes, peas and carrots from the same beds as the salad.

Saffron was shameless. She made no concessions to ladylike concern for her figure but tucked in like a ravening beast.

When the main course had been removed and the table cleared, a magnificent peach and raspberry pavlova was brought into the room and placed at the centre of the dining table, for all to admire the extravagance of meringue, whipped cream and fresh fruit. Hidden away inside it, as a special indulgence for a starving refugee from England, was a core of rich, home-made vanilla ice-cream.

All the courses were accompanied by local wines, made from grapes grown at Weltevreden, or in the other vineyards nearby, and the final treat was a cup of strong, rich Kenyan coffee.

Shasa chuckled to himself as he watched Saffron emptying her cup and then saying, 'Oh, yes, please,' as one of the staff approached with a silver pot, offering to refill it.

'I don't think you've said a word all meal, except "please" or "thank you",' he said, with only the mildest note of affectionate teasing in his voice.

'Oh, I'm sorry. Have I been terribly rude?'

'Not at all, darling,' Centaine assured her. 'You have clearly taken pleasure in the meal, and what hostess or cook could possibly be offended by that? You poor thing. Are the rations in England very bad?'

'Well, it's not as if we starve,' Saffron said. 'It's more that we only get enough to survive on and the way one gets anything nice to eat is through the black market. So we do get the occasional treat. But nothing like this dinner. Do you know, I think that was the best meal I have eaten in my whole life!'

'In that case,' said Blaine, 'we had better let you digest it. Saffron, I was going to suggest that you and Shasa and I had a bit of a chat, just to go over a few things. But on reflection, I can't see the point of ruining a delightful evening. Darling, can we commandeer your study for a meeting tomorrow morning?'

'By all means,' Centaine replied.

'Excellent. Saffron, might I be able to interest you in a drop of brandy? Awfully good for the digestion, you know.'

'Excuse me, sir,' Shasa piped up. 'I believe we've neglected something. I won a bet today. Now I want to collect my winnings . . . in full.'

Centaine sighed theatrically. 'Must I?'

'In full,' Shasa repeated.

'If you insist . . .'

Centaine pushed back her chair. She stood up, squared her shoulders and raised her chin as she said, 'Darling Shasa, I apologise. You were right and I . . .' She let the silence hang over the table, so that the other four found themselves leaning forward in their eagerness to hear the fateful words. And when they came, no great actress could have delivered them with more intensity or defiant pride as Centaine declaimed, 'I was wrong.'

Blaine leaped to his feet. 'Bravo! Magnificently said!'

All eyes turned to Shasa as he rose and walked, straight-backed and handsome, around to his mother's place at the table, where she was seated once again.

He bowed before her, as seriously as if before his sovereign. 'Thank you, Mama. It is my great honour to accept your most gracious apology.'

Blaine nodded. 'Spoken like a gentleman. Honour has been satisfied all round. And now I really would like a drop of that brandy.'

• • •

Saffron felt weightless, as if gravity had been sloughed off, as if she was floating in the depths of the ocean. And then she was in mid-air with her arms outstretched, rolling and tumbling with the innocence of a child. A fighter plane plummeted in a dive towards her, its guttural roar deafening, its cockpit canopy open. It was Gerhard, waving to her. Then he was by her side, holding her so tightly that the air was expelled from her lungs and she thought she was going to pass out, but he held her safely, her head up, and he kissed her with such tenderness their breath became one. She had never known such happiness.

Saffron awoke, having had the best night's sleep in as long as she could remember. She retrieved her canvas shoulder bag from under the bed and took out the photograph of her and Gerard in front of the Eiffel Tower. His shirt was open, and she could almost feel the sensuous sheen of his silk cravat between her fingers. His smile was radiant, guileless, and she wanted to kiss those eyes that lit up her world and ignited her heart. She felt the stab of loss that memory always brings and suddenly Gerhard was unreachable, a dissolving speck in the sky, dipping in and out of darkening clouds. She brushed away a tear.

Downstairs she demolished a full English breakfast and another two cups of coffee, and went into her meeting with Blaine and Shasa full of renewed determination.

• • •

Blaine had allotted himself the place of honour, behind what was normally Centaine's desk. As she walked in, Saffron could see him moving a vase filled with a beautiful arrangement of freshly cut flowers out of the way, with the disapproving frown of someone who was not used to having his work surface cluttered with such fripperies. Shasa was seated in another chair.

'Morning, Saffron,' he said, catching sight of her. 'Take a pew. I've got a plane to catch to Jo'burg, so we'd better get straight down to business. I assume you got the details of the young woman that we sent you.'

'Yes . . . Marlize Marais . . . Poor girl,' Saffy replied. 'Her sad life-story was received safe and sound. We have a Belgian passport in her name, backdated to 1937. In my legend, Marlize grew up in Jo'burg, so I'll need to get it stamped again, and backdated at the Belgian Consulate General there. Apparently the consul is passionately anti-Nazi. He'll make sure everything's done and then forget it ever happened.'

'What do you need from us here?'

'To get as close as I can to the key men in Ossewabrandwag, and I have to get physical evidence of that, something a third party can hold and look at and see with their own eyes that this young woman really is a committed fascist.'

'Hmm . . .' Blaine gave the matter some thought and then looked at Saffron again, not as a devoted, avuncular friend of the family, but as a man involved in serious business. 'Look, I appreciate the need for security. I respect it too, and if I were this Gubbins fellow, who claims to be your boss—'

'He really is,' Saffron assured him.

'Then I'm sure he'd be pleased to know you were sticking to the letter of the rules. But there's no point having rules if they make it harder to run an effective operation. We will help you to the utmost of our abilities. But we can't do that unless we have more to go on.'

Saffron nodded. 'I can see that. And I know that I can count on both of you to do the right thing. But I have to decide where to draw the line . . .'

'I understand.'

'Well, then, I will say this much . . . For reasons that I cannot disclose, I plan to penetrate the pro-Nazi political parties in Flanders and then, through them, the Netherlands. First, though, I'm going to present myself, as Marlize Marais, to the Germans in Lisbon, telling them that I've come from South Africa and want to go to the Low Countries.'

'My God, that's cheeky, even by your standards!' said Shasa.

'Maybe, but I think it will be easier to persuade the Germans that I am Marlize if I turn up at their consulate in Lisbon as someone who wants to join their cause.'

'It'll make a change for the Jerries to have someone wanting to travel in their direction,' said Blaine. 'Lisbon's packed to the gunwales with people trying to get away from them. Not too many going the other way. You never know, they might be pleased to see you.'

'That's what I'm hoping. But the key to it is that they have to believe in the reality of Marlize Marais, a young woman who was born and raised in South Africa, but had a Flemish mother, now deceased. Marlize lost both her parents. For various reasons, she blames the British and the Jews for hurting her parents and causing their deaths. This has led her into fascist politics in South Africa. Now she wants to do her bit for the Nazi cause, and that of the Greater Netherlands, by travelling to her mother's homeland and working in the women's wings of the fascist parties.

'In order to establish her credentials, I want her to be carrying letters, photographs and so forth, clearly linking her to men here of whom the Nazis are aware. Ideally, I'd have my picture taken cosying up to a well-known fascist bigwig, and come clutching a letter from him, on headed paper, saying what a thoroughly good Nazi *mädchen* I am.'

'There's a minor problem in that a significant number of those bigwigs are now in detention,' said Blaine. 'I take it McGilvray told you about Koffiefontein?'

'Yes.'

'There's something else too, sir,' Shasa interjected. 'Saffy might be able to persuade a German or a Belgian that she was an Afrikaner maiden, but I'm not sure she could fool an Afrikaner.'

'I'm working on it,' Saffron assured him. 'I was going to say that it would be a great help if we spoke Afrikaans when we were talking about this.'

'Fair enough,' Shasa said, and switched languages, for, like most white South Africans, he was fluent in both tongues. 'It's not what you say, but how you act. Your attitude isn't quite right. You're too independent, too sophisticated.'

'And too single,' Blaine added. 'The kind of girl who believes in the ideas these people peddle also believe that her first duty to the cause is to get married and produce as many white babies as possible. She stays at home looking after them while her man goes to the meetings.'

'Hmm . . . What if I'd like to be making babies, but my man has been locked up in Koffiefontein? That would make me hate the British even more. I could say I was fighting in my way because he couldn't fight in his.'

'That could work,' Blaine conceded.

'But again, sir, only with the Germans,' Shasa pointed out. 'We've got about eight hundred members of various subversive groups under lock and key. That's not very many. It certainly wouldn't be difficult for someone here to check whether your man existed. We've done our best to make sure that none of the guards at Koffiefontein is on the same side as the internees, but I'd be amazed if one or two haven't slipped through our net.'

'The Germans would have a hard time checking, though, wouldn't they?' Blaine said. 'Or rather, they could, but it would mean taking a lot of trouble to check out a woman who posed no apparent threat.'

'There's no reason why I can't have two different versions of the story: one for here and one for when I get to Europe,' Saffy pointed out.

'Why can't Saffron write to one or two of the top OB men in Koffiefontein – you know, chaps like Vorster, Erasmus and van den Berg?' Shasa asked. 'She sends them a letter telling them how much she admires them, maybe she even puts in a picture to think about when they're all alone in their beds at night. If she had letters from them, all signed and everything, that would be a start.'

'If I had handwriting samples and the correct paper – blank sheets, I mean – that would be a great help. I could do a lot with that. And I got the impression from McGilvray that there were still some OB people you hadn't put in prison.'

'There are plenty. We only interred men who had either taken part in, or actively supported acts of criminality and subversion. We didn't arrest people just because they said they didn't like us.'

'Which brings us to Johannes van Rensburg. Am I right in thinking he's the top man?'

Blaine nodded.

'Does he attend any social events?' Saffron asked. 'I don't mean party rallies, but more informal occasions where a person might bump into him.'

'I'm sure he does, but I don't have his diary to hand.'

'Don't worry, Saffy,' said Shasa, 'we've got people in place who are very close to the OB leadership, in and out of prison. It shouldn't be too hard to find out what van Rensburg is up to.'

'Could I meet any of these people of yours? I have a feeling that would be useful. Even a couple of hours talking to someone who understands the way that the OB and organisations like them operate, the way they talk to one another, the slang they use . . . all that sort of thing would tell me more than any amount of notes in files.'

'I can't let you meet our undercover agents,' Blaine said. 'We too have security procedures and I can't take even the risk of compromising their cover. But I can put you in touch with people – journalists, academics and so forth – who can help. Remind me, what were you reading at Oxford?'

'Philosophy, Politics and Economics.'

'Perfect. You can say that you're working on an academic thesis about fascist politics in South Africa. We can also supply you with files on significant OB supporters and sympathisers, though you'll have to come to my office in Jo'burg to read them because they cannot leave the building. What else?'

'Well, Marlize will need a South African passport, of course, because she's got dual nationality, and a birth certificate. Oh, and can you recommend a photographer? If I'm going to send saucy letters to randy, sex-starved prisoners, I might as well do the job properly.'

SS-Haupsturmführer Dietrich Horst was an ambitious young officer. Though he only held the equivalent of an army captain's rank, he had every intention of rising to the highest reaches of the SS apparatus, as high, indeed, as the man on whose door he was now about to knock. Horst steeled himself. He was in no way responsible for the news he was bringing, but he lived in a world in which the old saying 'shoot the messenger' might literally come true. He had no alternative. He was the duty officer, and *Brigadeführer* Konrad von Meerbach was the man whose orders were required.

Horst knocked.

'Enter!' barked the voice from within.

Horst did as he was told. He grimaced inwardly. Von Meerbach was looking more red-faced with alcohol and bile than usual.

'What is it?' he demanded.

'I have a report from Taganrog, sir. An incident in a bar. It involves treasonable speech insulting the Führer.'

'Then what the hell are you doing bothering me with this trivia? Why wasn't it dealt with there and then?'

Horst's collar was feeling tight around his neck. 'Two reasons, sir. In the first place the only witness willing to talk is the owner of the establishment, a Ukrainian. He is a useful source of information.'

'There were other Germans there at the time of this incident?'

'Yes, sir.'

'Then get hold of them, take statements and tell them they had better describe what they saw and heard, or they'll face the same punishment as the traitor.'

'Yes, sir . . . but there's . . .' Horst felt the sweat prickling under his armpits. 'There's something else. The man who said the words in question was, ah . . . Luftwaffe *Oberstleutnant* Gerhard von Meerbach, sir . . . Your brother.'

'I know who my brother is, *Haupsturmführer*. I'm not a complete imbecile. But I fail to see why you are informing me of this incident . . .'

'Well, sir, there was a belief in Taganrog and here in Berlin that you should be told because . . . ah . . .'

'Because I would want to do my brother a favour? Is that what you are suggesting?'

'I wouldn't say that, sir.'

'But you would think it all the same. Evidently you, and the others, imagine that I am the sort of soft-hearted sentimentalist who puts his family before his duty. Is that it?'

'I didn't think at all, *Brigadeführer*, I was doing as I was commanded by—'

'Enough! I don't want to hear any more excuses or explanations. What did my brother say?'

'We don't have a transcript yet, sir. The proprietor's command of German is far from perfect, and he was in his office, behind the bar at the time. But he thought he heard – and he swore that his barman confirmed it – that *Oberstleutnant* von Meerbach described the Führer as . . .' Horst paused. It shocked and terrified him to say the next words, even though they were not his. 'He described the Führer as "goddamned", he suggested that the Führer had lied about what was happening in Stalingrad and he called the Führer's sanity into question.'

'How exactly?'

'The proprietor wasn't sure, but he thought your . . . *Oberstleutnant* von Meerbach called the Führer a maniac, or a crazy person. Something like that.'

'Something like that . . . but he can't be sure because he's a snivelling, shit-for-brains Ukrainian sub-human and you don't have any proper German witnesses.'

'Well, it's not me, sir, it's Taganrog.'

'I know who it is!' shouted von Meerbach, smashing his fist on his desktop. "It's a bunch of incompetent, gutless officers who failed to do their duty and investigate an incident of treason-speech because they were frightened that I might object. Wouldn't you agree, Horst?'

'Yes, sir.'

'And now, because they sat on their arses doing nothing, all the men who were in that bar are now back with their units and we won't be able to track them down without combing the entire Army Group South warzone!' Von Meerbach's fist pounded onto the desk again. 'In the middle of the Russian winter! . . . With the damned Ivans attacking along the whole . . . length . . . of the front!'

Horst winced with each further crash of the *Brigadeführer*'s fist.

'I agree that the effort required would be considerable, sir,' he said, in a bid to pacify him.

'It would be disproportionate to the nature of the accusation,' said von Meerbach. 'It would be a fault the other way, on my part. People might say that I was pursuing some kind of grudge or vendetta against my brother.'

Horst knew better than to comment on that. He asked, 'So how would you like to proceed, sir?'

Von Meerbach sat back in his chair to consider the question, then responded, 'Have our people in Taganrog get the word out to all SD and Gestapo officers in the *Reichskommissariat* Ukraine that *Oberleutnant* von Meerbach is to be regarded as a potential threat to the Reich. Make sure he is watched. Have any suspicious activities, or improper opinions, noted, with witness statements. Keep a file on my brother. He has a long record of actions hostile to the state. He will trip himself up eventually. And then, Horst . . .'

'Yes, sir?'

'Then we will get him.'

'**M**orning, Vorster,' said the camp guard, handing out the mail. 'Looks like it's your lucky day, mate. Marlize has added you to her list. Thinks you're a general, too, the daft bint.'

At once the other men who slept in the bunks near Balthazar Johannes Vorster, prisoner No.2229/42 in Hut 48, Camp 1, of the Koffiefontein Detention Centre, clustered around him. They pushed and shoved for a better view of the large pink envelope, addressed in a rounded, girlish script and sprayed with an intense rose scent, that Vorster held in his hand. The envelope had already been opened and its contents examined by the camp's censors. It had been posted by a young woman called Marlize Marais, whom every man in the hut, and the others alongside it, now knew as Mooi Marlize, *'mooi'* being the Afrikaner word for 'pretty', for this was the third letter she had sent to the camp, as part of what appeared to be a one-woman campaign to improve morale among its inmates.

Vorster did not betray any signs of excitement. Another of the lawyers who were prominent in the ranks of Afrikaner politics, both legitimate and revolutionary, he had enjoyed a stellar start to his career. In his early twenties he had been clerk to the president of the South African Supreme Court, and within a few years had founded two law firms before his devotion to the Afrikaner cause began to outweigh his legal ambitions. Having joined the Ossewabrandwag in the early days, he had attained the rank of general within the organisation, yet claimed to have had no hand in the many acts of sabotage and criminality carried out by the OB's *Stormjaear* assault troops.

Vorster was a big, barrel-chested man. He had neat, dark hair swept back from a high forehead, the base of which, like bushes on a cliffside, sprouted a brace of thick black eyebrows. His face was fleshy, his eyes sharp, his normal expression stern. Yet he was still a young man, who had only celebrated his twenty-seventh birthday a couple of months earlier, and he could not suppress a degree of curiosity as he opened the envelope.

He pulled out the ten-by-eight-inch black and white photograph. As in the two previous photographs that she had sent his fellow inmates, Mooi Marlize was engaged in the good, clean exercise that was appropriate for a fascist maiden entering her prime breeding years. She wore the same costume that they had all seen in the newsreels of Nazi maidens cavorting for Herr Goebbels' cameramen: a short, white, sleeveless singlet, tight at the top, but flared at the hips to form a hint of a skirt that fluttered over a pair of matching white gym-knickers.

As Goebbels had been aware, this was an outfit that was virginal, redolent of healthy sporting activity – and flagrantly sexual. Marlize had grasped the point, because she had been photographed out of doors on a summer's day, smiling happily, with her legs apart, holding a large hoop above her head. The sex-starved camp inmates were treated to a splendid view of her breasts, lifted jauntily by her rising arms. They could run their eyes all the way up her long, sunkissed bare legs and, because her skirt had risen higher than usual, they could linger on the view between her legs, where her fresh white cotton pants pressed tightly against her crotch, folding with her flesh so that they could practically reach out and run a finger along the full length of the inviting gap between her labia.

'Oh, Jesus,' a man gasped. He turned, ignored the furious look that his blasphemy provoked from Vorster, and ran off like a startled hare, desperate to be first into the hut's only toilet cubicle. He wanted to derive the maximum pleasure from Mooi Marlize while her image was still fresh in his mind.

Vorster allowed the men to pass the photograph around, so that each man could feast his eyes. As much as he disliked pandering to baser instincts, he was enough of a realist to know that it would be good for their morale. When the picture was returned to him, he put it back in the envelope, saving it for private contemplation later. His attention turned to the letter.

Dear General Vorster,

I hope you do not mind that I wrote to the others first. But I was thinking of those wonderful Olympic Games in Berlin. The gold medal was always the last to be handed out. Of all the heroes who have been rounded up by the cruel British, you are the most important. So I give you the position of greatest honour!!

I know it is crazy! I am just an ordinary girl and you are one of the greatest, most important men in all South Africa. What right do I have to say anything to you? How can I expect you to pay any attention to little me? I cannot! But I am writing to you anyway because I want you to know that you are not forgotten.

Your courage and your suffering inspire me. I, too, believe that South Africa belongs to the people who have built our nation. My father's ancestors were Voortrekkers. My great-grandfather fought under Pretorius at Blood River. What right do blacks and Jews and British have to take away what we white Christian Afrikaners created?

I know that it is my duty to be a mother, so that I can raise more strong young men to defend our people. War and politics are men's work! But when the men are taken away, then the women must stand up in their place. So I want to do my part, before giving myself to my duties as a wife and a mother.

My mother, who died when I was sixteen, was Flemish. She always used to tell me about the bond between all the Dutch-speaking peoples, and of the close racial connection between we Dutch and our German cousins. I do not know how, but I want to help make that bond stronger, because we all believe in the same things and stand for the same ideals.

In the meantime, I can only say the words of 'Die Stem' –

We will answer your calling
We will offer what you ask
We will live, we will die,
We for thee, South Africa

I hope that maybe I have cheered your spirits a little bit. I send
you my very best wishes and pray for your release.
Yours sincerely,
Marlize Marais

Vorster considered this text with lawyerly detachment. What conclusions could he deduce from the evidence in front of him? It was clear both from its appearance and the quality of the Afrikaans in which it was written that the letter was the work of a young woman who possessed a modest degree of education. She was by no means stupid, but was neither intellectual nor sophisticated. Vorster considered these to be points in her favour. An attractive, healthy young woman, with plenty of common sense and an understanding of her true purpose, was always to be preferred to some over-educated, pampered, neurotic and decadent madam whose head was filled with ideas she could not possibly understand.

Granted, Miss Marais had ideas whirling around in her mind too. Her dream of uniting the Dutch peoples against their British enemies was patently absurd coming from an unknown Afrikaner girl, as if she were a South African Joan of Arc. But the principle was a sound one and in line with the sort of thing one heard coming from the mouths of senior men within the OB hierarchy. Vorster wondered for a moment whether this girl might have family connections with the movement. The fact that she referred to him as 'General Vorster' suggested that. His OB rank had been mentioned in newspaper coverage of his arrest as a means of justifying his detention. She had noticed and remembered, which suggested that she had a strong identification with the cause.

Unless the whole thing was a joke, or even a trap. Was someone in the Smuts government trying to trick him into revealing beliefs and allegiances that he had hitherto been careful to keep under wraps? Or were they trying to provoke him into writing something that could be used to threaten his marriage, or even leave him open to blackmail? Vorster doubted that either of these possibilities was realistic. Smuts was a damn traitor, a Boer commander who had betrayed his own people by reconciling with the British. He'd even campaigned for English to be the sole official language of South Africa. But he, too, had studied law. He believed in doing things correctly. As for those plum-in-mouth men at the Interior Ministry, Malcomess and his one-eyed sidekick Courtney, they would never have the cunning, or imagination, to set up some kind of entrapment scheme. They'd think it was beneath them.

On balance, Vorster concluded that the letter was genuine. He felt beholden to write a short, sober reply to Miss Marais. It made no mention of her physical appearance, since that would be both unwise and unseemly. Vorster took care to avoid direct expressions of support for Nazism or the German war effort, since that would be bound to catch the censor's eye. He thanked her for her support, congratulated her on her appreciation of what was best for her people and the country they loved, and wished her success in her efforts to bring unity and mutual understanding to the Dutch-speaking peoples of Europe and Africa, mentioning the Germans only in the most general and passing terms. He allowed the photograph of Mooi Marlize to be stuck onto one of the walls of the hut, for the benefit of his men, but he barely glanced at it himself.

B. J. Vorster dreamed of being the dictator of a one-party, Afrikaner state. He had much bigger things to think about than the fate of a young woman.

• • •

Saffron perched on the edge of Shasa's desk, in his office at the Interior Ministry, as she read Vorster's letter aloud. "'I share your belief in the supremacy of the white, Christian race, the common bond between the Dutch-speaking peoples, and the natural, racial affinity between them and the Germanic population.

May I wish you every success in your endeavours to promote this honourable cause . . ." Honestly, it'll be meat and drink.'

'I think you hit the jackpot with that, Saffy,' Shasa agreed. 'A hand-written letter from the great white hope of Afrikaner fascism, written on cheap prison notepaper and addressed from the Koffiefontein Detention Centre – and it specifically mentions the Dutch. Honestly, I don't think you could have done any better. It'll be meat and drink to all your Flemish and Dutch Nazis. They'll welcome you to the fold like a long-lost child.'

'It saves me the trouble of having to forge the thing myself.'

Shasa laughed. 'My God, Saffy, is there any dirty trick you don't know?'

'I haven't told you the half of it,' she replied cheerfully, while behind her smile she was thinking, *Darling Shasa, I haven't even told you a quarter.*

'Then the Special Operations Executive has trained you well.'

Saffron's eyes widened, her mouth dropped open and with a hoot of triumph Shasa crowed, 'You should see the look on your face!'

'How . . . how did you know . . . I'm sure I didn't . . .'

'No, you were very good. You maintained perfect discipline. Blaine and I were impressed . . . honestly, we were.'

'Then . . . ?'

'*Ou Baas* is not only a member of the Imperial War Cabinet and a Field Marshal in the British Army, he's been a close colleague and friend of Mr Churchill for thirty years. And you will be glad to hear that Winston has a soft spot for your outfit. He rates Gubbins damn highly, too. The word went out that if Gubbins wanted us to help you, then Winnie himself would see it as a great kindness. Smuts called Blaine and said, "Give this agent whatever she needs." We've got orders to push the boat out for you . . . literally.'

Shasa set out a journey, planned down to the last detail, that would get Saffron, in her guise as Marlize, from Cape Town to the port of Walvis Bay, on the Atlantic coast of South-West Africa, complete with a travel permit, issued because she claimed to need to go there to care for a dying grandmother.

'Of course, you don't need a permit to go anywhere in South Africa, or the colony of South-West Africa, but the Jerries don't know that and they probably wouldn't believe it,' Shasa said. 'We've arranged for a freighter bound for Luanda, in Portuguese Angola, to take you aboard as a passenger for cash. From there you can catch a ship to Lisbon. You'll be there by the end of the month.'

'That's wonderful, thank you so much!' Saffron leaned across the desk and planted a kiss on Shasa's face. 'What a wonderful cousin you are,' she said, before pushing herself back up. 'Would it be too much to ask about Marlize's identity papers?'

'Not at all,' Shasa replied. He searched through a pile of papers in a wire tray on his desk and pulled out a large envelope, which he passed to Saffron.

'Open it . . . You'll find the birth certificate of Marlize Christien Marais, genuine and proof against any investigation . . . until someone thinks of asking whether she has a death certificate. Along with that we have a genuine South African passport in her name, but with your photograph, and an almost genuine Belgian passport, issued by their South African consulate.

'So,' Shasa concluded, 'you've got almost everything you need.'

'Only van Rensburg to go.'

'Ah yes,' said Shasa, with the grin of a man who has been keeping one final piece of good news up his sleeve. 'I think we've managed to get you the sort of thing you need. The law faculty of the University of Pretoria is throwing a dinner and dance for its former alumni. It happens to be twenty years since van Rensburg received his Masters there, so he has accepted the invitation.'

Shasa pulled one of his desk drawers open and took out a piece of white card, covered in embossed, copper-plate print. 'This is your stiffy, inviting you to be a guest of the law faculty. Yes, dear Cinders, you shall go to the ball!'

• • •

A few days later, Saffron was in the august hall of the University of Pretoria. The crowded room reverberated with the low hum of self-importance and occasionally the higher register of feminine approval. Shortly after the last after-dinner toast had been proposed and the band prepared to strike up the first dance, Saffron took a bead on Johannes van Rensburg. Like a hunter lining up a shot, she strode across the banqueting-room floor towards him. She was wearing a strapless black evening gown that displayed her charms in a manner that had many of the older, more conservative female guests hissing in disapproval, though their menfolk seemed to find less fault. For Saffron this was a small mission in itself and a rehearsal for the more serious challenges to come. For the first time in her life, she was playing a role and she wanted to get it right.

Van Rensburg's wife had disappeared, along with a couple of the other women from their table. The three of them would be gone some time, Saffron reckoned, as they queued for the loos, used them, repaired their faces and finished their gossiping. Van Rensburg was sitting by himself, smoking a cigarette and nursing a glass of brandy. He looked like a man enjoying his temporary solitude.

Sorry, buster. No more peace and quiet for you, I'm afraid.

'Excuse me,' Saffron began, in a sharp, high-pitched voice that any South African would recognise as the whine of a privileged female member of the country's British community. 'Are you that van Rensburg fellow?'

Van Rensburg closed his eyes for a second, as if asking God to give him strength. Then he placed his glass on the table, stubbed out his cigarette and got to his feet, for he could hardly remain seated in the presence of a lady.

'Johannes van Rensburg at your service, madam,' he said, speaking English, with a thick Afrikaner accent. He was in his mid-forties, quite tall and held his head high, with an air of self-importance. 'Might I ask whom I have the pleasure of addressing?'

'Petronella Fordyce,' she said, with as inane a grin as she could manage.

'Good evening, Miss Fordyce, but please, I am not sure why you have, ah, blessed me with your company.'

'Oh gosh! Sorry, of course, silly me, I should have explained myself. Well, it's very simple. I think you're absolutely spot-on . . . with your opinions, I mean.'

Van Rensburg looked at her with a cautious frown. 'What opinions would those be?'

'About racial superiority and all that.' Saffron tilted her head conspiratorially towards van Rensburg and said, 'Look, of course I want us to win the war and so forth. I'm jolly well not a traitor . . .'

'Of course not.'

'But Herr Hitler has some very sound ideas about race.'

'I concur. I studied in Germany some years ago and was able to observe affairs there at first hand. I believe that the effects of National Socialism were overwhelmingly positive.'

'Well, he's right about the Hebrews. Ghastly people. But of course, for those of us here in South Africa, the real problem is the blacks. We can't have them getting the vote, or being educated at the same schools as us, or living in houses like ours, can we?'

'Not in my view, no.'

'It would be a disaster. They wouldn't have the first idea how to run a country. We have to have a white South Africa. It's the only way.'

'That's very perceptive of you, Miss Fordyce.'

'Gosh, thank you! All my chums in Sandown will be fearfully impressed that you think I'm perceptive!'

'Sandown, eh?' said van Rensburg. 'That's a very nice part of the world. Big houses, lots of money, stables and paddocks everywhere. What is it they call you, the "mink and manure set"?'

He spoke in what was intended to be a light-hearted style, but Saffron could hear the resentment and suppressed hatred in his voice. She ignored it, however, and brayed, 'Personally, I can't abide the smell of horse-droppings, but I do love a nice new fur coat!'

As van Rensburg gave a condescending smile, Saffron frowned, in the manner of a stupid person attempting to seem thoughtful. 'Look here, I quite understand that you speak for your people, but there are plenty of us on our side of the fence – British people, I mean – who wish that some of our leaders spoke the way that chaps like you do. I think you're a bit of a hero, actually.'

'Thank you . . .' A more contented look was coming over van Rensburg's face, for few middle-aged men can resist being flattered by a beautiful young woman.

'Look, I know this is very forward, but could I possibly ask you to sign my menu card, please? It really would be such a splendid souvenir.'

'Of course.'

Saffron handed over a menu, with the plain side up, and van Rensburg wrote his signature. He paused, his pen hovering over the blank white surface for a moment before adding some more words. When he passed her the card, Saffron saw that he had written: *My God, My Volk, My Land, My Suid-Afrika*, the motto of the Ossewabrandwag.

'Now, if you will excuse me,' van Rensburg said. 'It has been a pleasure meeting you.'

He stuck out his hand and, as Saffron shook it, smiling broadly, a camera flashed. She turned to look at the photographer, still smiling, and he took another shot before disappearing off into the crowd to capture more of the revellers on film. They were all happy to pose for him, for everyone knew that the photographs would be put on sale to provide souvenirs of the happy occasion.

• • •

'Who was the woman throwing herself at you, Hans – the one dressed like a whore?' Louise van Rensburg asked her husband as she returned to the table.

'Some Englishwoman,' he said, hoping his indifference would save him. 'She said she was interested in my political opinions.'

'Ha!' his wife snorted. 'That strumpet may be interested in many things, but I promise you politics is not one of them.'

'*Ja* . . . you may very well be right,' van Rensburg replied. 'Excuse me, my dear, but I think I see Charl du Preez over there. I just want to have a quick word with him. In private.'

Louise van Rensburg took her seat, satisfied that her words had hit their mark as Johannes made his way across the room towards a tall, grey-haired figure, who greeted him with a broad smile and a warm handshake. She saw how quickly the other man's expression changed as Hans started talking to him about the Englishwoman and smiled contentedly. *Now you're going to find out what happens to little vixens who try to interfere with my marriage*, she thought.

A waiter was gliding between the tables with a silver platter bearing glasses of brandy. 'Cognac, madam?' he asked.

'*Ja*,' Louise replied. 'A large one, if you please.'

Across the room, Charl du Preez, who held the rank of Deputy Commissioner in the South African Police, was nodding his head as van Rensburg finished his account of recent events.

'You're a lucky man, Hans, to have a wife who looks out for you the way Louise does. I think she's right. I smell a rat. Someone has been trying to get at you in some way. It could be blackmail, could just be political intrigue. These pictures of you with this girl . . .'

'I didn't even know they were going to be taken . . .'

'Ah, listen, I know you did nothing wrong, but we can both see how they could give a bad impression. But don't worry. We are old friends and, more importantly, we are of one mind on the issues that matter. Just leave it to me, eh? By the time the night is out, I will have answers for you.'

'Thank you, Charl. I won't forget this.'

• • •

Charl du Preez had arranged for a number of his men to pick up extra overtime for acting as traffic control, car-parking attendants and doormen at the event. One of them, a sergeant called Dawie Visser, was standing by the door to the banqueting hall. He had fifteen years' service and, more importantly, strong support for Nationalist, and even OB, policies.

It was clear from his flushed complexion and the concentration with which he snapped to attention at the senior officer's approach that Visser had been indulging in plenty of the alcoholic refreshment that the event had to offer. But he was a big, strong, experienced individual. Du Preez felt sure that he could handle his drink like a man.

'Hey, Visser, come here,' he ordered.

'On my way, *baas*,' Dawie Visser replied.

'Have you seen a young lady leave here in the last few minutes: tall, slender, black hair, blue eyes, black dress . . . showing a lot on top, if you get my meaning.'

Visser grinned. 'Oh, *ja*, I saw her all right. A little skinny for me, but she's a real little *boer* . . . you could smell it on her.'

'Well, I need you to get close enough to smell her again. Is your pal Piet Momberg still on parking duty?'

'*Ja*, he should be.'

'Then he'll know the car she left in. Take him and go after it . . . This woman said her name was Fordyce and she lived in Sandown, so she'll be on the Jo'burg road.' Du Preez looked Visser in the eye. 'Got that? Not too drunk to do your job?'

'Not me, *baas* . . . Never.'

'Then catch that woman. I know she was up to no good. You just find out what her game was and report back to me – directly to me.'

'This is unofficial?'

'Strictly.'

'You won't mind if we arm ourselves . . . as self-protection?'

'Whatever it takes, Visser. Just get it done.'

• • •

It was past midnight and the Johannesburg road was deserted when Saffron saw the lights in her rear-view mirror. She thought nothing of it, but then the lights drew nearer until she had to tilt her head away from her rear-view mirror to rid her eyes of the glare.

She sped up, hoping to get away from the dazzling light, but the car behind her kept pace. This wasn't another late-night driver. Someone was following her.

Saffron accelerated again. Shasa had loaned her a Ford Prefect from a collection of vehicles, seized during criminal investigations that were used for undercover work. It was a sturdy, comfortable vehicle, well-suited to an affluent house-wife. But it was no racing machine and as hard as she pressed the accelerator to the floor, it would not go faster than sixty miles-per-hour.

The car behind her came closer, then moved out into the other lane until it had drawn level. It stayed beside Saffron, matching her pace whether she sped up or slowed down. The word 'POLICE' was written on the passenger door and a man in uniform was looking out of the window, studying her while another policeman beside him manned the wheel.

There was something hostile about his gaze. He was trying to intimidate her and for a second he succeeded. Saffron felt a prickle of fear. She told herself to buck up. *Pull yourself together, girl. You've seen much worse than this.*

Then the police car disappeared and when she looked in her mirror, the lights were behind her again. Fear was replaced by relief. Had your fun, have you? Bored of gawping at a lone woman?

The headlights behind her came closer again and they were joined by the blue lights flashing from the roof of the police car. There was a brief wail of the siren, the headlights blinking repeatedly.

Saffron had no option. She slowed down and pulled over to the side of the road.

The police car came to a halt behind Saffron. The two officers emerged and began walking towards her. She glanced in the back mirror. They were big men, visible only as hefty silhouettes back-lit by the beams from their headlights. But that was enough to tell her that they were both armed: one with a pistol, the other holding a double-barrelled shotgun across his body.

South African police did not carry firearms on their regular duties. Whoever had sent these two was working off the books.

Saffron turned her eyes away from the mirror, not wanting to lose what remained of her night vision. She heard the policemen's footsteps, one on the tarmac to her right, the other on the gravelly earth at the passenger side of the car.

The man on that side marched around the front of the car and stood about ten yards in front of her bonnet. He was carrying the shotgun. He raised it to his shoulder and pointed it at her. He didn't say anything. The threat was self-evident: try to drive away and I'll blow your head off.

There was a sharp, metallic sound in her ear as the other policeman tapped the driver's side window with the tip of the pistol barrel. He made a few circles in the air with the barrel.

'Roll down the window,' he ordered.

She did as she was told. The policeman bent his head towards the car. He was thick-necked, with a fleshy face, and there was sweat across his brow.

'Show me your licence,' he ordered and the pungent odour of alcohol, cigarette smoke and halitosis hit her like a gas attack.

'I don't have it on me,' Saffron said, cursing herself for her lack of thoroughness. She hadn't counted on maintaining her Petronella Fordyce identity for any longer than it took to get van Rensburg's signature on a piece of paper and his face in front of the party photographer, who was one of Shasa's men. She would have to bluff it out.

'I'm awfully sorry,' she drawled, slipping into Petronella's spoiled, mink-and-manure accent. 'But I must have left it in another handbag.'

'Get out. And don't try any funny stuff, hey?'

He was speaking English, but the accent was Afrikaner. Saffron knew the type. If he wasn't raised on a farm, his parents had been. He'd have no love at all for the British and even less for rich *rooineks* who had made their money on land that belonged to his people.

'Now look here, officer,' Saffron protested. 'My husband is a close friend of your commissioner and I can assure you he—'

'Shut up, you lying bitch,' the policeman snarled. 'Don't fool with us.'

Saffron took a step towards the policeman.

'Hey, I said no funny stuff!' he shouted, raising his gun until the barrel was pointing at Saffron's chest, two feet away from her. 'Put your hands up!'

Saffron raised her arms. So far, it was all going perfectly.

'I've got you covered, Dawie!' the other cop shouted, edging around the front of the car.

'Don't you worry, Piet,' Dawie said. 'I can handle this bitch by my . . .'

Saffron had been watching his eyes. For a fraction of a second they were distracted. He couldn't help glancing towards his pal. It was basic human nature.

'. . . self,' Saffron muttered, finishing the sentence as she swung her right arm down hard onto Dawie's right wrist, pushing the gun away and twisting her body to the left, out of his firing line, pulling Dawie between her and Piet.

The pistol fired. The shot flew past Saffron and hit the car behind her as she brought her left hand onto the pistol and grabbed it firmly.

The barrel, still hot from the blast, was now sticking out between her thumb and forefinger. Her other fingers were wrapped around the front of the trigger housing. Her right arm was still around the policeman's wrist with her manicured nails digging into his skin.

Dawie was screaming incoherent curses. His partner Piet was shouting, 'I'll shoot! I'll shoot!'

They were both drunk. Saffron could not rely on them to behave rationally.

Having grasped the gun, her instinct, honed by hours of training at Arisaig, was to smash her knee into her opponent's crotch. But the long evening dress made that impossible, so Saffron improvised and raised her high-heeled foot as high as she could and then slammed it down onto the top of Dawie's foot.

He howled in pain. He bent over, facing Saffron, with his back towards his partner. As his grip on the pistol relaxed. Saffron wrenched the gun from Dawie's hand.

Piet saw that Saffron was now armed.

Dawie, hopping on one leg, straightened his back, blocking the view between Saffron and Piet.

At that same moment, Piet fired.

The full blast of a 12-bore shell, at point-blank range, ripped into Dawie's back, punching him forward.

Saffron threw herself out of the way as his body toppled like a chopped tree. She did her best to execute a controlled fall and roll, as Piet fired another wild blast where she had been standing. He missed.

By the time she had got back on her feet, with the pistol held out in front of her, Piet had thrown his gun away, collapsed to

his knees and was whimpering, 'Dawie, *boetie* . . . I'm so sorry . . .
I'm so sorry . . .'

Saffron walked towards him. 'Get up.'

He lifted his head, saw her standing over him with his partner's gun pointing down at his face and unleashed a short,
sharp stream of profanities.

Saffron whipped the gun barrel viciously across his temple.

Piet howled in pain, and crouched down with his hands raised
to his head in self-protection.

'Get up,' Saffron ordered him, stepping back, away from his
reach, but with the pistol still aimed towards the grovelling
policeman.

The gun was a Webley Mark VI revolver, standard issue for
British and Commonwealth troops during the First World
War, carrying six .455 rounds in its chamber. Saffron was
familiar with it from her small-arms training. It felt pleasantly
comforting.

Piet got to his feet, holding the side of his head.

'Do you have any handcuffs?' she asked.

He nodded.

'Cuff yourself . . . Do it!'

Piet began fumbling at the handcuffs with clumsy fingers.

Just then a terrible, scarcely human moan drifted across the
night air. The shotgun blast had not been fatal.

'Dawie!' Piet cried and took a step towards him.

Saffron fired a shot into the ground an inch in front of him.

'Cuff yourself,' she repeated.

'He needs help, you heartless bitch!'

'We can't help him. Put on the cuffs and I'll call for someone
who can.'

Piet looked at her furiously, muttered another expletive but
obeyed her command.

'Now walk, nice and steadily, to the back of your car.'

That meant walking past Dawie. His back had been blasted
away and a gaping hole revealed a horrific sight of minced flesh,

splintered bone and pulsing blood. Dawie moaned again, more softly this time, and his legs twitched feebly.

'Oh Jesus,' Piet said, then bent forward and threw up over the front of his shirt, down his trousers and onto his legs.

'Keep walking,' Saffron said, barely glancing at the wounded man.

They reached the police car. 'Wait,' Saffron ordered. Keeping her eyes on Piet, she switched the gun into her left hand, leaned towards the car and grabbed the keys, which were still in the ignition.

Piet had not tried to run away. He was being sick again.

'Move,' she told him. They moved to the rear of the car. 'Open the boot.'

He fumbled with the handle, then stepped back as the boot swung up.

'Get in.'

Piet was about to protest but thought better of it. He got in and curled into a foetal position.

Saffron slammed the boot shut, then locked it. She wiped the keys thoroughly on her dress and then dropped them on the ground by the car.

She cleaned the gun, and, holding it by the barrel, with the fabric of her skirt between her fingers and the metal, she placed it in Dawie's hand and closed his fingers around the handle.

There were no signs of life now. There was nothing to be done for him. If he wasn't dead, he soon would be.

Saffron leaned into the car again and turned off the headlights. She opened the glove compartment. There was a chamois leather inside. She wiped every surface she might have touched, replaced the chamois in the compartment, which she closed with the back of her hand.

Then she walked to her car, climbed in and drove away.

• • •

Saffron stayed the night at the Courtney family home out-side Jo'burg. Shasa was waiting for her when she arrived. He'd promised to stay up until she returned from Pretoria, to make sure that she was all right.

The moment he saw Saffron, he knew from the look on her face that something had gone wrong

'What happened?'

'My cover was blown. I don't know how, but van Rensburg must have guessed there was something fishy going on. Does he have friends in the police?'

'Almost certainly. Close to the top. Why?'

Saffron told him what had happened, leaving nothing out, making a point of describing where the shotgun, with Piet's fingerprints all over it, would be found.

'So the body is there, the murder weapon is there and the killer is in the boot,' Shasa said, wanting to make sure he'd got the essential details correct.'

'They were there about half an hour ago. What do you think we should do about it?'

'Let's think this through . . . Did this man Piet intend to kill the other policeman?'

'No . . . he was aiming at me.'

'So it was an accident, manslaughter at worst. Which means we can bury it with a clean conscience.'

'How do you plan to do that?'

'Simple . . . Somewhere high up in the South African Police is a senior officer who does not want it to be known that he sent a man to his death as a favour to his friend Dr van Rensburg. Agreed?'

'Why else would those two policemen have chased after me?'

'Exactly . . . And somewhere high up in the Ministry of Justice are a minister and his son-in-law who don't want any-one looking too closely into why a woman was present under a false identity at a university event, trying to chat the same van Rensburg up.'

'That's true.'

'We also have a police officer who doesn't want the world to know he shot his own partner while drunk on duty.'

'Not to mention that he and his partner were both over-powered by a woman . . .'

'Correct . . . Now, it is not good for justice to be impeded or perverted. In fact, it's a crime. But this was an accidental shooting. No member of the public was harmed, and the only person who could make a complaint would be you . . .'

'Which I have no intention of doing.'

'I say we give Dawie a full police funeral, as befits a man shot in the line of duty by thieves he interrupted in the course of a crime. We pack Piet off to Koffiefontein. That will keep him out of the way and he'll hardly complain about it if all other charges against him mysteriously disappear. We find out who gave the orders to the policemen and suggest that his retire-ment on health grounds, on a full pension, naturally, would be a good idea. And hey presto – nothing ever happened.'

Saffron smiled at her cousin. 'And people say I'm cold-blooded and calculating . . .'

Shasa returned a piratical grin. 'Nonsense! You're the most adorable creature in the world. But you're a Courtney . . . and you know what we're like.'

'Rogues and scoundrels, every one of us.'

'We've sorted out my end. What about yours?'

'It's time I made a discreet exit. I'll get the first train to Cape Town in the morning. That should get me in by lunchtime on Monday. I've got all the Marlize Marais stuff at Weltevreden. I'll pick it up and aim to be on a boat to Walvis Bay by nightfall.'

'I'll make sure there's a skipper waiting for you at Cape Town. And don't go to Mater's place. Probably best not to get her involved. I'll make sure everything is collected and brought to your boat.'

'Thank you, Shasa, you're a darling.'

'Hang on!' he said, as a thought struck him. 'What about the photographs that were taken this evening – won't you need those?'

'Send them care of the post office at Walvis Bay. I'll pick them up there. Now can I ask you one last favour?'

'Of course, whatever you need.'

'Is there a typewriter anywhere in the house? I need to write a letter, signed by van Rensburg. It could make all the difference to Marlize.'

The army officer who witnessed Gerhard's anti-Hitler speech and took down his name for future reference was Colonel Heinrich Graf von Sickert. The following day he called up an old school friend who was on the staff of the Fourth Air Fleet and made inquiries about Gerhard. A few days later, his friend called back with his findings.

Von Sickert did not find Gerhard's family background as impressive as some might. To a man of his aristocratic Prussian lineage, the von Meerbachs were newcomers to the world of wealth and social privilege. Gerhard's war record, however, was impeccable and perfect for von Sickert's purposes. He decided to make further enquiries among contacts in Berlin and Munich.

In early March, he had an opportunity to share his findings with a likeminded soul.

After a disastrous December and January, the tide had unexpectedly turned in the Wehrmacht's favour. In the south, Field Marshall Erich von Manstein had overseen a series of armoured assaults, executed with blitzkrieg vigour, which took back much of the territory seized by the Russians after the Battle of Stalingrad. Now von Manstein was preparing a new campaign, and the Führer had flown to the Ukrainian town of Zaporozhye, to bring what he saw as his unique military genius to bear on the next stage of operations.

In the improved mood, there was more time for socialising among the officers who were present. This enabled von Sickert to have a word with another old friend, a staff officer called Kleinhof from Army Group Centre. They armed themselves with schnapps and cigarettes and found a couple of armchairs tucked away in the corner of a reception room.

'I think I've found a possible recruit,' he said. 'Man called Gerhard von Meerbach.'

'One of the von Meerbachs who make engines?' Kleinhof asked.

'Yes, younger brother of the current head of the family.'

'You mean that fat swine Konrad? Are you sure your man is on our side? The older brother's a diehard SS man. He was Heydrich's toady-in-chief, and now has his thick skull rammed up Himmler's backside.'

'I'm informed that the two brothers have never been close. Young Gerhard never showed enthusiasm for the Party. He was an architectural student, more of a lefty, bohemian type. But then something happened, no one's quite sure what, but suddenly Gerhard had joined the Party and was working in Speer's architectural practice.'

'He couldn't have got that job unless he had the official seal of approval.'

'Quite so. But even then, a lot of people got the impression that the good-Nazi act was put on for show,' von Sickert said. 'They assumed brother Konrad had insisted on it for the good of the family business.'

Kleinhof nodded. 'Everyone was at it. Steel companies, Krupp and Thyssen, and all their friends were buttering up the Nazis like mad. Hardly surprising: the state was their biggest customer.'

'Then again, it's possible that von Meerbach was sincere in his beliefs until he saw what was happening here in Russia.'

'God knows that's enough to change anyone's mind.'

'He was at Stalingrad, right through the campaign. Von Richtofen didn't pull his last aircraft out till mid-January.'

'He should count himself lucky to survive.'

'Well, that's the thing. I happened to be in a bar in Taganrog about a month ago. Von Meerbach was there. I gather he'd recently discovered that his wingman had died of injuries received at Stalingrad. Then some damn fool of an infantry-man came up and called him a coward.'

'I'd horse whip any man who said that to me.'

'Von Meerbach didn't do that. But he laid into him verbally, I can assure you.'

Von Sickert gave a full account of everything Gerhard had said, keeping his voice as low as he could. It would hardly do to be overheard when the Führer was in the same building.

'Are you sure it wasn't just the drink talking?' Kleinhof asked.

'No.' Von Sickert shook his head. 'I considered that possibility. But in the first place, von Meerbach wasn't that drunk. A little tight, maybe, and he was angry at being insulted. But he knew what he was saying. One could tell from the way he looked around, almost daring anyone to disagree with him.'

'And did they?'

'Not so much as a whisper.'

'That says something too, you know.'

'I agree. But the impression I got from von Meerbach was of a man who was saying things that had been on his mind for some time, and not giving a damn about the consequences.'

'Well, if that's true,' Kleinhof said, 'then I agree that he is worth following up. I tell you what, when I get back to HQ, I'll have a word with Henning von Tresckow and we'll see if we can't find a way to put him and the von Meerbach fellow in the same place at the same time. Henning will soon work out if he's a likely ally.'

'It would be useful, for propaganda purposes if nothing else, to have a man like him on our side. The public love their fighter aces.'

'And, if we removed the big brother, he'd presumably be able to swing his business resources behind us too.'

'Give my regards to Henning when you see him,' von Sickert said, as the two men got to their feet. 'And to Frida.'

'Of course,' Kleinhof assured him. He looked around and gave a shake of the head before he remarked, 'Odd, isn't it, to be talking like this when he's so close?'

'Yes,' von Sickert agreed. 'I've been asking myself why I don't save everyone a lot of bother and get rid of him here and now.'

Kleinhof gave a weary smile. 'Everyone asks themselves that, and he knows it. That's why they take our guns away before we get anywhere near him.'

'Surely it wouldn't be hard to smuggle one in, though.'

'Calm down, Heini. It will happen. We have a great deal of planning to do. But I promise you that in the end, the man will get what he deserves.'

• • •

Within an office off the corridors of the Reich Consulate in the centre of Lisbon, a man was sitting behind a desk on the far side of the room, writing something on a pad. He looked up, his pen still in his right hand, and registered the presence of the woman sitting opposite him.

She was shabbily dressed, and in need of a hot meal, a bath and a good night's sleep. She was good-looking enough, though – underneath it all – with long legs and striking blue eyes. The man returned to his work.

After a few moments, the senior official stopped writing. He looked directly at the woman. He was a heavy-set man with a tough, sceptical air to him.

'And your name is?' he said.

'Marlize Marais,' replied the woman.

'I am Deputy Consul-General Schäfer.'

The woman did not believe that Schäfer was a consul. *What are you?* she thought. *Abwehr? SD? Gestapo? Something dirty, that's for sure.*

'I find myself in an unusual situation,' Schäfer continued. 'All day long we deal with the Jews, degenerates and criminals who seek to escape justice in the Reich by coming here to Lisbon and polluting the streets while they wait for a means of getting away. But here is a charming young woman, going the other way.

She seeks nothing more than the chance to enter the Occupied Territories of the Reich.'

'That is correct, Deputy Consul. I wish to do my duty.'

Schäfer shrugged. 'This photograph. The woman in it is clearly yourself. The man you are with is Johannes van Rensburg, leader of the Ossewabrandwag?'

'Yes, that's van Rensburg,' she said.

Schäfer nodded. He looked the woman in the eye again, maintaining a steady gaze. 'Here are two letters. One bears van Rensburg's signature. The other purports to come from a senior OB man called Vorster, in his own handwriting. Am I to believe they are genuine?'

'Yes, sir, I am an admirer of the two men.'

'The British are crazy,' Schäfer said. 'Why let prisoners write any letters at all?'

'They are weak. That is why they will lose,' she replied.

Schäfer leaned back on his chair and put his feet on the desk. He was going to play cat and mouse with her. She felt revulsion at his dominance, the cruel twist of the smirk that was crawling across his face. She would have liked to break his neck.

She had to forget those thoughts. They belonged to Saffron Courtney, but she was Marlize Marais. Her life might depend on how well she played that part.

'How do you know van Rensburg?'

Saffron kept as close as she could to the truth. 'I don't. We'd never met before that night. But I think he is a wonderful man who understands what our country needs and why it can never succeed so long as the blacks and the Jews have any say in it. I heard he was going to a party at Tukkies so I asked a friend to take me along as his guest. I wanted to say hello to Dr van Rensburg, but I was too scared to do it. Then I told myself not to be so silly and approached him. We talked for a bit and then a man came by. He was taking photographs of all the guests. He took that one of us.'

'Tukkies, eh? That's a nickname for the University of Pretoria, if I'm not mistaken.'

'That's right.'

'Are you a student there by any chance?'

'No . . . I should have been, but I couldn't go.'

'Why not?'

'Because my father lost all his money. The filthy Jews took his business, every penny he had. We lost our house, our car . . . everything.'

'This business of your father's,' he went on, 'what was it?'

'A school outfitters in Jo'burg. Uniforms for all the rich children who go to the private schools there.'

'And you lived in Johannesburg?'

'Yes.'

'With other Afrikaners around you – your family, your neigh-bours and so on?'

'Yes.'

'So why can I hear a distinct trace of English in your voice?'

Saffron had anticipated that someone might ask this ques-tion, though not until she reached Flanders or Holland. She was prepared. 'My father sent me to Roedean – have you heard of it?'

'No. I expect it's a fancy private school.'

'It's a college for English gentlewomen. For years my father served the mothers who sent their daughters to Roedean. He dreamed that if he worked hard enough, he could send his own daughter there. He thought that the Dutch and British could be reconciled. He wanted his girl to have the best that the British could offer, to become as good as them.'

'We Germans are already better than either of them,' Schäfer sneered.

Saffron shook her head sadly. 'Pappa was only doing his best. And after he had worked his fingers to the bone for years, he made enough that he could send me there, and learn to carry myself and talk "like a lady" – he always said it like that, in English. And I tried my best, because I knew how much it mattered to Pappa. I tried to talk like a lady . . . and it made no difference. The girls looked down their noses at me. I was a shopkeeper's daughter. "A dirty Boer", that was what they called me. And then my father lost everything and I had to leave, in my last year because he could not pay the bills. They would not let me stay for my final examinations. So yes, I was left with this reminder of my past in the way I speak. But believe me: I hate the British even more because they took my own voice from me.'

'I feel for you, Fräulein Marais,' Schäfer said. 'How did your father lose his business?'

'I told you, the Jews took it from him.'

'Which Jews? How?'

Saffron shook her head as if trying to get past a bitter, humiliating memory. 'My father wanted to expand his business. He planned to buy the shop next to ours in Jo'burg and knock them into one big shop. And he wanted to open another branch in Cape Town. So, in 1938, he borrowed the money from a Jewish businessman called Solomons. He bought the shop next door. He had plans drawn up. He hired builders. They started work . . . and then Solomons called in his loan. My father had to pay all the money back, but of course he had used it to buy the property, pay architects and builders. He only had about a quarter left . . . Because my father could not pay, Solomons took the shop. He made his nephew the manager . . . The filthy, scheming, greedy Jews.'

Schäfer frowned. 'Why did he call in the loan?'

'The excuse he gave was that there was a war coming and the risk of lending was too high.'

'In 1938? How did he know a war was coming then?'

'I don't know. Maybe the Jews know these things because they start the wars themselves. But it doesn't matter. That was just an excuse. Solomons deliberately got my father into debt so he could take the business. Pappa thought he was a friend.

But a Jew is never your friend. All he thinks about is himself and his race. So now he has the shop. My Pappa is dead. And all I want to do is help the fight against the Jew.'

Schäfer was stony-faced, unmoving, like a statue; he revealed nothing. He continued to stare at her, his eyes like needles probing deep into her soul. And then, as if flicking a switch, he said, 'Bravo!' and gave three slow, emphatic claps of the hand. 'Well said, fräulein.'

Saffron was unsure of her ground.

'Fräulein Marais, your papers . . .'

Saffron realised that she had passed the test. She was on her way to Belgium and it looked as though Schäfer was so impressed by her performance that he was sending her straight there.

She was in. Now her mission could begin. But in her mind she was offering up a silent apology to Isidore Solomons. *I'm sorry, Izzy. I used your name to help fool these Nazis. I told lies about you and your people. But I swear to you, old friend, it won't be in vain.*

• • •

Barely a week after her arrival in Lisbon, Saffron alighted from the train at Ghent-Saint-Peter's station in Belgium and begun her stay among the Low Countries' most abject collaborators and Nazi sympathisers.

To play her part convincingly, she was forced, as Hardy Amies had warned she would be, to adopt an air of conviction in an ideology and morality that she found abhorrent. It wasn't just a matter of parroting the vile, psychotic idiocies of Adolf Hitler, as if they were the products of the greatest mind the world had ever seen. It meant cheering when a drunken, red-faced VNV in a blackshirt uniform got up on the table at a bar in Ghent, filled with Nazi sympathisers, and said, 'We helped the SS round up a hundred and fifty Yids today and packed them off to the transit camp at Mechelen. Soon the rats will all be caught and Belgium will be Jew-free!'

It meant laughing when someone shouted back, 'Are they in time to catch the next train?' and the blackshirt replied, 'Oh yes, and they'll have plenty of company on their journey. They'll be packed in nice and tight!'

Over her first few months in Belgium she made her way to the heart of the VNV party hierarchy. The idea that someone had come all the way from South Africa to stand alongside them seemed to thrill the party's leader Hendrik Elias and his cronies. For all their bluster, they seemed aware that their politics were still hateful to most of the outside world, and to a great many people in their own country, too. Any gesture of friendship or solidarity was welcome, and when it came from an attractive young woman it was all the more warmly received.

Elias fancied himself as an eminent intellectual. A round-faced, bespectacled man of forty, he boasted of his studies in Philosophy and Law at the universities of Leuven, Paris and Bonn. 'I have two doctorates from three countries, so you can see I am both broad-minded and well-travelled,' he laughed, surprised at his own wit.

Saffron obliged. She decided that Marlize should be intelligent enough to interest Elias, but not so much that she was a threat to him. She affected an interest in politics and the VNV's role in the governing of Belgium under German occupation, while deferring to Elias' opinions and being grateful to him for his insights. She was at her most outspoken on the subject of the British and their arrogant, hypocritical view of the world.

'They talk about democracy and freedom, but they're wicked liars!' she exclaimed. 'They go all over the world, taking people's countries from them, robbing their precious possessions. Look at South Africa! My people found gold and diamonds on their own land. The British went to war to take the mines for themselves. They are like that everywhere . . . everywhere!'

A fortnight after her outburst, Elias took Saffron to one side and said, 'I have been thinking about your views on the subject of the British . . .'

'Oh! I hope I didn't say too much.' Saffron hung her head in shame. 'It wasn't my place to talk.'

'Nonsense, my dear, I thought you spoke well. Indeed, I happened to be speaking to General von Falkenhausen the other evening . . .'

Saffron looked at him in wide-eyed wonder. 'The Military Governor of Belgium himself?'

'The very same,' Elias said, glowing with pride. 'I mentioned your feelings about the British and the general said to me – and these are the words he used – "You may tell *Fraulein* Marais that the British will not be allowed to play their tricks in Belgium. They keep sending men here to work with subversive elements, and . . ."' – Elias paused before he delivered the punchline – '"we keep catching them!" There, how do you like that?'

'How wonderful,' said Saffron. 'How do they do that?'

'He has informants. One in particular is very important.'

'Who is he?'

'Oh, I can't possibly tell you, and besides, why on earth would you want to know such trifles?' laughed Elias.

Saffron noted that he didn't deny the informant's gender, and that Elias' smile had disappeared. She quickly changed the subject.

'I don't know how to say this . . .' Saffron enthused, though she felt more like weeping. 'I'm so grateful and so honoured that you spoke to the general about me. And that he should think me worthy of a personal message . . . I don't know what to say.' She allowed herself to shed a tear. 'I'm sorry, but I'm just overcome . . .'

'Of course you are, that's only natural,' said Elias, putting a paternal arm across Saffron's shoulders and drawing her close to his body. He held her for as long as was decent, and then a little longer before letting her go.

As Saffron wiped the tear from her eye, Elias said, 'Your words affected me in another way. You may have heard of the National Socialist Women's League in Germany. It does valiant work encouraging German women to set aside any foolish desire to enter the world of men, and preaching the virtues of staying at home as wives and mothers. There is no greater calling. The future of the Aryan race depends on the gift of new lives and new blood, which only mothers can provide. Women play a vital role, raising their children to have true, National Socialist values. I'm sure you agree.'

'Oh, I do, sir!'

'It strikes me that as a woman, with a gift for expressing political views in a simple, emotional way that women can understand, you would be the ideal person to set up such an organisation here in Flanders.'

'I can think of no greater honour,' Saffron said.

'Good, then you may set about the job at once. And after you complete your task you must get married and excel at motherhood.' He smiled crookedly and stared at her for too long.

• • •

Saffron got to work. Over the following weeks and months she wrote enthusiastic articles for the party-controlled newspaper, *De Schelde*, explaining why National Socialism was so beneficial to women. She addressed small meetings of women in towns all over Flanders and, to her dismay, proved effective at recruiting new converts to the pro-Nazi cause.

Every evening she went home to her digs in the house of a middle-aged woman called *Mevrouw* Akkerman, who was a known VNV supporter. Her room was shabby and almost permanently in shadow, for its only window faced onto a narrow cobbled street, no wider than an alley, with two- and three-storey buildings running down its full length.

At night Saffron would lie in bed and listen for the sound of bombers overhead, on their way to Germany, and pray that the anti-aircraft guns whose shells she could hear exploding in the distance had not found their target.

When she thought of the bomber crews, whose lives might at any moment be ended by a shell that would send them plummeting down to earth in a coffin of fire and steel, she could not help but think of Gerhard. However hard she tried to tell herself that it did her no good, for there was nothing she could do to help or comfort him, it was impossible not to wonder whether he was still alive, where he was, or what he was doing. She hoped that he was still in Greece, having an easy war, with no serious fighting and little more to occupy him than the flirtatious advances of the local girls. Just so long as he wasn't in Russia. He would never come home from that.

• • •

Every time she went off to another corner of Flanders to recruit more deluded women to the fascist cause, Saffron tried to make contact with any agents or Resistance groups that Amies believed were operating in the area. But it seemed that von Falkenhausen's claims of victory against SOE were no idle boast, for time and again she drew a blank. Only when she ventured into the French-speaking part of Belgium and visited Liège did she have some luck.

A bunch of students and teachers from the Free University of Brussels, led by an engineering graduate called Jean Burgers, had set themselves up as a team of saboteurs under the grandiose title of the *Groupe Général de Sabotage de Belgique*, which they thankfully shortened to Groupe G. Since many of them had scientific or technical backgrounds, they brought a degree of expertise to their work and specialised in putting electrical facilities out of action, from cables and pylons through to power stations. The power cuts they caused were localised and small-scale in themselves. But every time the lights went out in a Wehrmacht barracks, or the production line ground to a halt at a Belgian factory, the people and their conquerors were reminded that there were still some people who were willing to resist.

Groupe G's two main bases were Brussels and Liège. SOE had been instrumental in their creation and supported Burgers and his men with radios, explosives and other equipment, as well as large amounts of money.

'I was informed you might be coming to see me,' Burgers said, when they met for lunch in a place of his choosing called the Café Royal Standard. Their cover, should anyone ask, was that his family and Marlize Marais' mother's were old friends. 'I'm told you are highly capable.'

'I've been well trained.'

'And now we find ourselves in this madness.' He shook his head. 'What can one do? We have to speed up the process of change, don't you think?'

'Yes. That's the only way of getting back to where we started from.'

'And in the meantime, we are obliged to speak in riddles for fear that monsters will hear us. Pah!'

Burgers gave her a smile. He was twenty-five, good-looking, principled and brave. The young men around him were full of vitality and laughter.

They're not ashamed, like everyone else in Belgium, Saffron thought. *Resistance has given them life. It's set them free.*

Burgers leaned across the table, as if he were about to share a secret flirtation with her. She played along, giggling and moving her head towards his across the table.

'We have a radio, and a good operator. He's here now, in fact, if that would be of use to you.'

'Yes, it would be very useful indeed,' she replied and then leaned back with an expression of shock on her face and said,

'What kind of a girl do you think I am?' loud enough for the young men at the next table to hear and direct a few wisecracks at Burgers.

'But I forgive you,' she added, giving him a coy look that was the subject of more banter from what was now a captive audience.

'I think we should continue this conversation outside,' Burgers said, getting to his feet. He grinned at the others and added, 'In private.'

He walked to the counter to pay the bill. Saffron watched as Burgers chatted to a florid, pot-bellied man with a handlebar moustache – the owner, she presumed. The owner laughed at something he said, then picked up a dishcloth and light-heartedly flicked it at him as he walked back to Saffron, who was waiting by the door.

'You two seem like old friends,' she said.

'You mean Claude? I've been coming here for years; he's a good man.'

They walked out onto the pavement. The café was on the corner of a block, facing a busy avenue, with a narrow side-street, little more than an alley to one side. Burgers led Saffron around the corner, away from the crowds and into the shadows, as if he really was intent on her seduction.

'Claude helps us in any way he can.'

At the back of the café there was a high wall, with a solid wooden gate set into it. Burgers stopped by the gate and knocked twice, quickly, then twice again. One of the two panels of the gate opened and Burgers let Saffron in.

Claude was waiting for them inside. His smile had disap-peared and his face was tight with tension. His greeting was no more than a nod and a grunted 'In here'.

There was a small brick shed in one corner of the yard. It was dark inside. Saffron could make out shelves stacked with cans, bottles, sacks of vegetables – all the supplies a busy café would need. As her eyes adjusted to the gloom Saffron realised that the metal shelves at the far end of the shed, away from the door, were not positioned against the wall. There was a small space behind them, from which a faint light could be seen.

'Your friend's in there,' Claude said, and left the shed. He didn't want to see what they did next.

Burgers ushered Saffron into the space, which was illuminated by a single desk lamp bent low over a table on which stood a small brown leather suitcase, opened to reveal a radio set, linked to a Morse transmission key. A wire ran from the set to a small window on the wall behind the table and passed through a crack in the frame. That was the aerial.

Another young man about their age was sitting there, waiting for them.

'I won't introduce you,' Burgers said. 'It's safer that way.'

'Good.' Saffron looked at the radio operator. 'May I have your seat please?'

'Of course.'

He got up and Saffron took his place. She opened her handbag and removed a black notebook. If anyone chose to examine it, they would find that everything she had written within related to her work for the VNV. She tore out a blank page and placed it on the table in front of her. Then she reached into the bag again. Inside it had a false bottom. She lifted it out and extracted a square of silk the size of a handkerchief. It was covered in lines of numbers.

The radio operator looked at it with curiosity. He couldn't resist asking, 'What's that?'

'The new way of coding messages. It's unbreakable.'

The printed fabric was the innovation Leo Marks had promised to give Saffron. It was a 'one-time pad', a method he had devised to stop the Germans decoding incoming SOE messages, or sending fake messages back. It employed a complex numerical coding system with a unique key for each message. The only other copy of the pad was in Norgeby House.

Saffron began her message with the secret call-sign that identified her, and a set of numerals that indicated which number-pad she was using. Then she began encoding the following message:

IN PLACE WITH VNV. HAVE TRUST OF ELIAS. CONTACT ESTABLISHED WITH GP G. NO SIGN OF ANY BAKER ST FRIENDS. HAVE BEEN TOLD ALL INTERCEPTED, CAPTURED BUT NO PROOF. WILL KEEP LOOKING HERE AND HOLLAND.

The coding was complicated and it took Saffron over ten minutes to convert her text into code. Now came the dangerous part. The radio operator had to tap out the message in Morse Code as quickly as possible, before the Germans could detect his transmission and trace its source. The task was harder because he was working with meaningless jumbles of letters, each one of which had to be sent correctly.

He looked at Burgers and said, 'If you could leave me in peace . . .'

Burgers led Saffron back into the bigger section of the storage shed.

'Is this really necessary?' she whispered.

'Yes, that's how he always works.'

'How do you know he'll get it right?'

'Because he's been a radio ham since he was ten. He doesn't make mistakes.'

'I hope not.'

Burgers lit another cigarette. He offered Saffron the pack, but she shook her head. He said, 'Anything important about this message. Good news?'

'No news . . . that's the problem. Listen, you must be careful. Don't trust anyone who says they're from London unless you have been told to look out for them and you are certain, beyond doubt, they have not been turned by the Germans.'

Burgers sighed. 'My God . . . it sounds like *les Boches* are winning.'

'I don't know . . . not for sure. But this is only one small corner of the war. Look around the world and the war is going our way. Don't worry. You will be free.'

'I hope so . . .'

The tapping of the Morse key ceased, there were sounds of movement, followed by the snap of the suitcase being closed. The radio operator emerged with what looked like a normal, rather battered leather case in his hand.

'That was quick,' Saffron said.

He shrugged. 'It took two minutes to send thirty-five words. I used to be quicker than that. We should be going.'

'One moment,' Saffron said. 'Can you light this with your cigarette?' she asked Burgers, passing him the silk one-time pad. As he put the tip of his cigarette to the fabric, which started burning almost immediately, she scanned the shelves and the junk that lay here and there on the floor until she found what she was looking for: an empty tin can. She picked it up and held it out so that Burgers could drop the burning pad inside. They waited until the pad was ashes in the bottom of the can. Burgers stubbed out his cigarette on top. Now the can was an improvised ashtray. It would attract no one's suspicion.

'All right, we can go,' Saffron said.

She made to leave but Burgers reached out and took her arm. 'Look, I've been thinking,' he said. 'It's not our business to help agents. We exist to carry out acts of sabotage. But we're on the same side, you and I, and if I can help you again, I will. I come in here, most days after work, around five in the afternoon, so that's where you can find me. Or ask Claude. He'll know how to get a message to me.'

'Thank you,' Saffron said. 'You know you'd be risking your life for me?'

'You're risking your life for us, too. What kind of a man would I be if I turned my back on you?'

They left the shed. 'I'll see you,' Burgers said as he walked across the yard to the wooden gate.

Before she could answer, he had turned and was heading up the street with the radio operator, moving as fast as they could without breaking into a run.

Saffron departed in the opposite direction. Half a minute later, walking down a nearby street, she passed a furniture van, stopped by the side of the road. She paid no attention to it.

Inside the van a German radio technician took off the headphones though which he'd been listening to the 'ping' whose volume told him how close they were getting to the source of the signal he had detected five minutes earlier.

'No good,' he said. 'It's gone dead.'

The plainclothes Gestapo officer leaning against the inside of the van muttered a curse under his breath. 'Damn! I thought we had him this time. You're sure it was Otto?'

'I'd recognise his style anywhere. None of the others are as fast or smooth as he is. It's as good as a fingerprint.'

'Funny . . . we don't know who Otto is, or what he looks like. But we can detect his touch on a Morse code key. Let us hope we can one day put a face to the dots and dashes.'

'Oh, we will sir, don't you worry. We're getting closer. He can't keep getting away from us for much longer.'

• • •

The following morning, when she went into work at the VNV offices, Saffron was greeted by a beaming Hendrik Elias.

'I have excellent news, Miss Marais. We have been invited to take part in a conference of political parties from the Low Countries – the legal parties, that is. It will take place in The Hague, at the Binnenhof, the headquarters of the German administration.'

'How exciting!' Saffron replied. 'What's the reason for the conference?'

'To discuss the role of the Low Countries within the new Europe that will arise after the war. Our German friends will be arranging the event and I am assured that they will be informing us about the latest thinking in Berlin on the subject of the Greater Netherlands and the forging of bonds between the Flemish, Dutch and German peoples.'

'How fascinating . . . It is a great honour, Dr Elias, for you to be honoured in this way. I'm sure no man deserves this more than you.'

Elias puffed out his chest and lifted his chin to adopt a more statesmanlike pose. 'That's kind of you, Miss Marais. One feels very humble, even to have been considered worthy of an invitation, which comes, I might say, from the highest echelons. But I am not alone in the honour. I have been permitted to bring a deputation of eight party officials. I would be delighted if you could be among them. We must remember that women will form part of our future too, and you should represent your sex in The Hague as you do so ably in Flanders.'

Saffron gasped and lifted her hand to her mouth, as if overwhelmed by such a sign of favour. 'Thank you, Doctor Elias. This means so much to me, I can't put it into words. I won't let you down, I swear.'

'I'm sure you won't, my dear. Just be your usual charming self, leave the men to do the talking, and the Germans will form a very favourable opinion of you, and thus the party itself will benefit.'

'I will do my best. And I would not dream of interfering in the men's deliberations.'

'Well said. Now, I have a meeting to attend in my office. Bring me a cup of coffee, there's a good girl.'

'It would be my pleasure.'

Marlize Marais went off to make her boss's coffee, knowing how he liked it, having performed the same task many times before. When she brought it to him, the two other men in the room decided that they would like coffee, and she made it for them, too.

'You're very cheerful this morning, Miss Marais,' one of Elias' guests said, when she handed him his drink.

'I've been able to give her some good news,' Elias explained. 'And in a moment I will share it with you. That will be all, dear. You can go now.'

Saffron smiled and departed. She was indeed as happy as that man had suggested. Too many Special Operations Executive agents had seen the insides of various Nazi headquarters when taken there as prisoners. She was about to walk in as an invited guest.

• • •

They took the train to The Hague, in a carriage whose compartments had been set aside for the Belgian participants in the conference.

It's like a school outing, Saffron thought. The men from the fascist factions even acted like bitchy schoolgirls. There was the same sense of people who had known each other for years, almost indistinguishable from one another to a stranger's eye, yet divided by bitter rivalries, and ambitions that meant everything to them and nothing to anyone else.

The different groups pointedly arranged themselves in separate compartments, making no attempt to mingle. This separation persisted until the train arrived at The Hague, where Arthur Seyss-Inquart, the man Hitler had appointed as ruler of the *Riechskommissariat Niederlande*, as the Netherlands was now known, had set up his headquarters. But the moment they set foot on the station platform and greeted the Germans who had come to take them to the conference, the visitors discovered that their factions were of no interest in Holland. They were Flemish and they were fascist. No one gave a damn about the subtleties.

They were led to a small bus and driven a short distance to a hotel, located on a square near the Binnenhof. They passed under a banner, hung across the street that read: *V = Victory! Germany winning on all fronts for Europe*. She saw a vacant shop with the Star of David daubed in whitewash across its window and 'Filthy Jew' scrawled beside it. A mother hurried by, head down, crouched over the three children she was herding down the street. They all had yellow stars sewn onto their coats.

One of the VNV men pulled down the window beside his seat and shouted, 'We're coming for you, little Yids!' and sat back to hoots of laughter and slaps on the back.

When they arrived at the hotel, Saffron stood on the pavement by the bus, waiting for her case to be unloaded, casting her eyes across the square. White wooden signs on stakes had been placed at regular intervals around its perimeter. They said the same thing: *Voor Joden verboden*. Forbidden to Jews.

The only item on the agenda that day was a 'familiarity' session for the delegations from Flanders and the Netherlands. They were walked to the Binnenhof, a complex of buildings at the heart of which stood a structure whose facade could have been taken from a medieval Gothic cathedral, complete with a magnificent rose window, surrounded by other stained-glass windows. Two thin, round towers, with tall pointed roofs, stood either side of the main entrance, and from each tower hung a scarlet Nazi flag, with the white circle and black swastika at its centre. Here, at the heart of Dutch democracy and independence, was an unmissable symbol of the way things were now.

The Dutch national socialists were awaiting the arrival of their Flemish brethren in the main hall. A buffet of sandwiches, pickled herring, local cheese and pastries had been laid out, and white-jacketed waiters stood behind tables laden with beer and wine. Saffron realised that she was the only woman in the room. The men ignored her as they got down to the business of bragging and backslapping. The leader of the Dutch National Socialist Movement stepped up to a podium at the end of the room and gave a long speech filled with sycophancy towards the Nazi Party and insults towards its enemies. Saffron found it loathsome, but knew that Marlize Marais would lap it up and so applauded heartily at every opportunity.

Not to be outdone, Hendrik Elias replied with an oration whose prejudices were slightly less repellent, but which was even more tedious. Once again, Marlize was moved to raptures of enthusiasm.

The event seemed to be drawing to its conclusion when one of the few Germans present made his way to Saffron. He was over six feet tall and his SS uniform jacket strained to contain his shoulders and barrel chest. He had pale skin, white-blonde hair (even his eyebrows and lashes were so pale as to be near-invisible) and small, blue eyes. His face was fleshy, his lips full enough that as he got closer to Saffron his resting mouth appeared to be pouting. She could see that his uniform bore the insignia of a *Hauptsturmführer*, the equivalent rank to an army captain.

He stood opposite her, clicked his heels and said, 'Good evening, fräulein. I hope you will allow me to introduce myself. My name is Schröder . . . Karsten Schröder.'

'Marlize Marais,' Saffron replied.

'*Enchanté*,' Schröder said. He took her hand and bent to kiss it, though, to Saffron's relief, his rubbery mouth did not make contact with her skin.

He stood up straight again, cast his eyes around the gathering and remarked, 'This is hardly the most amusing way for a beautiful woman to spend a Saturday evening.'

'On the contrary, I found the speeches both fascinating and inspiring,' Saffron replied, judging that it was more important to establish her pro-Nazi credentials than respond to his efforts at flirting.

Schröder smiled. 'Then I commend you on your judgement and political understanding. Now, I fear I cannot stay and talk. I have other matters to attend to. May I ask, will you be attending the proceedings tomorrow?'

'Yes.'

'Very good. I hope we have the chance to talk at greater length then . . . and not only about politics.'

• • •

Marlize was a devout Christian. Saffron made a point of going to church the following morning, dressed in her Sunday best: a cheap cotton summer dress and a baby-blue cardigan. She wore white cotton gloves on her hands and her hair was covered by a straw hat, held on with a pin. Any good Reformed Church girl knew the words of St Paul's first letter to the Corinthians: 'every woman that prayeth or prophesieth with her head uncovered dishonoureth her head', and she always wore a hat or scarf when she stepped inside the Lord's house.

Afterward she made her way back to the Ridderzaal with the rest of the Flemish delegates. Chairs had been laid out in rows in front of the podium. More speeches were on the agenda. The first was given by a senior official of the German administration called Gruber. He was a small, thin, intense man, whose Nazi zeal extended to a toothbrush moustache that made him look like an actor, or even a comedian impersonating Adolf Hitler. Not that the suggestion of wit or good humour pierced the ironclad seriousness of his delivery.

'Heil Hitler!' he began. 'The paper I am delivering to this symposium is entitled: *Building a New Europe: The Low Countries and Their Role in the Greater Germanic Reich*. I will describe the development of the idea of the Greater Germanic Reich as a product of the Führer's genius, which will inevitably be made manifest as a political and territorial entity that will be the greatest of all the world powers.'

He did this in great detail for more than an hour, then took questions for a further forty minutes. Saffron said nothing. The task allotted to Marlize Marais was to do her best to understand what the men were discussing – Hendrik Elias had promised to explain anything she found too complicated – and then translate it into the simple, even childish terms that the women she worked with would understand.

Saffron took detailed notes. It gave her satisfaction that every word she jotted down was providing more intelligence for Baker Street. But what struck her most was how different she felt now, listening to Gruber, than she would have done a year earlier. Then his description of German efficiency and power would have filled her with fear, even despair. Now that the tide of the war had turned, it sounded like an absurd fantasy, a demented fairy tale that all the men in the room were going along with, which had no basis in fact.

In the afternoon, Schröder, the SS officer who had introduced himself to Saffron the previous evening at the Binnenhof, took his turn at the podium. His subject was: *The solving of the Jewish question in the Netherlands.*

Schröder's speech was neither a fantasy nor fairy tale. It was a living nightmare.

'The Dutch have occasionally shown a distressing willingness to make futile gestures of resistance,' he said. 'Politicians have been murdered by communist assassins. Workers have gone on strike. Events such as these must be dealt with. We have not been afraid to liquidate large numbers of hostages as a means of reminding the people of the folly of resistance. But I can assure you all, gentlemen' – Schröder paused and looked at Saffron – 'and, of course, ladies . . . that Resistance efforts have in no way hampered our sacred task of ridding Europe of the taint of Hebrew influence.'

Schröder cast his watery blue eyes around the room. He ran his tongue around his puffy lips when his eyes found her out again, a gesture whose obscene intent, though not obvious to anyone else, was all too apparent to her. He looked at the room again as he spoke in slow, emphatic terms: 'Thanks to the unstinting efforts of SS personnel, and our Dutch allies, I can now tell you, as a matter of fact, that no other Occupied

Territory in western Europe can match our success in detecting, apprehending and resettling Jews. None!'

The applause rang out more loudly than at any time that day. Two or three of the delegates rose to their feet to make their point more emphatically. Schröder nodded, a self-congratulatory smile spreading across his features.

'When the *Reichskommissariat Niederlande* was established in 1940, there were some one hundred and forty thousand Hebrew scum within its borders. Now, that number has been reduced to below fifty thousand.'

A look of determination settled on Schröder's face, the expression of a general steeling his troops for battle. His voice lowered. 'I tell you now that within the next eighteen months – that is to say, by the end of 1944 – all but an insignificant fraction of the Jews in the *Reichskommissariat Niederlande* will be transported out of this country for resettlement in the East. Holland will be Jew-free!'

Saffron forced herself to her feet to applaud, for she would have been the only person in the room who did not.

Schröder nodded, graciously accepting the credit for the achievement. He let the hubbub subside and the collaborators' backsides descend to their seats before adding his punchline. 'And may I say, since we are all friends here, that none of you need fear that these Jews will be occupying land that should belong to well-deserving Aryan folk. Nor will they be taking food from Aryan mouths. The Jew resettlement will be shortlived.'

As the men around her laughed, and she smiled uncertainly, as if not quite able to understand the joke, Saffron tried to come to terms with what Schröder had said. He was suggesting that Holland's Jews were being taken away to be killed. And if that were the case, then so were all the other Jews who were being packed onto trains in Belgium and the rest of Nazi Europe.

But there must be millions of Jews in Europe, she thought. *Are they really trying to kill all of them? Even the Nazis couldn't be that monstrous . . . could they?*

• • •

When the day's proceedings came to an end, the senior men in each party were invited to dine with Gruber, Schröder and the other speakers. As they were preparing to leave, Schröder approached Saffron.

'Ah, fräulein,' he said, with a smile that did not extend to his eyes. 'How nice to see you again.'

'And you too, *Hauptsturmführer* Schröder.'

'Ah, there is no need to be so formal. Please, call me Karsten. After all, the formal proceedings are over and now we can relax. I wonder if you would care to join us for dinner. I dare say you would find it rather boring to be struck in a room with a dozen old men . . .'

'You are far from old, Karsten,' Saffron said, forcing herself to be charming. Schröder might still be of use to her.

'That is why I too will be bored tonight. Unless, that is, you would join us. I'm sure your presence would be welcomed by everyone.'

Marlize would be thrilled by this offer, Saffron reminded herself. 'Oh, yes, thank you . . . I mean, if you're sure that would be all right?'

'Of course.'

'But I'm not dressed for dinner or anything.'

'Pah! This is not some high-society affair. You could wear an old potato sack and still look like Marlene Dietrich.'

Saffron giggled. 'That's a very nice compliment.'

'My pleasure. Would you care to accompany me to the restaurant? I have a car outside.'

'That would be lovely but . . .' Saffron leaned towards Schröder and whispered, 'I don't think *meneer* Elias would be happy. I think he would prefer it if I went with him.'

'Oh, I see. So that's how it is, eh?'

'No! It's not like that at all. Though I think he would like it to be . . .'

'Ah.' Schröder nodded. He put his head close to hers and whispered, 'Then we will have to be discreet, won't we?'

He placed a hand on Saffron's buttocks, squeezed gently and then gave them a playful slap.

'I'll see you at dinner, then, fräulein,' Schröder said, as if nothing had happened. He walked away, leaving Saffron feeling helpless and degraded.

Get a grip! she told herself. *You're a trained agent. You're tougher than this!*

But she was also a young woman of twenty-three who had been groped by a much bigger, stronger man, who had treated her as if she were a piece of meat.

Saffron had been taught the importance of staying calm under pressure. She forced herself to put her feelings of shame and vulnerability to one side.

Across the room, Schröder was talking to Elias. Saffron joined them.

'Ah, Marlize,' Elias said as she approached. '*Haupsturmführer* Schröder was telling me that you will be joining us for dinner.'

She smiled. 'Yes, he kindly invited me . . . if you do not mind, of course?'

'My dear girl, why would I object to your company at dinner?'

Saffron looked at Schröder as she said, 'I'm so glad. I'm thrilled to have the chance to join you all.'

'Excellent, excellent . . .' said Elias, steering Saffron away from Schröder towards the rest of the VNV contingent.

Saffron glanced over her shoulder. Schröder licked his lips, just as he had done before. Saffron let their eyes meet before she turned away. It was her job to cultivate someone who might be able to provide inside information on SS activities in Holland. But inside she was thinking, *That's the last time you catch me unawares, Herr Schröder. And if you try it again, I'll make you regret it.*

• • •

Saffron and the other guests were taken to a restaurant in a basement on Plaats, a triangular plaza, close to the Binnenhof. There was at least one man in German uniform at every table and it wasn't hard to see why. The place was decked out in the style of a Bavarian bierkeller, with whitewashed walls and ceilings, two long rows of wooden tables and waitresses in low-cut peasant blouses, with their hair in plaits and their skirts swishing against the guests' chairs as they walked by.

There were fourteen in the symposium group and several tables had been shoved together to make room for them. There was no need for anyone to order food for within minutes waitresses had appeared bearing plates laden with *rookworst* sausages, so stuffed with pork, veal and bacon that their skins were as close to bursting as a fat man's waistcoat.

'They are made here on the premises, with our own secret mix of spices,' the proprietor, who was personally making sure that everything was to Dr Gruber's liking, assured his guests. 'We smoke them ourselves over woodchips specially chosen for their aromatic qualities.'

The *rookworst* were served sliced over a bed of *stamppot*: mashed potato, rich with butter and creamy Dutch milk, mixed with chopped onions and kale. And there were glasses of cold, foaming Heineken, brewed barely twenty kilometres away in Rotterdam, to wash it down. The hearty food and plentiful beer quickly filled the men with good humour.

Schröder was on fine form. He had insisted on seating Saffron beside him, which had caused Elias to make a beeline for the seat on her other side. For much of the meal she felt like a spectator at a tennis match, turning her head from one side to the other as each man tried to outdo the other in displays of intelligence and wit, delivered in German, for they were speaking the rulers' tongue.

Even Marlize wouldn't be impressed by these two, Saffron told herself. *But I suppose she'd feel obliged to look as though she was bowled over by them.*

Encouraged by what he assumed were displays of girlish enthusiasm, Schröder held forth on the inevitable triumph of German military might.

'Don't be fooled by our so-called withdrawals on the Eastern Front,' he told her. 'I have it on good authority from friends in Berlin – men who are in a position to know the facts – that the Führer is only toying with the Bolshevik rabble. Soon we will be blowing the Ivans to hell.'

'Marlize takes victory in the East for granted,' Elias said, wanting to demonstrate how much closer he was to the female over whom they were fighting. 'What interests her is the destruction of the British.'

'Is that so?' Schröder inquired with a knowing twinkle.

Saffron nodded. 'Yes . . . of course I despise the Bolshies, they are mere subhumans. But I hate the British for what they have done to my people, and how they treated me.'

'You should hear her denouncing the evils of the British,' Elias said. 'I can assure you, Schröder, that our Marlize has a bright little brain behind that pretty face.'

'Oh please, Herr Elias, don't tease me!' Saffron giggled. She turned to look at Schröder and said, 'He doesn't mean that. I'm an ordinary, simple girl.'

Elias glared at Saffron and then turned his eyes towards Schröder, who was smiling with lascivious smugness.

'Oh yes,' said Elias, forgetting his usual servility towards Germans, 'you may lead the way in Holland, so far as catching Jews is concerned. But we in Belgium know how to catch spies.'

Schröder brushed away the boast with a flick of his hand. 'I congratulate my colleagues on their successes,' he said. 'But we in Holland have the advantage with regard to spies as well as Jews. The Security Police wing of the SS, working in conjunction with Major Giskes of the Abwehr, have, to date, arrested fifty agents, sent by the British into the *Reichskom-missariat Niederlande*. Almost all of them were seized as they landed, because those buffoons in London had no idea that the so-called "Resistance" men in Holland with whom they were dealing were our own radio operators. We have seized huge quantities of guns, explosives, radio sets and money. We have their complete plan for organising Resistance forces in

Holland. We know every detail of their recruitment, training, deployment and personnel. In short, we have it all. It is a total victory. What do you think of that, my dear Marlize?'

'Th-th-that's . . . amazing.' Saffron was so appalled by what she had heard that she could barely speak, but prayed that her wide-eyed stammering would be taken for awe rather than horror. 'I never thought I would hear anything so incredible. How . . . how did you do it?'

Schröder chuckled. 'Ah, well, that would be giving away professional secrets . . . but you can take it from me that it has been a long time since the Dutch department of what the British call their Special Operations Executive sent or received a message that we did not read and reply to ourselves.'

'I . . . I congratulate you most heartily,' said Elias, through gritted teeth.

Schröder gave a curt nod of acknowledgement, then added, 'Speaking of the British, we currently have three of their latest gifts to us in the cellars below the Binnenhof. We expect to complete their interrogation tonight, in fact.' He looked at his watch. 'Almost nine o'clock. I must be on my way.'

Schröder looked at Saffron. 'Perhaps you would care to accompany me, fräulein Marais. I cannot allow you to attend the interrogation, of course. But you can look at the prisoners in their cells. It may amuse you to see the pathetic wretches whom those fools in London have sent as their spies and saboteurs.'

'I'm not sure . . .' Elias began, but Saffron said, 'Thank you, Karsten, I would like that very much.'

'Excellent,' Schröder replied. 'Don't worry, Elias. Your, ah . . . colleague will be safe with me.'

• • •

Schröder waited while Saffron disappeared to the ladies' room. She reappeared with her face and hair freshened up and wearing her hat and gloves. They stepped outside into the late evening twilight. The streets were deserted, the air was warm and still, and the blackout meant that there was not a light visible anywhere.

Schröder offered Saffron his arm. As she took it she said, 'It's so quiet. Here we are in the middle of a capital city and it's like a ghost town.' She wondered why Schröder was not accompanied by a bodyguard.

'I know,' Schröder said, his voice low and throaty. 'We have the whole place to ourselves, with no one to disturb us.'

Plaats had buildings along two of its sides, but the third, which faced the Binnenhof, was open. Saffron looked across the rectangular, ceremonial lake, known as the Hofvijver, towards the old parliament buildings that rose on the far bank where high walls and steep roofs softened into an indistinct purple-grey mass by the deepening dusk.

It was a short stroll around the near end of the Hofvijver to the closest corner of the Binnenhof. But Schröder led her in another direction, towards an avenue of trees that ran along the longer bank of the lake, opposite the Binnenhof's facade.

'I'm afraid the cells are at the far end of the building,' he explained. 'But I hope the walk will be a pleasant one.'

They carried on in silence. As they walked between the trees, the sense of isolation from the rest of the world became even more pronounced. Saffron began to feel uneasy and it had nothing to do with being an SOE agent undercover in hostile territory. It was a primal female fear of being led into the dark by a large, potentially dangerous man. She noticed that, although Schröder was keeping his head still, he kept darting his eyes from side to side, as if checking that they were not being followed. That would be a basic precaution: he was a target for Resistance assassins. A decent man would not make that obvious for fear of upsetting the woman at his side.

But instinct told Saffron that Schröder's motivation was very different: *He's making sure there's no one around. He doesn't want any witnesses.*

Suddenly she felt frightened. She knew how to defend herself against an attack by a larger opponent. She could fight Schröder off. But Marlize Marais couldn't do that. Either Saffron accepted that her mission required her to let Schröder do what he wanted with her – and it was obvious what that would be – or she stopped him, and blew her cover.

She felt helpless in the face of that dilemma. *Don't think about that*, she told herself. *Concentrate on the job in hand. Be Marlize. What would she be feeling?*

That was easy. She'd be very nervous. She'd want to say something, anything to break the silence.

'Tell me about the spies you are interrogating,' Saffron asked.

'Why do you ask?' For the first time a note of caution, bordering on suspicion, had entered his voice.

'I want to know more about you, what you do.'

Schröder laughed. 'You were right. You are a simple girl. But even a simple girl may have her uses. Come . . .'

He grabbed her wrist, holding it tight, and led her towards a large tree, whose trunk was barely visible through the deep shadow of the overhanging branches. They walked under the canopy of leaves and as they reached the base of the tree, Schröder spun Saffron around and shoved her hard against the trunk. She felt the bark scraping her skin through the fabric of her light summer dress.

Schröder did not waste time on small talk. He pressed the weight of his body against Saffron. His right hand reached down, pulled up her skirt and then reached beneath it, forcing its way between her bare thighs. His left hand grabbed the hair on the back of her head and pulled it so that her face was jerked up to face his. He tilted his face towards her, pushed his lips against hers and forced his tongue, like a thick, slippery eel, into the depths of her mouth.

Be Marlize! she told herself. *Be Marlize!*

Saffron tried to twist her head away from Schröder's but he gripped her hair tighter, making her gasp in pain. She writhed her hips to try to escape his hand rubbing against her crotch. His fingers were playing with her through the fabric of her underwear. His breathing was hot and loud in her ear. He belched and the air in her nostrils reeked of stale beer and cigarettes.

Schröder withdrew his hand and for an instant Saffron thought he might be done with her. He'd bullied her, overpowered her, humiliated her: that was where a man like Schröder found his pleasure. But she realised he was undoing his belt and fly-buttons, pulling down his trousers and underpants. He'd only just started.

At that moment, the role-playing ended. Now it was a fight for survival. To free himself from his trousers, Schröder had eased the pressure of his lower body against Saffron's.

That was his mistake.

She did what Fairbairn and Sykes had taught her at Arisaig and powered her knee with every ounce of her strength into Schröder's exposed testicles. He grunted in agony, let go of her hair, and as he bent double she followed up with the next move in a sequence she had practised countless times and, aiming by feel and instinct in the near-darkness, drove the heel of her right hand into the left side of his chin as his head jerked down to meet it.

The blow propelled his head around, wrenching it violently up and to the side and knocking him off his feet. As he fell, barely conscious to the ground, Saffron kicked him in the way all Arisaig trainees were taught: not with her toes, as if kicking a football, nor even with a single downward stamp. She jumped in a two-footed 'bronco kick', aiming at his rib cage and shooting her legs out straight, immediately before she hit, so that the steel-tipped heels of her shoes slammed into his diaphragm.

Fairbairn's book *All-In Fighting* provided a mathematical explanation of the force exerted on an opponent's body by the full power of a jumping attacker's legs being applied through an area not much bigger than a tent peg. She had bronco-kicked into soft turf and seen what a deep dent her heels made.

The effect on Schröder was devastating. The air was driven from his body as half his ribs caved in. He flapped on the ground like a fish out of water, gasping for breath.

Saffron sat astride his chest, with her knees pinning down his upper arms. 'There, there,' she murmured softly. 'I know . . . your balls hurt, your guts hurt, your neck hurts and your poor little brain's been bouncing round your skull like a ping-pong ball in a bucket. Never mind, I'll make it go away.'

Saffron reached up to her hat and pulled out the long steel pin that kept it in place. She leaned forward, grateful that the faintest shred of moonlight had penetrated the canopy of tree-leaves, making it possible for her to place the point of the pin delicately on the innermost corner of Schröder's left eye.

It widened in alarm. Schröder tried to shout out a protest but could manage nothing more than a wordless gargling sound. Saffron looked at him and smiled.

'Oh, the things they taught us,' she whispered.

She placed her left hand over Schröder's mouth, in case he should recover the power of speech. One couldn't be too careful.

She pushed the pin with her right hand into Schröder's eye-socket, exerting an even, steady pressure as the needle-sharp point felt for the superior orbital fissure at the back of the socket through which a bundle of nerves travelled to the brain. The point scraped against bone once, twice . . . and then she was through into the mass of brain tissue and blood vessels. Keeping the end she was holding steady, she worked the point of the pin back and forth, causing maximum internal damage before she withdrew it.

Schröder's heart was still beating, but he was as good as dead. The internal bleeding in his brain would finish him off, even if all his other injuries had not.

Saffron's body was casting a black moonshadow over the dark grey form of the man she had murdered. She leaned back to take a better look. Her night vision was excellent, sharp enough to see the blood, oozing like a black tear from the wound in his eye. She got up and went across to where her bag lay on the ground, knocked from her arm in the first seconds of Schröder's assault. There was a small cotton handkerchief inside. She used it to wipe the blood away. If she had done the job properly, the wound would barely be visible. It would take until the post-mortem for anyone to work out what had killed him, and she would be long gone by then.

She looked around. There was no sign of anyone. Relieved, she turned her attention to Schröder as his life ebbed away. His trousers were around his knees and his genitalia were exposed. His body was sprawled on the ground. Even in the near darkness he looked like a man who had died while trying to rape someone. His would-be victim would be able to claim self-defence, but she would still be the only suspect.

Better do something about that.

Saffron grimaced in disgust as she put Schröder back in his underpants and did up his flies. That was more distasteful to her than killing him had been.

But then, I am a killer. That's why Mr Brown was interested in me. That's why SOE took me on. That's my gift.

She grabbed Schröder under his arms and managed to drag his massive body towards the tree until he was in a seated position, with his upper back and head slumped against the trunk. The ground was dry and hard, which would limit the scuff-marks, but Saffron used her hands and feet to smooth over the ground and cover any trail she had made.

As a final touch, she took Schröder's cigarette and lighter from the chest pocket of his uniform jacket.

Mustn't get lipstick on the cigarette . . . But surely his fat slobby mouth must have wiped it all off me.

To be on the safe side, she applied as little pressure as possi-ble from her lips as she lit the cigarette, breathed in just enough smoke to get it burning, then placed it between the fingers of Schröder's right hand. She put the lighter and the cigarette packet back in his pocket.

Now he was a man who'd stopped beneath a tree to smoke a cigarette. And even if his head slumped to one side and he didn't move, even if he looked very dead – *especially if he looks dead* – no Dutch citizen was going to go near a man in an SS officer's uniform. It would take another German to raise the alarm, and that hopefully wouldn't happen till the morning.

Somewhere in the distance a church bell rang the half-hour. It was only half past nine. There were at least seven hours before the first light of dawn. She thought about the three British agents in the cellars below the Binnenhof and whether she could try to rescue them. But she might simply end up with a bullet in her head. It would be child's play to steal a bicycle and even allowing for time spent evading German patrols and roadblocks she could be most of the way to the Belgian border by morning. But then what?

Saffron shook her head. That wasn't the way to do it. There was a better option. It would require a lot of luck, a cool head and a steady nerve. But it was the fastest and surest way out of Holland. First, though, she had to go back to the hotel.

• • •

'Your colleagues are in the lounge, miss, if you care to join them,' the night porter said as he let her in.

Elias and half a dozen of his cronies were sat in a circle of armchairs beneath a haze of cigarette smoke with glasses beside them and a couple of bottles of brandy on a table in their midst.

'Aha! Miss Marais, how good of you to join us,' Elias said. 'So . . . tell us about the British spies.'

Saffon looked down at her feet in embarrassment before she admitted, 'I didn't see them.'

'Oh . . . really?' Elias could not hide the triumph from his voice. 'Don't tell me that nice *Hauptsturmführer* Schröder tricked you in some way. What happened?'

'Well, we went for a walk along by the lake and we talked for a bit. He didn't seem to be in as much of a hurry as he'd said. And then . . . then . . . he tried to kiss me,' she confessed, shamefaced amidst mocking cries from the men. 'I had to push him off. And then I said, "No, I'm not that kind of girl." And he said, well, in that case, if I wouldn't give him what he wanted, he wouldn't give me what I wanted.'

'Sounds reasonable to me,' one of the VNV men remarked, to nods and laughs.

'Well, it didn't seem reasonable to me. It was horrible. It made me feel dirty. Because I'm not that kind of girl . . .' Saffron looked around the room with pleading eyes. 'I'm really not.'

'There, there, my dear, I'm sure you're very virtuous,' Elias said. 'But you only have yourself to blame. You kept calling him by his first name . . .'

Elias turned to look at the men around him. 'Oh yes, it was Karsten-this and Karsten-that,' he said, then returned to Saffron. 'You shouldn't be surprised if he thought you were leading him on.'

'But I didn't want to call him Karsten!' Saffron wailed. 'He told me to . . . An SS-officer told me how to speak to him – what was I supposed to do?'

Elias nodded sagely. 'Well, when you put it that way, I can see that it would be wrong not to act in accordance with the wishes of the SS . . . I hope for your sake that you haven't offended him too badly by rejecting his advances.'

Saffron shook her head. 'I don't think so. I think he thought it was a joke. I said I was going back to my hotel and he laughed at me, which made it worse. He said, "You can't blame a man for trying." Then he walked off in one direction and I came here in the other.'

'"You can't blame a man for trying",' another of the men repeated, chuckling to himself. 'I like that.'

'He's a good man, that Schröder,' someone else agreed.

'Well, if you don't mind,' said Saffron, looking downcast, 'I'm off to bed.'

When she got upstairs, Saffron tore her handkerchief into small pieces and flushed it down the lavatory. She checked her clothes and shoes for traces of blood. Her gloves were dusty from covering her tracks, so she washed them in her basin at the same time as her underwear, and hung them over the bath to dry.

She went to bed and tried desperately to fall asleep. The last thing she wanted was to appear exhausted in the morning. After all, she was an innocent woman with nothing to fear.

• • •

At half past one on Monday afternoon, Chief Inspector Rutger De Vries stood in the office of *SS-Brigadeführer* Hans Rauter, the Chief of the SS and Police in Occupied Holland, and he prepared to deliver a brief account of the early hours of investigation into the death of *SS-Hauptsturmführer* Karsten Schröder. Rauter, he knew, owed his position to his devotion to Nazism, rather than police work. But the other two men present at the meeting were more worthy of De Vries' professional respect.

Kommissar Wilhelm Lüdtke was the head of the Berlin Murder Squad, which had long been regarded as the finest homicide unit in the world. Its development of forensic science as a tool for detective work had been particularly influential. Beside Lüdtke was the Berlin police pathologist Dr Waldemar Weimann. Less than two years earlier he had helped Lüdtke identify and apprehend Paul Ogorzow, the infamous 'S-Bahn Killer', who had murdered eight women, and assaulted many more during a two-year crime spree. For the Germans to have flown these two star performers in from Berlin, less than eight hours after the dead man's body was first reported to The Hague's police, was a sign of how seriously they were taking the SS man's death.

De Vries had spent twenty years in The Hague police, most of them working in the homicide department. His hair was greying, his body worn down by drink and too many late nights, and his weary, heavily lined eyes had seen too many of the infinite ways human beings could find to hurt one another. This case, though, had a number of unusual features to it. Given the chance, he'd like to discuss them with Lüdtke over a few drinks. But that could wait. For now, the facts were all that was required.

'The body was first spotted at approximately seven-thirty this morning by two city council workers who were clearing litter from the area around the Hofvijver. In fact, gentleman, if you come to the window you will get an excellent view of the lake and the avenue of trees beyond it where the crime took place. If you look towards the far bank, slightly to your left, you will see the two police officers who are guarding the murder scene.'

The two Berliners did as De Vries suggested. When they turned away from the window he continued.

'At first glance, the men assumed that Schröder was asleep. They saw that he was wearing an SS uniform and they did not want to disturb him. It was only when they came back past the same spot an hour later, and he was still there, in the same position, that they became suspicious. One of the men stayed at the scene while the other proceeded to the nearest telephone kiosk and called their supervisor. He in turn contacted the police. By nine o'clock we were on the scene.'

'Was the crime scene disturbed at any point before your arrival?' Lüdtke asked. 'It was Monday morning, after all, with a lot of people going to work.'

'We don't think so. The council workers were adamant that they had kept passers-by well away.'

'Let's hope so. Carry on . . .'

'Schröder's wallet and papers were still on his person, so we were able to establish his identity at once.'

'No sign of any robbery?' Ludtke asked.

'No. There was money in the wallet. Hs still had his watch, cigarette lighter, gun – everything, in fact, that a robber might wish to take.'

'What was the condition of his body?' Weimann asked.

'I'll come to that in a moment, if I may, doctor,' De Vries said. 'But first I will run through the sequence of events. Thanks to the assistance of *Brigadeführer* Rauter and his staff, we learned that Schröder had been taking part in a symposium of National Socialist politicians from the Low Countries. He had dined with the more senior delegates at a restaurant on Plaats that has a predominantly German clientele and had left there at approximate twenty-one hundred hours with a young woman, Marlize Marais, who was part of the delegation from the Flemish National Union.

'The delegates had left their hotel and were on their way back to Belgium, but we were able to intercept and interview them at the station before they boarded their train. Miss Marais was among them. She told us that she had gone with Schröder because he had offered to show her three British spies who were being held here in the Binnenhof for interrogation.'

'I must say, I find that almost impossible to believe,' Rauter said. 'Most irregular.'

'Her account was confirmed by the VNV leader, Hendrik Elias, who was sitting with Schröder and Marais and took part in the conversation. He confirmed that they had discussed the successful efforts to apprehend British spies and saboteurs in Belgium. Schröder insisted that the fight against these intruders had been even more successful in Holland. And he wanted to prove it.'

'That's still no excuse for his behaviour.'

'Any man who saw Miss Marais would understand why he might want to impress her. She is unusually attractive.'

'Was she the last person to see Schröder alive?' Lüdtke asked.

'The last we know of, yes.'

'So what's her story?'

'She says Schröder decided to take her the long way round the lake. She began to worry about his intentions. Sure enough, he tried to kiss her. She said she wasn't that sort of girl and pushed him away. He said that if that was her attitude he was damned if he'd show her the spies. She went back to her hotel on Plein and that was the last she saw of him.'

'She didn't look to see where he went?'

'She made it plain she had no desire to lay eyes on him ever again.'

'This kind of behaviour is not what is expected of an SS officer,' Rauter said. 'Can anyone back this woman's story up?'

'There were no witnesses that we know of . . .'

'Unless Schröder's killer was lurking in the shadows somewhere,' Lüdtke pointed out.

'Quite so . . . But a number of people who were at the hotel when Miss Marais returned all confirm that she told them what had happened. Most of them seemed to think she had asked for it. Elias was particularly disapproving, saying that she had been calling Schröder by his first name, Karsten, throughout dinner. He admitted, however, that she had told everyone at the hotel that he had ordered her to call him that, and that she did not feel able to disobey him. The power of the uniform . . .'

'What do we know about Marais?'

'Her background is unusual. She appears to be a South African national, though she possesses a Belgian passport . . .'

'Genuine?'

'Yes. She is an Afrikaner and therefore, she says, strongly opposed to the British, with whom her people have been at war, on and off, for the past century. She arrived in Lisbon earlier this year and was interviewed at the German consulate. Having established her bona fides, they issued her with travel permits to go to Belgium, where she has been active in the VNV for the past few months. Elias confirmed that she has been setting up the party's women's organisation. He said she was a hard worker and was doing an excellent job.'

'How does she compare in size to Schröder?' Weimann asked.

'She's tall for a woman, at least one hundred and seventy centimetres, possibly one seventy-five. But she's slender. I'd say fifty-five, maybe sixty kilos. Schröder, on the other hand, was a very large man: height one-ninety, weight at least two hundred kilos.'

'So she could not have overpowered him?'

De Vries gave a smile. 'I'm sure you gentlemen have seen enough improbable murders in your time not to take anything for granted. I would say it is unlikely. Marais had no marks on her of any physical struggle. No bruises, no defensive wounds, no abrasions on her fists . . .'

'From what you say, any punch of hers would have bounced off Schröder,' Lüdtke said.

'Exactly. And I can also confirm that we had her examined and there was no sign of recent sexual activity. Whatever happened between her and Schröder, it didn't go beyond a kiss.'

'Where is she now?'

'Ghent, I imagine. We had no reason to detain her, or any of her companions.'

'Why the hell not?'

Because either she was innocent, De Vries thought, *or she really had killed the bastard, in which case I'm happy to give her a head start over the rest of them. But I'm not telling you that.*

He shrugged. 'There was no evidence to suggest that she had done anything wrong.'

'Why the hell do you need evidence, man?' Rauter snapped. 'Throw her into custody and then look for the damn evidence.'

'I'm afraid, sir, that many of us old-timers find it hard to adjust to the new . . . methods,' Lüdtke said. 'It is unfortunate, but old habits sometimes die hard. I speak from personal experience.'

'Thank you,' De Vries said.

'Well, you'd better hope you've not let a murderer walk free,' said Rauter. 'I take it you took her address, place of work and all other relevant contact details?'

'Of course.'

Rauter gave an angry, dissatisfied grunt.

'Excuse me, sir, may I make a further observation?' De Vries asked. He waited for Rauter's nod of assent and then said, 'I'm sure you would agree, Herr *Brigadeführer*, that a highly trained SS officer in peak physical condition would not be overpowered by a mere woman, little more than half his size. His superiority to the Marais woman was a significant factor in my deliberations.'

Rauter said nothing. He could hardly argue with that line of thinking.

'Excuse me,' Dr Weimann piped up. 'Now can you tell us about the victim's condition?'

'Yes, doctor,' De Vries replied, glad to change the subject from Marlize Marais. 'I have to say that it's hard to see what killed Schröder. Once we knew that you were coming, our pathologist carried out a cursory examination, not wishing to disturb the body in any way.

'He found slight bruising around the chin, a small smear of blood below the left eye and some indication of a possible wound to the inside corner of the eye, close to the nose. There appeared to be significant bruising to the torso, sufficient to break a number of ribs, but not likely to have killed him. Aside from that, no gunshot wounds, no sign of stabbing and no defensive wounds. Schröder was found sitting against a tree with a cigarette in his fingers. He doesn't seem to have gone down fighting . . . and we have no idea how he went down at all.'

'Hmm . . . how interesting,' murmured Weimann.

The *SS-Brigadeführer* looked from the Berlin detective to the pathologist. 'Well, gentleman,' he said, 'now you know why I sent for you.'

• • •

Saffron thought about Gerhard and imagined his charred body lying in the broken, burned-out wreckage of his aircraft. She thought about the day her mother died and the sight of her lying on a table in a small clubhouse beside a polo field in Kenya, while a doctor tried to hold down her thrashing limbs and the blood from her miscarriage turned her skirt crimson. She thought about how far she was from home, and how alone she was in this hostile land . . . anything to keep the tears flowing.

'I'm sorry,' she sobbed as Elias made tentative, half-hearted attempts to comfort her, while failing to hide his irritation at the nuisance she was causing. 'But it's all been so horrible. First that man doing what he did . . . then discovering he was dead . . . and being interviewed by the police . . . It's too much!'

'There, there,' Elias muttered. 'I'm sure you'll soon forget all about it.'

'I won't! I know I won't! Nothing like this has ever happened to me. I'm a good girl . . . I am!'

Elias sighed frustratedly. 'Yes, yes, I'm sure you are. Perhaps you should take a day or two off work . . .'

'But you need me to type up the notes from the congress.'

'I'm sure they can wait.' Elias cast around for something else to say that might get this caterwauling female out of his hair for a day or two. 'Do you have any relatives you could stay with until you feel a little better?'

Saffron made a show of calming herself enough to wipe her streaming eyes and nose with a handkerchief. She glanced up at Elias, hoping that her face looked as hot, red and unappealing as it felt and said, 'Well, I do have a great-aunt. My mother gave me the last address she had for her. It was just outside Antwerp, I think . . . I'm sure I have it in my address book somewhere.'

'Perfect!' said Elias. 'We'll be pulling into Antwerp soon. Why don't you get out there, go and find your great-aunt . . .'

'But she's not expecting me.'

'Then it will be a surprise for her. She'll be delighted to have you to stay for a few days. You can come back to Ghent when you feel a little better. How does that sound?'

As though you've said exactly what I hoped you would, Saffron thought.

'I don't know . . .' She hesitated, aware that it would be fatal to seem too keen to accept Elias' offer. 'I don't want to be any trouble to her.'

'Oh, don't you worry about that. She'll be happy to hear all your news from South Africa. Perhaps you can tell her about your work for the party. That will impress her.'

'Well, if you're sure . . .'

'Go ahead.'

'Thank you, Mr Elias. You're a kind, thoughtful man. I'll work twice as hard when I get back to make up for the lost time.'

Elias gave her arm a reassuring pat, then slumped back in his seat. He was exhausted by the emotional turmoil and unsettled by Schröder's death, and now he was relieved that he wouldn't have to put up with the girl's hysterics all the way to Ghent.

When the train pulled into Rotterdam, Saffron found the nearest pharmacy and bought some blonde hair dye and a pair of scissors. She returned to the station and bought a ticket for the first train to Liège. She had a short while to kill before the train departed, so she went to the cafeteria and bought a cup of coffee and what was advertised as a cheese roll, but which turned out to be a paper-thin sliver of yellow rubber encased in a stodgy bun that tasted suspiciously of sawdust. Eating it filled her stomach and passed the time until she boarded her train, which departed on time.

It was now a little after half past twelve.

• • •

With the station clock about to reach half past two, the train from Antwerp arrived in Liège. It took Saffron fifteen minutes to walk to the Café Royal Standard. Inside there were a couple of men in blue workers' overalls, finishing off their glasses of brandy in one corner. A waitress was leaning on the zinc- topped counter of the bar, reading a magazine.

Saffron approached, put down her case and asked, 'Is Claude here?'

The waitress looked up and examined the newcomer with a sceptical sweep of her eyes. 'Who's asking?'

'Tell him it's a friend of Monsieur Burgers. We met a short while ago.'

'If you say so.'

The waitress pushed herself upright with an exaggerated display of effort and disappeared through the door behind the bar. Less than a minute later she was back.

'He's in there,' she said, nodding towards the open door. 'Quick!'

Saffron went into the office behind the bar, where Claude looked after the business side of the place.

'Please do not think me rude, *mademoiselle*, but I was hoping never to see you again. I take it you want to see Jean Burgers?'

'Yes.'

'And you are in trouble?'

'Yes.'

'Of what kind? I believe I have a right to know.'

Saffron saw no point in lying. She had been amazed to escape The Hague. It could only be a matter of time before the Dutch police and their German masters worked out what had happened and started the hunt for her.

'An SS officer tried to rape me.'

'But you are here, apparently unhurt, so he did not succeed.' Claude stroked his moustache as he pursued his line of reasoning. 'And you are the one who needs help, not him. What did you do?'

'I killed him.'

Saffron delivered the words in a flat, matter-of-fact tone and Claude's response was equally understated.

'*Merde*,' he grunted. 'Well, then, I congratulate you. The world is better, I am sure, for that bastard's passing. But I am also concerned. I do not wish any of their fury to be directed at me, or my family.'

'I understand. I need to make contact with Burgers and then I will be gone forever. Can you reach him for me, please?'

'Not fast enough for your purposes, I fear. But he will be coming this afternoon as usual.'

'He said he gets here at around five.'

'That's right.'

'May I stay until then?'

Claude stroked his whiskers again. 'You may stay until half past five. If he has not come by then, and I mean exactly then, you must go. If the Germans turn up, I will deny all knowledge of you. I am not a hero. If they torture me, I will talk. Or if they threaten my family.' He shrugged his shoulders. 'You are a brave girl. I admire you. But my wife and children come first.'

'I understand,' Saffron said. 'While I am here, is there a bathroom I could use? I may be some time.'

'You have a gastric ailment of some kind?'

Saffron smiled. 'No. I need to change my appearance.'

'Ah, I see . . . You'd better use the family bathroom. It's in our apartment, upstairs. Follow me.'

A few minutes later, Saffron was standing in front of the bathroom mirror, naked from the waist up, with her newly bought pair of scissors in her hand. She had unpinned her hair, which hung in glossy black waves that fell to her shoulders and down her back. She ran her fingers through it and gave a shake of her head, to feel her mane against her bare skin.

She said, 'Oh well,' lifted her right hand, looked back at the mirror and started cutting.

• • •

Hendrik Elias did not return directly to his home, or the VNV offices when he arrived back in Ghent. Instead, he and a couple of his closest associates went off for a leisurely lunch. They had important party matters to discuss, and he needed a stiff drink after putting up with the police delaying their departure for over an hour, followed by the Marais woman's wailing all the way from The Hague to Antwerp.

'This is what happens when one allows women to become involved in politics,' one of the other VNV men said, when the conversation turned to the Schröder business. 'They are unable to control their emotions, they distract men from more important matters and they inflame sexual passions that have no place in our work. We have to get rid of her. I insist.'

Elias' second colleague took a more emollient tone. 'Miss Marais seems a decent girl, and I'm sure she's done good work with the women's groups. But let's be honest, they are an irrelevance, a sideshow at best. And she's doing us more harm than good. It's not right for people to see us being stopped at the station by the police. Even if we are innocent of any wrongdoing, the mud sticks. You must see that, old man.'

Elias nodded. 'I can't argue with you, gentlemen. The events of the past two days have been most regrettable and I can see good reasons for letting Miss Marais go. But there is no need to make an immediate decision. I have sent Miss Marais away for a few days. I assure you that I will resolve the situation by the time she returns.'

Elias had given his colleagues enough of a concession to keep them quiet for the time being. It was almost four in the afternoon before he returned to his office to find his secretary in a state of anxiety.

'There's . . . there's someone waiting for you in your office – a German. He seems keen to speak to you. He's been waiting for a while.'

One look at the man told Elias that he was a Gestapo officer. After three years of occupation he had learned to spot the signs: the suit that was as clean and neatly pressed as a dress uniform, the short hair clipped high up the back of the neck and the side of the head, and above all the air of assurance that came from knowing that their power was absolute. This officer could have him arrested, interrogated, tortured and thrown into a prison camp, without any reference to a conventional legal system.

The Gestapo man got to his feet as Elias entered the room. He was of medium height, thin, with grey eyes behind round, wire-framed glasses.

'Good afternoon, Herr Elias,' he said. 'My name is Feirstein. I am an officer in the *Geheime Staatzpolizei*. Please, be seated.'

Elias found himself saying, 'Thank you,' as if it were a kindness to be allowed to sit in his own office. 'How can I help you?' he asked.

'Where is your employee, Marlize Marais? She is not here and her landlady, Frau Akkerman has not seen her since she left her house on Saturday morning, to accompany you to The Hague. What has become of her?'

'Ah . . .' Elias felt a prickle of fear beneath his armpits. Even though he had done nothing wrong, he felt guilty. 'I don't know . . . not exactly.'

'Why do you say that?'

'Well, she did not return with the rest of us to Ghent.'

'Why not?'

'She was feeling indisposed. To be frank with you, Feirstein, she was in a state of nervous hysteria. I put it down to the strain of her encounter with the SS officer Schröder, and then the police interviews this morning. She was weeping and making a scene. You know how it is when women become hysterical . . .'

Elias was hoping for man-to-man sympathy, but Feirstein remained impassive.

'Go on . . .' the German said.

'I suggested she should take some time off. She mentioned a relative, a great-aunt, if I remember rightly, who lived near Antwerp.'

'Did she give you the name of this great-aunt, or an address?'

'Er . . . no, I'm afraid not.'

'You did not ask her for these details?'

'It didn't occur to me. I was glad to be rid of her.'

'She left the train at Antwerp?'

'That's right.'

'And you saw no reason to think this was suspicious?'

Elias frowned. 'No . . . why should I?'

'Because a man is dead and Fräulein Marais was the last person to see him alive. That, in itself, is enough to arouse suspicion. But when she engineers a reason to leave the train and disappear – does that strike you as the behaviour of an innocent person?'

'How do you mean, "engineer"? The woman was having hysterics. I saw it for myself.'

'And you are sure her tears were genuine?'

'Well, they seemed . . .' Elias stopped mid-sentence. 'Oh dear God . . . you aren't suggesting . . . Has she been fooling us all along?'

Feirstein said nothing. His look of contempt was enough. He walked to the telephone on Elias' desk, dialled the operator and gave the number to which he wanted to be connected.

'None of the VNV idiots know where the Marais woman is. She left their train at Antwerp, claiming that she wanted to visit a relative who lived near there. No, she did not provide a name or address. Listen carefully, I don't want our colleagues in Holland thinking we can't manage our business down here in Belgium. Get everyone in Antwerp working this case. Start at the station. Talk to anyone who might have seen Marais. She is twenty-three years old. Height, one meter seventy-three, slender build. She had blue eyes, long black hair, thick and glossy, said to be very striking. Wait . . .'

Feirstein looked across at Elias, asked, 'What is she wearing?' and then passed the description of her clothes and suitcase onto the man on the other end of the line. 'Get onto Antwerp and tell them to work fast. I can stall Holland for a couple of hours, but they're getting it in the ear from Rauter. I need something to tell them. Two hours, maximum, that's all I can wait.'

Feirstein put down the phone and walked to the door without another word. Only when he had opened it and was about to leave did he turn to Elias and say, 'You will be seeing me again.'

• • •

The Security Police office in Antwerp threw every available man at the task of tracking down Marlize Marais. A combination of Gestapo, Criminal Police and uniformed SS personnel flooded the station and spoke to members of the station staff, shopkeepers, waitresses in the cafeteria, flower- and newspaper-sellers. By half past five they had established that the suspect had been seen getting off the train from The Hague, purchasing a ticket for Liège and boarding the outbound train.

There was a gap of between ten and fifteen minutes between the times given by the ticket-office clerk who had sold Marais her ticket and the waitress who had taken her order for food and drink. This seemed odd, since it would only take two minutes at most to walk from one location to the other. But the officer collating all the evidence concluded that the discrepancy was most simply explained by one or both of the witnesses getting their timing wrong. In any case, it was not important. They had established that Marais was no longer in Antwerp.

She was someone else's problem now.

• • •

Shortly before five, Rauter, De Vries, Lüdtke and Weimann met again in the police mortuary and this time it was Weimann who did the talking. 'I am going to take you through the injuries in the order in which I believe they were inflicted. Let me direct you first to the area of the victim's genitalia. I have shaved the pubic region to enable you to see the traces of bruising above the genitalia, consistent with a blow, most probably with a knee.

'A man who has been hit in that vulnerable region instinctively doubles up. His head descends, leaving him open to a blow to the face. This is significant if the victim is taller than his assailant. Note the contusions to the lower left jaw, close to the chin. They are not particularly vivid, suggesting that the blow was not a punch with the fist, but a slap with the palm or heel of the hand.

'The effect of such a blow is dramatic. It spins the head on the neck, causing severe ligament damage. As the head turns it takes the body with it, so that even a large man can be knocked to the ground. And the motion causes the brain to knock repeatedly against the inside of the skull. This concusses the victim.

'Everything that I have described so far has taken place in a matter of a few seconds: five, maybe, ten at most. The victim has been taken by surprise. He has not landed a single blow: his knuckles show no sign of bruising. Now he is on the ground, lying on his back, and the third blow is struck. Look at the upper torso. Note the two vivid contusions side by side. Two identical objects have hit this man simultaneously. Tell me, Chief Inspector De Vries, when you interviewed Fraülein Marais, what kind of shoes was she wearing?'

De Vries closed his eyes to conjure a picture of the women in his mind and said, 'Perfectly ordinary, lace-up walking shoes, I think.'

'And did her toes and heels click on the floor as she walked?'

'I think so. I wouldn't have thought anything of it. Everyone's feet click. People reinforce their soles to prevent wear and tear.'

'Quite so. And it is unfortunate that you do not have those shoes in your possession because if you did, my guess is that the heels would match the marks on the victim's chest.'

'A "bronco-kick",' said Rauter, saying the phrase in English.

'I'm sorry, sir, what do you mean?' De Vries asked.

'As we know from our interrogation of enemy agents, the "bronco-kick" is the British term for a two-footed, jumping kick, which the handbook used to train agents in unarmed combat recommends, rather than a single blow from the toe of a boot. The same handbook also shows trainee agents how to attack a man by striking him first in the testicles and then in the face, with the flat of the hand, as Dr Weimann has described.'

'You mean, Miss Marais is a British agent?' Lüdtke asked.

'Yes . . . but that is impossible. Schröder told the truth. We have control of all communications between London and Holland. They could not have landed an agent in Holland without us knowing about it.'

'Perhaps that explains why they sent her to South Africa and then Portugal, and let us bring her to Belgium, without letting anyone in the Low Countries know she was coming. My guess is that Marais, or whoever she is, has been sent in to find out what has gone wrong with their previous agents. And now she knows the situation in both Belgium and the Netherlands, from the mouths of German officers.'

Rauter's face paled. 'My God . . . how could they have been so stupid? We have to stop her.'

Weimann coughed to attract the other men's attention. 'Before you do, sir, there is one thing you should know. None of the injuries I have so far described were fatal. Schröder would have been badly injured, but he would have made a full recovery. But Marais could not allow that. She took a hatpin, or a brooch with a long pin, and inserted it in the corner of the eye while Schröder was lying helpless on the ground. Then she pushed it through the back of the orbital bone into the brain, where she manipulated the tip of the pin to cause the greatest possible internal damage to the brain.

'*SS-Hauptsturmführer* Schröder died of a cerebral haemorrhage. And he died slowly, which explains the other mystery of this case, from a pathology perspective. The body was arranged beneath the tree so that people would take it for a resting man. But the victim was still alive when it happened: blood was circulating in his system. I can assure you, the internal appearance would have been very different had he been dead when he was moved.

'But how could the killer move and then arrange a large, fit, strong man who was still alive? Answer: because he was already dying and did not have the power to resist. Whoever committed this crime is a highly trained fighter, capable of violent action and then an act of slow, calculated homicide. The murderer then covered their tracks, buying time to get away.'

'She will not get away, Herr *Doktor*, you have my word on that,' said Rauter. 'Within the hour, every SS man and local police officer in the Low Countries will be searching for Marlize Marais.'

'You'd better tell them to be careful,' said *Kommissar* Lüdtke. 'I have dealt with a great many killers in my time. But few of them have been as dangerous as this.'

● ● ●

Saffron grinned as Jean Burgers' eyes widened in disbelief. 'What do you think?' she asked coquettishly, tilting her head to one side and then the other. Her long black hair was now a short, fringed blonde bob.

'I honestly would not recognise you. If you had been sitting in the café as I walked in, I would have walked right past you.'

'Good. I've changed my clothes, too, since this morning.'

'So . . . Claude told me what you had done. Do you think the *Boches* know it was you that killed that man?'

'We have to assume that.'

'Then we must also assume that they will go crazy trying to find you. The first thing to do is to get you out of Liège. There are bound to be roadblocks on every road out of the city, so we have to get past them on foot. Once we are beyond them, I will get us a car and then we will be able to drive across country.'

'Won't the Germans be watching the roads outside the city?'

'Not all of them. There are too many. Don't worry, I know my way around all the country lanes.'

'But where will we go?'

'The radio operator you met . . .'

'The one you wouldn't introduce me to?'

'Yes . . . His name is André Deforge. His parents have a farm about forty kilometres from here, between Malmédy and Spa. They feel the same way we do about the Germans. They will let us hide you there for a few days, but no longer. It would be too dangerous. They would never give you up, you understand. But if a neighbour hears cars driving by in the night, or strange people in the fields . . . It's very sad, but a lot of people are willing to help the Gestapo. They think things will go better for them if they do.'

'Will André be able to bring his radio out to us? I need to get in touch with London.'

'No . . . that would be too dangerous. Like I said, he has been crazy about radios since he was a boy. He has all his old equipment hidden away in a barn. Are you ready to go?'

'Yes, but I need to get rid of my suitcase.'

'Give it to me. Claude has a furnace in the basement. It provides all the hot water for the café and the apartment and heat in the winter time.'

Saffron handed it over.

'Are you sure you have taken everything from here that you need?'

'Yes. It's all in my handbag.'

'Then I will give this to Claude now. It will be ashes by dinnertime.'

• • •

The moment he received the news from Antwerp, Feirstein had contacted his opposite number in Liège, Inspector Fritz Krankl, explained the situation and told him that locating and apprehending Marlize Marais was now his number one priority.

'Is she the main suspect in the Schröder case?' Krankl asked.

'I don't know for sure. But let it be known that she is a killer on the loose. That will frighten people and make them more eager to report her.'

'That makes sense. But I worked with Karsten Schröder in Mainz before the war. He was a mountain of a man. A real bastard, too. Always happier using his fists than his brains. Hard to believe a woman could kill him.'

'Any man can be killed if his guard is down. All that matters is that we have lost one of our own and this woman is the only suspect. Let's find her first, then concern ourselves with the finer details.'

'Don't worry, Feirstein, my men are hard workers. We'll get this woman, you can be sure about that.' He determined to immediately contact the handler looking after Prosper Dezitter, 'the man with the missing finger', the Nazi's chief informer in Belgium.

•   •   •

As they left the Café Royal Standard, a black Mercedes with speakers mounted on the roof drove by. A harsh metallic voice announced: *'Achtung! Achtung!* A killer is on the run in your city. She is a young woman. She is tall, with long black hair and blue eyes, last seen wearing a dark blue dress and a maroon coat, carrying a suitcase. She is wanted for the murder of a German officer. If you see her, report it at once to the authorities. The sooner she is caught, the better it will be for everyone . . . *Achtung! Achtung!'*

Saffron shivered as the Mercedes drove away and the voice from the speakers faded. She clutched Jean Burgers' arm tighter and they walked down the road in the same direction that the speaker-car had taken. Saffron felt every eye on the street was looking at her and they could see through her pathetic disguise.

They passed a group of workmen, standing outside a bar with beer glasses in their hands, and one of them called out, 'Cheer up, blondie!' and another shouted, 'I'll make you happy if he won't!' And as the laughter and wolf whistles subsided, Saffron realised that the looks were due to her tarty blonde hair.

Burgers paid no attention. He was trying to walk as quickly as possible without drawing attention to themselves. 'We have to get across the river,' he said. 'Without that we can't get anywhere.'

They pressed on, breaking into a run down a couple of quiet, deserted side-streets, then emerged onto the Quai de Rome, the main road along the bank of the River Meuse. On the far side of the road, closest to the water, there was a broad path and Burgers led her onto it. He turned right. In front of them, no more than a few hundred metres away, the three cast-iron arches of a magnificent old bridge stretched across the river. There were two German army trucks parked in front of it. Soldiers were unloading poles, boards, sandbags and rolls of barbed wire from a truck under an officer's supervision. Saffron spotted a pair of plainclothes policemen, either detectives or Gestapo, scanning the people passing by them.

'A roadblock,' whispered Burgers.

'Leave it to me,' Saffron replied.

They were close to the bridge. One side of the road had been blocked off and the soldiers were putting a barrier across the other. It would be a minute or two before the barrier was fully operational.

Saffron saw a woman with dark hair, whose coat looked like the one she had been wearing. One of the plainclothes men had stopped her. He was demanding to see her papers. The woman was scrabbling in her handbag, scared out of her wits.

The other cop looked in their direction. Saffron smiled at him flirtatiously and then called out, 'Hello, boys!' at the nearest soldiers. The men stopped what they were doing and rewarded her attention with broad grins and a couple of whistles, until the sergeant in charge shouted at them to get back to work.

By then, Saffron and Burgers were on the bridge.

'I should have gone blonde years ago,' she joked. 'I had no idea what I was missing.'

His eyes were fixed on the road ahead. The bridge was sited at the point where the smaller River Ourthe flowed into the Meuse. There was a narrow sliver of land between the two rivers and a fourth arch took the bridge over the Ourthe. Only when they had stepped off the bridge onto the far bank did Burgers allow himself to relax.

There were more roadblocks as they made their way out of the city, heading southeast. On one occasion they had to shin up a drainpipe at the back of a shop that had closed for the day and clamber over the rooftops of the buildings next to it to get around the Germans below. On another they had to sneak through the gardens of some large Victorian villas on the edge of town.

'I think the way will be clear from now on,' Burgers said. 'Even the Germans can't close every road in Belgium.' He grimaced. 'Now I have to steal a car. I don't like that. I don't want to deprive a decent citizen of his prize possession.'

Saffron did not argue. She owed this man her life. It was hardly fair to criticise him for being too scrupulous. They walked for about a kilometre across country and came into a village with a square, around which stood a church, a café, several shops, houses and a *mairie*, or town hall.

A light was on in the *mairie*. A large Renault was parked outside it.

'The mayor must be working late tonight,' he said. 'There is his car. It must be his because, look, there is a sign saying the space is reserved. If he is the mayor then he is, by definition, a collaborator, because you cannot hold a public office unless you have been approved by *les Boches*. Therefore I do not feel bad taking his car. I am striking a blow for freedom.'

Saffron patted him on the back. 'Well said! Would you like me to break into the car for you?'

'You can do that?'

'I can.'

'I am impressed. But there will be no need. It will not be locked. Who would be crazy enough to take the mayor's car? And, before you ask, I am capable of starting the engine.'

Sure enough, the doors opened without being forced. Burgers reached beneath the dashboard, pulled out two wires, touched them together to complete the ignition circuit.

'Superb!' He beamed. 'Let's go!'

• • •

It was still light when they reached the farm where André's parents, Luc and Julie Deforge, lived. They took Saffron in without hesitation. Burgers soon left. He planned to drive most of the way back to Liège, leave the car a few kilometres from the village where it had originally come from and then catch a bus into the city.

'I will return with André tomorrow and we will contact London. Until then, *au revoir*!'

Julie climbed a ladder into the farmhouse attic, carrying an oil storm-lantern, and Saffron passed up blankets, sheets and pillows before following her up. She entered a dark, musty space that seemed like a repository for all the junk that any family accumulates. Saffron saw an old rocking horse, two small, child-sized wooden chairs and a pair of boy's bicycles in one corner. Elsewhere she noticed a stack of empty picture frames, a coat stand, the rusting components of an old iron bedstead and tea chests piled almost as high as the ceiling against the far wall.

Julie had placed the lantern on top of a small wooden table. Saffron assumed that they would assemble the bed that she had spotted. But instead Julie walked across the attic to one side of the pile of tea chests, placed her hands against them and pushed.

To Saffron's amazement the pile rolled smoothly across the floor in a single mass. She saw that they had been arranged in a rough, apparently random triangular shape, like a stepped pyramid. One side of it exactly matched the angle of the roof, so the boxes could slide all the way to the side wall. In the space where they had been standing was a door.

'That's marvellous!' she exclaimed.

Julie smiled. 'André's big brother, Henri, did that. He could always make anything, that boy. He found the chests, then screwed them together and put in little wheels, like the ones on the bottom of furniture, inside the boxes, where they could not be seen. He and André had their secret place where they could hide from everyone.'

Julie's face hardened, and she spat on the floor. 'The filthy *Boches* took him to work in their factories. They have turned our men into slaves. They'll be after André too, once he finishes his studies. Aahhh . . . what can any of us do, eh? Come.'

She led Saffron into a small room, which was lit by a skylight. 'It cannot be seen from the ground. The chimney is in the way. Now, look here . . .'

The edge of the box-pile protruded across the doorway. Saffron saw a wooden handle, facing the room. Julie took hold of it, pulled and the boxes rolled back across the open space. Then she closed the door. '*Alors* . . . now we are hidden.'

There were four mattresses on the floor, an empty chamberpot and a discarded newspaper. Saffron picked it up and saw that is was dated 14 March 1942. There was a picture of Hitler on the front page, over which someone had drawn warts, devil's horns and blacked-out teeth.

'You are not the first guest at our little hotel,' Julie said. 'Four of your pilots were here last year. We sheltered them until the Resistance came to take them away. I think there is a secret route to Spain. Maybe you could go the same way.'

'Yes . . .'

'Come with me, *chérie.*' Julie went through the same routine with the door and the boxes in reverse. A few seconds later, they were back in the attic and there was no sign whatsoever of the secret room.

'Let us go outside,' Julie said, leading the way down the ladder. 'No one will see us . . . and we will pick some flowers, to make your room less miserable. I have made a casserole of pork and apples for Luc and me to eat for our supper. We can get some broad beans and potatoes from the kitchen garden and there will be more than enough for three.'

'Please don't go short on my account. I know how hard it is for farmers with the Germans demanding everything you produce for themselves.'

'Pah!' Julie snorted disdainfully as they walked back down the stairs to the ground floor of the farmhouse. 'They are like locusts. If we only had what they allowed us, we would starve. But we are not as foolish as they imagine. Did you know that pigs and chickens are both woodland creatures? *Alors* . . . when we know *les Boches* are coming, we return one or two of the pigs and maybe six of the chickens to nature. They have a little vacation among the trees. Then they come back to the pigsties and the chicken runs and all their friends are gone. But we have meat and eggs, and even the Germans would not deny us our potager to give us vegetables and fruit.'

Saffron helped Julie gather a basket of supplies for her supper and a bunch of sweet peas for her room. They ate splendidly and washed the food down with cider made from the farm's own apples.

It became clear that Burgers had not told the Deforges why Saffron needed their help; they had known him since he was a boy and their trust in him was absolute. Still, she felt she owed it to them to know the truth, and made it clear that she would bear them no ill will if her presence was too great a risk to their own safety. But when they heard what had happened to her, the Deforges were united in their support.

Luc took his pipe from his mouth and pointed the stem at Saffron, emphasising his words with little jabs as he assured her, 'If a man tries to rape a woman, he deserves to die. And if a man joins those sons-of-whores, the SS, then he deserves to die, too. If he is in the SS and a rapist . . .' Luc sat back, feeling no need to complete the sentence. He turned to his wife. 'Bring us some cognac, my love – the good bottle. I wish to drink a toast to this brave young woman.'

• • •

That night, Saffron sat on the mattress on the floor of the secret room with her head in her hands. In front of her was the old newspaper, Hitler staring up at her, the defacement of his features doing little to alleviate the murderous intent in his eyes. The date of the newspaper was two years and eleven months since that Good Friday in 1939 in Paris when she and Gerard held each other close, a moment of transcendence when time itself stood still. She missed his touch so deeply that the emptiness inside her ached. The photo of the two of them by the Eiffel Tower was in her hand, a little faded now. She wondered if he retained those strong forearms, his delicate hands, his clear, bright purpose, whether his soul had been disfigured, scarred or even destroyed, or had he cheated death? She could never give up hope.

• • •

The following evening, Burgers returned, riding pillion on André's motorbike.

'The *Boches* are going crazy,' he told Saffron when they met up in the farmhouse kitchen. 'You know that poor woman we saw with the Gestapo at the bridge yesterday evening? Every female who is more than a metre-sixty tall and has even slightly dark brown hair is being stopped. They are offering rewards for anyone who has information, and threatening death to anyone who helps you. I have been made aware of a particularly dangerous informer who goes by the name of Prosper Dezitter . . .' Burgers hesitated, concerned by a sudden grimace on Saffron's face. 'What's the matter?'

'When I came to the café yesterday afternoon, there were two men there . . . and a waitress I'd not seen before. They could identify me. And that would be bad for Claude.'

'These two men, were they wearing overalls, like labourers?'

'Yes.'

'And did the waitress have the air of a woman who did not give a damn about her job, but only wanted to read her magazine?'

Saffron laughed. 'How did you know?'

'Because the men are Pierre and Marco. They are in the café every afternoon and they are passionate communists. They would never betray anyone to the Nazis. And the waitress was Madeleine, Claude's daughter. It is true, she and her papa have fights that you would not believe, but they love each other very much. You are safe with her. I will brief you later on Prosper Dezitter, dark complexion, black hair, around five foot six inches tall. His nickname is: *l'homme au doigt coupe*. His mistress is called Florie Dings – she too is not to be trusted.'

• • •

'André, let's go and inspect your radio gear. It's been stuck in that barn for three years. I hope it's not been eaten by rats.'

As they walked over to the barn, Burgers said, 'Have you thought about how you can escape? We could arrange for you to get false papers and travel permits, but I must be honest: the quality is not perfect, and the way the Germans are looking for you . . . I cannot believe you could get to Spain, or even Switzerland without being caught.'

'I agree,' Saffron said. 'I've been thinking about it. I have to get back to London. I've got too much information for a few radio messages. I must tell them in person. But if I try to get out overland, it could be months before I'm back in England. And I'll put too many lives in danger along the way. I have to get out by air.'

'Can they do that?'

'There's a special squadron that flies in and out of France all the time. They don't come over here, to the Low Countries. But where we are seems rural; maybe they could fly here. But would there be anywhere safe to land?'

Burgers called out, 'Hey, André, whatever happened to the field at La Sauvinière? You know the one that people used to fly from? Are the Luftwaffe using it?'

'Not as far as I know,' André replied. His voice was slightly muffled because his upper body and head were leaning under the bonnet of the old van in which the Deforges had taken their produce to market, before the Germans had removed that possibility by taking everything for themselves. 'No one round here is allowed to fly, of course. It's probably a cow pasture now.'

André lifted various bits of kit out of the engine bay and placed them on the ground. He stood up straight, wiped the back of his hand across his forehead and said, 'But it's on the road from Spa to Francorchamps. Hardly an ideal place for a secret rendezvous.'

'Yes, but it's a huge space,' Burgers countered. 'And I'm sure parts of it are hidden from the road by trees.'

André considered then nodded. 'I think so too.'

'There you go,' Burgers said to Saffron. 'Now you have an airfield.'

An hour later, André had reassembled his old radio and tuned it to the frequency used to call London. Meanwhile Saffron and Burgers had studied a local map supplied by Monsieur Deforge. She composed and coded her message and was ready to send it.

Following the codes that identified Saffron and the pad she was using, it read:

HOLLAND WORSE MARKS FEARED. TOTAL BLOW-OUT. HAVE VITAL INFO. AM HUNTED BY GERMANS. KILLED SS MAN SCHRODER. COVER BLOWN. REQUEST IMMEDIATE AIR EXTRACTION. SUGGEST FIELD AT LA SAUVINIERE 4KM ESE SPA BELGIUM OFF N62 ROAD TO FRANCORCHAMPS. PLS REPLY TONIGHT, 22.00 GMT

'Less than two minutes,' André said when he had finished transmitting. 'I'm getting better.'

• • •

The transmission was picked up by an operator for the *Funk-Horchdienst*, the German radio interception service, but they were unable to get more than a general fix on the source: eastern Belgium, not far from the border with the Reich itself. It was not an area from which they had previously detected any radio traffic to or from London. When the cryptographers were handed the text, they noted that the pattern of letters was unlike standard British coding. One member of the team recalled seeing something similar a fortnight earlier. But there was no time to break the code. The Führer had recently ordered that all radio and cryptographic staff had to be dedicated to Russian radio traffic. Army Group Central was about to be thrown at the Soviet front line in the biggest offensive action since Barbarossa, and that was all that mattered.

• • •

'What do you make of this?' Gubbins asked, holding a copy of Saffron's message. 'Is it genuine?'

'The coding is spot-on,' Leo Marks replied. 'And there's one other thing: our girls recognised the style of the chap who communicates with us from Groupe G. That ties in with what Courtney said in her first message.'

'Next question: Amies, do we have any information to corroborate this talk of the Germans hunting Courtney?'

'Yes, sir, I checked with Signals and there's been a lot of chatter about a British spy killing an SS officer: radio traffic between German units in Holland and Belgium, and radio broadcasts ordering the public to cooperate. There hasn't been anything about her being arrested. The Jerries would have wanted the world to know if they'd caught their quarry.'

'That makes sense. N, what about this Schröder chap?'

The head of the Netherlands section had only just found out that an operation had been run on his patch without his prior knowledge. He had been extremely put out by the news. But there was no point making a fuss. Self-pity was not an emotion for which Gubbins had any time.

'He is, or was, an exceptionally nasty piece of work, even by SS standards,' N said. 'He's led the death squads on at least two occasions when hostages have been murdered in reprisal for acts by the Dutch Resistance. I would class him as a significant loss to the SS in Holland.'

'Can I take it that we are agreed that this message was indeed sent by Ensign Courtney, that she did kill Schröder and that she is now in grave danger?'

Seeing no sign of dissent, Gubbins continued, 'Now, to the question of the intelligence she has gathered. What do you make of it, Amies? I must say that the idea that Courtney has had private chats with the Military Governor of Belgium does strike one as somewhat farfetched.'

'True, but she named Colonel Scholtz as her source for the news that our agents had been seized. I'll be honest, his name was new to me. So far as I knew, the local Abwehr was run by a chap called Colonel Servaes. But I have confirmed that she was right. Scholtz is the new man in charge. More importantly, sir, I do not believe that Saffron Courtney is the kind of fantasist who invents information to make themselves appear more valuable or important. The person who does that fears that they are insignificant. I doubt that girl has ever felt insignificant in her life.'

'I tend to agree with you,' Gubbins said. 'What's more, if she has found out what we wanted to know about our network in the Low Countries, even if it's bad news – in fact, especially if it's bad news – we need to know everything she has to tell us.

'Amies, you sent her and she's on your patch – I'm putting you in charge of getting her out. Send her a message. Keep it as short as you can. Tell her we're on our way, tomorrow night. She will receive instructions at twenty-one hundred GMT.'

'Tomorrow? The RAF may have a word or two to say about that. Short notice for them.'

'Then they'd better start work on it right away. Call Tempsford. Impress upon them the importance of the agent and the need for urgency. If they want any recce photographs, they'll need a plane in the air first thing in the morning.'

'Yes, sir.' Amies looked at Gubbins. 'May I speak frankly, sir?'

'Go ahead.'

'As you know, I have the highest opinion of Ensign Courtney, and I have no doubt of the significance of the intelligence she is carrying. But I feel bound to point out, as a devil's advocate, that this is a high-risk operation. If things go wrong, our enemies in Whitehall won't hesitate to use it against us.'

'I know that, Major. But let me ask you: if you were in my shoes, would you order this mission?'

'Without hesitation. There's a danger of losing Courtney if we try to get her out. There's a virtual certainty of losing her if we don't.'

'Then we'd better go and get her, hadn't we?'

• • •

Feirstein was not a senior Gestapo officer, yet circumstances had dropped the Schröder/Marais case in his lap and he had the ambition and initiative to take control of it. He was assembling scraps of evidence, like pieces of a jigsaw. He had not connected them all to create the entire picture. But he felt sure that it would not be long before everything became clear.

Piece one: Marais had taken the train to Liège. She had been seen leaving the station and spotted walking through the city, but her destination was unknown.

Piece two: that same evening a Renault car had been stolen from a village outside the city. It was recovered the following morning but its owner, a local mayor who was keen to cooperate with the German authorities, was able to confirm, both from the odometer and the fuel gauge, that it had been driven around one hundred kilometres since he had last seen it.

Piece three: a garage mechanic, working late, recalled seeing a black Renault travelling through the village of Cornémont, twenty kilometres southeast of the point where the car was stolen.

Piece four: a listening station had picked up a message, sent the next evening, from an area that was consistent with the journey taken by the Renault. The message had not been decoded, partly because the cryptographic staff had other priorities and because the code matched none that they had seen before.

Hypothesis: a person or persons unknown had helped the suspect Marais to get out of Liège, hidden her away in the countryside and then contacted her bosses in London. Now it was a matter of finding her.

Feirstein gave two sets of orders. The first underlined the importance of maintaining vigilance in all railway stations, and all cross-border trains between Belgium and France. Under no circumstances should Marais, or anyone answering to her description, be allowed to leave the country.

Having trapped her within Belgian borders, the second imperative was to locate her. Gestapo personnel were instructed to contact the thousands of Belgians living in an arc southeast of Liège, between the city and the border of the Reich, who had volunteered information to the Secret Police. Ask them about suspicious movements, anyone who was believed to be involved in subversive or resistance activity, and, in particular, anyone who might possess a radio transmitter capable of sending a message to London.

• • •

Fritz Krankl was a colleague, a comrade and, to some extent, a friend of Feirstein. But he had been trained to operate in a world that – on the strict orders of the Führer – ran on brutal Darwinian principles. Nazism did not believe in God, but it possessed a profound faith in the survival of the fittest. One service was pitted against another, units within services competed to see who could produce the best results, and men were in a state of constant conflict, even with their friends.

Krankl could see no good reason to be helpful to Feirstein. Of course, the spy Marais had to be apprehended. But it would be better for Krankl if he were the man to do it, and an act of lunacy to give Feirstein the means to do it himself. The suspect was believed to be hiding in an area of Belgium that fell under the control of the Liège Security Police Office, of which the Gestapo was part. Krankl was the officer assigned to the case. He would therefore be the one to arrest the woman.

He had a lead. Prosper had been useful. There was a woman, a farmer's wife called Fabienne Moreau, who lived near the town of Spa. So far as her wide circle of female friends knew, she was a delightful, charming, sweet-natured soul, in whom they could confide all their secrets. But Madame Moreau harboured secret resentments. Her husband was a drunk. She was convinced he was having affairs with local women. The other women in her set regarded her as a saint for remaining loyal to her feckless man. But she seethed with hatred at the way they looked down on her, deceived her, stole what little was left of her pleasures from her own bedroom. The thought of her husband coupling with these women enraged and disgusted her, filled her with bitter betrayal. And when the Gestapo offered her the chance to get back at them, she had leaped at the opportunity. But her information had value and she was determined to find the best price.

The Gestapo officer who had contacted her gritted his teeth and clenched his fists. 'OK,' he said.

'You should go to the Deforges' farm,' she told him. 'I remember, one of their boys was always tinkering with radio sets.'

'What was the name of this boy?'

Madame Moreau thought: *which of them was it? There was Henri, the older one, and then the younger brother . . . What was he called?*

'The name, please,' the Gestapo man insisted.

No, it can't have been him, anyway. Henri was the practical one, forever making things, or fixing his father's car. It must have been him.

'Henri Deforge,' Madame Moreau said. 'I've got their address, if you want it.'

• • •

The next morning, Saffron had opened the hideaway door and was about to pull the boxes aside when she heard vehicles, a truck and car, coming down the drive that led from the road to the farmhouse.

She closed the door and sat down on her mattress.

There was nothing she could do except sit and wait, and pray that no one decided to find out what lay behind that pile of tea chests.

• • •

Julie Deforge was standing at the front door, peering out at her courtyard and doing her best to remain calm as she watched the soldiers get down from their truck. The passenger door of the car opened and Krankl emerged. He was wearing a plain business suit. That frightened Julie even more than the gun that the soldier next to him was carrying. It meant that he was Gestapo.

She heard Luc walking down the hall behind her, then felt his hands on her shoulders as he gently moved her out of the way, saying, 'I'll deal with this.' He stepped outside.

Julie followed her husband through the door. Luc was a good, brave man, but his nature was too honest, too direct. She loved him for those qualities as a husband. When dealing with the Germans, however, honesty was rarely the best policy, and he could panic under pressure. He might need her to protect him from himself.

Luc stood in front of the door, legs apart, hands in his pockets, looking Krankl in the eye as he asked, 'What do you want?'

'Are you Luc Deforge?'

'Yes.'

'And this is your wife, Julie Deforge?'

'Yes, what of it?'

'You have a son, Henri, correct?'

'Yes.'

'And he is a keen radio ham?'

Without thinking, Luc responded, 'No, that's—'

Before he could finish the sentence, Julie dashed forward, grabbed her husband's arm and said, 'Don't, Luc! Don't try to deny it!' She looked into his eyes and prayed to God that he understood what she was doing. 'Don't you see? It's not worth it.'

She turned towards Krankl and said, 'Yes, it's true. Henri has been keen on radios since he was a small boy. Why do you ask?'

'We have intercepted radio transmissions being sent by British spies to their masters in London. The transmissions came from this area.'

'Well, Henri can't have sent them, officer.'

'Why not?'

'Because he's in Germany, working in a factory. Your people called him up and sent him away.'

'I see . . .'

Krankl inwardly cursed the informant who had sent them on this pointless mission. But all might not be lost. 'It is possible that someone else may have used his equipment. Show it to me now . . . or my men will find it and believe me, you will regret your non-cooperation.'

'Yes, of course, officer,' Julie said. 'Follow me.' She had taken charge now and Luc, seeing what she was up to, was letting her get on with it.

Krankl turned to the senior sergeant next to him. 'Stay here, Schmitt. Make sure your men are ready if I need them.' He went into the house with the Deforges.

Julie led Krankl to André's bedroom, which was much as it had been when he was a boy. A basic crystal radio set was sitting by a window that looked out onto the garden.

'That's my son's radio,' she said. She gave a laugh and said, 'But I don't think it could reach London. My son had enough trouble speaking to his friends in the village.'

'Is this all there is?' Krankl asked.

'I think there are some more parts for it in the table drawer, but don't ask me what any of them are.'

Krankl opened the drawer and was met by a mass of wires, old valves, a radio crystal and some screwdrivers and other tools.

'I hope that reassures you, officer,' Julie said. 'We are good people. We want a quiet life. We don't want to cause any trouble.'

She could see the German weighing up what to do next. *Please, God, don't let him search the house*, she prayed. *Don't go up to the attic. Don't try to look in the tea chests.*

Krankl sensed Julie was nervous, on edge. But that meant nothing. Anyone the Gestapo ever met was terrified.

He walked downstairs. Everything the Deforges had said was unremarkable, and it would only take a couple of hours to check whether their son was in the country or not. He would have done that basic background check already if there hadn't been such a hurry to solve the case. There was something nagging him: *Why did the wife interrupt her husband like that? What was he about to say?*

He looked back at the farmhouse. There was something going on here, he was sure of it. But there was no point interrogating the Deforges if he didn't know the right questions to ask, nor in tearing the house apart if he didn't know what he was looking for. It would create further resentment among the locals.

The better option was to make them think they'd got away with it and then let them hang themselves.

Krankl walked towards his car, telling the sergeant, 'Let's go.'

Once he got to the car, he told the driver, 'Take me to the police station in Spa.'

The car set off, followed by the truck. When they reached Spa, Krankl spoke to the chief inspector who ran the local police station. He gave him the address of the Deforge's farm.

'I want it watched,' he said. 'Round the clock. Be discreet.'

He headed back to his vehicles. Fabienne Moreau had not been the only informant claiming to have information about radio users. Word of the money they had paid Moreau passed from house to house. And Prosper had given them another six leads to check.

• • •

The pilots of RAF 161 (Special Duties) Squadron were based at Tempsford, in Bedfordshire, an airfield whose existence was as secret as the work they did there to the Nazis. For it was 161 Squadron's task to fly by night, ferrying the agents working for SOE and various other intelligence agencies in and out of

Occupied Europe. The few men and women who knew what they were up to called them the Moonlight Squadron.

In his office, Wing Commander Percy Pickard, known to all his men as 'Pick', perched his lanky figure on the edge of his desk, one hand in his pocket. Opposite him sat one of his best men, Flight Lieutenant Bobby Warden, whom he'd called in to discuss an urgent assignment that had been dropped into the squadron's lap.

'It's a rush job, Bobby, can't pretend otherwise, but I thought it would be up your street,' Pick began. 'A damsel in distress needs a knight in shining armour to rescue her. Damned good-looking damsel too, from what I hear.'

'I hope she's suitably grateful, sir,' Warden had replied. 'Happily ever after, and all that.'

'Seriously, old chap, this one's top priority. Baker Street wouldn't go into any details, you know what they're like. But they made it plain that this young lady's picked up some damned important gen. The Photographic Reconnaissance Unit have sent a Spit over the area; should have the pictures mid-afternoon. Feast your eyes on them before you take a shufti down to Tangmere for fuelling and the final check-up.'

'I can't help noticing that you haven't told me where I'm going.'

'The destination will tell you how desperate they are to get this girl back to Blighty . . . You're going to Belgium.'

Warden could not believe his ears. 'Belgium? But I thought it was a matter of policy: no drops or pick-ups from the Low Countries. Too crowded, too little open country, too much ack-ack.'

'That is the policy, yes. But not tonight. Here are some crumbs of comfort: the moon's almost full tonight, and the weather men are predicting clear skies most of the way, so visibility shouldn't be an issue. As an added bonus, Bomber Command have got a big show on tonight. Seven hundred Lancasters and Stirlings bound for Frankfurt. They'll be flying over Belgium, so that should keep the local ack-ack and Luftwaffe boys busy, provide a spot of diversion for you.'

'Well, it should be an interesting ride, sir. We'd better hope she's worth it.'

• • •

An hour or so after Krankl's visit to Spa, one of the local police took up his station outside the Deforges' farmhouse. At lunchtime, Luc rode a bicycle through the gates of his property. It had a basket on the front, inside which were a bottle of home-made cider and a ham baguette. He waved to the policeman, dismounted and wandered over, carrying the provisions.

'*Salut*, Pierre!' he said. 'Julie thought you might like some lunch.'

'Ah, Luc, my friend, you're a lucky man to have a wife like that.'

'Oh, I know, believe me. So, you're watching us, eh?'

Pierre shrugged. 'Pah! What can I do? Some Gestapo son of a bitch said you were to be put under observation, round-the-clock.'

'I wonder why?'

'Who knows what goes on inside their crazy Nazi heads?'

'You won't have much to observe, I'm afraid.'

The policeman chuckled. 'Even if I did, I'd be sure not to see it.' He looked around to make sure that he could not be overheard and added, 'Whatever it is they think you're doing, I hope it goes well.'

'Thank you, Pierre, I hope so too. Whatever it is. I'm going to Manu's bar to get some cigarettes. Do you want any?'

The policeman shook his head, unwrapped the paper that surrounded the bread and ham, and took his first, delicious bite.

At the bar, Luc bought his cigarettes and used the payphone to call the university laboratory, where his son was studying for a Master's degree.

'Hello, André, it's Papa. We're very much looking forward to seeing you for dinner. I thought you should know that we have some unexpected guests. We'll see you at eight.'

• • •

Unlike Tempsford, RAF Tangmere was anything but secret. During the battle of Britain it had become famous as one of Fighter Command's key bases and since then it had been home to two of the RAF's most celebrated aces: Douglas Bader and Johnnie Johnson. It was also the base from which 161 Squadron flew missions that required agents to be delivered or picked up from the ground in Europe, as opposed to those who were parachuted in. But the Moonlight Squadron's presence was so clandestine that its pilots never entered Tangmere's officer's mess.

They prepared for their missions and relaxed after they had been completed at a cottage outside the airfield gates. It was a charming, rustic place, with low ceilings, black-painted beams and roaring log fires to ease the chill of the cold night air.

On this evening, Bobby Warden, who had flown any number of missions in and out of France, was sitting at a table in the cottage living room, doing his best to familiarise himself with the route to Belgium.

Over the eighteen months of their squadron's operational activities, Warden and his comrades had learned that a man's survival had little to do with his daring or skill as a pilot, but depended almost entirely on the thoroughness of his preparations.

That afternoon, at Tempsford, he had been provided with a number of charts, which showed the land and water he would cover on the three-hundred-and-fifty-mile flight to the landing point near Spa. He had drawn the line of his course across the charts in a thick grease pencil. Around the line were notes, arrows, stars, exclamation marks and other symbols reminding him of any threat, like a Luftwaffe base, or a known anti-aircraft battery that he had to steer clear of.

He had cut out a series of rectangular sections of the chart, each of which showed a portion of his course, and the terrain, or water, on either side of it. Finally, he stuck the sections of his course onto pieces of cardboard of matching size, numbered them and piled them in sequence, with the first section of the journey at the top.

Experience had shown that this was the handiest way for a solo pilot, in a cramped cockpit, who could not unfold and examine charts, to give himself some chance of navigating his way across the Channel or North Sea and across long stretches of hostile territory to destinations that tended to be in the middle of nowhere.

Warden also had a selection of the reconnaissance pictures taken earlier in the day. They revealed both good news and bad. The good news was that his destination should be easy to spot, since it was off a main road, with the town of Spa a few miles to the northwest and the Spa-Francorchamps motor-racing circuit to the southeast. This, however, was also the bad news. He was going too close to too many people for comfort.

Another of the squadron pilots wandered over to where Warden was sitting and looked over his shoulder at the charts he was butchering. 'Where's that?' he asked. 'Doesn't look like anywhere I know.'

'Belgium,' Warden replied.

'Bloody hell.'

'Precisely.'

'Never mind, old boy, look on the bright side. They'll give you a slap-up dinner before you go – bangers and mash tonight, from what I gather – and all the eggs and bacon you can scoff when you get back for breakfast. Where else can a chap get a deal like that these days?'

'And a pretty girl to pick up when I get there,' Warden said.

'Sounds like a splendid show.'

An hour later, fortified by food and coffee, Warden walked out to the dispersal area where his matte-black-painted Westland Lysander was waiting. The Lizzie, as all the pilots called it, was not an impressive-looking machine. The fuselage was as short and stubby as a half-smoked cigar and was slung beneath long, lozenge-shaped wings that were angled forward, like a gull. The Lizzie was slow, not agile, and, when configured for special duties, carried no guns to defend itself. As a combat aircraft, it was a sitting duck. But it had one gift that made it perfect for this type of mission: it needed little space in which to land and take off. Nor was it fussy about the ground beneath its wheels. For getting agents in or out of tricky situations, there wasn't a better plane.

Warden ran through his final checks. The aircraft was in fine fettle. His chart and torch were present and correct. He had a clear idea of where he was going and what he should look out for when he arrived.

As the engine spluttered into life, the propeller whirled and the Lizzie trundled like a portly banker towards the Tangmere runway, Warden gave his craft one last word of encouragement.

'Here we go, old girl. Up, up . . . and away.'

• • •

At eight in the evening, it was Julie Deforge's turn to go down to visit the policeman who was on watch outside their property. She carried a tin plate of her splendid pork-and-apple stew and a bottle of *vin ordinaire*.

The policeman was new to the area, but as he had come on shift, the officer he replaced had assured him that he could expect to be well looked after because the Deforges were fine people and understood how things should be done. At first he refused the offer of wine, since he was not supposed to drink on duty. But Madame Deforge had insisted that one glass couldn't do any harm and he had, on reflection, agreed.

• • •

While the sentry was distracted, Jean Burgers and André Deforge entered the farm at a rear entrance. They ate supper while Saffron explained what their role would be when the plane came to pick her up. Shortly before ten in the evening, their time, they went across to the barn.

The message from London came in on time. She decoded it and it read:

AIRCRAFT DESPATCHED TO AGREED LOCATION. ARRIVAL 23.30 GMT. CHALLENGE W. REPLY P. GOOD LUCK

Saffron replied:

MESSAGE RECEIVED. UNDERSTOOD. SEE YOU TOMORROW

Saffron and the two men went out into one of the Deforges' fields and rehearsed the landing procedure until all three were confident in their respective roles. She rested for half an hour, not trying to sleep, but lying still, breathing slowly, relaxing her body and emptying her mind.

At half past eleven local time, an hour before the pick-up, they set off for the landing field on foot. The journey was less than three kilometres and best undertaken across country, in silence, taking advantage of any hedges or woodlands that would hide them from prying eyes.

They arrived at the field with half an hour to spare and settled down to wait.

The half hour passed without sight or sound of the plane, though the sky echoed to the drone of passing bombers, high overhead.

Another fifteen minutes went by.

Saffron tried to keep the apprehension she could feel growing within her at bay. So many things could go wrong. The plane could have been hit by anti-aircraft fire aimed at the bombers, or shot down by a Luftwaffe nightfighter.

'How much longer should we wait?' André asked.

'As long as we have to,' Saffron replied. 'He'll be here. I know he will.'

But five more minutes passed, and still there was no sign.

• • •

Michi Schmitt had been an industrial welder before the war. He was a union man, in the days before Hitler banned them. The workers at his factory in Mainz elected him as their shop steward because they knew he would always fight for their cause with the bosses. Management respected him because, as tough and unyielding as he was, if Schmitt gave his word, they knew that he would keep it.

When he was called up to the army, Schmitt swiftly rose up the ranks. By the time the war in Russia had entered its second year, he was an *Oberfeldwebel*, or master sergeant, in a regiment of panzer grenadiers – motorised infantry who fought alongside the tanks at the sharp end of any attack.

His unit had spent eighteen months as part of Army Group North, most of them camped outside Leningrad in a siege that seemed doomed to last forever. There came a point when they had lost so many men, and those who remained were in such poor shape, that they had to be withdrawn from the line. Now they were in Belgium, stationed at Spa to rest, recuperate and reinforce their numbers with new men before they headed back to the front.

Spending a day at the beck and call of a Gestapo man on a fruitless search for a radio set, and a British spy who might have been in their area, and which might possibly be connected, was not the kind of duty that Schmitt enjoyed. Too many of his communist friends had been arrested by the Secret Police to make him feel comfortable doing their dirty work, even if they were on the hunt for a genuine enemy.

When they'd returned to base and come off duty, Schmitt had obtained his company commander's permission to go for a drink with a couple of other sergeants and a dozen or so men, all veterans of the war in the east. They'd taken the truck they'd been driving around behind Krankl and headed off to a country inn outside Spa, where the food was good, the beer was brewed on the premises, and the landlord didn't mind staying open into the early hours.

They were armed, because they'd served in Russia and seen what partisans could do to soldiers who had been caught napping. Only a fool went unarmed in occupied territory. But Schmitt didn't expect to be seeing action that night.

It was a warm evening, so he and two friends – old comrades who'd been fighting alongside one another since the Polish campaign in '39 – were sitting outside the inn, as they drank their beer, smoked their cigarettes and looked up at the night sky as the bombers droned overhead.

'I hate those bastards,' Schmitt said. 'They're too shit-scared to fight like men, face-to-face. They'd rather kill our women and children.'

'Don't waste time on them, Michi,' one of the other sergeants said. 'There's no point. Nothing you can do.'

'On the other hand, you could get us all a drink,' another NCO said. 'It's your round, you tight bastard.'

Michi went into the inn to get the beers. As he came out, he was halfway to the table where his friends were sitting when he stopped and listened.

'Do you hear that?' he asked.

'What?' one of the others asked.

'An aeroplane engine.'

The man laughed. 'No? Really?! For hell's sake, man, there've been hundreds of planes flying over us all night . . .'

'No, this one's different. Listen.'

The men were silent, and now they understood what Schmitt had been talking about. Something was up there. But this wasn't the roar of a four-engine bomber; this was the thinner sound of a small, single-engine plane.

'Sounds like a Storch,' someone said.

'That's a reconnaissance aircraft. Why would anyone be up in one now?' Schmitt asked.

'No, they take passengers, too. The top brass use them for transport. I heard Rommel has his own, done up how he likes it.'

'Maybe . . .' Schmitt said.

'Can we have our beers, or are you going to stand there all night?'

'Ah . . .' Schmitt brought the drinks to the table. The men returned to drinking and talking, with much of the conversation dedicated to their distaste for being lackeys to the SS and all its offshoots.

Then it returned, the same aircraft noise.

Someone laughed. 'That idiot's got shit for brains, going round in circles.'

'Maybe he's as drunk as you,' another said.

'Or maybe he's lost,' Schmitt said, 'because he doesn't know where he is . . . because he's a damned Tommy.'

'God in heaven – what if that Gestapo bastard was right about that enemy agent?'

'Whatever he's looking for, it must be round here. That's why he's been circling.'

'Only one way to find out,' Schmitt said. 'Tell the lads we're moving out, now.'

The engine noise was fading to the south. Schmitt pointed after it. 'And that's the way we're going.'

• • •

'Damn and blast!' Bobby Warden cursed his rotten luck and his even more rotten navigation. For reasons he could not begin to explain, he had found himself north, rather than south, of Spa. That meant he had to take a long detour around the town to take him back towards the landing zone, which in turn resulted in him approaching it from the wrong direction, and thereby missing all the landmarks that he was counting on to guide him in.

The most obvious of these was the Spa–Francorchamps road, and the only way to find that was to circle over the general area and hope that the line of the road at some point cut across his course. He went all the way around once without success, aware of the time ticking by. He was going to be late for the pick-up and the later he was, the greater the danger for all concerned.

There was nothing for it but to try again. This time, to his relief, he saw the silvery-black line of the tarmac in the moonlight. He was about to bank the Lizzie in the right direction when he caught sight of something out of the corner of his eye. He turned his head to see the faint glow of light spilling from the door of what looked like the Belgian version of an English country pub. He saw men in uniform, sitting around a couple of tables, drinking, and in the road beyond them an army truck.

Bloody Germans! And unless they're deaf and blind they've spotted me.

Bobby started doing sums in his head. He was a couple of miles from the landing ground. He'd be there in under a minute. Say it took them a minute, at the most, to get into their truck and get going, and say the truck went at thirty miles an hour – once they got on the main road, they'd be bound to see him land. And they'd drive that truck to the limit of its speed.

Then it would be a race.

They would take maybe four, five minutes to get there. In that time, he had to locate the pick-up spot – which was easier said than done, in his experience – land, come to a halt, turn the plane, taxi to where the girl would be waiting, get her aboard and then take off.

'Christ,' Warden muttered. 'This'll be a close-run thing.'

• • •

There was a set procedure that Saffron, like all Baker Street agents, had been taught for the preparation of a field for use as an impromptu airstrip. It required three lights, or torches, known as A, B and C, which were arranged in the shape of an L, with A at the end of the longer side, C at the end of the shorter side, and B at the corner where the two sides met. The L measured 150 metres by 50 metres.

The agent stood at point A. When the aircraft approached, the agent flashed the challenge letter in Morse code: tonight it would be 'W'. The pilot then flashed his reply letter, in this case 'P'.

Now each party knew that the other was genuine.

At this point the three marker lights were lit. The pilot, who by now had probably made a circuit of the site, then came into land, aiming to touch down at Point A and then aim for the midpoint of B and C: down the long side, to the centre of the short side, in other words.

Bobby Warden had been trained in the same procedure and had carried it out on more than a dozen missions to France.

Everyone knew what was supposed to happen.

But only Warden knew what was actually going on.

He'd seen the truck. It was barrelling down the Francorchamps road.

Forget four minutes. Make that less than two.

• • •

Saffron stood at Point A, with Burgers at B and Deforge at C. The noise of the incoming aircraft was getting louder, and then she saw it, a black shadow against the sky, coming in low over the trees beyond the main road.

Saffron flashed W: dot-dash-dash.

There was no response.

The aircraft kept flying towards them, descending as it went. But there was no glimmer of a reply letter, no sign that the pilot was genuine. It could be a trap. And it was coming into land.

• • •

Schmitt saw the aircraft too, travelling so slowly that he could not believe it could stay in the air, flying across the road ahead of them, barely higher than the trees on either side of the carriageway.

'There it is!' he shouted.

'I see it!' the driver replied. He pressed his foot hard on the accelerator and the truck picked up speed with the lumbering bulk of a rhino pushing itself into a charge.

The aircraft was less than a kilometre ahead of them. The truck's speedometer was straining up towards 60 . . . 70 . . . 80 kph.

Schmitt called out, 'We can get them!'

The driver grinned. 'Can't wait to see that Gestapo man's face.'

'Come on,' Schmitt shouted. 'Go . . . go!'

. . .

Warden had no time for the usual landing rigmarole. Get in, turn around, grab the girl, take-off. That's all he could do.

If he was lucky.

But first he had to remind himself: less haste, more speed.

The Lizzie could stay airborne at remarkably low speeds, and the slower Warden came into land, the sooner he could stop and turn the plane, ready to take off again.

Warden wasn't going much faster than the truck as he came into land.

He'd seen it as he crossed the road. It was too close for comfort.

He could only pray that the agent and the men with her would work out what was going on.

. . .

Saffron was paralysed by indecision. The aircraft was close enough for her to be sure it was a Lysander. But what if it was one that the Germans had captured? What if the Abwehr found a way to read the one-time pad code? Were they in charge of this operation, just like all the others?

She thought of Leo Marks. He had been certain that the Germans had cracked the old codes, and he'd been right. He was also convinced that he'd found a way to beat them. Saffron had faith that he'd be right about that too.

She waved her torch over her head, signalling to the two men to turn on their lights.

The aircraft was over the field, coming down, and then it was passing her at barely more than head height. She could see the blue, white and red RAF roundel painted on the side and the identification letters. And though there was still a voice in her head saying, *This could be a trap*, she forced herself to believe. *No, this is real. He's come to take me home.*

She watched the plane break to a halt in what seemed like no distance at all. It began to turn and start taxiing back towards her. Burgers and Deforge were running from their posts, coming to say goodbye.

Saffron waved at them, smiling now, feeling sure that everything had worked out. And then Burgers stopped and a second later so did Deforge. Burgers pointed past the plane, towards the road. They hesitated and then turned tail and dashed the way they had come, heading for the shelter of the trees on the far side of the field.

Saffron swung around to see what had frightened the two Belgians.

At the edge of the main road a truck was turning onto the field and driving towards them.

Now she understood why the pilot had not bothered with the regular landing procedure.

She saw a black shape emerging from the side of the truck. Then a series of bright pinpoint flashes and an instant later the rat-a-tat-tat of automatic gunfire.

Saffron started running for the plane.

• • •

'Get in!' Warden leaned as far as he could out of the cockpit, gesturing frantically towards the ladder, fixed to the fuselage, that led up to the rear of the cockpit.

Saffron was running hard towards the Lizzie, forcing herself to go across the line of gunfire, moving like an athlete with high knees and pumping arms. But she could never win a race against the truck, which was speeding towards them across the field. It was still four or five hundred metres away, but at the rate it was going, it would cover the ground in less than twenty seconds.

• • •

Schmitt had his head and shoulders out of the side window of the truck, blasting away with his submachine gun in the direction of the aircraft and the running woman. The truck was bouncing like a jackrabbit and both his targets were moving. The odds against him hitting anything were long. But gunfire distracted and frightened even the most hardened soldier and all it would take was one lucky shot to kill the agent or the pilot of the plane.

• • •

Saffron had reached the foot of the ladder. She pulled herself up onto the second rung, grabbed the bottom of the cockpit, which was hinged on the far side to open across the fuselage, and she flung it open. In an instant there was a spark on the metal fuselage in front of her, a high-pitched clanging sound and a whirring, grabbing sensation as the bullet that had ricocheted off the side of the plane passed through the hair at the nape of her neck. Her body was untouched, a finger-width away from death.

Barely five seconds had passed since she'd first grabbed the ladder, but the truck had come at least a hundred metres closer.

Saffron threw herself into the cockpit, banging her knees and shins against the metal frame, ignoring the pain. She pulled the hatch down over her head.

Before she had time to buckle herself into her seat, or put on the flight helmet that would give her oxygen and a voice link to the pilot, the Lizzie had started moving.

• • •

In the split second that the cockpit hatch crashed into place, Warden opened the throttle and let the Lizzie rip. The manual said the Lysander required 279 metres of runway to take off and reach a height of fifty feet. The truck was no more than 50 metres away and the gap was closing from both sides.

• • •

Schmitt had emptied his magazine. He slid back into his seat. There was no time to reload. The windscreen was filled with the sight of the onrushing aircraft.

• • •

Saffron was pulling the belts of her Sutton harness over her shoulders. She could feel the aircraft pick up speed. Within the next few seconds it would lift into the air or collide with the truck like a pair of onrushing trains. There was nothing she could do.

• • •

The truck was so close that Warden, looking over the upturned nose of the Lizzie, could only see the top of its cab and the canvas awning of the load-bay.

Wait, you bastard . . . wait . . . Warden forced himself to fight the instinct to pull back the joystick. He'd only get one attempt at a take-off. It had to be right first time. He had nowhere else to go but up. Every fraction of a second, every mile-per-hour of speed, every inch of ground covered increased his chances of lift-off.

But they also brought him closer to a fatal collision.

Warden held his nerve.

• • •

'Keep going, keep going!' Schmitt shouted.

The driver's knuckles were white as they gripped the wheel, his face wide-eyed, his mouth open in a terrified scream.

• • •

Warden could wait no longer. He pulled the joystick with every ounce of strength that his arms and shoulders possessed.

The Lizzie groaned and strained as it struggled into the air.

The truck driver's courage broke. He wrenched the steering wheel to the right.

The truck was side-on to the aircraft as it clawed against the air.

The Lizzie fought its battle to the death against gravity.

Its wheels let go of their grip against the earth. They rose a few feet into the air, and then a few more.

They tore through the canvas awning of the truck, hitting two of the men inside it and knocking them aside like a bowling ball through skittles as Warden rode his aircraft into the night sky. He continued to climb on full throttle until he levelled off at five thousand feet and spoke into his headset.

'You all right back there?'

'Very comfortable,' Saffron replied.

Warden laughed. 'Splendid. Welcome aboard the Tangmere Express. We'll have you home in no time.'

Below them, Jean Burgers and Andre Deforge, crouching in the canopy of trees on the far side of the field, watched the Lysander disappear. They stood and shook hands vigorously before melting into the darkness.

Eight months had passed since the German army was driven out of Stalingrad. Since then, they had retreated twelve hundred kilometres. Kiev was about to be added to the list. Week by week the fighter wing that Gerhard commanded found itself moving from one base to another, each a little closer to home than the one before.

These days he spent as much time behind his desk, doing paperwork, as he did at the controls of a combat aircraft. One day in late October 1943, he was working his way through a pile of requisition forms. He paused to look out of the window as the incessant autumn rain turned the airfield into a deep, sticky quagmire, when a clerk came in to tell him, 'There's a general here to see you, Herr *Oberst* . . . General von Tresckow.'

'You'd better show him in,' Gerhard replied, getting to his feet.

Von Tresckow appeared, wearing the scarlet collar tabs and epaulettes on his uniform that indicated an officer of the general staff. He was about forty years old, with receding hair, a high forehead and strong, regular features that gave him an air of distinction.

Gerhard gave him the obligatory 'Heil Hitler' salute.

Von Tresckow responded with a perfunctory lifting of the hand, but no 'heil' to go with it. He glanced at a folding wooden chair with a canvas seat and back that stood opposite Gerhard's table and asked, 'May I?'

'Of course, Herr *Generalmajor*,' Gerhard said. 'Can I get you anything? A cup of coffee? It's ersatz, I'm afraid – ground acorns and brown shoe-polish. Or perhaps something stronger . . . I have vodka that's real enough.'

'That's kind, but no. I shan't be staying long.' Von Tresckow took out a silver cigarette case engraved with a heraldic crest, selected a cigarette, and offered the case to Gerhard, who declined.

'You don't mind if I smoke?' he asked. He had the voice and manners of an aristocrat, to go with the name and the family crest. Von Tresckow was a member of the Prussian nobility that had for centuries sent its sons away to command the German army.

'Not at all, sir,' Gerhard replied. 'What can I do for you?'

'I'm here because of an argument you had in a bar, several months ago . . . in Taganrog. Perhaps you recall the occasion?'

'Ah . . . I was wondering when I would get a visit about that. Although I must confess I was expecting someone from the SS or Gestapo – one of my brother's creatures. I feel honoured that I merit a visit from someone of your standing.'

Von Tresckow smiled. 'Do you imagine that I am here to interrogate you? I suppose that's understandable. From what I gather you were very frank in your opinions and they were far from flattering towards our country's leadership.'

Gerhard had long ago decided that when they came for him, he would not try to deny what he had said. 'I was in Stalingrad from the moment the city was attacked. I got out one step ahead of the Russians. I had earned the right to say my piece.'

Von Tresckow nodded, breathed out, and, as the smoke drifted across the table, he asked, 'And did you mean what you said?'

'Yes.'

Von Tresckow inhaled, stubbed out the cigarette, and said, 'Good. I was hoping you would say that. You see, I agree with you. So do a lot of men, including some of the most senior officers in the Wehrmacht. We can all see that the Nazis are monsters. Do you have any idea what they have been doing here in Russia . . . the killings?'

Gerhard gave a grunt, thought for a second and added, 'I saw them using a gas truck once. Up close . . . I could hear the people inside. Saw what was left of them afterwards. So yes, I know what they've been doing.'

'And you know that the war is lost?'

Gerhard gave a mirthless laugh. 'I told you. I was in Stalingrad.'

'Now you are here, in Kiev. A year from now, if you're lucky enough to live that long, you will probably be flying from bases in Germany itself. The barbarians will be at the gates of Berlin. Unless we stop this whole thing now.'

'There's only one way to do that.'

'Yes.'

'How would you get to him?'

'We have people who are close, people willing to risk and even sacrifice their lives in the cause.'

'Then what? Will Bormann, Himmler, Goebbels, Göring, all that gang roll over and hand you their Reich?'

'No, but we have plans. We believe we can take it from them before they realise that it's gone.'

'You and your generals, you have power. Then what?'

'We sue for peace.'

'The Allies will demand unconditional surrender.'

'If the Nazis are still in power, yes. But if they are gone, they may be more reasonable. That jumped-up Austrian housepainter was right about one thing: the real enemy is Bolshevism. The British and Americans may not believe that yet, but they soon will. They don't want to wake up one day and find that Stalin's tanks have reached the Rhine, because they won't stop there. They will need a strong, free Germany as a bulwark against the Reds.'

'What do you want from me?'

'Nothing . . . not yet. But when the day comes, if we should succeed, then we need to know that there are Luftwaffe formations we can count upon. Can you deliver your fighter group to us?'

'That depends on my men. Some of them are still diehard Nazis. But most want to live long enough to see the end of the war. If I tell them that this is the best way to bring peace and save the Fatherland from total destruction, they'll follow my lead.'

'Excellent. There is one other thing . . . We need to bring the people with us. It will be a great help if they hear our message from a genuine hero, a dashing fighter pilot with medals on his chest and rows of kills painted on the side of his plane.' Von Tresckow paused and looked inquiringly at Gerhard. 'Why are you smiling like that?'

'Because that is what the propaganda boys at the Air Ministry told me, when they sent me off on a tour of the country a couple of years ago.'

'I'm not surprised. Fighter pilots are modern-day knights in armour. Everyone wants you on their side . . . So . . . Are you on our side?'

'Yes,' said Gerhard. 'I am on your side.'

'Good. Then you will hear no more from me. But when the day comes, we will be counting on you to do your part.'

'I understand.'

Von Tresckow got up to leave but stopped and added, 'You understand, this is our country's last chance. If we don't do something soon, it will be too late, and Germany will be like a modern Carthage: every brick torn down, salt ploughed into the soil . . . wiped from the face of the earth.'

I t was midday on 1 April 1944 when the door to Saffron's office at Baker Street opened without a knock and Leo Marks burst in, a thunderous look on his face, waving a piece of teleprinter paper in the air.

'Have you seen this?' he asked, too filled with righteous fury to bother with social niceties. 'It's Herr Giskes' little April Fool's jape.'

Saffron got up and walked around her desk to meet him.

'Here you go,' Marks said, handing her the paper. On it was printed the text of a telegram, which read:

YOU ARE TRYING TO MAKE BUSINESS IN THE NETHERLANDS WITHOUT OUR ASSISTANCE. WE THINK THIS IS RATHER UNFAIR IN VIEW OUR LONG AND SUCCESSFUL COOPERATION AS YOUR SOLE AGENTS. BUT NEVER MIND WHEN EVER YOU WILL COME TO PAY A VISIT TO THE CONTINENT YOU MAY BE ASSURED THAT YOU WILL BE RECEIVED WITH SAME CARE AND RESULTS AS ALL THOSE YOU SENT US BEFORE. SO LONG.

'Ha!' Saffron gave a mirthless laugh as she handed the message back to Marks. 'I suppose this must be the Abwehr's idea of a joke.'

'Cheeky sod, isn't he? He sent it from ten of our own radio sets simultaneously, letting us know that he's had them all this time. On the other hand . . .' Marks took a few steps towards the door, closed it and returned. 'You didn't hear this from me, but at the very moment Giskes was playing his joke, we were sneaking onto his patch. There were two separate drops over Holland last night, four agents in total. And he didn't know they were coming.'

'I hope they've got a good supply of your one-time pads.'

'They have indeed . . . and all because of you, dear wife of mine, proving that they worked.'

'Anything to help you, darling husband.'

The pretence that they were married had remained a running joke between Saffron and Marks in the months since her return to London. When she arrived back from Belgium, she had been thoroughly debriefed. She explained to Gubbins and Amies in forensic detail about what had happened to her, how she had responded, her impressions of every encounter, event and place, in case there were nuances that could be gleaned from her information. She told them about Schröder's speech at the Ridderzaal in The Hague and the Nazi's plan to solve the Jewish question in the Netherlands, and, it would appear, their monstrous ambitions to eradicate all the Jews in Europe.

She informed them of Jean Burgers' suspicions about Prosper Dezitter and his mistress Florie Dings. Burgers was convinced they were German spies and were compromising Groupe G's activities in Belgium by infiltrating Resistance groups, running fake safe houses and informing on agents' activities. They were highly effective double agents. Dezitter was a master of aliases and bluff but could be clearly identified by the missing first joint or two joints of the little finger on his right hand. It was a feature he could hide most of the time, but not all of the time.

In the weeks that followed, Burgers had published Dezitter and Dings' description in underground newspapers and Amies had organised Operation Rat Week to use agents to assassinate traitors in Belgium. Dezitter and Dings were top of the list. The exiled Belgian government in London was unhappy with the idea of execution without trial, and the campaign was officially cancelled. However, Saffron heard reports that Dings was found dead outside her flat, killed by twenty-two blows from a pointed hand tool. Dezitter had fled Belgium and was being pursued by the Resistance.

Saffron had been promoted to the rank of captain and given a new role: handling agents who were being sent into Belgium, planning their missions and watching over their activities once they had been sent into the field. This meant that she was in contact with many of the local Resistance groups in Belgium, whose activities were becoming more effective, as the tide of the war turned against Germany, and as Baker Street itself became more experienced in the way it went about its business.

Saffron's job demanded long hours and brought a heavy burden of responsibility. She took the safety of her agents personally and feared for their safety more than she had ever done for her own. Even when Baker Street was doing the best job, the life of an agent in Occupied Europe was fraught with terrible danger, for there were still turncoats, collaborators and double agents scattered among the ranks of the Resistance forces. Two of Saffron's agents had been betrayed to the Gestapo and their loss had hit her hard.

There were triumphs to set alongside the disasters. Less than three months earlier, Groupe G had pulled off an astonishing coup: a series of simultaneous bomb attacks on the Belgian electricity network that left the country without power for the following day. Offices, factories, mines and railways all shut down – some not getting back to full operation for a week. The enemy war effort was hit by a serious blow, and the country received a clear message that their occupiers were no longer in full control. The news had thrilled Saffron and the fact that Jean Burgers had helped organise the scheme made the triumph all the sweeter.

'So, are you going to this pow-wow with our American cousins?' Marks asked, changing the subject.

'Yes, Amies asked me to represent T Section.'

'I'll see you there. I'm giving a talk to the assembled company on our new cryptography methods . . . In the meantime, how are you coping? With that Dutch business, I mean . . .'

It was not the done thing in Baker Street to admit to the physical or psychological after-effects of missions. Saffron had found it hard to rid her mind of the events of the night when she had killed Karsten Schröder, but had never made a fuss.

Leo Marks was the one person in whom she had confided. But even with him, she felt compelled to underplay her feelings.

'Oh, it's all right,' she said. 'Nothing to worry about.'

Marks was not so easily fooled. 'Are you still getting the nightmares, old girl?' he asked, his flippancy replaced by genuine concern for a friend.

'Sometimes . . .' Saffron sighed. 'I feel as if that bloody man's haunting me. Maybe that's what a ghost is – a presence of the dead in the dreams of the living.'

'Hmm . . .' Marks murmured appreciatively. 'That line is almost worthy of one of my celebrated poems.'

Marks was almost as well-known in Baker Street for his poetry as his codes.

'You can have it,' Saffron said, 'for the price of a four-ounce steak. I was raised to be a carnivore. I need red meat to survive, and more than the ration book can get me.'

'Then we have a deal: your words for my beef. I shall consult my sources at once.'

'Oh, thank you, darling, what a wonderful provider you are! Now I must get back to work. I don't want those Yanks thinking that I don't know my stuff.'

• • •

Two days later, having lunched in a Lyons Corner House, where they tested one another on the presentations they were about to make like school pupils preparing for an exam, Saffron and Marks walked down Whitehall towards the War Office and through its grimy black arches. They were in fine spirits. The meeting concerned the coordination of the various Resistance movements in Occupied Europe with the forthcoming invasion. A campaign of sabotage and guerrilla warfare, organised in large part by the Special Operations Executive, would sweep through Holland, Belgium and France, cutting railway lines, blocking roads, blowing up bridges and doing everything possible to prevent the Wehrmacht from bringing reinforcements to the beaches on which the British, American and Canadian forces would be landing. There was a time when Baker Street would have struggled to meet that challenge. But now the organisation was buoyed by its ability to get agents in and out of Europe; to supply Resistance forces with guns, munitions, radio equipment and money; and to plan campaigns of sabotage and subversion.

The success of the invasion depended on being able to secure a foothold on French soil. Baker Street would play a vital part in ensuring that was possible, and Saffron was looking forward to laying out the contribution that the Belgian section would make.

She and Marks proceeded up a spectacular white marble staircase that rose to a half landing, before splitting into two separate flights that ascended to the left and right, around the central atrium, before meeting again at the first floor landing. An ornate, golden clock hung on the wall in front of them and above it a balcony protruded from the colonnade that ran around the top of the staircase. Saffron could see men in the uniforms of different countries and services, some smoking, others holding cups of tea, chatting to one another before the formal proceedings began.

One man caught her eye. He was wearing the dark blue service dress and white peaked cap of the US Navy. The cuff of his jacket bore the single quarter-inch stripe, between two half-inch stripes that signified a Lieutenant Commander. He was leaning against the carved stone balustrade that ran around the balcony with a relaxed, easy-going stance that seemed familiar to Saffron.

She stopped dead on the stairs, her heart suddenly racing. *No, it can't be him!*

The Lieutenant Commander turned his head and looked towards the stairs. Their eyes met and locked together with a connection that sent a shock deep into her stomach.

'Danny,' she gasped.

Marks had paused when Saffron did. He'd seen how she and the American had looked at one another and the way that the sight of him had affected her.

'Anyone you know?' he asked, as casually as he could.

Saffron didn't say a word. She nodded. She chewed her lower lip. And, lost for words, she walked to the top of the stairs.

Another Baker Street officer was waiting for them. 'Where have you two been?' he asked. 'The show's about to start, but the old man wants to give us a pep talk first. You've kept him waiting . . .'

'Ah,' Marks said. They knew how strongly Brigadier Gubbins felt about punctuality. They were hurried away to an ante-room, where Gubbins and a few more SOE people were waiting.

Gubbins didn't say anything to Saffron and Marks. He didn't need to. One freezing stare from those ice-blue eyes put them in their place as effectively as a verbal rocket from any other man.

'Right then, now that we are all here, let's make sure we're on the same page,' Gubbins said. 'Each of you has a contribution to make to the day's programme. Make it. Read your lines. Do not be tempted to improvise. Do not engage in displays of humour.'

'Is he talking to me?' Marks whispered to Saffron.

She did not respond. Her mind was reeling from the sight of Danny. Part of her wanted to dash out the door of this dingy little room, run across to the balcony and throw herself at him. Another part of her was thankful she had been denied the opportunity to make a fool of herself.

She had not been listening to Gubbins, but she sensed, more than heard, that he was coming to the end of his remarks. 'Yes, sir,' she said, along with the others, when he asked if they'd got the message.

'Right then,' Gubbins said. 'Follow me.'

He led them into a conference room that had dark, wood-panelled walls beneath a vaulted white ceiling. Two bronze chandeliers, suspended on chains from the ceiling, hung over an oak table long enough to have a dozen chairs on either side. The British and Canadian representatives were directed down one side of the table. Their American counterparts faced them on the other.

Saffron took her place. She was the only woman in the room, aside from a stenographer, sitting to one side, who was taking notes of the proceedings. She spent a few seconds extracting everything she needed from her bag and making sure that she had her report on Belgium, a notepad and a pen all handy.

She looked up, across the table, straight into the eyes of Danny Doherty. He smiled at her: that lazy, confident, devastatingly seductive smile that she remembered with such clarity from Arisaig. Almost two years had passed, but when she saw that smile, and the way his eyes crinkled, it might as well have been two minutes.

It took all the self-control she possessed to get through the day. She found herself grateful for Gubbins' half-heard instructions. All that was required was for her to sum up T Section's current operations and those being planned to coincide with the invasion in a straightforward way. When she was asked questions, she answered them as thoroughly as she was able. Otherwise she kept her mouth shut and did everything she could to pay attention to whomever else was speaking, and not the face of the man across the table. It was hard not to wonder what Danny had been doing since they had last met. For all she knew he had married his girl in Washington DC. There was no ring on his finger, but plenty of married men did not wear one. He could already be a father, for all she knew.

Eventually the meeting ended. The three-star general, who had chaired proceedings, summed up everything that had been agreed, looked towards Gubbins and the SOE contingent, and said, 'You know, Brigadier, I have to admit I was kinda sceptical about your outfit. I guess I'm a traditionalist. The way I wage war is, I get a bunch of hairy-assed bastards in uniform, train the heck out of 'em, get 'em the best equipment Uncle Sam has to offer, and put 'em up against the other guy's bastards. The idea of sending civilians, including female civilians, into harm's way, to kill the enemy and sabotage his operations, well, that never sat too well with me. But I've gotta admit, the results you're getting are damned impressive.'

His eyes fell on Saffron. 'Tell me, Captain, you spoke well about the Resistance movement in Belgium and its effectiveness as a weapon against the Germans. Have you been there and met these people for yourself?'

'I'm not sure if I'm allowed to answer that question, sir,' Saffron said. She glanced towards Gubbins. He gave a fractional nod of the head. She addressed the general again. 'Yes, sir, I have. I spent some months in the Low Countries last year. I met a few of the key members of the Resistance . . . and of the German administration.'

'Well, I'll be damned. Here we are, gentlemen, dreaming of the day we set foot on Occupied Europe and this little lady has beaten us to it. My congratulations, ma'am.'

'Thank you, sir.'

Saffron heard a cough to her right. Marks was passing her a note. *Fair warning!* it read. *From now on I plan to call you Little Lady.*

Saffron considered it for a few seconds and then, as the general stood to leave, scribbled back: *Also fair warning. Am trained to kill.*

• • •

'You made a conquest there,' Danny said.

He was waiting outside the door of the meeting room as Saffron walked out.

'I can't talk,' Saffron said. 'Gubbins wants us all back to Baker Street for a debrief.'

'I have to see you, Saffron.'

She tried so hard to resist. And then she thought, *Why? Why do I have to deny myself? Gerhard's probably dead. If Danny's married, that's his responsibility. Why do I have to be so bloody alone all the time?*

'I should be able to get out by half past eight,' she said.

'I'll be there, outside.'

'No, don't. People will see us. Listen, I'll take the bus from work to Knightsbridge. I'll meet you outside the Scotch House. It's at the corner, opposite the end of Sloane Street. You can't miss it.'

'I know it.' He smiled. 'I bought a tartan blanket for my mom.'

'I'll try to make it by nine. But I can't guarantee I'll be on time.'

'I'll wait.'

It was almost quarter to ten when Danny saw Saffron get off the bus. He was leaning against the side of a doorway, in the shadow, so as she looked around she couldn't see him. He watched her hesitate, saw her shoulders droop when she thought he wasn't there.

Then he stepped out onto the pavement. Her face lit up, her whole body seemed to stand up straighter, and then she was running towards him and the look on her face was exultant. But there was desperation, too. He opened his arms to take her and she threw herself into them. She nestled her head against his shoulder, not looking at him, wrapping her arms around his waist and pulling their bodies tightly, almost fiercely together.

He held her and felt her body quiver in his arms. She was crying. He stroked her hair and murmured, 'It's OK.' He bent down and kissed the top of her head and the scent of her filled his nostrils. She made a sound, a soft, wordless moan.

Danny couldn't work it out. He felt an overwhelming need to protect this girl, who tried so hard to be strong; he wished he could keep her safe so she didn't ever have to try any more. He wanted to be her wall against the world, her knight in shining armour. And at the same time, he wanted to take her and strip her and ravish her and hear her scream.

For now, though, he knew he had to let her take her time. He held her tight and, after a while, she raised her face to him, and there was a look in her eyes that he had never seen before. She wasn't the tough, highly trained spy, or the rich, sophisticated debutante. Her face had softened and it showed him all the pain and vulnerability and loss of the motherless daughter she was and went to such great lengths to conceal, from herself and everyone else. He felt as if he was seeing the true Saffron Courtney. She had trusted him enough to show him her soul and he did not know what to do in response except take her head in his hands and kiss her and hope that his love could somehow heal her wounds.

They remained locked in their embrace as around them the Tube-goers flooded in and out of Knightsbridge station and the cars and buses picked their way through the crossroads.

It was Saffron who finally pulled away. She took Danny's hand and said, 'Come with me.'

They walked arm in arm to Chesham Court, then managed to keep their hands off one another as they shared the slow, rattling lift up to Saffron's floor with an elderly lady and her Pekingese. The lift reached its destination. Saffron and Danny emerged and walked, hand in hand, to her door.

'Not yet,' she whispered as Danny tried to put an arm around her. 'Someone might see.'

The self-restraint was agonising. Saffron was aching for him and her frustration only made her desperation all the more intense.

She turned the key. They went in. The second the door closed behind them and the instant the latch clicked, Saffron pulled herself tight against Danny's body as she felt him hard against her. They stumbled to her bedroom, still locked together, then tore themselves apart.

Saffron won the race to be free from their uniforms. She didn't care any more about anyone or anything except for herself and Danny and the craving to feel him inside her. She spent all her life being dutiful and responsible. She didn't want to think, or make decisions, or care about anything except pleasure.

His body was lean, broad-shouldered and strong, and he was looking at her with the fierce determination of a hunter.

Saffron looked him in the eye and said, 'Here I am.'

• • •

Later that night, Danny told Saffron that he had managed to get a transfer back into the regular navy. 'I've been away so long, I can't remember which end of the ship is which.'

'The pointy end is the front,' Saffron said.

Danny laughed. 'The front – that's starboard, right?'

They didn't talk about the war, or others in their lives. Danny didn't tell Saffron whether he was married and she didn't ask him. They had three nights together, and two days when Saffron found it almost impossible to concentrate at work for the tremors that ran through her body like an earthquake's aftershocks whenever her mind turned to the night before.

Then the third morning came, and this time Danny's kit-bag was lying on the living room floor of Saffron's flat when she walked over to the kitchen to make him a cup of coffee. When he got out of bed, there was no tempting him back into it because a Jeep was coming to pick him up at 08.00, on the dot, and he had better be on the pavement to meet it.

He was gone as suddenly as he had appeared. Saffron kept herself together as she waved him off. She wanted his last memory of her to be a good one. Only when the Jeep had disappeared down the road, and she had taken the rickety old lift up to her flat and closed the door behind her once again, did she give in to the tears.

In time, though, they passed, and as the sun comes out from behind the darkest clouds once a shower has passed, so her mood lifted again and she felt almost cheerful as she rode the bus to Baker Street. There was, she had to admit, nothing like making love, frequently and ecstatically, to make a body feel alive.

What it came down to, though, was the stripping away of her uniform and the revelation of her naked body. The war was almost five years old. She had spent that time as a driver, a fighter, an agent and an officer. But for those three nights, she had been nothing but a woman. And it was utterly marvellous.

• • •

Konrad von Meerbach's father Otto had been relentlessly unfaithful. He had made no effort to be discreet, nor done anything to lessen the private pain and social humiliation that his conduct caused his wife Alatha. He wanted to leave her. He made no secret of the fact. Yet he never managed to obtain a divorce. Alatha's devout Catholic faith meant that she would not countenance such a step under any circumstances, and her husband had, for once in his life, been obliged to go along with her wishes.

Looking back, Konrad found his father's conduct towards his mother contemptible. He did not, of course, object to all the years of cruelty and neglect. So far as he was concerned, his mother had failed to satisfy her husband and deserved any punishment he chose to inflict upon her. What made Konrad despise his father's conduct was the old man's weakness in failing to find a way to divorce his wife, irrespective of her wishes.

When the opportunity arose to rid himself of his first wife Trudi, Konrad did not waste any time. Trudi was a pretty, docile but insipid blonde, whose most appealing feature was that she was a great-niece of Gustav von Bohlen und Halbach, or

Gustav Krupp of the great Krupps steelmaking and armaments company. Despite the status and business advantage Trudi conferred on Konrad, she was a disappointment in bed and he had numerous affairs. He informed her that she would concede to a divorce, on whatever terms he chose to grant her.

'And what if I do not agree to your terms?' she asked.

'Then you will spend the few remaining days of your life in a slave-labour camp.'

Even now, there were times when the depths of Konrad's depravity could take his wife unawares. 'But . . . but . . .' She could hardly get the words out. 'I am the mother of your children. How could you take their mother from them?'

'Easily. It would be your choice, after all. If you want your children to have a mother, you will give me the divorce.'

The divorce was finalised within the month.

Konrad was free to marry Francesca von Schöndorf. Francesca was his mistress and she had married Konrad as an act of bitter revenge on his brother Gerhard, who had rejected her for Saffron. The more he observed the effect of hatred on her personality, the greater the pleasure he took in finding new ways to corrupt her. He knew she did not love him in any feeble, fairy-tale sense. He could tell that there was a part of her that hated herself for allowing him to take possession of her. But that only made the act of sex with her more thrilling, for it was akin to rape and therefore more satisfying than a voluntary act of copulation, for it involved the application of power.

She submitted to Konrad because she had become addicted to everything he could provide. Even before the divorce, she had long since become the mistress of Schloss Meerbach, with an army of staff at her beck and call. She dressed in the finest clothes that Paris could provide. She moved in the highest reaches of Nazi society. She counted Eva Braun and Magda Goebbels among her closest female friends. Even the Führer had declared himself charmed by her. For a girl raised in a family whose fine name was not matched by any great fortune, these were giddy heights, made intoxicating by the prodigious consumption of alcohol and narcotics in the court of the tee-total, non-smoking, vegetarian Führer.

Konrad and Francesca married on Saturday, 15 July 1944, and he took a week's leave so that they could honeymoon at Schloss Meerbach. Five days later, they were sailing on the lim-pid waters of the Bodensee, (for Konrad fancied himself to be an expert yachtsman), when their peace was disturbed by an armed motorboat racing at speed towards them. It came to a halt ahead of the bows of Konrad's skiff, forcing him to tack hard and then loosen his sails, coming to a halt in the water rather than crash into its hull.

'This is an outrage!' Konrad shouted, standing up in the stern of his boat and waving his fist at the motorboat. 'I am on my honeymoon. I gave strict orders not to be disturbed.'

A young officer emerged from the motorboat's cabin and came to the rail on the skiff, which was now lying alongside his vessel.

'I apologise, Herr *Brigadeführer*. I am under orders to escort you to shore as quickly as possible.'

Konrad's first instinct was to fear that someone in Berlin had stabbed him in the back. He suddenly felt frightened, for the struggle for power at the top of the Reich was, by the Führer's own design, a continuous fight to the death. Because of that, it could be literally fatal to show any sign of weakness. He decided to brazen this out.

'By God there had better be a good reason for this,' Konrad shouted, 'or you and every one of your men will find yourself wearing army uniforms and serving on the Russian Front.'

'Yes, sir. My orders come directly from Berlin. I am to inform you that this is an urgent matter of state, involving the safety of the Führer.'

'The Führer? Has something happened? Has he been injured, or . . .' Konrad could not bring himself to end the sentence.

'I don't know, sir,' the young naval officer replied. 'I was not given any information about the Führer beyond what I have told you. I can only tell you that you are to make your way to the nearest secure telephone and call SS headquarters at once. Please, Herr *Brigadeführer*, if you and the Countess would come aboard, we can attach a line to your boat and tow her to shore. It will only take a few minutes.'

Less than a quarter of an hour later, Konrad was in his private study at Schloss Meerbach, where he had a secure line to Berlin. He was told a bomb had been detonated at the Wolf's Lair, the Führer's field headquarters in East Prussia, from which he was directing the fighting on the Eastern Front, and on the new battleground of Normandy, where the Allies had launched their invasion of France. By a miracle the bomb had been placed against a heavy table leg that had deflected the blast away from the Führer. The hunt for the plotters was already underway. All senior officer were required immediately at their posts.

'I am sorry, my dear, but our honeymoon is at an end,' Konrad informed Francesca. 'You will have to amuse yourself here. I must return at once to Berlin.'

'How is the Führer?' she asked.

'He has survived an assassination attempt and is in good health. I can assure you that the same will not be true of the men who tried to murder him.'

• • •

On 21 July Major-General Henning von Tresckow committed suicide on the front line, near the village of Królowy Most in eastern Poland, by detonating a hand grenade held under his chin. The following morning, as SS men went through his belongings, searching for clues that might lead them to other plotters, an officer – whose civilian rank was that of inspector in the criminal police – was reading a small notebook that had been found underneath von Tresckow's bedding when he came across something that made him stop. He put the notebook down and smoked a cigarette while he contemplated what to do next. He came to the same conclusion as any middle-ranking individual in any large organisation: move the problem up the chain of command.

He took the diary to his direct superior and said, 'Excuse me, *Sturmbannführer*, but I have discovered something I think you should see.'

The ex-policeman found the entry to which he was referring and explained its significance.

Sturmbannführer Franz Minke had acquired his rank more by political sycophancy than competence and greatly depended on his junior's experience and worldly wisdom.

'What do you think I should do?' he asked.

'I would go to Berlin, insist on a personal meeting, explain why you are there and say that you felt it was vital that he should see this first, since it should surely be his right to decide how best to proceed.'

'He won't be pleased when he sees it.'

'Perhaps not, but he'll be very pleased that it's him that's seeing it, rather than someone who could use it against him.'

'He'll be pleased I came to him, then?'

'Yes, sir . . . and relieved . . . and very grateful.'

Within the hour *Sturmbannführer* Minke and von Tresckow's notebook were on their way to Berlin.

• • •

For a few heart-stopping moments, *Sturmbannführer* Minke feared that he had made a terrible miscalculation. *Brigadeführer* von Meerbach was not known for his sweetness of nature. He was reputed to possess a streak of cold, ruthless cruelty that was exceptional even by SS standards. But then von Meerbach did something that took Minke entirely by surprise. He burst out laughing. He hooted. He guffawed as if he had seen the world's funniest comedian tell his best joke.

Minke tittered nervously, uncertain whether he should respond in kind to the senior officer's amusement.

'Oh, this is priceless . . . absolutely priceless,' von Meerbach said, pulling himself up straight and wiping a tear of joy from his eye. 'What did you say your name was again?'

'Minke, *Brigadeführer*.'

'Well, Minke, you have made my day . . . and my dear wife's too, when she hears about it. Here is proof that my smug, self-satisfied, conceited, Jew-loving brother is the traitor I always thought he was. Oh, he thought he had everyone fooled, the handsome fighter ace with his medals around his neck. But he didn't fool me. I knew that if I left the trap open long enough he was bound to walk into it. And here it is, in this notebook, proof that he was in league with von Tresckow, one of the key men in the conspiracy against the Führer.

'Look here,' von Meerbach said, striding over towards his aide-de-camp, who had been standing discreetly in a shadowy corner of the office. He held the notebook under the ADC's face and jabbed at the open page. 'My brother's name, the date and place of their meeting and then a single word, "Ja". A mere two letters, but they say everything.'

The ADC frowned. 'Excuse me, *Brigadeführer*, perhaps I am being stupid today, but what do those letters say?'

'That my brother said yes to von Tresckow, of course. He agreed to join the conspiracy. Naturally, he doesn't spell it out. He would not need to for himself, and he would not want to make it obvious if someone found the book. But in hindsight, now that we know what he had in mind . . . Oh, I have no doubt at all what that "Ja" means, and nor will the People's Court. Have my brother arrested. And Minke, tell me, who first came across this entry?'

Minke gave the ex-policeman's name and added, for he saw that he could afford to be generous now, 'He understood at once, just as you did, what the entry meant.'

'Then he is a fine officer, as are you, Minke, for having the wit to bring this to me. I will not forget your good work, you can be sure of that.'

'Thank you, Herr *Brigadeführer*.' Minke beamed.

'Not at all . . . Now, we had better call the People's Court, while we're at it. The sooner my brother receives the justice he so richly deserves, the better.'

Gerhard was no longer flying missions over Russian soil. Army Group South had been pushed back into the Balkans and his fighters were engaged in constant missions against the Russian and American bombers, which were trying to knock out the Romanian oil fields and refineries that were the principal suppliers of Germany's fuel. The first he heard about the 20 July assassination attempt was when he returned from a mission and found his base abuzz with rumours that the Führer was dead and a coup had taken place.

He thought back to his meeting with von Tresckow. He wondered whether this was any of his doing. But then news came through that the Führer had survived.

More's the pity, Gerhard thought, and it was clear from the mood of many of his pilots that he was not alone in that opinion.

Within a couple of days, the plot against Hitler was all but forgotten. They had more urgent matters to think about. The days when the Luftwaffe had command of the sky were long gone. The Russians had better aircraft now, produced in massive quantities. Each time he took to the sky, Gerhard felt his lease on life growing shorter. Somehow he had survived, but the odds on him going much further were getting longer by the day.

One afternoon in the first week of August, he climbed from his plane and was greeted not by his ground crew, but by a man in a suit – Gestapo, Gerhard realised at once – accompanied by half a dozen soldiers from the Waffen-SS.

Gerhard was arrested, bundled into the back of a lorry, taken to Berlin and thrown in an underground cellar. For three nights he was questioned. The interrogations seemed strangely half-hearted, as if no one really cared what answers he gave. No torture was used, but he was beaten up a number of times. Even then, he was roughed up, but not seriously injured.

His captors accused him of plotting against the Führer, but their questions were oddly unfocused. They were not trying to make him confess to something they felt certain he had done. They were attempting to establish whether he had done anything at all. And as the interrogation went on Gerhard concluded that their only evidence was a single notebook entry, in which the key word appeared to be, '*Ja*'.

There was not enough evidence to prove a crime beyond being rude about the Führer during an argument in a bar. Gerhard's interrogators seemed untroubled by their failure to pin a more serious offence upon him. Far from becoming more aggressive or desperate in their questioning, their attitude changed to casual indifference, until they ceased dragging him out of his cell for questioning.

A week went by when he was left alone in his tiny cell, with nothing to mark the passing time but the increasing hunger that gnawed at his belly. He was fed twice a day and the meals were so unpleasant – potatoes, pinkish from mould, rotten cabbage, sawdust and flour bread, blutwurst, a rock-hard sausage made from congealed animal blood – that it was all he could do to force them down.

Then one morning his guard informed him that his trial would be in two days' time. 'Your lawyer will be coming to see you today,' the guard said. He laughed and said, 'I'm sure he'll do a good job.'

Even after a dozen years of Nazi rule, Gerhard still believed a criminal lawyer was a brilliant man, motivated by belief in the system of justice, whose fierce intellect was devoted to his client's defence. The man who came to meet him, clutching a manila file that contained two sheets of paper on which the charge against him was laid out, was short, shabbily dressed, with slightly protruding teeth and hair greased flat against his scalp. His voice was thin, his accent coarse. The Nazi Party badge on his lapel indicated where his loyalty lay.

'My name is Karpf,' he said. 'I expect you're wondering what will happen at the trial.'

'I expect you to present my case,' Gerhard replied. 'I played no part in the attack on the Führer. The only evidence against me consists of a two-letter word in the diary of an army officer I met once in my life. I am no lawyer, but I've always assumed that courts operate on the basis of evidence and proof. In my case, there is none. I am not guilty.'

Karpf's rodent face was twisted into a pained grimace. 'Ah . . . yes . . .' He pulled the document from his file. 'You've been serving on the Russian Front, I see.'

'Yes. That's why I couldn't have had anything to do with this bomb plot. I was in mid-air when the damn thing went off.'

'I suppose that would explain it.'

'What?'

'Your failure to understand the purpose of the People's Court. Had you been closer to home you would know that the court has no need to establish innocence or guilt. The fact that you stand before it is proof enough. The court exists so that the righteous fury of the people can be directed at those who seek to undermine the Führer, the Party or the Reich. The people need to see that their enemies are dealt with so that they can feel safe themselves.'

'A show trial, in other words.'

'You should not use that phrase, Meerbach, it reeks of Bolshevism.'

'My name is Colonel von Meerbach.'

'To you, maybe, but not the People's Court.' Karpf replaced the paper in the file. 'Well, I am glad that we have had this chance to talk. I will see you again in two days' time. Naturally, I will be pleading guilty on your behalf. Good day.'

• • •

Gerhard's initial reaction was fury at the injustice of his situation and frustration at his impotence. Now he understood why his interrogators had behaved with such indifference. Evidence was irrelevant. Justice had ceased to exist.

But as the hours went by, his thinking changed. Now his anger was directed at his own stupidity. How could he have expected anything different? His country was ruled by leaders who locked naked men and women into a van and gassed them, then passed the time until the last of their victims had died by drinking coffee and nibbling pastries. Its leader would allow an entire army to die of hunger and frostbite, rather than lose face by allowing them to retreat. In such a world why would anyone expect there to be justice?

He lay awake all night, wondering what his fate would be and how he would greet it. He presumed that the penalty for his supposed treason would be death. But he had seen so much of it inflicted in so many forms that the prospect of oblivion no longer held any terror. Besides, it was inevitable at some point. And execution, whether by the firing squad's bullets or the hangman's noose, was a quicker and more merciful exit than most men could expect.

In the morning, a second visitor came to the cell.

He was a Luftwaffe major by the name of Bayer, who was, in every respect, the opposite of the lawyer Karpf. Bayer was tall, well-built and as handsome as a department store mannequin. His uniform was immaculate, his grooming impeccable. The snap of his 'Heil Hitler' salute was worthy of the parade ground.

'I work at the Air Ministry,' he said. 'I have the great honour of serving on the private staff of *Reichsmarschall* Göring, so you may take it that what I am about to tell you comes from the highest levels. Do I make myself clear?'

'Yes,' Gerhard replied. An unfamiliar sensation he could not quite identify was fluttering in his belly. It took him a second to recognise it as hope.

'I am sure that I do not have to tell you that, as Vice-Chancellor of Germany, second only to the Führer himself, the *Reichsmarschall* utterly condemns the cowardly, treacherous plot against the Führer's life and against the Reich itself.'

'Of course.' Gerhard nodded.

'That said, concern has been expressed at the eagerness with which certain elements in the SS have pursued the case against you. They note the contrast between the frankly inadequate evidence of any treachery on your part and the years of your gallantry and service to the Fatherland.'

Gerhard said nothing, but a fractional nod of his head sufficed to acknowledge Bayer's compliment.

'There is also a strong feeling of dismay that one department of the Reich should go to such lengths to besmirch the reputation of a man from another department. The Luftwaffe is dishonoured by the attack on your honour. It cannot be a good thing to make a public attack on a man who has been presented to the people as a hero. It will confuse them and make them question all heroes. None of this does any service to those who truly care about the wellbeing of the Reich.'

'Where is this leading?' Gerhard asked.

Bayer gave a half-smile. 'A fair question. The answer is as follows. Representations have been made. Negotiations have taken place. As you can imagine, the Justice Ministry and SS are equally jealous of their reputation. A lot of busy men have dedicated a considerable amount of time to your case . . .'

Bayer looked at Gerhard to emphasise the point. He was now in other men's debt. He owed it to them to justify their efforts.

'An agreement has been reached that satisfies all parties. You will admit in open court that you met with the traitor von Tresckow, that he made his anti-Führer sympathies plain and that you neglected to inform the proper authorities of this meeting. This is correct, no?'

'Will it incriminate me if I say yes?'

'On the contrary, it will save you.'

'Then yes, that is the truth.

'In exchange, the court will accept that you had no knowledge of, or role in, the plot of twentieth of July and bear no criminal responsibility in that regard.'

'That is also true.'

'Very well then, you will be found guilty of some minor charge – the precise wording is still under debate – and sentenced to thirty days' solitary confinement, under Luftwaffe supervision.'

Bayer glanced around the cell. 'You will have proper food, sanitary facilities, books to read. It will seem like a grand hotel after this . . . And compared to what would happen to you if the People's Court has its way.' Bayer shook his head in disgust. 'Tell me, what do you think they will do to you?'

'Firing squad . . . hanging, maybe.'

'And you do not fear that?'

'Not particularly.'

'I understand. You are used to facing death. But you won't be that lucky. The People's Court will send you to one of the camps, like a criminal or a Jew. You will die . . . eventually. It will be a terrible death and it will be slow. That is why I plead with you – accept the offer.'

'But you haven't told me all of it. If this was all there was to it, there would be no need to plead. Only a fool would refuse it.'

'You're right. There is one more condition, and it is one on which the Luftwaffe and the other parties agree. You must stand up in court and affirm your loyalty to the Führer, your absolute faith in his leadership and your unshakeable confidence in our certain victory.'

'Ah . . .'

'Listen to me, Colonel. Anyone who knows what is happening understands why you might find those words sticking in your throat. Day after day, night after night, more Allied bombers attack our nation. And we have fewer aircraft and fewer pilots with which to oppose them. Even if we have fighters, we don't have enough fuel for them. Even if we have pilots, most of them are inexperienced and unfit for combat. We know that there is only one possible ending, but for now . . .' Bayer shrugged. 'We have to deal with life as it is. Say the words – if not for your sake, then for the people you love . . . for your comrades, whose own reputations will be stained by association with you . . . for the Luftwaffe itself. Just say the damn words.'

Gerhard thought of his mother and of Saffron. *Do I not owe it to them to try to survive?* He remembered Berti Schrumpp and all the other friends he had lost over the past five years. *Do I have the right to cast a shadow over their reputations?*

He considered the alternatives Bayer had laid out before him. What good would be achieved if he condemned himself to suffering in a concentration camp? What purpose would be served? The Reich was falling apart. The only thing that mattered now was survival.

Gerhard looked at Bayer and said, 'Please pass my sincere gratitude to the *Reichsmarschall*. Tell him he has his deal.'

• • •

The judges marched into the People's Court in Berlin with Nazi eagles embroidered onto their robes. They gave a 'Heil Hitler' salute and took their places.

Gerhard was commanded to stand. He had not been allowed to wash or shave for days. He had been given a shabby, ill-fitting suit to wear. The only possession he had managed to keep was his photograph of Saffron, which he folded and slipped into one of his socks when no one was looking. He had been wearing his flying boots when he was arrested. Now he had a pair of unpolished shoes, worn at the heels. One of the soles was coming loose at the toe.

The image he presented to the court was not that of an elegant Luftwaffe officer, with his uniform emblazoned with awards for gallantry. Instead they saw a dirty, scruffy, malodorous scoundrel, represented by a weasel who looked little better.

Gerhard surveyed the packed courtroom. He saw army officers, SS men and party officials; reporters, or rather propaganda-writers, pens hovering over their notebooks; well-dressed Berliners here for a day's entertainment. Several senior Luftwaffe officers were seated side-by-side, close to the front of the court.

Have they come to support me, keep the judges in line, or make sure I don't go back on the deal? Gerhard wondered.

The he saw Konrad, with Chessi next to him. She smiled at Gerhard with a look of cold, malignant triumph, while Konrad sat and gloated at the culmination of his long campaign to crush his younger brother. Gerhard saw that they were the reason he was in the dock. His true crime had nothing to do with his meeting with von Tresckow. It was leaving Chessi for Saffron, and foiling Konrad's schemes to do him down.

The proceedings began and Gerhard realised that he was not in a courtroom at all. He was in a madhouse.

There were three men sitting in judgement: an army general, Hermann Reinecke; a prosecutor, Ernst Lautz; and sitting between them, presiding over the lunacy, the president of the court, Dr Roland Freisler.

As Gerhard discovered, Freisler was the only one of the trio who counted. He played the role of prosecutor, judge and jury. A beaky, unattractive man of almost fifty, with wiry dark hair surrounding a bald pate, he liked to begin his cases by berating the defendant before him. And the moment Freisler began this particular diatribe, Gerhard knew who had been feeding him his lines.

'You come from a parasitic life of privilege and wealth. You take money that would feed an honest German family for years and squander it helping your Jew friends. You reject German women in favour of British whores. The Führer reaches out a hand of friendship to you and you repay him with treachery.'

As he spoke, the volume and pitch of his voice increased until it was a harsh, grating screech. 'You have been heard insulting the Führer in terms so vile that I will not repeat them in this courtroom! Drunkenly insulting him in public, spitting in the face of loyal German soldiers as you do so! You are a wastrel, a lecher, a traitor and a coward! I dare you to deny it!'

Gerhard said nothing. He was too tired, too hungry to argue with this gibbering maniac, and there was no point. The deal had been done and they both knew it.

'Your silence condemns you!' Freisler shouted. 'You are a known associate of the traitor von Tresckow and his loathsome gang of assassins, conspirators and subversives. There is proof, overwhelming proof, that you met with von Tresckow and agreed with his views. It is also beyond dispute that you failed to report your meeting either to your superiors, or those of the traitor, so that proper measures could be taken against him. Your inaction was treasonable. By saying nothing you placed our beloved Führer in danger. A loyal pilot fights for his Führer. But you do not fight for him. You fight against him. You are a disgrace, a criminal disgrace!'

Still Gerhard said nothing. The mood in the courtroom was changing. There was a general sense of dissatisfaction. The show had not been following the approved script. One of the performers was failing to play his role. Most defendants would be begging, grown men in tears, pitifully admitting their guilt and pleading for mercy. They were not supposed to stand in silence, refusing to acknowledge the judge's harangue.

Freisler could sense it too. But he knew that there was nothing he could do. He had received his orders from on high and if he dared dispute them, the next time he returned to the People's Court it would be as the accused rather than the judge. He took a deep breath, did his best to maintain a commanding, assertive air and said, 'Gerhard von Meerbach, you stand accused on three counts of anti-social behaviour . . .'

Freisler paused. It was impossible to ignore the sound of murmuring among the spectators, or the mood of surprise and disappointment at what he had said. The people had expected charges of treason, sedition and even attempted assassination. They were looking forward to a death sentence, not a petty crime and a slap on the wrist.

'Silence!' Freisler shrieked, hammering his gavel. 'There will be silence in this court!'

He waited until the hubbub had subsided and continued. 'Firstly, you are accused of making derogatory remarks about the Führer and his conduct of the war. On this first count, how do you plead?'

'Guilty,' Gerhard replied.

'Secondly, you are accused of taking a private meeting with a known traitor. On this second count, how do you plead?'

'Guilty.'

'Thirdly, you are accused of failing to report this meeting or what was said by the traitor von Tresckow. How do you plead?'

'Guilty.'

The admissions of guilt seemed to have mellowed the mood in the room. Freisler was more confident as he continued. 'These are serious matters and the accused has admitted his guilt. But the court is aware of his war service and will show mercy, so long as the accused now pledges his unconditional loyalty to the Führer, his willingness to fight and die in the cause of National Socialism, and his confidence in the certain victory of the Reich against all its enemies.

'Gerhard von Meerbach, will you solemnly swear this vow in this courtroom, making your oath of loyalty in front of this court, for all the world to hear?'

The silence was profound as the spectators waited for Gerhard's answer. He looked around the room. The Luftwaffe officers were staring ahead, confident that their man would keep his side of the bargain and preserve the honour of their service. Konrad was not hiding his fury at being outwitted at the last moment. Chessi was looking at him with poisoned daggers in her eyes.

It struck Gerhard that once again the case had come down to the same two letters: '*Ja.*'

Freisler was becoming impatient. 'Give the court your answer,' he demanded.

Gerhard drew himself up straight. He stood to attention. He told himself that all he had to do was to keep his side of the bargain and stay alive, by any means possible, until the Allies won, Nazism was crushed and Germany was rid of the evil that had enslaved it.

And then he knew, more surely than he had known anything in his life, that he could not make that vow. He saw that this was not a deal for his freedom, but for his soul. If he said 'Yes' he would betray himself so profoundly that he would never be able to look at his own reflection again without seeing a man who had condemned himself. What was the point of surviving if he made himself so contemptible that he could never look Saffron, or his mother in the eye again? What could betray Schrumpp's memory more utterly than this?

Once before, Gerhard had given in to a Nazi's blackmail and betrayed his principles in the name of expediency. Never again.

'No,' he said. 'I refuse to take that vow.'

The silence turned at once to uproar. Konrad clapped his hands at his brother's wilful self-destruction. The Lufwaffe men were standing and shouting at him, one or two of them waving their fists.

The judges looked aghast, then turned inwards and consulted with one another, heads bowed in conference with only the occasional hand gesture to give a hint of what they were feeling.

Gerhard smiled to himself. He had pleaded guilty to a series of minor crimes. They could not now insist he should be accused a second time of more serious ones. But then he understood. They did not have to charge him again. They could sentence him as if he had been guilty of treason.

Then three heads separated. Freisler looked across the court. 'The prisoner accused has held this court in contempt,' he declared. 'He has spat in the face of his mercy. He has made his hatred for our Führer, our party and our fatherland all too plain.

'Very well then, Gerhard von Meerbach, you have made your choice and you must pay the price. This court will show you how it deals with traitors, anti-social conspirators and enemies of the state. You are to be sent to Sachsenhausen camp to serve a sentence of hard labour. I will not set a term of imprisonment.

There is no point. By the time that even the shortest term is over, you will long since have died from starvation, exhaustion or disease.'

A few of the spectators burst into applause. One or two cheered. The show had been saved by the twist in its tail.

'Take him away!' Freisler commanded. 'And let us move to the next traitor to be tried.'

• • •

Gerhard was removed from the court, placed in the back of a van and driven with three other prisoners north out of Berlin to the town of Oranienburg. It was a distance of around thirty-five kilometres and when they arrived at the town, the van drove past a series of large white buildings, which contained the administrative headquarters of the Reich's concentration-camp system. It approached a gatehouse, also white, into which were set iron gates bearing the slogan of the concentration camps: *'Arbeit Macht Frei'* or 'Work Sets You Free'.

A small clock tower stood on the roof of the central section of the gatehouse and Gerhard could see the long, thick barrel of an 8mm Maxim machine gun protruding from the entrance gate guard tower. The gunner was sighting the prisoners as if preparing for target practice.

The prisoners were pushed into a room and told to strip. When naked, they lined up in a row and one of the men was turned around by a guard to face the wall. He ran his hand through the thick black hair on the back of the prisoner's head, grabbed a handful and slammed him against the white tiles of the wall. From the corner of his eye Gerhard saw the crimson spray against the tiles.

'Too much hair,' said the guard. 'You break the rules.'

The prisoners were sprayed with a hose, the water ice cold. One by one, they were seated on a wooden crate, their bodies shaking. Their heads were shaved. Gerhard felt the nicks of the razor on his scalp, trickles of wetness on his forehead. They were marched into another room.

They were notified that they no longer had names. In future they would be known only by their numbers. If asked for their identity they would give their number. If they failed to do so they would be punished. If they failed to respond when their number was called, they would also be punished.

'You will give us the Sachsenhausen salute!' one guard declared, with a grin.

The guard peered closely at each of the prisoners in turn, his expression a mixture of fascination and disgust. He spat in the face of the prisoner whose nose continued to bleed.

From this moment on, Gerhard von Meerbach no longer existed. He was prisoner No. 57803. The number was printed on a patch crudely stitched onto the striped prison uniform he was given. An inverted red triangle marked him out as a political prisoner. To his relief he kept his shoes and socks. The photograph was still safe.

As they were led out of the van and into the building where the uniform was issued, Gerhard had caught a glimpse of some of the Sachsenhausen inmates, milling around a large, open space. Though it was a baking hot August day, a few of them had jackets and even coats over their uniforms. He understood now why that was: any item of additional clothing was a precious treasure, for in winter it could be a lifesaver.

Gerhard identified the most senior of the guards supervising their arrival at the camp. The man was an *SS-Rottenführer*, a corporal in military terms. Ten days ago he would have jumped to attention at the sight of Gerhard in his lieutenant colonel's uniform. Now their positions had been reversed and it was Gerhard who adopted a subservient, respectful tone as he asked, 'Please, sir, may I make a request?'

'You just did,' said the *Rottenführer*. He and the other guards burst out in laughter. 'Would you like to make another?'

'Yes please, sir, if I may.'

'What's your name?'

Gerhard stopped himself in time. He glanced at the patch on his uniform. 'Prisoner 57803, sir.'

'Almost had you, didn't I, eh? Spit it out then. What do you want?'

'May I keep my jacket?'

The *Rottenführer* picked up the jacket and examined it with distaste. He smelled it and recoiled in mock horror. 'God in heaven! Smells like a tramp's wiped his arse on it. Is that what you are, then, a tramp?'

Gerhard longed, more than anything else, to say what he really thought, to assert himself as a man and put this tawdry bully in his place. But he knew that there was nothing to be gained from that. All that mattered was getting the jacket.

'Yes, sir, if you say so, sir. I'm a tramp.'

'Did you wipe your arse on your jacket, tramp?'

'Yes, sir.'

'Then you'd better have it, in case you do another shit.'

'Thank you, sir. Thank you so much.'

Gerhard and the other prisoners were marched off to the barracks hut where they would now be housed. It was a long, low building. Inside its dimly lit interior, two unbroken lines of wooden bunks ran the length of the building, with a narrow aisle between them. The bunks were three levels high. The prisoners slept on the bare wooden slats, without mattresses or blankets, two or even three to each bed.

Gerhard was allotted a space on the bottom level of one bunk, and was exposed to any fluids, be they bodily waste, blood or pus that might drip down from the levels above. He shared the space with a former Social Democrat politician, No. 36419, who introduced himself as Karl.

'We still use names between ourselves,' he said. 'That's the only way we remember them.'

He was painfully thin. His eyes stared from his fleshless face. When he grinned, his teeth were yellow-brown.

'How long have you been here?' Gerhard asked, thinking he must be one of the longest-serving prisoners.

'I arrived in March,' Karl replied. 'What's the date today? I don't know what month it is any more.'

He asked Gerhard what his crime had been. They talked about their separate experiences of the People's Court and Gerhard described how he had been able to keep the jacket that had been issued to him for the trial.

'By the way,' he added, 'when we were being given our numbers, one of the guards mentioned something about the Sachsenhausen salute. What's that?'

Karl gave a wheezy laugh that turned into a hacking cough. 'You get down on your haunches with your arms held straight out in front of you. You stay like that for as long as they want, hours at a time. For a fit man that is hard enough to do for a few minutes. For men in our condition . . .' He shrugged. 'That's Sachsenhausen.'

Over the next few days, Karl helped Gerhard get his bearings. The main body of the camp was laid out inside a huge triangle, outlined with a barbed-wire fence and guarded by a watchtower from which an old First World War machine gun was trained on the prison below.

At the base of the triangle, by the gatehouse, was a large semi-circular parade ground, where roll calls were held, and on which stood two sets of gallows. All the barracks buildings radiated outwards from this open space.

'Each hut was built to house one hundred and forty prisoners,' Karl said. 'But the Nazis are such busy boys, arresting everyone they don't like, that now there's around four hundred poor bastards in every hut. Sometimes you get a lot of deaths, so the number goes down. Sometimes there's a lot of new arrivals, so it goes up. But four hundred's about normal. There are some women's huts, too.'

He looked at Gerhard and gave another of his wheezing laughs. 'Don't get hopeful. There's not a lot of romance around here. And if you think our guards are bad, you should see the bitches that guard the woman. One other problem – they don't seem to have increased the rations to match the numbers. I mean, look at us . . .'

Along with the huts, the two major buildings inside the triangle were the Gestapo prison, where suspects arrested by the Secret Police were brought for interrogation and torture, and the punishment cells.

'They stick you in solitary,' Karl said. 'Tiny cells, pitch black, no light, no air, even less food than you get out here. Most people who go in never come out. Those that do are so sick and so crazy they don't last long.'

Outside the perimeter of the triangle were two other blocks. One contained the 'Special Camp' for high-level prisoners. The other housed British and American officers, who had been caught trying to escape from conventional POW camps, or were being held as spies, rather than military prisoners.

'We get Russians, too, thousands of them. But they mostly seem to be killed and shoved in there . . .' He pointed to a tall chimney from which grey smoke was drifting. 'The crematorium.'

There were a number of industrial facilities beyond the triangle where prisoners were sent to work. The hardest labour was in the brick works, where building materials were manufactured for the proposed *Welthaupstadt* or 'World Capital' Germania that Hitler had been dreaming about since the pre-war days when Gerhard was a young architect, assigned to Albert Speer's studio. It would have been a pretty irony if Gerhard had been set to work amidst the choking dust and infernal heat of the brick kilns. Instead, he was given another oddly appropriate task and put to work in the factory that made parts for Heinkel bombers.

Karl was on the same production line. 'Some of the men deliberately make faulty components,' he said. 'They like the idea that they could make one of those goddamned bombers crash.'

'I can't do that. I know the men who fly in those planes. They're ordinary fellows, trying to get through this war. It's not their fault that their leaders are maniacs. Besides, there's no need to sabotage anything. We'll have lost the war soon, whatever anyone does here.'

'How long do you think it will be?' Karl asked.

'The rate the Russians are advancing in the East, they could be in Berlin by Christmas. I don't know what it's like in France. But if the British and Americans move as fast as we did, when we invaded in forty, they'll be across the Rhine by the autumn.'

Karl's eyes gleamed with hope. 'It could be over this year? Is that what you're saying?'

'It could be. But if it isn't . . . you may have to wait a while. The Allies will take their time over the winter, build up their forces. They'll wait till the spring before they strike.'

'And then?'

'The Third Reich will collapse like . . .' Gerhard was about to say 'a pack of cards'. Then a memory came to him from his childhood and he said, 'I have an older brother. He's high up in the SS. It's thanks to him that I'm here, in fact.'

'Not a very nice brother.'

'A bully, always has been. When I was a small boy, I used to make buildings out of wooden blocks. I spent hours on them. My brother would wait until I'd finished and the whole thing looked perfect. Then he'd kick it as hard as he could and send the bricks flying across the playroom. That's what's going to happen to Germany. Once the Allies come, they will smash our country into pieces.'

'But that will be the end of Hitler, and the SS, and camps like this . . . so it will be worthwhile.'

'That's why I intend to live to see it happen.'

Karl gave a weary smile. 'Don't build your hopes up, my friend. We live in the shadow of death here. It can come at any moment in any number of ways: starvation, sickness or an

SS man deciding, for no reason, that you are the poor soul he wants to kill today.'

'I understand,' Gerhard replied. 'I was at Stalingrad. I have seen hell once and survived it. I swear by God, I will survive it again at Sachsenhausen.'

'Can you believe this is the seventh calendar year of the war?' Leo Marks observed as he and Saffron walked down Baker Street, on the way to work on New Year's Day 1945.

'But the last year, surely,' she had replied.

'In Europe, certainly. This time it really will be over long before Christmas. But I'm not so sure about the Far East. Look how the Japs are defending scraps of rock in the middle of the Pacific. Can you imagine what they'll be like when we try to invade their own islands?'

'No need for T section to worry about that, thank God.'

Nowadays, the subject that consumed more and more of Saffron's time was what would happen in the aftermath of Hitler's now inevitable defeat. There were still dozens of SOE agents held captive in German hands. Every effort was being made to trace all their whereabouts, so that they could be rescued as soon as the Allies entered Germany.

'Not long now till the big push across the Rhine,' Amies said, one day in early February. 'Monty will lead our chaps and the Canadians, striking into northern Germany. The Americans are taking the centre and the south. Gubbins wants us to be behind the advance. We're not going to let our people spend one more second in captivity than they have to.'

But twenty-four hours later came news that three of F section's agents, Violette Szabo, Denise Bloch and Lilian Rolfe, had been executed at Ravensbrück, a concentration camp for female prisoners an hour's drive north of Berlin. The news struck everyone at Baker Street hard, so Saffron was not surprised when she was summoned to Amies' office the following morning to find him looking preoccupied and downbeat.

'Sit down,' he said, and then asked the secretary who had shown Saffron in, 'Could you please make tea for us both?'

The secretary nodded and hurried away, avoiding Saffron's eye when she looked towards her. Baker Street people weren't usually evasive in the face of professional disaster. The tension in Amies' expression wasn't normal either. This was personal.

A sickly feeling of dread was already spreading over her before Amies said, 'I'm afraid I have some bad news for you . . .'

Saffron's first thought was that her father must have died. *Who else could it be?*

'It's about Lieutenant Doherty . . .'

'No,' she gasped, holding her hands to her face.

'I'm afraid he's been killed in action, off the Philippines. I'm so sorry . . .'

Saffron sat, numb and immobile, as if she had not heard what Amies had said. Then she bent double in her chair as she burst into tears, sobbing so hard that she had to gasp for breath.

Amies came around his desk and pulled up another chair beside hers. He reached out and stroked the back of her neck and her back. 'My dear girl, I'm sorry,' he said. 'I wish there were another way to say this sort of thing, or that it never had to be said at all.'

The door to the office opened and the secretary placed a tray on the desk. She started pouring the two cups of tea.

'Plenty of sugar, I think,' Amies said, for if there was one belief that united the British population it was that nothing restored a person's morale like a cup of hot, sweet tea.

By the time the drink was made, Saffron had managed to bring herself under control. She wiped her face with her handkerchief, managed a wan smile as the cup was pressed into her hands and took a sip of the drink.

'What happened?' she asked.

'One of those blasted kamikaze attacks,' Amies replied. 'The aircraft hit the bridge of the cruiser on which Doherty was serving while he was on duty. The bomb it was carrying didn't go off, thank God. But the impact was enough to kill everyone in the immediate area. I dare say it's little consolation, but it all happened in an instant. He didn't suffer.'

'Oh Danny . . . Danny . . .' Saffron found herself crying again, but she forced herself not to give into the grief, not yet. There was something she had to find out before she could allow herself that release. 'How did you hear the news? I don't understand . . . How could they know about me?'

'They found a letter in his locker. It was inside an unsealed envelope. He hadn't finished writing the letter, but the envelope was addressed . . . to you, here at Norgeby House.'

'Why here?' she asked, as much to herself as to Amies. The fact that she asked the question implied that Doherty had known her home address.

'Perhaps he thought it would get to you quicker if it was sent to a military address,' Amies suggested.

'Oh . . . yes . . . I suppose that makes sense. What . . . what did it say?'

'I don't know. But I have it here, along with a note from his commanding officer. Let me get it for you.'

Amies stood up and leaned across his desk to reach a large brown paper envelope that he passed to Saffron. 'They're both in here. Listen, I have to go to some blasted meeting or other, but why don't you stay here, read everything in private? I'll make sure you're not disturbed. No need to rush . . .'

'Are you sure?'

'Of course. Think nothing of it. We go back a long way, you and I . . .'

Saffron waited until Amies was out of the room. She finished her cup of tea and then opened the envelope and pulled out its contents: a typed letter folded around a second envelope. She saw her name: *Captain Saffron Courtney GM, First Aid Nursing Yeomanry . . .*

The sight of his handwriting was a painfully visible reflection of him. The thought that he had been alive as he drew the pen across the paper and the image that formed so clearly in her mind of him writing the words was too much for her to bear.

She wept once more, and duly pulled herself back together, knowing that this was a cycle that would trap her for a long time to come. She read the first letter.

Dear Miss Courtney,

I know that there is little that can be said at times like these that will lessen the grief or loss. But I pray that these few words may go some small way to ease your pain.

Lt-Commander Daniel P. Doherty was a highly competent and courageous officer, in the finest traditions of the US Navy. He was greatly admired by his brother officers and greatly respected by the men. He served with distinction in the heat of battle and died with honor at his post.

He never for one second regretted his determination to transfer back into active service, nor doubted the cause for which we all fight. I am certain that even had he known what fate had in store for him, his decision would have been the same.

On a personal note, I would like to add this: Danny only spoke about you to me once, but he did so with such affection, respect and admiration for you that I was in no doubt of how much you meant to him.

With my very deepest condolences.
Yours sincerely,
James F. Vinston (Capt. US Navy)

The memories were flooding back to Saffron: the first time he had strolled into her room at Arisaig; the walk over the dune to the sea at Camusdarach; the smile on his face, like a boy who had got away with something tremendously naughty as he looked down at her, after they had made love for the first time.

She wondered if Amies kept a bottle of Scotch, or brandy somewhere in his office; most of the senior officers did. She felt she needed something stronger than tea before she read

Danny's letter. She told herself not to be so bloody feeble. He deserved better of her than that. She took it out of the envelope and read:

My dear sweet Saffy,

I've started God knows how many letters to you and haven't finished a damn one yet. Maybe this time I'll get lucky. I'll say the thing that I've been too chicken to say before.

Baby, I'm crazy about you.

You know that first time we spent together, the night before I left Scotland? Remember how you asked me if I'd ever been in love? I said I don't know. How can you tell?

You said, you don't even have to think about it. Love fills you right up. You can't miss it. And I said I envied the guy who made you feel like that.

I got back to the States, and I knew I didn't feel that way about Meg and I never would, even though she's pretty and sweet and if I married her all the other guys would envy me for having such a cute wife. But if I didn't feel love, the way you described it, how could I marry her?

I guess I forgot about love for a while, and I worked like crazy, and had fun when I could. Nothing serious.

Then I came to London. I couldn't decide if I should look you up. I didn't know if you'd be pleased to see me. But I guess Fate made that decision for me. There you were, across that conference table. And right there and then – bam! – it hit me like a lightning bolt.

I was in love. With you.

I had to see you. I had to be with you. But I knew I was shipping out any day. I told myself, 'Don't be crazy. This can't happen. You know she doesn't feel the same way about you. There's another guy. The whole damn Jap navy's waiting to blow you to kingdom come. Don't talk about love.'

I don't know if I did the right thing. But I want you to know that . . .

Damn! Battle stations. Back soon!!

By the time Amies returned, Saffron had cried herself out, for the time being at least.

'I'm sorry, I must look a fright,' she said as he walked into the office.

'Well, that's one good sign,' he replied. 'When a woman has recovered her vanity all is not yet totally lost. Now, my dear, you've had the most ghastly shock. Would you like to take the rest of the day off? There are no flaps on. We can manage without you for once.'

Saffron shook her head. 'No,' she said. 'Danny Doherty died doing his job. The least he deserves is for me to carry on doing mine.'

'Well said . . . By the way, I can't say I knew Doherty well, but he always struck me as a thoroughly good man. And, if I may say so, devilishly handsome.'

Saffron smiled. 'Yes, sir, he really was handsome . . . and devilish, too.'

• • •

Konrad von Meerbach told himself that there were few, if any, men in the Reich who had done more than him to make the Final Solution possible. He had not been given the opportunity to stand on a shooting line on an anti-Jew operation in the East. Nor had he been given a command role at any of the killing centres where Jews from all over Europe were processed. But he had made an essential, if not so visible, contribution.

Himmler had told him, 'If you had not kicked those *Reichsbahn* pen-pushers into line, we would never have got a single train into Sobibór or Treblinka. And without them, there could have been no Auschwitz-Birkenau.'

That was true. The relationship between the SS and the *Deutsche Reichsbahn* railway authority was a constant source of frustration. Timetables were drawn up with almost no consideration for the practical needs of the men and women who would have to meet the trains at their final destinations and deal with the disposal of their cargoes. There were endless wrangles over money. The *Reichsbahn* was paid for every kilometre covered by every Jew. When von Meerbach contemplated the enormous sums that the railway people were making, he was tempted to march to their headquarters, shove all the board of directors against a wall and inform them that they could make a simple choice: charge less or be shot.

They were not the only pigs getting their snouts into the trough of the Final Solution. The chemical companies, oven manufacturers and construction organisations were profiteering, even though they were dependent on the foreign slave-workers who could not be rounded up without the aid of the SS. But did they show any gratitude for that when the time came to present their bills? No, they did not.

Von Meerbach was fortified by the knowledge that his efforts were being made in the service of a great and noble cause. Week by week the processing figures came in, the tally rose higher and the extermination of the Jews from the mainland of Europe drew a little closer. There was further compensation. Von Meerbach had visited all six of the major extermination camps in Occupied Poland, enabling him to get to know the men who ran them and form the relationships that were essential to the efficient running of any major industrial operation, which this most certainly was.

But the SS was concerned with more than the Jewish Question. It was responsible for the concentration camps that housed anyone else who had displeased the Reich authorities in Germany or its conquered lands.

Von Meerbach took great pains to let the staff in these camps know that Berlin had not forgotten them: that good work would be rewarded and inefficiency or disorder punished. He underlined the point with personal inspections of camps across the nation. Today he was making just such a visit. He had been looking forward to it for many weeks and now that the day had come, his mood was sunnier than it had been in months.

The news from the front, both in the East and West, was unrelentingly awful. The threat to the Reich grew greater every day. The Russians were barely sixty kilometres east of Berlin. The British and Americans were on the west bank of the Rhine. But for now such cares could be forgotten. For this one day Konrad von Meerbach could afford to indulge himself.

Gerhard shuffled into the doctor's surgery. The snow lay thick on the ground outside. Even indoors, his faltering breath hung in the air. An orderly took a note of his number, wrote it down on a form and barked, 'Roll up your sleeve.'

Gerhard looked at him dumbly. He was finding it hard to understand what had been said, still less translate the words into actions. The cold, his constant, gnawing hunger and the crushing fatigue brought on by the impossibility of proper sleep in the overcrowded bunks had numbed his brain, along with his ability to reason.

The orderly slapped him across the face. He felt a tooth come loose. There was pain somewhere, but his senses were dulled.

'Roll up your sleeve!' the orderly shouted.

Gerhard heard him this time but his clumsy fingers would not do as he commanded. The orderly pushed Gerhard's jacket and uniform sleeves up his emaciated stick of an arm, grabbed his wrist and dragged him to the doctor, who was holding a metal and glass syringe.

'How the hell am I supposed to stick a needle in that?' the doctor muttered, looking at the fleshless limb. 'Bend the elbow,' he said to the orderly. 'As if he's showing off his bicep.'

The orderly did as he was told. A scrap of muscle could be seen above the bone. The doctor jabbed it with the needle. The orderly pushed Gerhard and he tumbled forward to the far side of the room where a *kapo*, one of the prisoners who worked for the camp administration, was waiting. He was a big man, well fed, nice and warm in his fur-lined coat.

Gerhard recognised him, not with any conscious thought, but in the way an animal recognises a human that it knows and fears, because that human has mistreated it. A reflex born of repeated punishment told him this *kapo* was a cruel and violent man, so he bent over and lifted his arms to protect his head as he went past.

The *kapo* kicked Gerhard in the backside, sending him sprawling on the floor. He kicked him again in the ribs as he shouted, 'Get up, you piece of shit!'

To his surprise, prisoner 57803 jumped to his feet. It was as if someone had sent an electric shock through his skeletal physique.

Gerhard's reaction came as a shock to him too. He could not understand it. He suddenly felt alive again: his body filled with energy, his mind sharper than it had been in months. He looked at the *kapo* and thought, *I know you. You're one of the Russian POWs. You were in a criminal gang before the war. That's why the SS recruited you to be a* kapo. *They value sadists. They're useful allies in the war against humanity.*

• • •

Back in the dispensary the doctor noticed that the camp commandant, Anton Kaindl, had entered the room.

'Are we ready for the experiment?' Kaindl asked.

'Yes, *Standartenführer*. The prisoners have been injected with our performance–enhancing formulation D-IX. It is a mixture of the narcotic cocaine, the methamphetamine stimulant Pervitin and the opioid painkiller Eukodal. This should greatly increase their confidence and energy levels, while also raising their pain threshold.'

'They will perform in a more animated fashion than usual?'

'Correct. However, we cannot make any definitive statements until the results have been collected and compared with standard figures. But if our working hypothesis is accurate, this will result in a significantly improved performance.'

'And what do you expect the consequence of this to be?'

'The prisoners have been weakened by malnutrition and disease. Their strength is reduced; no drug can alter that fact. They will therefore expend their resources more intensively than they would otherwise do, with much more drastic consequences.'

'Describe those consequences, please.'

'To summarise, they will walk more quickly. They will ignore the pain from their blisters and cuts. And then their hearts will explode and they will drop dead.'

Kaindl beamed. 'Perfect. We have an important visitor today, doctor. I have promised him first-class entertainment. I would not wish him to be disappointed.'

● ● ●

The official reason for making prisoners walk as much as forty kilometres per day in ill-fitting military boots was to test footwear before it was given to fighting men. The second reason was to test the people who were walking. Doctors wanted to know how long a human body could keep going when it was malnourished, wracked with sickness and fatigue, and on the verge of death. As Stalingrad had demonstrated, it was possible for frontline soldiers to find themselves in that state. Their generals needed to know what they could accomplish under such circumstances.

But the real reason the commanders of Sachsenhausen and their staffs put the men and women under their control through this, and all the other pitiless torments and degradations that the camp had to offer, was that cruelty was the guiding principle of the camp and its staff. The point was not merely to punish, or even kill, the Reich's internal enemies, but to rob them of dignity, humanity and identity. The struggle for the prisoners was not only to survive, but to retain some sense, no matter how diminished, of their own humanity.

Gerhard tried to walk with his head up, maintaining a steady pace, even though every cell in his body was crying out to be allowed to stop, curl up into a ball on the ground and weep with pain and humiliation. Today that task was easier than usual. He knew that his feet were bleeding from the blisters and lacerations left by previous forced marches because he could feel the blood between the sole of his foot and the inside of the boot. Today, the boots he had been issued with were too big. It was moot which was worse: too big or too small – they never seemed to be the right size. The small ones hurt from the moment one put them on, but the confinement in which the feet were trapped, however agonising, kept the foot inside the boot. A bigger pair was easier at first, but as the foot slipped against the toe, the skin was rubbed, like wood under sandpaper, and the wounds were worse.

With only three kilometres completed and many more to come, each step should be a moment of torture. Yet he felt no more than a dull ache. The tin cup of watery black liquid that purported to be coffee and the lump of buckwheat bread he had consumed that morning could not possibly provide him with enough energy. And yet he felt capable of more effort than before. He even experienced a strange sense of euphoria.

The men around Gerhard looked similarly revived. One was whistling a tune as he walked. Gerhard reasoned that these were the effects of the drug they had been given, and its purpose was to keep the men of the Wehrmacht fighting when a sane man would surrender. He remembered the sights he had witnessed at Stalingrad and thought, even now, even here, *I'm not worse off than those poor bastards.*

Gerhard kept walking, and he kept his eyes in front of him, instead of gazing sightlessly at the cold, hard earth beneath his feet. He looked across the expanse of the parade ground and saw the camp gates open and motorcycle outriders sweep through, ahead of a large black staff car. He realised that Kaindl was there with a reception party, waiting as one of his men opened the passenger door of the car and everyone snapped to attention. A uniformed SS officer got out of the car. Kaindl stepped forward to greet him. The two men exchanged, 'Heil Hitler's.

All the while Gerhard had been telling himself, *It's not possible . . . it can't be*. But as the SS officer walked down the line of men who had been presented for his inspection, there could be no doubt as to his identity.

In all the pharmacies of all the doctors labouring to produce wonder drugs for the Reich, there was not a single substance that could cure the sickening blend of helplessness, shame and impotent fury that now squatted like a cold, malignant toad in the depths of Gerhard's guts.

• • •

'You must be feeding him too well, Kaindl,' Konrad remarked as they paused to watch his brother walk by. 'Look at him strolling along as if he owns the place.'

Kaindl gave a nervous laugh. 'Have no fear, *Brigadeführer*. That is the effect of the drug with which he was injected this morning. I am assured by our medical staff that when we next return to observe your brother, he will be in a far more satisfactory condition.'

'I should hope so. What else have you got to show me?'

They passed a punishment squad of female guards who were supervising a dozen women. All had been deemed guilty of minor breaches of camp discipline and were being forced to give the 'Sachsenhausen salute'. They squatted with their arms held out straight in front of them and the guards berated their shaven-headed victims with a steady, screeching stream of insults and commands, and any of the women who let her arms drop, or lost her balance, was set upon with boots and wooden batons.

Elsewhere, two lines of male prisoners were standing to attention, their sequence interrupted at intervals by bodies lying motionless on the ground.

'Who are those men?' Konrad asked.

'They are the male prisoners who claim to be unfit for work. They must spend the working day standing to attention. As you can see, it provides a useful form of attrition. We expect to lose around half a dozen a day in this way.'

'What is your fatality rate?' Konrad asked.

Kaindl pursed his lips as he considered the question. 'If one sets aside executions – for example, we have terminated more than one hundred dissidents and saboteurs from the *Reichskommissariat Niederlande* alone – and considers it as a process of attrition, then we lose on average five thousand men and women a year. That would be a daily rate of, let me see . . . roughly fifteen every day. My predecessor, Albert Sauer, showed great foresight in installing a crematorium to deal with the remains.'

'Did you use the gas facility he also constructed?'

'It has its uses, although it is only a small facility. For processing on a large scale, however, we still use shooting.'

'The old ways are often the best.'

The tour of the camp took in the brick kilns, where prisoners made bricks, and the aircraft component workshops. Then they arrived at a workplace of particular interest to Konrad: the rooms where forgers, working under SS supervision, were producing hundreds of millions of pounds' worth of fake, British £5 notes.

'These may come in useful in the days and months to come,' Konrad observed.

'The men have almost mastered US dollars,' said Kaindl, handing Konrad a $100 bill, decorated with a profile portrait of Benjamin Franklin.

Konrad was rarely impressed, but he could not hide his admiration for the work the forgers had done. 'Remarkable . . . It even feels like real currency.'

'Here,' Kaindl said, 'please accept this as a gift, with the compliments of Sachsenhausen.'

He gave Konrad another note. The man whose portrait it bore was a nineteenth century Secretary of the Treasury and Chief Justice called Salmon P. Chase. The denomination inscribed upon it was $10,000.

Konrad beamed with pleasure. 'I heard of these notes before the war, when I did business in America. I must say, Kaindl, that is a very agreeable souvenir of my visit.'

'Now,' said his host, 'would you care for some lunch?'

• • •

Gerhard gasped as his chest was seized by an excruciating agony. It was as if his heart was being squeezed by a steel claw. His lungs had seized up. His throat was caught in an invisible garrotte. Though his body desperately craved air, he could not make himself breathe. He thought he was going to die.

He fell to his knees, his hands clasped to his ribcage, unable to make any cry of distress except for the sound of his frantic gagging for air. Nothing happened. He still could not breathe. His heart seemed to have stopped beating.

And then some deep, primal survival instinct, far beyond his conscious control, kicked in. The pressure on his throat relented, he sucked in air with the urgency of a drowning man breaking the surface of the water and he felt the faint beat of his heart once again.

All the clarity of thought and perception briefly returned, along with vestiges of energy and strength. That same animal compulsion to live, which had restarted his breathing, told him that he had to keep moving.

Gerhard tried to get to his feet. But his body refused to obey his commands. He could not make his limbs do what was required to stand upright, let alone walk. He couldn't remember how it was done.

But he could crawl, though it was little more than a slow, grovelling motion, resting on his knees and elbows, with his head almost touching the ice and dirt beneath him.

Gerhard began to worm his way around the parade ground. He barely noticed the mocking laughter of the guards, or felt the stones that they threw at him until, while his comrades cheered him on, one of the SS men marched up behind him, prepared himself like a footballer about to take a penalty, took a short run up and kicked Gerhard as hard as he could, sending him sprawling face first onto the ground.

It was Gerhard's second kicking of the day, but this time he did not spring back up. Instead, whimpering softly, the frozen, emaciated, skeletal remains of the man Gerhard had once been remained immobile on the frozen earth, as the dregs of his life ebbed away.

• • •

The staff of Sachsenhausen ate better than their inmates, but they were still on reduced rations, for the whole Reich was going hungry. Kaindl had done his best to put on a decent spread for his distinguished guest. Konrad, however, paid no attention to the food. He cleared his plate quickly then ordered everyone out of the dining room, with the exception of Kaindl.

Konrad waited, saying nothing until the camp's officers had left, some casting nervous looks over their shoulder. He knew what they were wondering: *who is in trouble – the boss or one of us?*

Only when he was sure that they were alone did Konrad address the camp commandant, who was by now agitated. 'We must make contingency arrangements,' he began. 'Of course, we still have faith in our Führer's genius . . .'

'Yes, fervently,' Kaindl agreed with an urgency born of the knowledge that many of his prisoners, including the *Briga-defführer*'s own brother, were there because they had shown insufficient faith in their leader.

'Nevertheless,' Konrad continued, 'the international Jew still weaves his treacherous plots, in alliance with the Bolsheviks, the malcontents, the perverts and the saboteurs. We must con-sider the possibility, however unlikely, that the Reich, or large areas of it, may fall into enemy hands. We must be prepared for any eventuality.'

'I'm sure you are right, *Brigadeführer*.'

'Detailed preparations are being made by men such as ourselves, whose commitment to National Socialism remains absolute and unflinching, to ensure that the fight will go on, no matter what. For more than a year, under the personal direction of *SS-Reichsführer* Himmler, plans have been made for the creation of an Alpine Fortress in the mountains of southern Bavaria and the Austrian and Italian Tyrol.'

'I had no idea . . .' said Kaindl, tactfully not remarking upon the fact that if the plans had been in circulation for more than a year, then the higher echelons of the Reich had already anticipated defeat by the end of 1943.

'For obvious reasons, these plans have only been discussed within a select group of senior officers. I am adding you to their number.'

'I am truly honoured, *Brigadeführer*.'

'Now, your inmates include a number of individuals who possess a high value as hostages. Some are rich and might fetch a high price if ransomed. Others have political or social status in their homelands, or are valued intelligence assets and so might be used as bargaining chips in any future negotiations.'

'Ah, you mean the inhabitants of our Special Camp. We have always taken particular care of them . . . in case they are useful at any point. We have numerous enemy officers, too.'

'Good . . . You are to draw up a list of any prisoners who you believe fall into the categories I have described. In the event that this camp is threatened by the enemy, they are to be moved to a safer location. You must be ready to have them transported by rail at a moment's notice. Do I make myself clear?'

'Yes, *Brigadeführer*. Do you wish me to include your brother on that list?'

Konrad considered before giving his answer. 'On reflection, I believe he would be a tradable asset, even if I can say with absolute assurance that his own family would not pay a single *pfennig* for his safe return!'

Kaindl chuckled politely at Konrad's little joke.

'Others, however, might be willing to make arrangements on his behalf. He was not without wealthy friends. Include him. But I insist: no special treatment. He must be kept under the same conditions as the other prisoners on the list.'

'And if he dies?'

Kaindl feared the consequences of such an eventuality, but Konrad was happy to reassure him. 'Then he dies. It is of no matter to me. Who knows, we may yet see him perish today.'

There was a knock on the door. Kaindl looked at Konrad, who nodded. 'Let them in, our business is done.'

The doctor who had administered the injections entered the room. 'I apologise for disturbing you, *Brigadeführer*, but I have news that may interest you. The effects of the substance that was administered to the prisoners have worn off rather earlier than expected, perhaps because of the physical condition of the experimental specimens. But the after-effects are quite marked. I believe you will find them of particular interest, *Brigadeführer*.'

All three men knew at once what that meant. A smile spread across Konrad's meaty face. 'In that case, Herr *Doktor*, it will be my pleasure to see the results of your research.'

• • •

Gerhard had found the will not to die. He had forced himself onto his knees. But the drug had left him confused. He knew he was supposed to go somewhere, but could not understand where he was or which direction he should take. He remained on all fours, looking around with uncomprehending eyes, trying to find a sign of what to do next while the guards took bets on which direction the pathetic, brainless beast in front of them would eventually choose.

'I don't think it'll go anywhere,' one of them said, with the air of a man who knows best. 'I say it dies right where it is. All the others have.'

The rest of the guards were obliged to acknowledge this conclusion, for the track around the parade ground was littered with the dead bodies of the other prisoners who had set off on the march that morning. This was the only survivor.

One of them was having a hard time holding back his Alsatian, which was barking and straining at the leash as it tried to get closer to Gerhard. 'He thinks it's a bitch,' he said, shouting over the noise of the dog. 'He wants to fuck it.'

'Maybe he wants a bone to chew on,' said another.

But before the matter could be debated further, one of them hissed, 'Shit! Look who's coming.'

The others threw away their cigarettes, straightened their uniforms, beat the dog into a sitting position and snapped to attention as the doctor and the two officers approached.

'As you can see,' said the doctor, 'the drug appears to have astonishing powers in the short term, but a price is paid in due course. This one' – he consulted the clipboard he was carrying – 'number 5-7-8-0-3, is the only survivor. I gather you know the prisoner, *Brigadeführer*.'

'Yes . . .' Konrad said. It gave him a pleasure so intense as to be almost sexual to see his younger brother in the pitiful state that now met his eyes. Here was the cocky young architect who had once been praised by the Führer in person for his designs, the handsome young buck who had always got the prettiest girls, the dashing fighter ace whose uniform had once been adorned with so many medals for gallantry, now reduced to a subhuman bag of bones, snivelling at his feet.

It was an affectation of Konrad's that he always carried a horsewhip when on official business. He felt it matched the riding boots of his uniform and the essence of what it meant to be an SS officer. He flicked it across Gerhard's face. The blow was not a strong one, but Gerhard's skin was so thin and so taut across his bones that a thin line of blood started seeping down his cheek.

A look of incomprehension passed across Gerhard's face. He tried to raise a hand towards his wounded skin, but before his fingers could reach the cut, he lost his balance and toppled onto his side.

One of the soldiers laughed, then stopped himself. He looked nervously towards Konrad, but then he burst out laughing too and a second later all the men were in stitches as Gerhard tried to right himself with the helplessness of a beetle trapped on its back.

With a blundering effort that required every scrap of concentration and strength, the feeble wretch known as 57803 managed to resume its previous crawling posture. But now it was back at its starting point, unable to work out where to go next.

Konrad had the solution. With a few flicks of his whip on Gerhard's haunches, he was able to make him turn until facing the correct direction. Then he addressed his admiring audience, saying, 'Now, gentlemen, observe how the dumbest animal can be trained to obey a command.'

He stood in front of Gerhard with the toes of his boot beneath his brother's chin.

'Lick my boot,' he said.

Gerhard shook his head, though whether it was because he was refusing to obey the order or did not understand, it was hard for the onlookers to say.

Konrad hit him with the whip across the back.

'Lick . . . my . . . boot.'

Gerhard's head remained where it was, unmoving.

Konrad whipped him again. He placed the end of the horsewhip under Gerhard's chin, lifted it and saw, to his delight, that there were tears running down his grimy face.

Konrad looked him in the eye and said, 'Lick.' Then he made a grotesque, exaggerated licking motion by way of instruction.

He removed the whip and Gerhard's head fell again.

'Lick . . . my . . . boot.'

Konrad raised his whip, ready to strike again. Then Gerhard lowered his face onto Konrad's boot. He licked.

A ragged cheer went up from the watching men.

Konrad reached with his gloved hand, ruffling the top of Gerhard's head as he would a dog's, and said, 'There's a good boy.'

He took a step back, tapped his boot with his whip and said, 'Here!'

Gerhard lifted his head and looked at him, not understanding the word or the gesture. But when Konrad raised his whip again, Gerhard, with painfully slow movements, shuffled across the metre or so of ground until his face was once again over Konrad's boot.

'Lick!'

Gerhard licked.

'Congratulations, *Brigadeführer*!' the doctor exclaimed. 'Pavlov himself could not have conducted a more persuasive demonstration of animal psychology!'

'Thank you, Herr *Doktor*,' Konrad said with a nod of the head. 'Kaindl, I must return to Berlin. It has been a most instructive visit. I want the prisoner led around one entire circuit of this parade ground in the manner that I have demonstrated. If he obeys, he is spared. If he does not obey, he is hit. And before you ask me again – no, it does not concern me if he dies before the end of the circuit.'

• • •

In mid-April, troops of the US Seventh Army entered Nuremberg, not far from the estate on which Francesca von Meerbach had grown up. As the invaders added another German city to their list, she and Cora, her lady's maid, were driven from the Schloss Meerbach to the family's factory complex. Behind the Mercedes limousine followed a small van.

The motor works that had earned the family its vast fortune had been the target of a dozen or more raids by American bombers. Yet there were still a few signs of life in one corner of the several square kilometres that the works occupied. At the private airfield where so many aero-engines had been put through their paces by test pilots working for the von Meerbachs, a large hanger was still fully staffed and properly maintained. Beside it were bunkers surrounding tanks that contained many thousands of litres of aviation fuel.

This liquid was perhaps the single most valuable commodity in the remaining territory of the Third Reich, since it was in huge demand and almost impossible to come by. But Konrad Meerbach had the full authority of the SS behind him and could afford to pay any price for what he wanted.

Francesca's car drove into the hanger. As she got out, she saw two aircraft. The first looked like an oversized fighter plane, with a streamlined fuselage and a single propeller at its nose.

'I've found just what we need,' Konrad had told her at Christmas, when they'd first discussed their escape plans. 'It's a Heinkel He 70 "Lightning". It was designed to be a small, express airliner and to carry airmail, so it's damn fast. The Luftwaffe's been using Lightnings for courier work, but a squadron captain had one he didn't need and I possessed a bag full of gold teeth, so now it's mine.'

'Gold teeth?' Francesca asked.

'Yes, their owners had no further use for them.'

'I'm glad to hear those people can be good for something.'

Her husband had laughed. 'By God you're a cold-hearted bitch.'

'That's what you like about me.'

Konrad gave a contented smile of agreement, then said, 'Anyway, the Lightning can carry four passengers and their baggage. There'll be room for you and that woman of yours, as well as our valuables.'

The Heinkel had been painted khaki and emblazoned with broad white bands around its wings and body, on which large red crosses were painted. Any potential aggressors seeing it would assume it was carrying sick or injured passengers and, with any luck, leave it alone. Only the closest examination would reveal the faint shadow of the black Luftwaffe crosses beneath the red and white.

The other aircraft looked like nothing Francesca had ever seen in her life. It was not particularly large, but it carried an extraordinary air of menace. This was due in part to its black paintwork, on which there were no markings: no serial number, no Luftwaffe cross, nothing to indicate its identity or allegiance.

The fuselage was a smooth, sleek tube with a slightly bulbous, glazed nose that, to Francesca's eyes, gave it an unmistakably phallic appearance. From the wings hung four pods, clustered in pairs on either side of the fuselage, both open at either end. She had a sense that these were the engines, but how they worked she had no idea. What was obvious, however, was that this looked like a craft from an entirely new age of history. Not only would it take one further and faster than any ordinary aircraft could ever hope to do, it looked as if it could fly all the way to the stars.

Francesca shook her head at her fanciful thoughts. She had more practical matters on her mind.

'Be careful with those cases,' she snapped as a pair of mechanics in white boiler suits set about moving her luggage from the van to the Heinkel. There were two large, metal steamer trunks and an assortment of smaller cases.

'Oof!' one of the mechanics grunted as they struggled to heft the trunk onto a trolley beside the car. 'What have you got in here, ma'am? Lead pipes?'

Gold sovereigns, actually, Francesca thought, *lying beneath my dresses and fur coats*.

The other trunk contained more clothes and shoes, and three leather tubes in which were rolled the canvases bearing masterpieces by Raphael, Vermeer and a Renoir that Konrad reviled as 'sentimentalist, Impressionist, chocolate-box trash', but Francesca unashamedly adored. The best of the family jewels filled two large hatboxes. And as well as her handbag, Francesca carried a briefcase filled with the two million US dollars in bearer bonds that Konrad had acquired on his trip to Portugal, three years earlier.

The total value of all the assets contained in Francesca's luggage was enough to ensure that she and Konrad could live a life of luxury and ease for the rest of their days. When she arrived in Switzerland, however, this treasure would take its place in the bank vault that contained the far greater wealth secretly squirreled away by Konrad, before and during the war. He had been looting his family's firm since his first day at its helm. Since 1939 he had been party to the plundering, looting and thieving that had accompanied every Nazi invasion and that was such a huge part of the Final Solution. Even now, it was not enough: not for Konrad.

Francesca was distracted from this train of thought by the von Meerbachs' personal pilot, Berndt Sperling, who coughed politely to signal his presence, and said, 'Excuse me, my lady, but the plane is now ready for take-off.'

Francesca smiled graciously. 'Thank you, Berndt. How long will the flight be, do you think?'

'I'm expecting a nice smooth flight, so I should have you across the Bodensee and into Switzerland within ten minutes of take-off, and landing in Zurich less than half an hour after that.'

'Will you be returning to Germany immediately?'

'Yes, your ladyship. I promised the Count I'd be available in case he needs me.'

'Very good then, Berndt, let's be on our way.'

• • •

Sachsenhausen, like the Reich, was falling apart. The dead lay where they dropped, for the guards had lost interest in clearing them up and the prisoners were too weak to do the job themselves. The closest anyone came to disposal was to make piles of the dead, heaped on top of one another like skeleton puppets whose strings had been cut. They lay around the parade ground, as casually strewn as discarded socks on a bedroom floor. In overcrowded huts, where prisoners were crammed three or four to a bunk, the living lay trapped and unable to move between the dead and dying. Even those who were nominally alive were no more than rotting, breathing corpses.

Disease had spread out of control, as it had in every other concentration camp. The latrines were overflowing with the diarrhoea that spurted from dysentery sufferers whose shattered digestive systems could not extract a meagre amount of energy from the ever more pitiful rations before they voided themselves again. The lice that infested every man and woman in the camp spread the typhus, which began with symptoms of fever, headaches and chills, before appearing as a rash that spread from sufferers' bellies and chests, until it covered every inch of their body, and only their faces, the palms of their hands and the soles of their feet remained unaffected. By then they were delirious, babbling incoherently before they fell into their final coma.

Day after day, Russian, British and American planes flew overhead, bombers and fighters alike, apparently untroubled by any resistance from the Luftwaffe. Word had spread around the camp that the Russians were about to make their final march on Berlin. The guards were behaving more brutally than usual, shooting prisoners on the slightest pretext, on a whim, as if they knew their time was up too. Meanwhile the usual routines were collapsing: the Germans no longer bothered with the daily roll call. The workshops and the brick kilns ceased operations. And then came rumours that the SS were going to march everyone out of the camp, to remove the living evidence of what they had done, though those few prisoners who were able to reason wondered what good that would do them when the dead gave such damning testimony.

Gerhard didn't know how, but his heart was still beating after crawling a circuit of the parade ground. Gerhard had one thought on his mind: food. The daily rations were brought from the kitchens to the huts by teams of prisoners, tethered like oxen to a cart on which sat the steel canister of gruel and the baskets of bread that were supposed to feed the inmates.

There had been a time when the food was distributed properly. It would be brought into the huts and people would line up to receive their paltry ration. Care was taken to ensure that everyone received their fair share, no matter how small. If any dregs of soup or crumbs of bread were left, they were the perks of the men who brought the food. Now there was hardly anyone left to bring the food, or serve it. The half-empty canisters were left outside the huts, with the bread on the ground beside then.

Men died in their beds and were left to decompose where they lay, for there was no one to move or bury them. Those with typhus became too weak to get out of bed, push aside the corpses beside them and make their way outside. They were unable to eat and became more deprived and more certain to die. In this hellhole, survival depended on the ability to make one's way to the canister and seize whatever sustenance was available, even if that meant fighting off other starving men intent on doing the same thing.

And through it all, the cold refused to release its grip and let spring bring some warmth to the bones of men and women whose fingers and toes were blackened by frostbite and whose bodies had not stopped shivering in the endless, bleak, dark months of this winter without end.

And then one day there was a roll call, summoned as the breakfast rations were being dumped in front of the huts. When it was over, a number was read out and the guard said, 'Gather up your belongings and report back to the parade ground immediately.'

The number in question was 57803.

Gerhard had reached the point where he responded to his number automatically and the sound of his name would have confused him. His only possession – his photograph – was safe inside his jacket. He had no belongings to gather. He was about to say as much to the guard when he overheard one man say to another, 'I wonder where they're taking him.'

'Nowhere good,' the other replied.

The cart on which breakfast had been dragged towards the hut was standing outside. The coffee canister was empty. The pieces of bread had been taken from the baskets. But experience had taught Gerhard that it was always worth scavenging. He looked under the cart and saw a piece of bread, and beyond it another. As a nervous pickpocket, he shoved the bread into his jacket pockets: one hard, stale crust on either side.

Having reported back as instructed, he was led away, out of the main camp to another area where a group of people were being lined up beside some trucks. They were prisoners but were dressed in suits and military uniforms, and they seemed healthier and better fed than him. He could see them look at him as he approached, wondering why someone so filthy, no doubt crawling with lice and riddled with disease, was doing with them. One of the men backed away when Gerhard was placed next to him in the line.

He did not want to do anything to attract anyone's attention. He wasn't going to waste energy on anything that was not essential. His dignity was irrelevant. The only thing that mattered was survival.

They were driven to a railway yard and loaded aboard two covered goods wagons. The train set off, passing what looked like the west of Berlin and then onwards. Still the winter would not break and the only warmth in the wagons came from bodies pressed together. Gerhard, however, was excluded from the huddle. He was unclean and a risk to health. He was left to huddle in a corner, alone.

Progress was slow, for the journey was frequently interrupted without warning and in random locations. The train would stand motionless for hours and, if they were lucky, the prisoners would be allowed out to relieve themselves, a blessing when the only toilet in each wagon consisted of a foul-smelling, overflowing bucket.

When the engine started moving again, the train would retrace its steps before taking another line: one whose tracks and bridges had not been destroyed by Allied bombers or local partisans. The endless delays meant that a journey that should have been completed in hours stretched into several days. Rations ran out and Gerhard was pitifully grateful for his hoarded bread crusts and the isolation that allowed him to nibble them in secret, without the others knowing what he was up to.

On the fourth night, they stopped outside a village. The local people must have heard voices coming from inside the wagons, for after a few hours they emerged from the woods on either side of the track, bearing bread and vegetable soup and even cheese for the prisoners. They spoke the Czech language. The SS guards, who were almost as cold and hungry as their surviving charges, tried to stop the villagers, even threatening to shoot them. But one of the locals, speaking German, offered a simple deal: if the SS allowed the prisoners to be fed, they could share in the meal as well.

The villagers were poor and had little enough to live on themselves. They could only provide each hungry mouth with small amounts of food. But it was just as well, for any larger meal might have killed the man or woman who consumed it: their digestive systems could not have coped.

The food they had received kept almost all the surviving prisoners alive as the train continued on its journey, until it stopped at a station. The signs on the platform said Flossenbürg.

'End of the line; everybody out!' an SS guard announced, and they clambered from the wagons before being herded into trucks for another two days of driving, stopping, waiting and moving again.

'We're heading south,' someone said. 'I can tell from the sun.'

'Perhaps they're giving us a holiday in the Alps,' another croaked.

Gerhard was feeling sick with headaches that seemed to be splitting his skull down the middle. He lay in the back of the truck in a foetal curl, a shaven-headed subhuman identifiable only by his number, completely numb, indifferent to his surroundings, indifferent to life itself.

The truck turned into a side-road that passed through an opening in a barbed-wire fence. It stopped. Gerhard heard shouts, barking dogs, the rattle of chains being unlocked and the slam of wood against metal as the backs of the trucks were dropped open.

Somewhere a voice shouted, 'Where in hell's name have you come from?'

'Sachsenhausen,' another man replied.

'Sachsenhausen? Shit, we were expecting you days ago.' Gerhard heard a mirthless laugh, and then, 'Welcome to Dachau.'

D ay by day, week by week, the grief of Danny's passing eased. Saffron had once trained herself to endure progressively longer cross-country runs at Arisaig, or learned how to survive on little sleep. Now she trained her emotions. She made herself go an hour without thinking of Danny Doherty, then two, then a morning. She disciplined herself not to cry in public when a poignant memory struck her out of the blue, and, by degrees, not to cry at all.

She had done it before after all. She had thought that Gerhard was dead, then for an instant recovered him. But as the years had gone by and the chances that they would both survive the war, let alone meet again, grew slimmer, she had told herself not to think of a future with him. It was almost easier that Danny was gone. There was no possibility of suffering from the occasional tremors of hope that even now sometimes took her unawares when she found herself dreaming that she might yet see Gerhard.

It was a foolish delusion. Danny was gone. Gerhard was gone. Soon the war that had done for them both would be over.

And then I will start again.

For now there was work to be done. The Allies had crossed the Rhine in late March, as Amies had said they would. The Germans had fought hard at first, but their line seemed close to collapse as the pace of the Allied advance increased. Meanwhile the Russians were drawing a noose around Berlin. Soon Hitler would be isolated. It was said that he lived underground, hardly ever emerging from his bunker.

On 15 April 1945, advance units of the British 11th Armoured Division, advancing into Lower Saxony, reached Bergen-Belsen, the first concentration camp liberated by the Allies invading Germany from the west.

They encountered a scene of unimaginable horror. No matter how evil they may have thought Hitler and his Nazi followers were, the inhumanity of the camps was beyond the powers of any normal mind to conceive.

Two days later, the BBC broadcast the first radio report from the camp. Saffron recalled SS officer Schröder's speech at The Hague, the banality of his words, the Nazi's absurd fantasies: 'we have not been afraid to liquidate large numbers of hostages', 'Hebrew scum', 'the Jew resettlement will be short-lived'. Now here was the reality. Saffron, along with the rest of a sickened nation, heard about a hellish world of dead bodies left to rot on the bare earth, while the surviving but half-dead inmates wandered aimlessly between them and mothers driven mad by suffering and grief begged for milk to give the dead babies they were carrying in their arms.

The men and women of Baker Street had been through the war, endured the Blitz and the V-1 rocket attacks, seen good men and women sent off to Europe to die, and, like Saffron, suffered personal losses of their own. Saffron had briefed them on her fears of Nazi genocide on her return from Belgium, but this was a crime too dark to be fathomed by any imagination. This was a door being opened onto a bottomless abyss.

A new urgency seized Saffron and the other members of the team who were working on prisoner recoveries. One morning she was summoned to meet Gubbins in the briefing room.

The years of unrelenting overwork and nervous stress had aged the man who'd been the heartbeat of Baker Street. But his eyes retained their crystalline clarity and his energy somehow seemed undiminished.

'How do you fancy going back into the field, Courtney?' he asked her. 'Nothing undercover. I want you to go into Germany, track down a group of our people.'

'I would like that very much, sir.'

'Thought I'd never ask, eh? Well, here's the situation . . .' He walked across to a map on the wall, on which pins marked the positions of the Nazi camps whose locations were known to the Allies. With each appalling discovery made by the advancing armies, the number of pins increased. Gubbins picked out one north of Berlin, to the east of the British Army's current forward positions.

'This is a place called Sachsenhausen. It was set up by the Nazis before the war to house their political prisoners: communists, liberals, pacifists, dissenters of every sort. Since the war began, they've used it, among other things, to house political prisoners from countries they've overrun – leaders of parties hostile to National Socialism, that sort of thing – and also some of our chaps. That's where you come in. They've got some of our people, British and Danes, as well agents from SIS and a few military types who angered them by their insistence on trying to escape from POW camps.

'Two of the prisoners, including one of ours, are called Churchill. No relation to Winston, but the Germans don't know that. Anyway, there are a lot of people – in Number 10, Broadway and elsewhere – who want our people back. But there's a complicating factor . . .'

The map told Saffron what that was. 'You mean the Russians, sir?'

'Yes. We believe they'll be liberating Sachsenhausen today or tomorrow, if they haven't done so already. But "liberating" is not the right word for what the Russians are doing. There's a view in certain circles, and I don't disagree, that we will soon be exchanging one war with a vile, dictatorial regime bent on world domination for another that's just as bad.'

'Oh God. . . . Can't we ever live in peace?'

'Let us hope so. In the meantime, we don't want our people falling out of German hands, right into Russian ones. I want you to fly to Germany. Our closest units to Sachsenhausen are elements of Twelve Corps. I want you to get to the divisional headquarters of their forward units. Put your ear to the ground. Find out how the land lies . . . We'll be within a stone's throw of the Russians by the time you get there. If you can find a way to make contact with them, so much the better. If you can get to Sachsenhausen, that would be best of all. Use your initiative.'

'Yes, sir,' said Saffron, unable to keep the smile off her face. Only now that she was presented with this opportunity did she realise how much she had missed the adventure of being in the action, rather than watching it from afar. 'May I make a request, sir?'

'That rather depends what it is.'

'It would be a great help if I had some sort of proof of my bona fides, and of the importance of my mission. I'm sure that if I were a soldier, busy trying to end a war, and some strange woman turned up at my HQ distracting me with talk of prison camps and captured VIPs, I'd be tempted to tell her to take a running jump.'

Gubbins smiled. 'You aren't the first person to have had that thought. Here . . .'

He handed her a small ring-bound folder. It contained two documents, typed on headed notepaper from Number 10 Downing Street, each slipped into a clear plastic cover. On one, a short statement was written, to the effect that Captain Saffron Courtney was on a mission of national importance, attempting to recover prisoners captured by the SS, and was to be given every assistance that she might require.

It was signed, *Winston S. Churchill*.

'Golly,' she said. 'That ought to do the trick.'

'One would hope so. The second sheet gives the same message in Russian.'

Saffron examined a page of impenetrable Cyrillic script.

'I had one of the chaps from our Czech section cast an eye over it,' Gubbins assured her. 'He reads Russian and assured me it made sense.'

'When do I leave?'

'First thing tomorrow, by Dakota from RAF Northolt. Twelve Corps know you're coming, so there'll be someone to meet you. I want you to keep me posted on what's happening. Code all messages as per usual. The war may almost be over, but we can't be too careful. One word of warning: I'm told the weather in central Europe is unseasonably cold this year. Wrap up warm. You will be provided with a small amount of American currency.

The dollar will be the most useful currency in Germany at the moment. But use it sensibly, and account for every bit of it. You may carry a gun for your personal protection. The armourer will issue you with a service revolver and holster. I hope you are not obliged to use it.'

• • •

The day was damp and cold. The sound of the Russian guns was getting louder. It would not be long before Berlin was in Stalin's hands.

How the hell did it come to this? Konrad von Meerbach thought as he watched Adolf Hitler proceed down the line of teenage boys, assembled to meet him outside the Führerbunker. *Look at him! He's a gibbering drug addict, hiding his hand behind his back so that people can't see it shaking. This is his fifty-sixth birthday. He looks more like seventy-six.*

As Hitler pinned another medal on a proud young chest, the sight of those boys, dressed in a motley assortment of battle dress and caps, depressed von Meerbach more. The years he had dedicated to the SS and the glory he had witnessed had been reduced to this: the desperate recruitment of untrained children because all the good, strong, Aryan men were gone.

The ceremony ended. The cameramen rushed off to develop their film, though God alone knew who would see it, for there were no cinemas open in the fragments of the Third Reich that had not fallen into enemy hands.

Von Meerbach finished his cigarette, savouring the pleasure in his lungs, for smoking was forbidden in the bunker, on the strict instruction of the Führer. He followed the rest of the entourage who had attended the medal ceremony down the spiral staircase into the concrete catacombs.

He entered the guardroom, where a clerk was sitting behind a desk.

'Papers,' the clerk said.

'It's less than an hour since you last checked them,' von Meerbach objected, though he knew it would do no good. 'Good God, man, my pistol's still in that locker behind you.'

The clerk's face was emotionless. He repeated, 'Papers.'

Von Meerbach handed them over. In the corridor beyond the guardroom he saw Hermann Fegelein, Himmler's personal liaison officer, with the headquarters staff. Fegelein was gesturing at him. Von Meerbach managed a terse nod in return. Fegelein was an unprincipled careerist, a man who had married Eva Braun's sister Gretl to get closer to the Führer's inner circle. To make matters worse, his move had worked. Fegelein was now an SS general, giving him seniority over von Meerbach.

The clerk returned the papers. Von Meerbach walked past the desk and down the corridor. Fegelein did not wait to greet him.

'Follow me,' he said and strolled through the long waiting room that ran down the middle of the main bunker, and turned right into the toilets. Fegelein checked that none of the cubicles were occupied. He opened the door at the far end that led into the washroom. That too was empty. He locked the main toilet door.

'Now we can have some privacy,' he said. He took a packet of cigarettes out of his breast pocket. 'Smoke?'

Von Meerbach wondered what would happen if they were caught, concluded it could hardly be worse than what was happening to them all anyway, and said, 'Thank you, General.'

'Ach, no need to be formal, Konrad. We old SS men have to stick together.'

Fegelein sounded like a man who was about to ask a favour. Von Meerbach's rank might be inferior, but his personal resources were infinitely greater.

Instead, Fegelein said, 'I thought you should know: Himmler's leaving Berlin today. He isn't coming back.'

'But I heard him, this morning, swearing his loyalty to the Führer. He promised he'd stay to the bitter end.'

Fegelein gave a sardonic smile. 'What else could he say? The fact is, he's getting out, and you should do the same. Tempelhof is still open, but it won't be for long. Himmler's departure will give you the justification to follow him. You are following your SS commander-in-chief's example. Who's to say he hasn't ordered you to go?'

Fegelein stubbed his cigarette out in a sink, washed away the ash and pushed the butt down the plughole, like a naughty schoolboy hoping that a teacher won't catch him.

He stood up straight again and said, 'Listen, it's a matter of your personal safety. You're going to be needed when the war is over. You can help rebuild for the future.'

Von Meerbach nodded, and asked, 'And you? Are you going too?'

'I can't. I'm still supposed to be manning my post with the high command. That's what comes with being part of the family, eh?'

'Hitler won't let himself be captured alive, or Eva. He could demand the same of you.'

'Oh, don't you worry. I'll have sneaked out before it gets to that stage. I've got it worked out.'

'Then I wish you luck.' Von Meerbach disposed of his own cigarette. 'I dare say we're going to need all the luck we can get.'

• • •

Von Meerbach was driven to the Reich Main Security Office on Prinz-Albrecht-Strasse, a cluster of buildings that served as the headquarters for the Gestapo, the SD intelligence service and SS. Smoke was wafting through the air as he walked up from the entrance, but it was not caused by enemy bombs or shells. Every scrap of space in the yards between the buildings and even in the gardens at the back of the complex was being used to burn secret, or potentially incriminating, documents. Male and female staff could be seen standing at open windows, throwing out bundles of paper that drifted and fluttered to the ground, where men gathered them up like autumn leaves and threw them onto the bonfires.

Von Meerbach made his way to his outer office, where his two secretaries, Heidi and Gisela, were waiting for him, and though he normally gave no thought at all to his subordinates' well-being, he found himself touched by their loyalty.

Heidi asked whether he wanted a cup of coffee. Gisela, who was holding a notepad and pencil, reported that he had a number of messages.

Von Meerbach waved his hand. 'There isn't time for any of that.' He glanced at Heidi. 'Fetch my briefcase.' Then to Gisela he said, 'Follow me.'

She went with him into his inner sanctum. 'Remove the photographs on my desk from their frames,' von Meerbach said. As Gisela did so, he went to a safe that was set into one wall, spun the dials to the correct combination and opened it.

By now Heidi had returned, bearing the briefcase. Von Meerbach transferred another million dollars in bearer bonds from the safe to the case. This was followed by three bundles of American notes in various denominations that amounted to approximately $15,000.

'The photographs, please,' von Meerbach said.

Gisela handed them to him: signed and dedicated pictures of Hitler, Himmler and Heydrich; one of Francesca; and another of his son and daughter by his first wife, Trudi. Both the secretaries were looking agitated, close to tears. It was obvious that von Meerbach was about to make his getaway, leaving them to the Russians. And they knew, as did every woman in the Reich, what fate the Russians had in store for them.

Von Meerbach saw that they were expecting him to say something: to tell them what was happening, reassure them that all would be well – anything would do. He began, as was his nature, with himself.

'It may seem that I am running from the fight. On the contrary, I am leaving here, where the situation is hopeless, so that I can help the fight back, when it comes. I believe in our cause. I am proud of the work I have done . . .'

It struck von Meerbach that his words were not impressing his two secretaries as he had hoped. Only now did he think, *They are women. They need sweet words, flattery, nonsense with which to fill their empty heads. Well, if they insist . . .*

'And, of course, I am deeply grateful for your help over these past few years. I could not have achieved all I did without you.'

He looked at the safe. There was another block of notes in there, worth several thousand dollars. Germany was about to be thrown back to the stone age: no power, no light, no fuel, no housing, no clean water or working sewers, and no food. But this would be more than enough to make sure that Heidi and Gisela could at least buy black-market food.

'Here,' he said, roughly dividing the pile in two and giving each of them one half, 'take this. Use it wisely. This money could be your ticket out of the city. It will buy you food and shelter. But for God's sake, whatever you do, don't let the damn Cossacks know you have it . . . no matter how much you may be tempted to buy them off. Understand?'

The two women nodded, then Heidi said, 'Is it really the end? Can the Führer not save us?'

Von Meerbach shook his head. 'No. He cannot save himself. Give me your hands . . .'

They reached out and he took their hands in his. 'Listen to me: go to the deepest cellar you can find. Take every drop of water, every scrap of food you can muster. You can start with all the bottles in my drinks cabinet: the brandy and whisky will keep you warm on cold nights. You know where my personal food is kept: the cans of paté, foie gras and caviar. They're no use to me, take them all. If the worst comes to the worst, at least you can have a party before the world ends.'

Gisela looked at him with a puzzled, uncertain expression on her face, as if expecting this was some kind of trick. 'Why . . . why are you being so kind to us?' she asked.

Von Meerbach had been wondering the same himself.

'I don't know . . . I suppose I can't see the point in being unkind. You have never done me harm. Other people, however, have harmed me, and you may be sure that if I get the chance to harm them in return, ten times over, I certainly will. Does that answer your question?'

'Yes, I believe it does.'

'Then I will say goodbye to you both.'

Von Meerbach did not waste time with hugs or kisses. He returned to his car, clutching his briefcase, and said to the driver: 'Tempelhof.'

Sperling would be waiting there. Von Meerbach had always expected that this moment would come, although not perhaps so soon. He had told his pilot to be ready to fly at a moment's notice. He settled into his seat and looked out of the window at the ruined city. One of the few buildings that was still standing had a propaganda slogan written in whitewash on its front wall: *Every German will defend his capital. We shall stop the Red hordes at the walls of our Berlin.*

Did anyone ever spout more crap than Goebbels? von Meerbach wondered. They passed a platoon of old men bearing *panzerfaust* anti-tank rockets over their shoulders, like the rifles they would have carried if they had been real soldiers in an army that could still fight. Up ahead he saw a line of lamp-posts, miraculously left standing. Bodies had been strung up on them, one for every streetlight: old men, young men, a couple of boys, a woman. They had been executed by the mobs of party fanatics who were wandering the streets, looking for scapegoats to blame for the death of the Thousand-Year Reich.

Each one had a placard around their neck with an accusatory statement scrawled upon it: 'I am a gutless coward', 'commie whore', 'I hid while brave men fought', and so on.

Von Meerbach grinned at the thought of the pleasure that the brainless thugs who had carried out the summary executions must have taken in their actions. It was a senseless, pointless addition to the mass slaughter all around them. It would have no effect on a battle that had long since been lost. But it would give them the pleasure of exercising power over another human being – the ultimate power of depriving them of life – and if that gave them a scrap of pleasure before the curtain fell, who could begrudge them?

And then it struck him: the answer to that stupid girl's question. He had given those two secretaries the money because he could. His act of charity was a demonstration of power and status.

Von Meerbach grinned at the logical corollary of that realisation. All charity was essentially a demonstration of power and an underlining of relative status. All the pious do-gooders who made a show of their generosity to the poor and needy were wallowing in their power as much as their virtue. They were all filthy hypocrites. He, at least, von Meerbach concluded, had the virtue of being honest.

He was greatly cheered by this thought.

When he reached Tempelhof he found Sperling taking a nap by his plane, but the pilot sprang into action. They flew south out of the city, over the heads of the advancing Russians, with Sperling straining to extract top speed from the Lightning, and by late afternoon they were landing at the Meerbach Motor Works field and taxiing into the hangar.

When von Meerbach stepped out of the aircraft that had taken him from Berlin, he looked at the strange, futuristic machine standing on the other side of the building.

He gestured to Sperling to come over and asked, 'You're sure you can fly it?'

'No question. I helped test it, after all.'

'And you're sure it has the range?'

'Normally, no. But with the drop tanks we've added, it should be fine.'

'And it can outrun anything the British or Americans can put in the sky?'

'Oh yes. Nothing short of a V-rocket goes any faster.'

'Good. We fly tomorrow morning. Be ready at dawn.'

• • •

Gubbins was right. The biting east wind that whipped across the North German Plain had come all the way from Siberia and Saffron was glad of the thick woollen jumper she was wearing under her battledress and the woollen skiing tights under her trousers. She was travelling light, with a small army rucksack to go with the canvas shoulder bag that had been her companion since her first days as Jumbo Wilson's driver in Cairo, back in 1940. It contained her purse, the folder with her signed letters from the Prime Minister, and a number of personal items that included the picture taken of her and Gerhard at the Eiffel Tower. She hardly ever looked at the faded photograph any more, but it had been with her everywhere she had gone. Even in the Low Countries, she had slipped it into the hidden compartments where her one-time pads had been kept.

Saffron slung her bag across her body and hoisted her rucksack over one shoulder. She intended to carry both pieces of baggage with her at all times, wherever she went. If her mission went well, she would have to make unexpected journeys at a moment's notice. She didn't want to leave anything behind.

A number of other army and RAF officers had been on the plane and there was a scrum of people at the foot of the steps, waiting for heavy baggage to be handed out, or looking for the drivers who were meeting them. Saffron was doing the same when she heard a voice beside her say, 'Afternoon, ma'am.'

The man who addressed her was a sergeant. He was tall and broad-shouldered, with strong, bony features and the healthy, ruddy complexion of a countryman who has spent his whole life outdoors.

'Sergeant Dunnigan, ma'am. Cumberland Fusiliers. I'll be taking you to divisional HQ.'

'Is it far?' she asked as Dunningan led her to his Jeep.

'Depends, ma'am,' he replied. 'Could take an hour, could take all day. You know what they say: there's a war on.' There was a regimental badge on his beret and Saffron recognised it at once.

'The Cumberland Fusiliers,' she said, smiling at the memory of the trip to South Africa.

'That's right, ma'am. I was on the *Capetown Castle*, that's how I recognised you, though I wasn't one of the lucky beggars that saw you give your talk. I had to listen to it over the ship's tannoy. Those were the days, eh?'

In the end the journey lasted a little over two hours. The landscape was battered and pockmarked with shell holes, smoke drifted from burning vehicles, buildings and scorched vegetation, yet sometimes they passed forests of evergreens rising majestically and untouched. And then they would round a corner and what used to be homes were rubble; schools, churches, shops and playgrounds were smashed and destroyed; and people were standing, immobilised by shock. It was a vision of ruined humanity, failure on an epic scale.

As Dunnigan drove, he told Saffron about his wife, his daughter and the young son, born after his last home leave, whom he'd never seen. He talked about his sheep farm in the hills near Keswick and, most passionately of all, about his love of hound racing.

'Ten miles the dogs run, over hill and dale, jumping over walls – nothing'll stop the little beggars. All the bookies are there; make a bloody fortune, they do. You should see it, ma'am.'

'I'd like that,' Saffron said, meaning it, and then described the Kenyan hills where she had grown up and the herdsmen whose cattle roamed across them.

She was interrupted by Dunnigan saying, 'Here we are,' as he turned off the road and through a gate on which there was a painted sign. Saffron caught the word '*Akademie*' and then they were pulling into a courtyard in front of a red-brick building.

Trucks and motorbikes and Jeeps were lined up across a large open tarmac space to one side that Saffron realised must have once been a playground.

Dunnigan jumped out of the open Jeep, lifted Saffron's rucksack from the back and hefted it over his shoulder as he led her towards the door. 'Oh, I forgot to mention, ma'am. The general sends his compliments, but he won't be able to see you today. Major Farrell, his ADC, will be looking after you instead.'

They walked into the old school hall that was now the division's nerve centre. Saffron saw an officer with rosy cheeks and a boyish shock of fair hair calmly issuing orders amidst an atmosphere of frantic activity. Though he barely looked old enough to have passed out of Sandhurst, Dunnigan led Saffron towards him and said, 'Captain Courtney for you, sir.'

Standing opposite him, Saffron could see that Farrell's youthful appearance was tempered by the lines and dark shadows printed on his face by war. But he smiled and his face lit up as he said, 'What a delightful surprise. They told us to expect a Captain Courtney, attached to the War Office. I assumed it would be some ghastly desk-wallah, come to check we were using the correct number of paper-clips, or something.'

'Well, here I am, sir.'

'So, what can we do for you?'

Saffron explained her mission, and then handed Farrell the letter from Downing Street.

'Well, if Winnie is on your side, who am I to argue? Where is this Sachsenhausen place, exactly?'

'Oranienburg, twenty-five miles northwest of Berlin. I expect it's in Russian hands by now.'

'Ah . . . so near and yet so far. We're getting closer to the Russkis every minute that passes, as they are to us. But there's a fair number of Germans caught between the two advancing armies, most of them trying to surrender to us before Uncle Joe gathers them into his arms . . . Actually, that gives me an idea. Come with me . . .'

Farrell led her down a corridor lined with cork boards to which children's drawings were still pinned, knocked on a door and let himself in without waiting for a reply. Saffron found herself in what must once have been a classroom. There were maps tacked to the walls and spread over a long trestle table that had been set up in the middle of the room. In one corner two operators sat at another table covered in radio gear. Two NCOs were sitting at school desks, typing out reports. A bespectacled man with a high forehead, thin sandy hair and round spectacles got up from his desk and walked towards them.

'Andy,' said Farrell, 'may I introduce Captain Saffron Courtney of the First Aid Nursing Yeomanry? Saffron, this is Captain Andrew Halsey of the Intelligence Corps. He's one of those rare creatures for whom the phrase "military intelligence" is not a contradiction in terms. He was a don at Cambridge before the war.'

'How interesting,' said Saffron as they shook hands. 'What was your subject?'

'German political history,' Halsey replied. 'And here I am seeing it made before my very eyes.' He looked at Farrell. 'So, what can I do for you, sir?'

'It's more what you can do for Miss Courtney,' Farrell replied. 'As you've probably deduced by now, she's not here to take your temperature or soothe your fevered brow. She's on a mission to track down a few of our chaps who were taken to a camp called Sachsenhausen. Have you heard of the place?'

'Yes, it was one of the first camps the Nazis established for political prisoners, after they took power.'

'Well, it occurs to me that there may be personnel from Sachsenhausen hidden away among the Jerries we've captured. Put the word out among the other intelligence chaps that we're looking for anyone who has reliable information about the British prisoners at the camp. Let it be known that we'll look favourably on anyone who helps us.'

'Everyone's pretty busy, sir. I'm not sure whether they'll have time to do this right away.'

'Then tell them to make time. This is important. Churchill's taking a personal interest.' He glanced at Saffron. 'Show him the letter.'

Halsey scanned the document, whistled softly and said, 'Ah, right, that does cast a rather different light on things. I'll get down to work right away. I doubt we'll have anything for you today. Perhaps we could reconvene tomorrow morning and I'll report anything that's come to light.'

'Fine. We'll meet here at oh-nine-hundred. And you can let your chums know that Twelve Corps HQ will be seriously unimpressed if they don't have some answers for us. Clear?'

'Crystal.'

'Good man. Now, Captain Courtney, you look as though you could use a spot to eat. I'm afraid our catering is pretty basic, but if you've wondered how many ways a man can cook bully-beef, you're in for a treat.'

• • •

As the first light of dawn washed over the Meerbach Motor Works, Berndt Sperling stood on the concrete apron in front of the main hangar, looked up at the menacing, ebony outline of the jet-powered Arado Ar 234 P-1 bomber that he was about to fly and asked himself: *How did we lose another war, when we can produce something like this?*

'Beautiful, isn't she?' said the chief mechanic in charge of the plane's maintenance.

'If only we'd had a thousand of these in forty-one or forty-two. The Ivans wouldn't have stood a chance.'

'Well, it's a bit late now, eh? Still, you've got to hand it to the Count. He's got himself a plane even the Luftwaffe don't have.'

Von Meerbach had spotted the potential of the Arado when the first models rolled off the production line a year earlier.

There was one problem: the plane was designed for a single-man crew. But a few months later, over a business lunch with some senior staff at Arado, he discovered that the company had plans for a two-man version and had gone so far as building the bodies for a few prototypes. They'd even taken delivery of the engines they planned to use. But the way things were, there was no chance of them ever being completed.

'Tell you what, I'll buy one of those prototypes, and four engines off you,' von Meerbach had said. 'I'll see what my lads can do. We'll assemble the thing, and tweak the engines, see if we can't get some more performance out of them . . .'

There was no point putting any Reichsmarks in anyone's pocket. Everyone knew they would soon be worthless. But that only made the gold that von Meerbach could offer even more desirable.

A deal was done, the aircraft's components were delivered to an area of the Meerbach Motor Works that was still intact. And here she was, as swift and sleek as a black panther waiting to be let off her leash.

'Here he comes,' the mechanic said as von Meerbach's limousine purred into the hangar. 'Best be off to do those final checks.'

'I'll just say hello to him, then I'll run through them with you,' Sperling replied.

He went to greet his boss. Von Meerbach seemed remarkably calm, under the circumstances, but purposeful.

'Have you set the course?' he asked.

'Yes, my lord. We'll be flying almost due south over Switzerland and northwest Italy, most of which is still in our hands, crossing the Mediterranean coast between Genoa and San Remo, before we change course to the west. From there on we will be in Allied airspace. But we will be flying so high and so fast that even if they spot this aircraft on their radar, they won't be able to do anything about it.'

Von Meerbach nodded his approval. He was kitted out in a flying suit, leather helmet, goggles and mask. He clambered into the glazed nose and was strapped into his seat, with his briefcase shoved onto the cockpit floor beneath his feet. Sperling checked that his passenger was comfortable and then fired up the engines.

They responded with a deafening roar, overlaid by a frenzied, high-pitched whine, a sound produced by no other craft in the history of aviation, for no other four-engine jet had ever taken to the skies.

Von Meerbach felt a jolt of excitement and trepidation at the thought of the flight ahead of him. The Arado started moving, taxiing to the end of the runway, turning, pausing and, as Sperling opened the engines up to full power and the noise became even more shattering, it rolled down the runway, picking up speed at an astonishing rate until the world on either side of the runway was little more than a blur. On and on they went, hurtling to the very limit of the runway before the aircraft leaped into the sky.

Von Meerbach was pushed back into his seat and there seemed to be a huge weight pressing down on him as the Arado made its vertiginous ascent. Up and up they climbed, until Sperling flattened out. His voice came crackling over von Meerbach's headphones, barely audible over the noise of the jets.

'We've reached an altitude of ten thousand metres. We could fly right over Mount Everest! And we'll be cruising at eight hundred kilometres an hour.'

He paused to let that sink in and then added, 'Congratulations, sir, you have successfully made your escape.'

• • •

'We're in luck,' Halsey told Saffron and Farrell when they met again in the requisitioned classroom. 'One of the chaps at the holding camp on Lüneburg Heath drove round the place yesterday evening with a loudhailer, asking for anyone who'd been at Sachsenhausen. He said that whoever had information could count on fair treatment. More than fifty men came forward. It took all night to interview them and of course they were almost all bogus, trying it on in the hope of wangling a soft deal.

'But there was one man who sounded promising, man by the name of Mikhail Shevchenko. According to his story, he was a Russian POW, though he made a point of saying he was Ukrainian and hated the Russians. He was taken to Sachsen-hausen because his original camp was about to be overrun by the Red Army. Most of the men he was with were killed when they got to their new place, but he was given the chance to avoid execution by becoming one of the trusties who were put in charge of the other prisoners. Apparently you'll understand why the Jerries chose him the moment you clap eyes on him.

'Shevchenko says he knows about a group of special prison-ers, who were taken from the camp about two weeks ago. He says he thinks there were some British among them. But he won't say any more unless he's speaking to someone who can make a deal with him. I think that means you, Miss Courtney.'

'How far is the camp from here?' Saffron asked.

'About fifteen miles.'

'Could take you a while to get there,' Farrell said. 'If you meet an armoured division coming in the other direction, you'll find they have the right of way.'

'Then the sooner we start the better,' Saffron said. 'I wonder if I could ask you formally for a favour, Major? Could I have the use of your sergeant and his Jeep?'

'By all means, be my guest.'

• • •

The holding camp was a field covering several acres, sur-rounded by a barbed-wire fence, within which German troops and those who had worked for them milled around like grey-coated sheep. Tents had been put up to provide field kitchens and medical treatment for the prisoners, as well as workspaces and quarters for the Allied personnel who were guarding them. Not that there were many guards. Two British soldiers met the Jeep at the gate and waved them through, but there were no guard towers, no machine guns trained on the prisoners, and the hastily built fence could have been charged down if the men inside had made a concerted effort to get out.

'Aye, but they don't want to get out, do they?' said Sergeant Dunnigan, when Saffron mentioned the lack of security precautions. 'They've got away from the Russkis, they're getting fed and no one's shooting at them. They know the war will be over any day now. Might as well stay here till it is.'

They were met at the camp administration tent by another Intelligence Corps officer, who introduced himself as Lieutenant Hart and took them to a smaller tent that was being used as a makeshift interrogation room. Two men were waiting outside the entry. One was an armed military policeman. The other was a small, moustachioed individual with black-brown eyes under intense, frowning brows.

'This is Corporal Panchewski,' Hart said. 'He's Polish, speaks Russian and even a spot of Ukrainian, isn't that so?'

Panchewski nodded.

'Do you mind if I sit in on the interview?' Hart asked. 'I'd be grateful for any information about the camps. Feel one ought to know.'

'Of course,' Saffron replied.

They went into the tent. It contained a small table with two chairs on one side, facing away from the entrance, and another chair on the other side. At least, Saffron assumed there was a chair. But none of it was visible beneath the enormous bulk of the biggest human being Saffron had ever seen.

Mikhail Shevchenko made every other person in the tent look like a small child. His shoulders were almost as broad as the table itself, his arms as thick as any normal man's legs and his bald head was dominated by the Neanderthal ridge of his browline. His bulk was even more exaggerated by the thick sheepskin coat he was wearing, the mark of his privileged status as one of the men trusted by the SS. It had faded to grey, but there was a black rectangular spot on his left breast where the patch bearing his camp number had been sewn.

This man is as big and bone-headed and dangerous as a Cape buffalo, Saffron thought, knowing, as any African would, that an angry buffalo could be as deadly as any lion.

She sat down, with Panchewski next to her. Hart and Dunnigan stood behind them, watching proceedings. She looked at the man-mountain and asked, '*Sprechen sie Deutsch?*'

Shevchenko shrugged and did not speak so much as rumble, in a voice so deep and indistinct that she could barely make out the single word that came from his mouth: '*Bisschen.*' A little.

She addressed Panchewski. 'Please tell him that I want us to speak in German, because I want to know what he's said. But if he cannot find the words to answer me in German, then he should talk to you and you can translate.'

Panchewski let fly with a volley of Russian, to which Shevchenko responded by looking at Saffron and replying in German, 'Why should I talk to the little girl?'

He leaned back, staring Saffron down with an arrogant, insolent defiance that came from certainty in his own physical power. She could tell how his mind was working. One thing Sachsenhausen would have taught him – if the rest of his life hadn't done so long before he arrived there – was the difference between the small number of people he had to fear and the multitude he could bully.

In Shevchenko's eyes Saffron would look like one of the weak. He would never tell her anything until she had persuaded him otherwise. Verbal argument wouldn't do that. She had to prove it to him in as concrete a fashion as possible.

She stared back, holding his gaze, challenging him as she replied, 'Because I am the only person here who has the authority to make a deal with you,' she replied. 'And also . . .' She leaned forward, flicking her fingers to let him know he should do the same, drawing her hand back to lead him forward.

She was a beautiful young woman, encouraging a man to draw closer. Shevchenko could not help but oblige. He tilted his giant head towards her.

Saffron struck him as hard as she had ever hit anyone in her life, the same way she'd assaulted Schröder that night in The Hague: heel of the hand to the side of the chin. It felt like hitting a wall of granite, covered in the sandpaper of his stubble.

Shevchenko's head jerked back. He fell into his chair, blinking in surprise. Then the shame of being sucker-punched by a woman turned the shock to anger and he rose to his feet, threw the table aside and looked up . . . into the barrel of Saffron's service revolver.

She was holding it, steady, aiming at the centre of his forehead.

'I know how to use this,' she said, speaking calmly, making him aware she was serious. 'And I know how to kill with it.'

He stood, the rage building inside him, the pent-up energy visible in every fibre of his being as he calculated the odds.

Panchewski scuttled away to the back of the tent, terrified of what Shevchenko might do.

'I've got you covered, ma'am,' Dunnigan said, raising his own gun. He was trying to sound reassuring, but he could not hide his own tension. Saffron could not count on him holding his nerve.

'That won't be necessary, Sergeant,' she replied, not taking her eyes off Shevchenko.

'Pick up the table,' she said to the Ukrainian. 'Slowly. Don't try anything, or you die.'

Shevchenko had been a *kapo* at Sachsenhausen. He knew how easily human life could be extinguished. He did as he was told.

'Now the chair . . . Sit in it.'

Saffron turned to Panchewski. 'You can come back now. It's safe. Mr Shevchenko and I understand one another. If he gives me good information, I will be reasonable. If he tries anything foolish, I will kill him.'

'But the Geneva Convention . . .' Hart protested.

'If you have an objection, you may discuss it with me afterwards.' Saffron sat down. 'Now, Shevchenko, please tell me about your duties at Sachsenhausen . . .'

Over the next few minutes, occasionally switching to Russian as the things he wanted to describe exceeded the limits of his German, the *kapo* outlined what the camp had been like and what role he had played. He did his best to understate the truth of it, and to insist that he had taken no part in any of the atrocities. But even so, there was no way of hiding the unspeakable nightmare that the SS had created there, as at so many other camps.

'Now, can you please tell me what happened to the prisoners at Sachsenhausen once it became clear that the camp was about to be liberated by the Russians.'

'The Germans did not want any witnesses who could testify to what they had done.'

'Wasn't the camp itself enough evidence? You said yourself it was filled with dead bodies?'

'The dead cannot talk. Almost all the prisoners were marched away from the camp. A "death march", the SS called it. They wanted as many people to die as possible.'

'Where did this death march go?'

'I don't know. Not exactly. They started walking to the northeast. I was with them, but I got away.'

'How?'

'How do you think? I killed a guard and ran. Some others from the march tried to follow me, but I think they were shot.'

'Were there any British prisoners on this march?'

Shevchenko shook that massive, buffalo head. 'No, I don't think so. I think they were with the other prisoners. The ones that left earlier. But if you want me to tell you about them, I must know what I get in return.'

Saffron was about to speak, but Shevchenko held up a hand to stop her. 'Don't say I must talk or I die. If I die, you have no chance of finding your people. Only if I live do you have a chance. What do you offer?'

'A head start,' said Saffron. 'When the war is over people like you, who collaborated with the Germans in the camps, will be hunted down as murderers and war criminals.'

'I had no choice!'

'They will all say that . . . Now, I cannot give you a pardon, or say that you will never be brought to justice. But I can say this: tell me something that proves to be accurate and you can walk out of this camp. After that you are on your own. And one other thing . . .'

'Yes?' Shevchenko sounded almost hopeful, as if she was about to add something to her offer.

'On reflection, it would be foolish for me to kill you today. We British are not like the Nazis. We don't approve of murder, and there are three witnesses who would be obliged to give evidence against me. Correct, Lieutenant?'

'I'm afraid so, ma'am, yes,' Hart replied.

'But there is a fate that would be worse for you than death, Shevchenko, and legal. You served in the Red Army?'

'Yes.'

'Then it would be proper for us to return you to your own people. That's right, isn't it, Lieutenant?'

'It is,' Hart agreed. 'It's probably obligatory, actually.'

Panchewski, seeing where Saffron was going, translated the exchange between her and Hart into Russian.

Shevchenko's eyes widened in horror. He was more frightened by that thought than he had been by Saffron's pistol. 'No! Please! I beg you . . . not that. If they find out what I did . . .'

'Talk to me and they won't.'

'There was a small group of prisoners, maybe fifty or sixty. I had to help round them up and take them to the train.'

'A train?'

'Yes . . . just a small one, two wagons.'

'Did you know who these prisoners were?'

'No, there were no names in camp, only numbers. But most were from the Special Camp, where they kept the prisoners who were important people – you know, on the outside. I heard two officers talking. They were being taken away as hostages, so that maybe . . .'

He jabbered a few sentences in Russian to Panchewski, who told Saffron, 'He says that the idea was to take these away to the fortress where the SS were preparing their last stand. Then they could be used as bargaining chips with the Allies, exchanging the prisoners' lives for those of SS men.'

'What kind of fortress?' Saffron asked.

'Excuse me, captain, but I may be able to help here,' Hart said. 'We've heard people talking about this, too. They've referred to an "Alpine Fortress", by which they mean a large area of mountains in the Alps that could be defended against the enemy.'

'Is that where they were going – to the mountains?'

'No,' Shevchenko said. He looked uncertain. 'There was a change of plan. They went south, but not to the mountains, to another camp. I don't know the name exactly, but it began like "Dak-something".'

'You mean Dachau?' Saffron asked.

'Yes . . . Dachau . . . that is the one. I am sure. I speak the truth, I swear it.'

'Stay there,' Saffron told Shevchenko. Then she spoke to Dunnigan. 'Keep an eye on him. If he moves, and you feel threatened, you have my permission to shoot.'

'Yes, ma'am.'

'Lieutenant Hart, a word, please.'

They walked outside the tent.

'That was jolly impressive,' Hart said. 'The way you went for Shevchenko. It took me by surprise, I must say.' He grinned.

'One had heard rumours about all the things you SOE people got up to. I have to admit I didn't believe them. But—'

'I have no idea what you're talking about,' said Saffron briskly. 'Now, Shevchenko could be telling the truth. There've been reports of other British prisoners being taken to Dachau. And some of the people I'm looking for would certainly be seen as "important people" by the Germans.'

'If he is, that may not be good news. We had reports this morning: the Americans have just liberated Dachau. Apparently the scenes there were indescribably ghastly. The worst yet.'

'Who's in charge of the place now?'

'Units of Fifteen Corps, part of the Sixth Army Group, under General Devers.'

'Can you put me in touch with Devers' HQ, please? I need to find out what they know. See if anyone's found our people.'

'I can, but . . . may I give you some advice, Miss Courtney? If Dachau is as bad as they say, and if our experience at Belsen is anything to go by, then I doubt anyone there has the first idea who any of the prisoners are, and I doubt they're going to be inclined to go looking for you, on the basis of a radio message . . . whatever that letter from Number Ten might say. The best way to get to the bottom of this is to go there yourself. By the time you've got there, the Yanks may have established some order, and I'm sure they'll be more helpful if they get the request from you in person.'

Saffron considered what Hart had said. 'In that case, could you please put me in touch with Major Farrell at Divisional HQ. I'm going to need Sergeant Dunnigan and his Jeep for a while longer. And if you could spare me a decent map of Germany, and a few days' supply of basic army rations, I'd be much obliged.'

'Certainly, ma'am. But what about Shevchenko? You aren't going to let him go, are you? I mean, after all the things he must have done.'

'No . . . I don't like to break my word, even with a man like him, but I think we should stick to proper procedure. We can't have the Russians kicking up a fuss because we haven't handed back one of their people.'

'It could cause a diplomatic incident – very embarrassing.'

'Then we must do the right thing and return him to the bosom of his people.'

'Yes, ma'am . . . I most heartily concur!'

• • •

Saffron studied the motorist's road map of Germany, found by Hart in an abandoned Volkswagen Beetle, a "Strength Through Joy" car that he had passed to her. She reckoned the distance from the camp on Lüneburg Heath to Dachau was about six hundred kilometres as the crow flew, so three hundred and seventy-five miles. But the fastest route, and the safest, since it curved away from the battlefront, would be to get onto the autobahn that ran south from Hamburg, down past Frankfurt to Stuttgart. Then they'd pick up another autobahn that ran from Stuttgart to Munich, a stone's throw from the camp.

If this had been the spring of 1939 and Saffron had been sitting beside Gerhard in the front of his thrillingly fast Mercedes Cabriolet, he would have comfortably completed the drive in a single day, and arrived at some wonderfully smart hotel in plenty of time to bathe and change for dinner. She tried hard not to remember the joy of sitting beside him, gave in to the temptation, wallowed briefly in the memory of the feel of his body close to hers and the strength of his hands on the wheel, and then cursed herself for being so stupidly self-indulgent.

He's not here, he's probably dead, we'll never meet again and I'm not a spoiled little girl, going to some divinely luxurious hotel. I'm an SOE officer on her way to hell on earth. She sighed. *We might as well get on with it.*

She saw Dunnigan approaching with a khaki rucksack over one shoulder. He heaved it into the back of the Jeep, where it landed with a sound of rattling tin, and he rubbed his shoulder ruefully.

'Weighed a fu—' He stopped himself. 'Sorry, ma'am. It weighed a lot, what with all them cans and all.'

Saffron laughed. 'It's all right, Sergeant. I'm used to military language. I won't faint at the sound of a swear word.'

'Right you are, ma'am.' Dunnigan grinned.

'So, how are we set?'

'The Jeep's been filled with petrol, and I've got three more full jerry cans, so we should be able to make the journey, even if I can't scrounge any more along the way. We've got another large can of drinking water. You know what it's like. Once you've fought in the desert, you never go anywhere without water.'

'Probably just as well. I shouldn't think there's much clean water anywhere in Germany.'

'I've got a stove and plenty of tea, so we can always brew up. And there's a tent for you, ma'am, in case we're out overnight.'

'What about you?'

'I can kip in the Jeep, or under her if it's raining.'

'I wouldn't worry. I'd rather not stop for the night anywhere unless we have to. We can drive in shifts . . .'

'Yes, ma'am. The sooner we get there the better, eh?'

'Quite . . . And the longer we take, the greater the chance we don't find the people I'm looking for, or they're dead when we do.'

'Hop in, ma'am, and we'll be on our way.'

• • •

They drove out of Lüneburg, heading for the nearest autobahn junction. It was slow going at first, pushing against the tide of the oncoming British army. They were travelling across a rural landscape covered with shell and bomb craters, and littered with ruined houses and dangling power and telephone lines; the wrecks of burned-out tanks, some blown onto their sides or upside down; artillery guns pointing blindly to the sky; abandoned trucks; and, here and there, the bodies of dead soldiers that no one had found the time to bury.

The air was filled with warplanes, from beautiful, nimble Spitfires to lumbering Lancaster bombers, streaming north to pummel the last remnants of the German war machine into the cold, frosty dirt. And all the time British vehicles kept coming towards them, filled with cheerful, occasionally wolf-whistling troops.

'They'll have the grins wiped off their faces soon enough,' Dunnigan said. 'Thirty Corps had a hell of a job taking Bremen and Hamburg's still holding out.'

After four hours, they stopped to stretch their legs and make a hot drink from an Army 'Tea Block' that came ready mixed with powdered milk and sugar. Saffron opened a packet labelled 'Biscuits, Plain' and another of 'Chocolate, Vitamin Fortified'.

'That's what I call a proper feast,' Saffron said as they packed up. 'Now get in the passenger side, Sergeant, and feel free to have a snooze. It's my turn to drive.'

Saffron kept going as the evening drew on, aiming into the setting sun, for if she headed west long enough she was bound to hit the autobahn eventually.

Suddenly, in the last light of the day, with the sky and the land reduced to shades of grey, a sign loomed up directing traffic *Nordern*, or north, to Hamburg. She ignored it and drove a little further until she caught sight of another sign, drunkenly tilted to one side because one of its supporting poles had been smashed, which said *Süd* to Hanover and Frankfurt.

'That's the one!' she said to herself and followed the slip road onto the autobahn.

It was deserted. The clouds that had hung heavy in the sky all day parted to reveal a full moon, and there was the road, broad, inviting and stretching away into the distance, begging to be driven upon. And with silver moonlight illuminating the scene, it no longer mattered that the blackout rules meant she couldn't use her headlights, for it was almost as clear as day.

Saffron gave an exultant smile as she pressed the accelerator to the floor, shifted into third gear, the highest the vehicle had to offer, and raced away down the highway.

The Jeep was a nimble creature, whose 'Go Devil' engine was loved by soldiers for its performance, and Saffron soon had this one cruising at almost sixty miles per hour. Ten miles went by, then twenty, and it occurred to Saffron that if they kept up this rate of progress, they would be at their destination by the morning. Beside her Dunnigan was asleep; soldiers as experienced as him had long since acquired the ability to grab any kip that was going, no matter where or when.

Saffron had been driving for almost fifty miles, maintaining her pace, though the monotony of the road seemed to be making it harder for her to keep her eyes from closing.

Just a little while longer and then we can switch places, she thought.

As she crested a shallow hill, something caught her eye a few hundred yards ahead, lower down the slope. There were large black shadows scattered across the road on both carriageways, a dozen of them or more cutting right across her path.

She blinked, tried to focus, did her best to prod her weary brain into making sense of what she was seeing.

The shadows were getting closer.

If they were shadows, then something had to be casting them. She looked up. The only clouds in the sky were light and high overhead, scudding across the heavens.

Saffron was exhausted. Something nagged at her brain. *The clouds were moving . . . The shadows are motionless . . .*

She was almost on them, repeating in her head: *the shadows are motionless . . .*

And then it struck her: *not shadows . . . bomb craters!*

Now she was awake.

She slammed on the brakes, but the little car was heavily laden, going downhill at top speed and it barely slowed at all. As the first of the craters loomed open in front of her, opening its jaws to swallow them up, Saffron yanked at the handbrake and heaved the wheel to the left.

The car slewed wildly, turned, skidded and skimmed around the rim of the crater, its tyres inches from the drop.

Dunnigan was thrown against Saffron's shoulder, almost knocking the steering wheel from her hand. She shoved him away and he banged headfirst against the metal frame of the windscreen. He shouted in pain, and was flung the other direction as Saffron slalomed the Jeep with an opposite turn.

The land had started to flatten and their speed was slowing, but only a little, and there was another, slightly smaller crater. She was able to swerve around that, and a third one, this time a little more steadily, until the car finally came to a halt.

Saffron got out of the car, holding onto the side as she secured her feet and cleared her head. She looked around. The car had ended up about halfway across what must have been an entire string of bombs dropped from a single plane. It was as if they were stuck in the middle of a giant piece of Swiss cheese, resting on one of the thin, solid sections, with great holes all around them.

She realised why no one else was on this section of the autobahn. The RAF had made sure it was unusable by convoys of tanks and trucks to inhibit German troop movements.

Dunnigan stood by the other side of the car, rubbing his head. 'Mind if I make a suggestion, ma'am? If ye going to drive like a bloody maniac, probably best to do it in broad daylight.'

He looked around at the lunar landscape. 'Now, ma'am,' he said. 'It's my shift, and I'm never one to shirk. I'll take the wheel . . . once we're on that nice, solid road over there. Excuse me impertinence, ma'am, but tha' can bloody well get us from here to there, 'cause I'm bloody not.'

'You're right, Sergeant,' Saffron said. 'That was impertinent . . . but entirely deserved. Hop in and I'll get us across . . . nice and slowly, don't you worry.'

When Gerhard and the other surviving prisoners from Sachsenhausen had arrived at Dachau, they'd been assembled into a line alongside their trucks. They were marched through a familiar landscape of bare earth, strewn with scrawny corpses, to a hut that looked, from the outside, exactly like the ones in which they'd been imprisoned at Sachsenhausen. But when the door was opened, Gerhard stepped into a room that seemed to come from a dream, a distant memory of the past made real. It was furnished with comfortable chairs, sofas, side-tables and lights with crimson satin shades. There were pictures of beautiful women on the wall, a carpet on the floor, glass in the windows and brightly patterned curtains.

The SS officer who was waiting for them in the hut seemed amused by the baffled stares of the new inmates. 'Our facilities are somewhat overcrowded at the moment,' he said. 'But this unit is no longer required. You gentleman may be sad to discover that the original inhabitants have departed . . .'

His wit received no response. The officer sighed irritably at his unappreciative audience. 'For heaven's sake, cheer up . . . This is the Dachau brothel.'

They were placed in solitary confinement, locked in the rooms that the camp whores had once occupied, each of which contained the unimaginable luxury of a bed – a simple metal frame with creaking springs and a horsehair mattress – which felt like paradise to Gerhard after the crammed slave-bunks of Sachsenhausen. The food was better than Gerhard had eaten in months, with an entire bread roll in the morning, soup that had the occasional shred of carrot or potato floating in it for lunch, and a buckwheat gruel, dotted with scraps of gristly, fatty meat in the evening.

Gerhard needed no conscious thought to make him eat. His body demanded it. But his physical condition was worsening as the typhus that had killed so many of his fellow prisoners took its hold on him. His body ached. He was gripped by burning sweats, followed by teeth-chattering chills. But when, after several days, the order was suddenly given to move out, he was still just strong enough to stumble out of the brothel and slowly, painfully, follow the others across the camp to where a motley convoy of trucks and old buses was drawn up.

More prisoners were waiting: another hundred or so, around a third of them women, who had already been at Dachau when the Sachsenhausen transport arrived. A few were as malnourished as Gerhard, but most, like the prisoners from the Special Camp at Sachenhausen, merely looked thin by normal standards. To Gerhard's eyes, they seemed enviably plump and well-nourished. He could hear several languages being spoken. Some, like English, French, Italian and Russian, he recognised. Others were less familiar.

They were herded aboard the vehicles and Gerhard found himself in one of the buses. The seat was hard and his knees were jammed against the back of the seat in front. But after the squalor of the wagons and trucks that had brought him to Dachau, he had no complaints.

The vehicles drove south, each one of them guarded by armed SS men. But their presence did not deter the passengers sharing information about themselves in whispered messages, passed up and down the bus when the guards weren't looking.

Gerhard learned that the prisoners with whom he was travelling included the former Prime Ministers of France and Austria, as well as a Mayor of Vienna and other political, military and industrial figures. There were also almost forty 'Kin Prisoners', as the Nazis had termed the wives and relatives of men who had been involved in the 20 July plot against Hitler.

There was one rumour, which spread more quickly than any other through the convoy. The officers in charge had been overheard receiving their final orders, just before they left Dachau. One of those orders had been: 'If, at any point on your journey, you are in danger of being captured by the enemy, kill all the prisoners.'

Gerhard could hear the two men behind him, both speaking English, trying to decide whether the rumour was true or not.

'It doesn't make sense,' one murmured, keeping his voice low so that the guards could not overhear him. 'Why would they have kept us alive all this time, only to kill us?'

'Because the war is lost. We're no longer any use to them.'

'In that case why haven't they killed us already?'

'I don't know. Nothing these animals do makes any sense.'

'I say we are of use to them. We're bargaining chips. They'll threaten us, to make our countries give them what they want. But they won't kill us. I'm sure of it.'

The Englishman was speaking a little louder now. It was the only way he could make himself heard over the sound of Gerhard's coughing.

The Arado jet carrying Konrad von Meerbach to freedom had landed as planned at an airfield outside Girona in the northeast corner of Spain, less than fifty kilometres from the French border. Konrad was met by a deputation of officers from the *Brigada Político-Social*, or BPS, the Secret Police unit established by the Spanish dictator General Franco in 1941. Himmler was pleased to answer Franco's request for assistance, and the BPS had been established and trained with help from SS advisors. As a result, the BPS was only too happy to return the favour and help Konrad in his hour of need.

'*Madre de dios!*' the senior BPS officer exclaimed as Konrad emerged from the Arado. He slipped into the German he had learned from his instructors to say, 'I congratulate you, Count – what an aircraft! What a testament to German genius!'

'Well, consider it yours. I have no further use for it. I'm sure you will obtain an agreeably high price if you let the Russians and Americans know that it is for sale.'

'The Generalissimo would not like us making deals with communists.'

'Need he ever know? I certainly won't tell him.'

The BPS man smiled. 'Ah, Count, you are a man of the world, I can tell. Now, your transport is all arranged. We will drive you to Barcelona. It would be our great honour if you would join me and a few of my colleagues for lunch. Afterwards we will put you on a train to Madrid, arriving in time to catch the sleeper service to Lisbon. Private compartments have been reserved for you on both trains.' He looked at his watch. 'You are ahead of schedule. We could not believe it when you said how short your flight time would be, and yet . . . Incredible.' He gazed at the Arado once again. 'Perhaps we should keep it for our own use, after all.'

'It is entirely your decision.'

'And what about . . . ?'

Konrad glanced in the direction that the Spaniard had indicated and saw Sperling having a relaxing smoke after his flight. The pilot had done the von Meerbach family a great service, extracting both the Count and Countess from Germany and depositing them safely in their respective destinations. On the other hand, that meant that he knew where the search for either of them should begin.

'Make him disappear,' Konrad said.

'Of course.'

He had an agreeable luncheon with like-minded souls, slept like a log on the train to Lisbon and checked into the suite he had reserved at a luxurious hotel on the seafront at Estoril. He sent a telegram to Zurich, telling Francesca that he was safe and asking her to join him as soon as the war in Europe had ended and it was safe to travel.

That evening he visited the casino and had considerably better luck at the *chemin-de-fer* table than he had done the last time he was there. Konrad's nation had suffered a crushing defeat. His beloved leader would soon be dead, if he wasn't already. The Nazi Party to which he had dedicated more than fifteen years of his life was, for now at least, on the verge of annihilation. But he was alive, well, and very rich. He was in an excellent mood as he began piecing together a master plan of revenge, each component exquisitely dissected, as if with a surgeon's knife.

● ● ●

After her narrow escape from the bomb craters, Saffron accepted that it might be a good idea to stop and rest, for a few hours at least. But by five in the morning the first light of dawn was seeping into a stone-grey sky. She and Dunnigan ate a breakfast of tinned ham and biscuits, washed down with sweet tea. They boiled some water to wash with. Dunnigan extracted a razor from a battledress jacket and shaved. And then they were on their way again.

Over the next eighteen hours, Saffron was given a vivid snapshot of a defeated nation. The armies invading Germany from the west had sliced through it in several distinct columns, spreading out across the country, some adhering to a straight thrust into the heart of Germany, others wheeling north or south into every corner.

Wherever the armies had marched, and been resisted, the wreckage of war was plain to see. But when traffic or road damage forced them off the autobahn onto the country lanes that ran alongside it, they would leave the lines of march and arrive in villages whose wood-framed, medieval buildings, straight from a book of fairy tales, were untouched by war. They drove past cows contentedly grazing in the fields, chickens in the farmyards, and pigs with fat bellies crusted with mud.

This was a land of women, for all the men had been called away to fight. Once Saffron stopped to ask the way and found herself chatting to a lonely farmer's wife who could hardly believe that her first experience of the invading enemy was an agreeable conversation with a fellow woman – and one who could speak German. She was exhausted by the years of conflict, just as women in England were, and devastated by the destruction of the Reich she had been assured would last a millennium.

'I am old enough to remember the last war,' one woman said. 'How could we have let the same thing happen again?' She looked at Saffron with an expression in which she could see the grief, bafflement, humiliation and anger of a spurned lover. 'He lied to us. He told us we would be great again and like fools we believed him. And now this . . . How will we ever recover? Ah well . . .' She sighed. 'People like me are the lucky ones. You got to us before the Russians. At least we are safe with you.'

She offered Saffron some fresh milk, eggs and a piece of homemade cheese for her journey, and was thrilled when Saffron insisted on paying her with a five-dollar note.

'This is better than gold,' she said.

The first town of any size they came to was Bielefeld. It was an old medieval city, overlooked by a castle on a hill, with two tall Gothic churches, a fine town hall and an old marketplace surrounded by attractive buildings with steepled roofs. It had possessed a viaduct that carried the railway towards large marshalling yards, and a gas works, all of which had been strategic bombing targets.

The damage was extensive across the city and when she saw the ruins of the railway viaduct, Saffron remembered newspaper reports she'd read only a couple of weeks earlier. This was where the most powerful bomb ever created by man had been dropped: the 'Grand Slam' earthquake bomb, otherwise known as 'Ten Ton Tess'.

'Made a hell of a mess, didn't it?' said Dunnigan, casting his eyes over the rubble to which the viaduct had been reduced.

'What a waste . . .' Saffron mused. 'Think of all the time, and thought and effort that went into designing that bomb, just so it could spread destruction.'

'Not a waste from where I'm standing, ma'am,' Dunnigan replied. 'Not if it made this bloody war one day shorter, or saved the life of one of our lads.'

They drove through the hills of the Teutoburg Forest, past Dortmund and then south towards Frankfurt. They were in the American sector now and suddenly everything seemed to be on another scale. The Americans had more of everything than the British. Their trucks were bigger, the men inside them seemed better fed, better dressed and better equipped.

'Aye, and five times better paid,' Dunnigan observed sharply. 'Mind, we fought alongside the Yanks in Tunisia and they did all right. Not bad fellows, once you get to know them.'

Whenever the Jeep became stuck in a jam of American traffic, Saffron found herself the object of the soldiers' attentions. The sound of their voices, the open, unabashed way they had of presenting themselves, unlike the awkwardness and reserve of the British, made her think of Danny. But their good humour was so infectious, it was hard to stay gloomy for long, and she decided to treat it as light relief from what she feared might prove to be a distressing mission. It didn't hurt that there was a constant supply of cigarettes, bottles of Coca Cola and chocolate bars provided by the passing Americans.

'I'll make a bloody fortune flogging all this when I get back to the regiment,' Dunnigan said, as the loot piled up in the back of the Jeep.

The mood was different when they passed the long columns of German, which was almost as common a sight as the advancing Americans. Some groups still marched in order, as if determined to preserve their dignity as fighting men, even after the ignoble act of surrender. Others were amorphous crowds of men, shepherded by American military policemen.

Saffron was struck by how many of the captured Germans were young boys, whose faces bore expressions of bafflement and shock brought on by the grim disparity between the promises of glory with which their masters had enthused them, and the horrifying realities of war and defeat. Beside them walked men old enough to have been veterans of the First World War, for whom the surrender of 1918 was being repeated in even more crushing circumstances. Most of the troops seemed healthy enough, though she spotted many bandaged heads, arms in slings and men swinging themselves along with crutches, while others bore their more seriously wounded comrades on stretchers, a man at each corner.

Most still wore their peaked forage caps; some had greatcoats flapping about their legs; others walked with arms crossed over their chests to keep warm. For the weather remained cold and in places there was fresh snow on the ground.

Saffron's mind turned to Gerhard. Was he walking across Germany somewhere in a column such as this? Was he bound for incarceration in a camp deep in Russia, never to return? Perhaps he was dead.

Whether he was alive or not, she felt herself resigning to never seeing him again, and perhaps that was just as well. What man could tolerate being so humiliated and brought low in the eyes of the woman he loved?

As the evening was drawing in, they came to Frankfurt. Or rather, they came to a wasteland that had once been a city called Frankfurt, but was now a desert of ashes and rubble.

Saffron had become accustomed to bomb damage. But even in London, the city was a functioning, living entity where people could live and work and carry out the normal activities of modern life. The lights went on when you pressed the switch. The water ran when taps were turned. But this was desolation so total that she could not imagine how any of the shadowy figures walking along the lines of what had once been streets, or picking through the rubble of shattered buildings – looking, she supposed, for possessions, or perhaps people that they had lost there – could possibly have survived the Armageddon that had been visited upon them.

Dunnigan was driving. 'Mabye this'll teach 'em, eh?' he said. 'Maybe now they'll learn to give war a rest. And if this doesn't do it . . .' He sighed and looked at Saffron. 'Give us a cigarette, pet. Reckon I need one . . .'

She didn't make a fuss about being called 'pet' instead of 'ma'am'. There were times, and this was one of them, when they weren't a captain and a sergeant, but a man and a woman in a car, travelling through a strange land in which none of the old rules applied.

'Thanks,' Dunnigan said, taking the cigarette. 'You're right, you know . . . about all this smashing things up. I'm sick of it. Just makes me want to get back to my farm.'

They passed through Frankfurt and onto the autobahn for Munich as quickly as they could. This time they did not stop for the night but kept moving, taking turns at the wheel while the other slept.

In the first light of day, they arrived at Dachau.

• • •

They smelled the camp before they saw it, a thick, cloying scent that became at first nauseating and then all but overpowering: the reek of raw sewage mixed with the putrefaction of a myriad of unburied bodies. It was the aroma of human annihilation.

Saffron had to slow the Jeep to a walking pace as they approached the gates of the camp. Ahead of them a long queue of German civilians was walking slowly down one side of the road, escorted by American soldiers. Only as they came closer did they realise that the civilians were being marched past corpses, an unbroken line of them, some showing signs of fatal wounds, their skulls half blown away, but most dead for no obvious reason. Except that when she looked again, the corpses were little more than skin and bone, garbed in striped rags.

'The Yanks are making them witness what their blessed Reich was all about,' said Dunnigan.

'But they're not, are they?' Saffron said, for almost every pair of eyes, men and women alike, was fixed firmly forward, unable to confront the truth of what had been done in their name.

Saffron entered Dachau and forced herself to look, though the shock of what she saw was so great that her mind struggled to make sense of it. Her impressions fragmented into disconnected images, like random pictures crammed onto a ruined gallery wall.

She saw SS men, still in their uniforms, with corpses draped across their shoulders – literal bags of bones – as they took them to huge open pits for burial. A group of local dignitaries were forced to watch as a bulldozer pushed the dead – tens, hundreds of them – into one of the pits. An American soldier, not much more than a boy, with vivid red hair and freckles across his nose, ran to one of the camp guards, who was returning from the pit to fetch anther body, and shouted, 'You dirty Kraut bastard!' then started hitting him with wild, uncontrolled punches. The guard made no attempt to defend himself and threw up into the dirt. Two other Americans grabbed their buddy and dragged him away.

Saffron walked to a hut. Another GI – older, unshaven – held out an arm to block her as she was about to open the door and said, 'Believe me, you don't want to go in there, ma'am.'

'I'm looking for . . .' Saffron's mind whirled. *Who am I looking for? What am I doing here?* She pulled herself together and said, 'I need to speak to whoever's in charge.'

The soldier shrugged. 'The major's over there, ma'am.' He pointed to an American, standing by the dignitaries. 'But he's real busy. They say Ike's coming by this afternoon, wants to see the place for himself.'

Saffron nodded, muttered, 'Thanks,' and went off to find the major. She explained her mission and showed him the letter from Churchill.

'Is that for real?' he asked.

'Mr Churchill is taking a personal interest in this. There are members of his own family involved.'

'OK, I guess you'd better go across to the administration building, right over there. That's where they're interviewing the SS. Maybe one of those bastards can help you.'

Saffron followed the major's instructions. A group of SS was lined up outside an office, waiting to be interviewed. A US Army lieutenant was walking down the corridor towards her.

'I need some information. One of those men may be able to help me. Mind if I ask them a few questions?'

'Knock yourself out.'

She stood opposite the SS men, Dunnigan beside her. 'I want to find a group of prisoners. They arrived here from Sachsenhausen, no more than two weeks ago, maybe less. They included a number of important individuals. What happened to these men? Can anyone help me?'

No one answered. But Saffron sensed that it was the stubborn silence of men who are withholding the truth, rather than the ignorance of men who don't know it.

Saffron nudged Dunnigan. 'Could you give me your packet of cigarettes?'

'Are you giving it to these buggers?'

'Yes . . . if it saves a man's life.'

Dunnigan grimaced, then handed over an almost-full packet of Lucky Strikes.

Saffron held them up. 'These, for anyone who tells me what I need to know.'

They were tempted, she could tell. The smell of tobacco would mask the stench of the camp. 'Come on . . .' she encouraged. 'No? Oh well . . .'

She turned to give the packet back to Dunnigan, then a voice said, 'Wait, I can help you.'

There were muttered curses in German and she heard him snap back, 'What the hell difference does it make? It's over . . . all of it. Over.'

'Find us an unoccupied room, please,' she said to Dunnigan.

He walked along the corridor, opening and closing doors. On the third try he struck lucky and waved at Saffron.

She led the SS man to the room, sat him down and said, 'Don't waste my time. Talk.'

'There are one hundred and thirty-nine prisoners in a convoy of motor vehicles. They left here only hours before the Americans arrived. And they are going south.'

Now he too bargained, as Shevchenko had done. 'Give me the cigarettes if you want to hear the rest.'

Saffron handed the packet over. 'Now talk.'

'What I can tell you is this: they were going to a camp at Innsbruck, in Austria, to wait for orders directing them to their final destination. The name of this place is the Labour Education Camp. But there is no point trying to follow them there.'

'Why not?'

'Because the men in charge of the transport are under orders: if you are in danger of capture, shoot all the prisoners. If you, or any of your American friends, get close to the transport, then everyone on it will die before you can save them. And if they are alive, that is only because no one has found them.' He smiled as he concluded, 'Either way you lose.'

Gerhard's body was wracked by fever. His temperature rose so high that he would sweat through his clothes. Then it plunged, leaving him shivering in his seat. He found himself spending more and more time dozing, then dropping into periods of dreamless unconsciousness.

One of the Englishmen behind him said, 'Do you think we ought to give him some of our soup? I know he's a Kraut, but he must have done something to make Adolf cross, or he wouldn't be here.'

'He's a human being. We should try to help him. That's what makes us better than them.'

Gerhard came to from one blackout to find that the coach had stopped. There was a hand on his shoulder, shaking it. He opened his eyes and turned to see one of the Englishmen leaning over the back of his seat behind him, holding out a lump of bread in one hand and a tin cup in the other.

'Food,' he said in English, 'to eat.' He mimed the act of chewing and then said, 'Yum, yum.'

'Thank you,' Gerhard replied. He took the bread and the cup, which was filled with a thin, watery, buckwheat gruel. It tasted both nondescript and unpleasant, as he knew it would, and Gerhard felt so ill that he had no appetite. But the soup was hot, liquid and would provide a small scrap of energy, so he tried to force it down.

'You speak English?' the man asked.

'A little . . .' Gerhard looked out of the bus window. He saw huts and a barbed wire fence, so it was a camp, but smaller than Dachau or Sachsenhausen. He had to close his eyes. It was sunny outside and the glare was unbearable. It made his head hurt even more than usual.

'Where are we?' he asked, turning away.

'Innsbruck.'

'Are we getting out here?'

Gerhard finished the soup and nibbled the bread as the Englishman replied, 'Good question. Our SS chums seem to be arguing about that very point. Have you met *Obersturmführer* Schiller?'

Gerhard shook his head. He suddenly felt very dizzy and could barely keep his eyes open.

'He's the chap in charge of our Cook's Tour of the Alps.' The Englishman turned and peered out of the window, as he went on, 'From what I can gather, he seems keen that we should disembark and find some digs here. But the local chap, who's evidently in charge of this dump, seems to feel that he's full up as it is. Reminds me of Joseph arriving at Bethlehem and being told there's no room at the inn.'

'You're wasting your breath, old boy,' the other Englishman said.

The two of them looked down at Gerhard, who was unconscious in his seat.

'Ah, right, poor chap's dropped off.'

'It's a bit more than that. I'd say he's fallen into a coma.'

'Poor bastard, he looks all in.'

'Not long for this world, I'd say.'

'No, probably not . . . But then again, which of us is?'

They watched the SS officers arguing for a few more minutes. Then Schiller stormed off towards the staff car in which he was leading the convoy.

'Looks like he's been given his marching orders.'

'Then we'll be on our way any minute . . . but where to?'

The bus was coughing and shaking as its engine was turned back on and the convoy was on its way, still heading south, ever deeper into the Tyrolean Alps. An hour later it was travelling through the Brenner Pass, on the border between Austria and Italy.

'Stunning scenery, isn't it?' one of the Englishman said as they drove past the meadows that ran along the bottom of the pass, with mountain peaks soaring upwards on either side.

'Rather . . .' the other replied. 'Oh, hang on. I think our German friend is coming to. Look, I've got a drop of that soup left, cold now, of course.'

One of the men propped up Gerhard's head so that the other could pour a few drips of soup into his mouth.

'Thank you,' Gerhard croaked in a voice so weak they could barely hear it over the engine.

'I say, old chap,' the man with the cup asked, 'what's your name? So we can pass on your details . . . if the need arises.'

Gerhard closed his eyes and frowned, as if making an enormous effort of concentration. 'Five . . . seven . . . eight . . .'

'No, not your prison number. We can see that for ourselves. Your name . . . Oh Lord, how does one say it in German?'

'Ah, something like . . . *Was ist dein Name, bitter?*'

Gerhard nodded. 'Von Meerbach . . . Gerhard von Meerbach.'

Then he closed his eyes and passed out.

'Did you catch that?' asked the Englishman with the cup.

'I think so . . . more or less, anyway.'

As she was leaving the administration building at Dachau, Saffron heard a cheer from one of the offices. She opened the door, peered in and saw four American soldiers clustered around a radio set. Before she could say a word, one of them exclaimed, 'Hitler's dead! That dirty, no-good son-of-a-bitch was killed yesterday. The Krauts have announced it on their radio . . . Adolf goddamned Hitler is dead!'

It was as if a huge black cloud that had been hanging over the world for years was lifting. The death of one man was meaningless in the face of the slaughter of millions, but it was now possible to hope, to believe in change, to see the terrible darkness of cruelty and bloodshed begin to fade and light emerge like a new spring.

Saffron felt numb. Her senses wanted to shut down as she and Dunnigan drove through the southern Bavarian landscape of thickly wooded hills and sparkling lakes, towards the mountains that rose in the distance. She wondered if the experience of the camps had scarred her forever, if she could ever know beauty again. She felt corrupted and soiled, but out here nature was surely renewing itself.

Almost to herself she said, 'The air is so fresh and clean.'

'Not to me, ma'am,' Dunnigan said. 'I don't think I'll ever get the smell of that place out of my head, I . . .'

He fell silent and for a moment Saffron's attention was distracted by a bomb or shell crater up ahead, which she spotted immediately and steered around without any great drama, for it had become a familiar activity over the past few days. Only once she was back on the smooth road surface again did she glance across at the man in the passenger seat, and the moment she did she had to pull in at the side of the road.

The tough, battle-hardened sergeant was bent over with his head in his hands, sobbing helplessly.

Saffron leaned over and put a hand on his back. 'What is it, Dunnigan? What's the matter?'

He took a deep breath, wiped his face and looked at her with eyes still wet with tears. 'That place . . . that bloody place . . .'

'I know . . .' she said. 'I understand.'

'You know what war's like. You see terrible things. Mates blown to bits in front of your eyes. Lads with their legs blown off, their guts hanging out. But that . . . that was the worst . . . that was like driving through the gates of hell . . .'

He sat up in his seat. 'Still, I'm glad I've seen Dachau. I've seen the worst and I'm proud I fought against it, and now I'm going to make sure it never happens again.'

They reached Innsbruck in the late afternoon, only a few hours behind the US 103rd Infantry Division who had entered the city without any significant resistance. Saffron located the divisional headquarters and set out to find the intelligence officers, while Dunnigan went to get fuel for the Jeep.

A combination of initiative, persuasiveness and regular use of the name 'Winston Churchill' enabled her to locate the major in charge of divisional intelligence, explain her mission and tell him about the Labour Education Camp.

'Yeah, I believe I know the place you're talking about. We keep an eye out for these camps now . . . after Dachau. But this one wasn't like that, thank God. It was pretty much deserted. The SS had all skedaddled and if there was anyone being held there before, they sure as hell ain't there any more.'

Saffron sighed and her shoulders sagged. 'I've gone from one end of Germany to the other, now into Austria. I'm so close to finding these people . . . I refuse to give up now.'

'Look, it's getting late. Why don't I find you a place to sleep? What rank is your driver?'

'Sergeant.'

'OK, I'll get my staff sergeant to make sure he's fixed up with some chow. I don't know about accommodation, though. We only just got here.'

'That's all right. He'll feel happier sleeping by his Jeep. He wouldn't like anyone else getting near it.'

The major laughed. 'Yeah, guys can get real possessive about their wheels. But here's what I'll do: I'll have one of my guys put the word out. We pretty much control everything around here now. Believe me, if there are a hundred and some prime ministers, princes, millionaires and aristocrats sitting on a bunch of trucks somewhere in this theatre of operations, someone will as sure as hell have found 'em . . . dead or alive.'

Saffron took food at the headquarters field kitchen and a bed at a hotel that had been requisitioned for senior officers. The following morning, she ate a hearty breakfast, then went looking for the major.

He greeted her with a broad smile. 'Captain Courtney – just the lady I was looking for. I have news for you, but I don't think you're going to believe it.'

'Why not?'

'Seems we've found your missing prisoners. One of them – a Limey, come to think of it – walked across country till he bumped into units of the forty-second Infantry Division. He led them back to meet the rest of his people. They were safe in the care of some German army officers, who were holding them' – the major paused for dramatic effect, and then concluded – 'in a luxury hotel.'

'What?' Saffron gasped. 'An actual hotel? Is this some kind of a joke?'

'I kid you not. The people you are looking for are safe, and most of them are well. The regular German troops took them into protective custody away from their murderous bastard SS guards, who had orders to kill them if it looked like we were winning this war. And if you come with me and look at this map, I will show you where to find them . . .'

• • •

They had been on the road for three hours and covered around eighty miles when Dunnigan spotted a signpost marked ST. VEIT and said, 'Reckon this is the turn, here.'

They were used to the scenery by now, the unfolding of yet more glorious views as they drove along a valley floor dotted with wooden farmhouses and barns. Seeing new vistas of hills and mountains no longer made their mouths open in wonder as it had done when they began their drive through the Tyrol a day earlier. They came to the end of the road, and there stood their destination.

The Hotel Pragser Wildsee resembled three huge Swiss chalets, built of stone and joined together: two larger buildings on either side flanking a smaller one in the middle. Steep, pine-covered hills rose on either side of the hotel and in the distance behind it Saffron could see the harsh, imposing mass of a precipitous, bare rock face, its summit still covered in snow.

All around them, US Army Jeeps and trucks were parked, with soldiers wandering between them, looking relaxed. Many wore dark glasses and had their torsos bare to catch the sun. An MP stopped their Jeep and inquired after their business.

'We got Limeys here, ma'am, that's for sure,' he said when she told him. 'Dunno if they're the ones you're looking for. But you're sure welcome to take a look-see.'

They parked the Jeep. Dunnigan stayed beside it to brew a cup of tea and have a smoke while Saffron walked towards the entrance, which lay beneath a canvas awning decorated with bright yellow-and-white stripes.

As they stepped into the foyer, a smartly dressed man smoking a pipe walked by with a pretty blonde girl on his arm. Two women, a blonde and a brunette, their clothes a little shabby but their manner and accents unmistakably upper-class, were chatting to one another in German. Beyond them a group of men in military uniform were strolling towards the back of the building, laughing as they went.

Saffron found it impossible to think that these people, who seemed at ease with the world, could have had any experience of the concentration camps. But this was where the prisoners had been sent, so who else could they be?

Saffron approached the women and asked, 'Excuse me, were you on the transport from Dachau?'

The two women stiffened. 'Why do you ask?' the brunette inquired.

'I'm looking for some British prisoners who were taken from Sachsenhausen to Dachau. I believe they were brought here.' Neither of the women had softened. Saffron offered up a silent prayer and played her trump card. 'I'm here at the personal request of Winston Churchill.'

'Can you prove that?' asked the blonde.

'Yes,' said Saffron, and showed them the signed letter.

The blonde relaxed. 'I suppose you had better speak to another Churchill. Darling,' she looked at the brunette, 'have you seen Jack lately?'

'I believe he's on the terrace. You can't miss him: a tremendously good-looking man in military uniform. I believe he is a colonel. And *so* amusing . . .'

The blonde laughed. 'Do you know, his men called him Mad Jack because he insisted on going into battle wearing a sword?'

'He says an officer isn't properly dressed without one!' her friend interjected.

'He also carried a bow-and-arrow and played the Scottish bagpipes! A remarkable man. He walked most of the way to Verona to fetch the Americans . . . He will tell you all you need to know. The terrace is through there . . .'

She pointed in the direction the three men had been walking. Saffron made her way through the hotel, pushed open some glass doors and emerged into a vision of a lost world. Before her was a terrace, filled with more neatly turned-out civilians and a score of military men representing almost all the Allied nations. Beyond them stretched a small Alpine lake, surrounded by mountains. A jetty ran out into the water and American GI's were jumping off it to the shouts and cheers of their friends.

Saffron scanned the crowd on the terrace until she saw a tall, slim, moustachioed man in khaki British Army battledress, with the crown and single pip of a Lieutenant Colonel on his epaulettes. He was as handsome as the women had promised, with swept-back sandy hair, strong features and a dimpled chin.

She approached him and asked, 'Excuse me, sir, but are you Lieutenant Colonel Churchill?'

'I am,' he replied. 'And who might you be?'

'Captain Saffron Courtney, First Aid Nursing Yeomanry, sir.'

'Tell me, is that a piece of decorative ribbon on your left tit or do you have the George Medal?'

'It's the medal, sir.'

He nodded approvingly. 'And what is a FANY doing all by herself in the Tyrol?'

'Looking for you, sir, among others. I've been sent to track down prisoners of particular interest. I followed your trail from Sachsenhausen, to Dachau and now here.'

'Hmm . . . I see you're armed. Hardly the usual FANY style. I take it you know how to use that gun.'

'Yes, sir.'

'Are you in the same game as my namesake Peter, by any chance?'

'I'm afraid I'm not at liberty to tell you, sir.'

Churchill laughed. 'That's what he says, too.'

'May I ask how you all ended up here, after Innsbruck?'

'Well, we kept heading south. All this time the Germans' whole show was falling apart, organisation and discipline going to pot. Made us distinctly concerned that the SS were going to bump us all off.'

'They were. They had orders to shoot everyone if they were in danger of being captured.'

'Yes, we thought as much. Anyway, a few chaps in our group were senior German officers who'd fallen out with Adolf. Some were involved with that whole Stauffenberg show, another was imprisoned for ordering a retreat on the Russian front. Cut a long story short, we got word to the German army. They came along and chased the SS off and we were brought here.' He chuckled. 'A group of Jerry generals had decided to see out the war in comfort. We rather barged in on their holiday.

'After a few days, the Germans disappeared. Dare say they planned to make their way discreetly home to their families, rather than become POWs. I went to see if I could fetch our American cousins. A few of our number needed medical help, one or two rather seriously. I'm afraid I may not have brought it on time. Ah, here's Peter . . .'

Churchill waved towards a bespectacled man in an ill-fitting suit and beckoned him over. 'Peter,' he said. 'Meet Captain Courtney. She's a FANY. Come all the way from England to find you.'

Peter Churchill shook her hand. 'Where in England, exactly?' he asked. He seemed distracted.

'Baker Street . . . on Brigadier Gubbins' orders.'

'Aren't you going to give one another the secret handshake?' Jack asked with a grin.

'Look, I'm very sorry, Courtney, but I can't talk at the moment. Something's come up.' He looked at Jack. 'It's von Meerbach – the doc thinks he's close to the end.'

Saffron gave a strangled cry.

'I say, are you all right?' Peter asked.

Her face suddenly ashen, her eyes staring, she grabbed his arm. 'Did you say von Meerbach?'

'Yes, but why on earth . . . ?'

'Gerhard von Meerbach?'

'Good Lord,' Jack said. 'You're not looking for him too, are you?'

'I have to see him!' she cried. 'Please, I'm begging you. Take me to him now!'

This moment had been foretold. Four years had passed since Saffron climbed to the top of a mountain that rose from the plains of her father's lands. There she consulted Lusima, the tribal queen and sorceress after whom the estate was named. Lost to the material world, in the trance of second sight, the venerable seer had told her, 'You will walk alongside death, but you will live. You will look for him, but if he is ever found, it will only be when you have ceased your search, and if you see him you will not know him, for he will be nameless and unknown, and if your eyes fall upon his face they will not see it for they will not know it to be his. And if he is alive, it will be as if he were dead. And yet . . . and yet . . . you must keep search-ing, for if he is to be saved, only you can save him.'

Now, standing in a room in the Pragser Wildsee Hotel, Saffron finally understood the meaning and the truth of those words. She gazed upon the shrivelled, shaven-headed, barely human creature who lay in the bed with an intravenous drip in his arm. Every scrap of flesh had been starved from his face. Above his protrud-ing cheekbones his temples were as concave as saucers. Below them the cheeks were parchment-thin skin, stretched to breaking point. The bare arms that lay unmoving on the sheet with which he was covered were livid from top to bottom with a scarlet rash, as were his shoulders and neck. She could not see or hear if he was breathing, so weak was the rise and fall of his chest. And yet she knew it was him.

'Is this who you're looking for?' Peter Churchill asked.

'Yes,' Saffron replied, without the faintest tremor of doubt in her voice.

'How can you be sure?'

'Because . . .'

Saffron fell silent. How could she explain the prophecy? The men might be polite to her on the surface, but she knew what they would be thinking inside: another foolish woman believing in nonsense and mumbo-jumbo. Then something caught her eye, a piece of card, brown with age and dirt, folded into quarters, sitting on the table beside the bed. She picked it up and unfolded it. She wanted to scream, to weep, to rend her clothes in Biblical mourning. But she forced herself to stay calm and blinked back the tears as she put the card down on the table and smoothed it out so that it could clearly be seen as a photograph, though the image upon it was worn and faded to grey.

Saffron reached into her bag and took out the photograph that was always with her. She placed it on the table, next to the other one. 'Look,' she said.

The two Englishmen and the young American doctor, who had been standing beside the bed when they walked in, bent over the photograph.

'Good Lord,' murmured Jack Churchill.

'Unbelievable,' said the doctor.

Peter Churchill straightened. 'I can see that's you, but is the man you're with really him?'

'Yes, in Paris, the spring of thirty-nine.'

The doctor took her by the arm and led her to one side. 'Ma'am, I have to tell you that Mr von Meerbach is close to death. He has typhus fever. I administered penicillin as soon as we found him, but . . . well . . . I fear we were too late.'

'No,' Saffron said, and now her voice was firm and unwavering. 'That's not true. I know it's not. He has to live. I . . .' She wondered how she could explain the faith she had in the prophecy and decided there was no point even trying.

'He has to live,' she insisted.

'Ma'am, I feel for you. Truly I do. But sometimes we have to accept the inevitable.'

'We do. And I'm telling you that it is inevitable that Gerhard von Meerbach will survive. And I will be the one to make sure he does.'

• • •

For three days and nights, Saffron stayed at Gerhard's bedside. A camp bed was brought in and set up along one wall for her to rest on for the few brief moments of sleep she allowed herself. When the fever came upon him she soothed his brow with cold compresses. Then she replaced the soaked sheets with fresh ones while the doctor, or one of the Churchills, lifted Gerhard up in their arms, for he weighed no more than a child. When he was chilled, she covered him in eiderdowns and blankets.

All the while, the doctor made sure that the glucose/saline drip kept Gerhard hydrated and provided him with enough energy to keep his body functioning.

'I have to warn you,' he said, 'malnutrition on this scale is enough to cause sudden, total organ failure by itself, let alone when it is accompanied by a disease as serious as typhus fever. He could go at any moment.'

'He won't,' Saffron insisted. Yet she knew that Gerhard was still just existing, rather than living. He remained unconscious and immobile, deep in a coma from which there seemed no escape. But she refused to let him slip further into the final blackness of death. She talked to him, telling him about her life in Baker Street; her training in Scotland; her adventures in North Africa, Greece and the Low Countries – everything except Danny. She had books from the hotel library brought up and read to him in both German and English.

Somewhere inside he can hear my voice, Saffron told herself. *That's what will wake him up.*

But he did not wake and then, on the fourth night, Gerhard's body was swept by fever. And this time it did not go away.

'This is the crisis point,' the doctor told her. 'I guess you could say it's make or break.'

The hotel maids brought her a pile of bedsheets and towels. Saffron spent hour after hour doing everything she could to cool Gerhard's temperature and keep his bedding fresh. Night became day and still the fever raged. Gerhard's frail body seemed to be burning itself up from within. It did not seem

possible that he could become any more reduced and yet he was
visibly losing weight.

At eleven the following morning, Gerhard's temperature
began to go down. Within the hour, it was back to normal. He
seemed more peaceful. But still he was deep in his coma.

'There's nothing more you can do for him now,' the doctor told
Saffron. 'Like I said, it's make or break . . . Now we have to wait
and see which.' He looked at her, as if examining her as another
patient, and said, 'You're exhausted. You should get some rest.'

'I can't.'

'Sure you can. You have to. You're no use to him like this.'

It was the only argument that could have persuaded her, and
the doctor knew it.

Saffron kissed Gerhard on the brow. 'I'm going to have a
little doze,' she said. 'But don't worry. I'm still here. I'll never,
ever leave you.'

She lay down, not wanting to sleep, fearful that he might die
without her beside him. But her body was shattered and seized
the sleep it so desperately required.

Two hours later the doctor came in, felt for Gerhard's pulse
and shook his head, for it was fainter than ever. He looked at
Saffron's unconscious figure, then back at the dying man. He
paused, considered his options, then let her be and left the room.

• • •

Saffron was dreaming that she and Gerhard were together.
He was as handsome and full of life as he had been before
the war, laughing and holding out his hand, saying, 'Take it.
Come with me.'

But she could not take it. She couldn't lift her arm. It wouldn't
move, no matter how hard she tried. Then she found a way to
raise it, but she couldn't reach Gerhard's hand. He seemed far
away and his voice was so quiet that she couldn't hear it as he
summoned her to join him: 'Saffron . . . Saffron . . .'

She couldn't bear it, the frustration was too awful.

Saffron forced herself awake. And then she heard it again, so muted that it was as if she were still dreaming it: 'Saffron . . . Saffron . . .'

She was fully awake, leaping off the camp bed, dashing to where Gerhard lay. His eyes were open, looking at her. He blinked again, unbelieving, and said, 'Saffron, my darling . . . is that really you?'

She fell to her knees beside the bed and took his fragile, bony hand in hers as she said, 'Yes, my love . . . I'm here.'

Tears were pouring down her face, but they were tears of joy, tears that released all the emotion she had kept buried deep inside her for so long. 'I love you,' she said. 'I love you so much.'

'I love you too.' He smiled weakly, but somehow it told her that the real Gerhard was still there.

From the open window, she heard a cheer ring out and she laughed through her tears as she thought, *Can they be cheering for us?*

The cheering grew, and it spread so that she could hear it all around her, from every part of the hotel, people shouting and clapping and whooping with joy.

There were footsteps running up and down the corridor outside.

The door opened and the doctor stuck his head into the room and asked, 'Did you hear? The Germans have surrendered! The war is over!' He paused as a huge smile of disbelieving joy spread across his face. 'We won!'

Saffron looked down at Gerhard. She knew now that the prophecy had come true. She had found her lion and brought him back to life. Now nothing on earth could part them.

'Yes,' she said triumphantly. 'We won.'

WILBUR SMITH

Readers' Club

If you would like to hear more about my books, why not join the WILBUR SMITH READERS' CLUB by visiting www.wilbursmithbooks.com/subscribe. It only takes a few moments to sign up and we'll keep you up-to-date with all my latest news.

ON LEOPARD ROCK

The first ever memoir from the Number One global bestselling adventure author

Wilbur Smith has lived an incredible life of adventure,
and now he shares the extraordinary true stories
that have inspired his fiction.

From being attacked by lions to close encounters with deadly
reef sharks, from getting lost in the African bush without
water to crawling the precarious tunnels of gold mines,
from marlin fishing with Lee Marvin to near death from
crash-landing a Cessna aeroplane, from brutal school days
to redemption through writing and falling in love,
Wilbur Smith tells us the intimate stories of his life
that have been the raw material for his fiction.
Always candid, sometimes hilarious, and never
less than thrillingly entertaining, *On Leopard Rock*
is testament to a writer whose life is as rich and
eventful as his novels are compellingly
unputdownable.

Available now

Discover the rest of the epic Courtney Series . . .

'A MASTER STORYTELLER' *SUNDAY TIMES*

WILBUR SMITH
WHEN THE LION FEEDS

BROTHERS BY BIRTH. ENEMIES BY BLOOD.

'A MASTER STORYTELLER' *SUNDAY TIMES*

WILBUR SMITH
THE SOUND OF THUNDER

SOME WILL WIN. AND SOME WILL LOSE.

'A MASTER STORYTELLER' *SUNDAY TIMES*

WILBUR SMITH
A SPARROW FALLS

'A FATHER BUILDS. A SON DESTROYS.

'A MASTER STORYTELLER' *SUNDAY TIMES*

WILBUR SMITH
THE BURNING SHORE

LOVE IN A TIME OF WAR.
HOPE IN A TIME OF DANGER.

'A MASTER STORYTELLER' *SUNDAY TIMES*

WILBUR SMITH
POWER OF THE SWORD

A POWERFUL FAMILY. A TIME OF WAR.

'A MASTER STORYTELLER' *SUNDAY TIMES*

WILBUR SMITH
RAGE

THE FUTURE OF A COUNTRY.
THE END OF A FAMILY.

'A MASTER STORYTELLER' *SUNDAY TIMES*

WILBUR SMITH
A TIME TO DIE

HUNTERS. HUNTED.

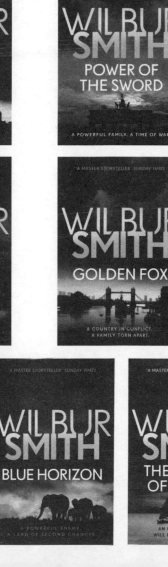

'A MASTER STORYTELLER' *SUNDAY TIMES*

WILBUR SMITH
GOLDEN FOX

A COUNTRY IN CONFLICT.
A FAMILY TORN APART.

'A MASTER STORYTELLER' *SUNDAY TIMES*

WILBUR SMITH
BIRDS OF PREY

A SIMPLE MISSION. A BATTLE FOR THEIR LIVES.

'A MASTER STORYTELLER' *SUNDAY TIMES*

WILBUR SMITH
MONSOON

THEY LEAVE AS BROTHERS.
THEY MUST RETURN AS MEN.

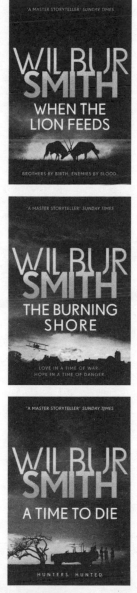

'A MASTER STORYTELLER' *SUNDAY TIMES*

WILBUR SMITH
BLUE HORIZON

A POWERFUL ENEMY.
A LAND OF SECOND CHANCES.

'A MASTER STORYTELLER' *SUNDAY TIMES*

WILBUR SMITH
THE TRIUMPH OF THE SUN

AN UNIMAGINABLE ENEMY
WILL BRING THEM TOGETHER

'A MASTER STORYTELLER' *THE SUNDAY TIMES*

WILBUR SMITH
ASSEGAI

FOR KING AND COUNTRY.
NO MATTER THE COST.

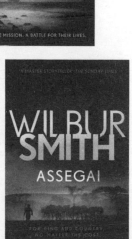

Want to read
NEW BOOKS
before anyone else?

Like getting
FREE BOOKS?

Enjoy sharing your
OPINIONS?

Discover

READERS FIRST
Read. Love. Share.

Sign up today to win your first free book:
readersfirst.co.uk

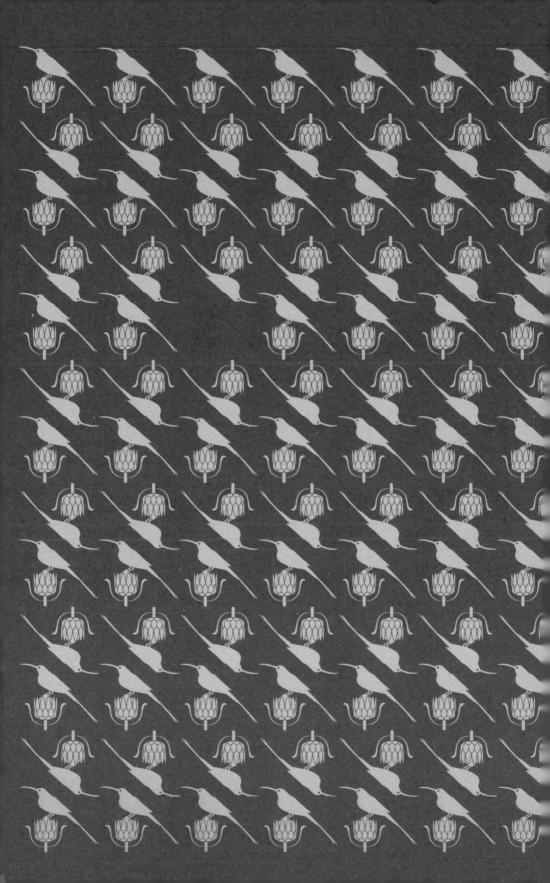